PRAISE FOR
OLIVIA STRAUSS IS RUNNING OUT OF TIME

"With heart, humor, and sparkling insight, *Olivia Strauss Is Running Out of Time* poses a powerful question: If you knew the date that you would die, how would that change the way you live? In her bighearted and dazzling debut, Angela Brown takes readers on a moving journey of second chances, new beginnings, and the timeless power of love. Readers will fall head over heels for Olivia Strauss as she explores the intimate beauty and honesty of a life well lived. In these pages, Brown has crafted a hopeful yet hilarious story of ambition, marriage, female friendship, community, and more. I couldn't put it down!"

—Becky Chalsen, author of *Kismet*

"Olivia Strauss is my new best friend. She is hilarious, honest as a diary. We meet Olivia in 'the last year of her youth.' Her story becomes a brilliantly lighthearted take on a taboo subject: the time we have left. This is dazzling entertainment, even as it considers our potential to change, how identity and dreams evolve. This is the rare comedy that feels profound. It's quick wit meets Mitch Albom, with revelations that will stay with me. I enjoyed every single page."

—Madeleine Henry, author of *Breathe In, Cash Out*

OLIVIA STRAUSS IS RUNNING OUT OF TIME

OLIVIA STRAUSS IS RUNNING OUT OF TIME

A NOVEL

ANGELA BROWN

Little
a

Text copyright © 2024 by Angela Brown
All rights reserved.

No part of this book may be reproduced, or stored in a retrieval system, or transmitted in any form or by any means, electronic, mechanical, photocopying, recording, or otherwise, without express written permission of the publisher.

Published by Little A, New York

www.apub.com

Amazon, the Amazon logo, and Little A are trademarks of Amazon.com, Inc., or its affiliates.

ISBN-13: 9781662516351 (hardcover)
ISBN-13: 9781662516344 (paperback)
ISBN-13: 9781662516337 (digital)

Cover design by Alicia Tatone
Cover image: © The Voorhes / Gallery Stock

Printed in the United States of America

First edition

For Hadley, who inspired me to finally start,
and for August, who inspired me to finally finish

These are the days that must happen to you . . .

— Walt Whitman, *"Song of the Open Road"*

There will be time, there will be time . . .

— T. S. Eliot, *"The Love Song of J. Alfred Prufrock"*

The problem is no one knows. Or that everyone knows. But not when or how or who. Maybe tomorrow. Or next year. Or in one hundred years. Or never! Well, not never. But it sometimes feels that way, doesn't it? Never. Never me. Never you. Never us. Not now. Now. We still have time. Time to put it off. To try again. To leave the job. To take the trip. To have more sex. To sleep. God, to sleep. To buy the supplements. To take the supplements. To put on the good shoes. Time to throw away the cigarettes. What? Fine. To really throw away the cigarettes. To apologize. To meet for coffee. To take someone's breath away. To say I love you. To kiss good night. To whisper good morning. There's time. Time to revise life. Time to put it all off. Time to live. Time to change. Time to evolve. Time to quit. Time to try.

Time.

That's the problem. There's never enough.

We're running out.

DEATH

ONE

On the eve of my thirty-ninth birthday, back when this whole mess started, I assumed I had decades (emphasis on the plural) left to live. I was getting older, yes, but still thought of myself as young. Not *young* young. But I was still at a point in life when I could wear sleeveless shirts (sometimes) or go makeup-free (sunglasses—a must!) without making a scene. I hadn't even had my first mammogram. I'm no philosopher, but if your breasts are youthful enough to skip being smashed by a giant imaging machine, that's saying something.

Back on the night of Suzanne's party, death still felt like an abstraction, like one of those sad stories on the news that you remind yourself happens only in faraway places. Real but not real. Death, I had determined, was a rule to be followed by everyone else, something so far in my future it seemed acceptable—logical even—to put off thinking about it in any sincere sense. It was like paying taxes.

Or it was, until that manila folder (death to *it*!) found its way into my hands. Of course, once I saw the information printed inside it, I could never *unsee* it, the details forcing me to acknowledge that the rules *did* apply to me, that my time on this planet would actually, inevitably, end. And for better or worse, thanks to that ridiculous folder, I knew precisely when.

I don't want to mislead you. I don't have a disease. I don't anticipate any charity walks or fundraising pages being organized in my honor anytime soon. In fact, as I blew out the single pink candle on my cupcake that night at Suzanne's, I was, for all intents and purposes, healthy. I didn't smoke (regularly). I didn't drink (define "regularly"). All my important medical abbreviations (BMI, BP) were just right.

Plus, I didn't do ridiculous things like not wear my seat belt. Okay, so I didn't work out as much as I should (translation: never). And over the years I'd gotten far too much sun (no shortage of vitamin D here!). For the record, no, I didn't take those articles about parabens seriously. I'm not a monster. It's just that I didn't want to wash myself with coconut and cashews. I mean, shampoo made from trail mix? I don't know. Maybe it's me.

It was all Marian's fault. Marian is my best friend. We met about a trillion years ago at a poetry reading our first year at NYU. We were basically babies who'd been handed dorm room keys. Marian was sitting beside me at the reading. She was wearing the T-shirt of a band I wasn't cool enough to know about and a pile of vintage necklaces that made her look bohemian but would have made someone like me look like a clown. Before we'd exchanged a single word, I knew she was one of those rare people who'd been born cool, who would eternally stay cool. Marian was not the sort of person who would ever buy a minivan. She would never own a household gadget you could describe as "practical." Some people are just like that.

"You want to get out of here?" she'd whispered to me, bits of poetry fluttering around us like moths. I couldn't believe she was talking to me. "I know a bar on Second Avenue that doesn't check IDs."

I know it sounds unlikely, but I think I knew even on that first night that we'd always stay friends.

A few weeks after the poetry reading, we met Andrew, the man who would eventually become my boyfriend and later my husband. We were at a dive bar known for selling buckets of Pabst Blue Ribbon. Purely classy stuff back in those days. I couldn't work up the courage to talk to him. Marian made me chug a PBR, then grabbed my hand, pulled me through the crowd, and forced me to introduce myself. Andrew just laughed and shook his head, then offered us each a beer from his aluminum bucket. After some senseless bar chatter, we realized we were all enrolled in the same writing program. Andrew handed us each another beer. The three of us became inseparable after that.

But I digress. I guess what I want you to know is that there was once a part of me that believed I was invincible, that everyone I loved was invincible. But who doesn't think that to some degree? I'm not guilty of a cardinal sin. I'm only guilty of being human: a human who can, and it turns out *will*, die.

There. I said it.

The thing is, there are so many ways to go. There are the obvious ones, like diseases, botched surgeries, and car wrecks. But there are also not-so-obvious reasons. Like tripping over the laundry basket, tumbling down the stairs, and landing precisely the wrong way. Or getting a paper cut and contracting a deadly blood infection. Or being stabbed by a flying metal umbrella at the beach. One minute, you're slathering on your SPF, and the next minute—sayonara! If you stop to think about it, you'll begin to realize that practically everything in life is a potential threat.

Which is how this story really begins, I guess. You see, at the end of the day, dying wasn't my problem. My problem, it turned out, was how.

TWO

I t started with a list.

I've been a list maker my whole adult life. Lists have always made me feel in control, like I could easily manage any earthly calamity so long as I organized the solution into the appropriate number of bullet points. Over the years, I've made shopping lists and meal-planning lists, lists of important dates (the point being to actually acknowledge them), lists of potential date nights and family nights, and lists of books to read on "me" nights (ha!).

Of course, after the initial list-writing buzz wore off ("I *will* do this" quickly became "Eh, I *might*, so long as there's nothing good on TV"), I mostly abandoned them. Still, the cycle repeated. When something in my life felt out of reach, there was a good chance I'd pick up paper and pen. Up until a few months ago, if you'd taken a peek inside my purse or desk drawers, you'd have found crumpled-up lists everywhere.

But there was one list I never crumpled: my annual birthday list, which I wrote in a little pink notebook I stored inside my nightstand. I started the tradition in my early twenties. Ever since, every year on my birthday eve, I'd pull out that same notebook and write a list of all the things I hoped to improve about myself and my life in the coming year. It was meant to be motivational. A New Year. A new page.

You get the idea. I always titled it based on my upcoming age—"Year Twenty-Seven," for example—and then underlined the words with a clean, sharp line.

It's strange to have this record of myself, to maintain the ability to flip backward through my life and to have concrete reminders of how consequential so many inconsequential things once seemed to me. For instance, a life goal for year twenty-two: "Take a shot at every bar in Manhattan!" (impossible when you consider how regularly bars shutter and new bars take their places, though I certainly did try). And for year twenty-three: "Do something dramatic with my hair! (Blonde? Pink? Anything but brown!)." Clearly a noteworthy moment in my existence.

But as the years passed, new, more significant trends emerged on those lists. First, they were becoming longer (probably a bad sign). And second, I had started to write down the same items every year (*definitely* a bad sign). In retrospect, maybe I should have kept a separate notebook where I listed all my excuses. Still, I never felt very affected by those untended items. If I ever did, I only had to flip through the empty pages that lay ahead. They were like neat little rectangular reminders of the many sunrises and sunsets that still lingered on my horizon line, all the time I still had stretched before me to daydream and procrastinate and list out my life instead of actually living it.

Mentally speaking, that's about where I was at last year, back when this whole fiasco—everything with that folder and Marian and that ridiculous party and the flamingos (yes, as in the tropical birds, but I'll get to that)—got underway. It began on a night in June. I'd been seated on the edge of my bed, still dressed in my work clothes with only minutes to spare before I had to rush out the door yet again. I was always rushing. No matter the task, it always felt like some other pressing issue was weighing on me. Anyway, that's when I pulled out that familiar pink notebook, turned to a fresh page, and told myself I had a whole two minutes to jot down my goals for the upcoming year. Thoughtful, I know.

Learn to cook (not just collect recipes from magazines). Exercise (reminder: exercise means breaking a sweat). Stop smoking porch cigarettes (I mean, really. You're how *old?). Stop rushing. Stop cursing (Tommy can hear you!). Stop procrastinating. Quit your job.* Start to *write* again. *Fix the table so you can eat like an adult. Read a new poem every night before bed. Go out with Andrew more. Play with Tommy more. Take care of yourself more. Iron your clothes (not just the fronts; the jig is up). Take a proper family vacation (see: "tiny paper umbrella cocktails"). Organize the house (i.e., stop living in a giant playroom). Laugh more. Garden? Try one of those breathing apps.*

As I did every year, I failed to consider how I'd achieve the items I'd listed. Instead, I stared at the page and convinced myself that I'd figure out how to cross off each item, even though I'd never once done so in the past. But that's the thing I've only recently come to understand about birthdays. They're not about presents or streamers. They're not about parties or pictures or petite pastel candles on your cake. They're about having a brief sense of hope. For that one day, we're able to close the door on our mistakes and cling to the false idea that we'll approach the next year wiser. We make wishes. We blow out candles. We tell ourselves *this* will be our year.

When I was done staring at my list, I slid the notebook back into my nightstand. I threw on a pair of jeans and the least wrinkled shirt I could find, gathered my long, mousy hair into a messy bun, and slid on my tortoiseshell eyeglasses. What can I say? It was my signature look: *frazzled-chic.* I sprinted into the hallway. When I was halfway to the stairs, one of Tommy's stray LEGOs impaled itself into the bottom of my bare foot.

"Fuuuuuck!" I shouted, loud enough for our whole block to hear.

"We heard that!" Andrew yelled from downstairs.

"Mama has to put money in the curse jar!" Tommy squealed.

"Sorry!" I shouted and then plucked the red plastic piece from my skin. My foot aching, I flicked the LEGO back onto the floor. I tried

9

to ignore the fact that it'd taken me mere seconds to abandon one of my bullet points. Fine. Two bullet points, technically.

Tomorrow, I told myself. *The list starts tomorrow.* I sprinted down the hallway and leaped over a pile of toy cars. *For fuck's sake, just not today.*

After all, like always, I was running late.

~

"Mama! Look! Daddy's a pony!"

I arrived at the bottom of our stairs, my foot throbbing, and strategically navigated the obstacle course of toys, unfolded laundry, and couch cushions my family had scattered across the floor. Tommy, his face hidden behind a superhero mask, rode through the living room on Andrew's back. I squinted and looked closer at Tommy's ensemble. "Are you using one of my work dresses as a cape?"

Tommy widened his eyes into saucers and kicked his father's hips. "Giddyup!" he shouted. "The villain is onto us!"

"Hey, babe." Andrew galloped across the hardwood floor. "If this game keeps up much longer, you might need to draw me an ice bath."

"Sounds like one of us is getting old." I turned over my bag and dumped out Tommy's many toys and snacks in one giant, satisfying heap. I batted my eyelashes. "Lucky for you, it's not me." I reached into the refrigerator for the appetizer platter I'd hastily assembled earlier that day.

"You look nice," Andrew said as he pulled himself off the floor. "New shirt?"

"Oh, um." I was like an awkward teenager anytime someone paid me a compliment. I chipped some dried Play-Doh from my blouse. "Not exactly."

Andrew smirked and then pretended not to watch as I flicked the clay from my fingernail. "In other news, Dr. White's office called. Something about your blood work." Andrew stretched his back, then adjusted his favorite moth-eaten T-shirt. With the exception of the commas that had formed around his eyes, he still maintained the same boyish charm that had drawn me to him back in college. "I think."

"Vampires!" Tommy shouted at no one in particular.

"Sorry, kiddo." I tossed Tommy a hunk of crunchy bread. "No vampires." I turned to Andrew. "I have my annual lady visit." That's what I called my yearly OB-GYN appointment. When it came to my body, I was still more or less an embarrassed adolescent. "They probably called to say they received my labs." I directed my attention to Tommy. "Hey, buddy." A rogue toy flew through the air. "Take off my dress cape and toss it back in the laundry basket, okay?"

"I can't," Tommy declared, plain and simple.

"Why?" I rummaged through our drawers for the plastic wrap.

"Because I'm a superhero space cowboy," he explained matter-of-factly.

I wrestled a piece of plastic into a flat sheet. "Well, how much longer do you plan to be a superhero space cowboy?"

"Until at least tomorrow morning," he announced. "Maybe longer."

I stepped over a giant package of snacks I'd recently picked up at the local big-box store and still hadn't put away. "Fine." I wrapped the platter and slammed the refrigerator shut with my backside. "You have until breakfast time."

Tommy slid the mask onto his head, his soft blond hair sticking up like spikes. "Mama, where are you going? It's pizza night. You love pizza night." Food that comes delivered in a box. What can I say? "I already set the table for us." Tommy gestured to three construction paper place mats on our table. Andrew and I exchanged a glance. "I picked flowers, too," Tommy said and then pointed to a drinking glass full of wilted dandelions.

I bit my lip. It was slick with lip balm, my go-to beauty product. "The thing is, that table is still pretty busted." I nodded toward a wooden leg wrapped in Bubble Wrap and duct tape. The leg had begun to wobble weeks earlier, after I'd piled a dozen boxes of bulk pantry staples on the tabletop. Like me, it seemed our table could barely handle the weight of our life. "You've made a beautiful spread, though." I turned to Andrew. *We're fixing that next weekend,* I mouthed, though I suspect we both knew that the hunk of wood would remain broken for weeks. Months, probably.

Tommy wrapped his arms around my thigh. "Why do you have to go?"

I rumpled his hair. "Because one of the neighbors is having a party for the mommies—"

"A party!" Tommy squealed. "On a school night?"

Weeknights were the only times the neighborhood moms got together. The weekends were too packed with errands and chores as we all hustled to prepare for the new week.

"Will there be cake?" Tommy asked.

Damn it. I hadn't thought of that. "There'd better not be," I mumbled.

"I want to come!" he pleaded.

"Trust me. You don't." I gave him a squeeze. "No one does."

Andrew circled his hips like he was wearing an invisible Hula-Hoop, then kissed me. "Mama has to go buy foot lotion in Mrs. Johnson's kitchen."

Tommy scrunched his face. "Why would Mama buy foot lotion in a kitchen?" Then he laughed wildly, the mere thought of buying beauty products next to a bowl of bananas the most comical thing he'd ever heard. "Everyone knows you buy lotion from a *store.*"

While Tommy was right, our neighbors failed to agree. Every few months, the women of Ferndale Lane were called to gather around one of our kitchen islands to contemplate beauty products no one wanted but all attendees were forced to buy. The parties, I'd learned, were how suburban women dealt with midlife crises. Instead of shaving their heads or investing in impractical wardrobes like normal people, they threw themselves into pyramid schemes and then acted like peddling lipsticks beside crudités platters was their life passion. It was a problem.

"Why do you have to go?" Tommy asked.

"Because if I don't," I informed him, "then everyone in the neighborhood will spend the whole night speculating about why I'm not there."

Tommy tossed a rubber ball above his head. "What does 'spec-u-looting' mean?"

I couldn't help it. I squeezed him again. I loved him and his innocence so damn much. "It means to talk badly about someone when she isn't present to defend herself."

"But you're not supposed to talk about your friends," Tommy said.

"I know, buddy." I grabbed his chin and kissed him. "Adults are terrible. Promise me you'll always stay young."

"Nope!" he shouted. "Superhero space cowboys make no promises!"

"Fine." I reached into my bag and dropped some coins into our curse jar—an oversize mason jar on our counter—then quickly sifted through our mess of unopened mail. *Bill. Crap. Another bill. More crap.* I stopped on a thin envelope. *Metrics Literary Magazine, New York, NY.* I tore it open. *Dear Mrs. Strauss, Thank you for your submission. Unfortunately . . .*

I'd been submitting my writing to literary journals for years. Decades, actually. Over time, the good ones had developed the courtesy to reject my work electronically, so my crushed dreams only had to exist in the metaverse. But the small journals—the ones no one outside academia knew—still believed in mailing me my failures. I don't know. Maybe it was part of the poetic experience for me to sometimes have to feel the weight of them.

I crumpled up the paper before anyone else saw it. "Anyway," I said to Tommy as I dug through a pile of plastic figurines until I found my shoes—a pair of neutral flats I'd worn for so long I wasn't even certain they were still in style—"just promise me you two won't play dodgeball in our living room while I'm gone."

"We won't," they announced in tandem, and I knew instantly that they would.

I shook my head, blew them air-kisses, and touched the doorknob. From the corner of my eye, I saw Tommy chuck the ball full force at Andrew. I closed the door behind me just in time to hear something shatter. But I didn't turn back.

After all, some things are better left as mysteries.

THREE

"Christ! Thank God you're here." Suzanne's door swung open before I'd even knocked. She had a bottle of wine tucked under her arm like a football. "Vikki is in there talking about Peter. *Again.*"

Beyond Suzanne's wide porch, I heard the cacophony of other female voices inside. Naturally, I was the last to arrive. "That's one way to say hello."

Suzanne rolled her eyes so far into her head I feared they might never return. "Maybe we should all finally tell her we know her son is gay," she said, more to herself than to me. "It's torture to watch her flounder like this." Suzanne likes to pretend she's having a two-way conversation when, in reality, she's mostly talking out loud to herself. Her whole life is one ongoing monologue. "She does *know*, right? I mean, how could she not?" She paused, weighing out her words like expensive produce. "Oh, shut up," she said, even though we both knew I hadn't said anything. "I *adore* Peter." She smoothed her smart button-down. "You know what I mean." I stood there holding my platter. Suzanne glanced at it, nodded her approval. "Fine. You're right. We can talk about Peter later. In the meantime, there's one more thing before you come inside." Suzanne smirked. "Happy birthday, Liv."

I forgot to tell you. That's the irony of this whole thing: the fact that my nickname is Liv. *Live. To live!* And yet . . .

"Oh. Right. Thanks," I said as I tried to smooth out my blouse. It was no use. "But you're a day early."

"Well, I figured you'd have plans all weekend. Plus, next week is a damn nightmare."

She was right. The last week of the school year meant everyone's calendars were a frenzy of parties and picnics and field days and frantic phone calls in which desperate parents begged teachers to give their crappy children higher grades. I should know. I'm a teacher at Blakely. It's one of those fancy private schools with iron gates and ivy growing all over everything.

"It's not a big deal," I told her. "Thirty-nine isn't exactly a milestone. I don't think they even make special greeting cards for it."

"Not a milestone? *Pfffft.* Of course it is."

Behind me, I heard the sprinklers come to life, the distinct *click-click-cliiiick* sounds, followed by the subtle scent of water on grass. "Maybe next year, once I'm officially over the hill," I suggested.

Suzanne rolled her eyes again. That was her signature look: head tilted back, eyes lost somewhere inside her skull. When her eyes rolled back down, reappearing like the images in a slot machine, she held up her free arm and waved. "Look at that beauty!" she shouted, surprising me. It took me a minute to realize she was addressing someone behind me.

I turned and saw one of our neighbors, Annie, an elderly woman who loved her hydrangeas more than life, out on her evening walk with her dog, Jack. I waved to Annie as a courtesy, though I didn't make a big deal about Jack. Frankly, between all the midnight barking and the public defecation, he was becoming a pain in the ass.

"That dog is a pain in the ass," Suzanne whispered, as though she could read my mind. "I hear him barking every day when I'm out for my walk." That was another thing about our neighborhood. The women on our block believed in their daily walks the way some people believe in their faith. I still wasn't sure if their goal was to walk toward or away from something. "He shit on our curb last week." Suzanne kept waving. "Nice night!"

"You know," I said while adjusting my eyeglasses, careful not to drop my platter, "I'm still young in dog years."

"For now. Until you wake up and are as old as her." Suzanne nodded toward Annie, who had nearly disappeared at the end of our block. "Doesn't it feel like yesterday that you were twenty?" She leaned against the doorframe. "If that's any indicator, we'll be sixty in a flash."

"You really ought to be a motivational speaker," I joked. Nearby, a group of neighborhood teens zipped past on bicycles, likely heading home for the night. "While we're on the topic of potential career paths, I've been meaning to ask if you've—"

"Not now." Suzanne swatted my comment away before I could finish it. "I don't want to get into it tonight."

A few days earlier, while we were drinking wine on her backyard swing set, Suzanne had told me that, back in ancient history, before her closet looked like an L. L. Bean catalog, she'd worked as a designer for a company that made apparel from recycled soda bottles. I had no idea. I'd never thought about who Suzanne was before we'd met. Adulthood is funny. Once you hit a certain age, everyone stops talking about their pasts. I hardly knew where the women on our street had gone to college. I didn't know their maiden names. Anyway, Suzanne had left that job after she'd learned she was pregnant. She swore she'd go back. Years passed. That night on the swings, she told me she was finally ready. She needed to unlock that piece of her identity again.

"But back to you," she said as she adjusted her wine bottle. "As a forty-one-year-old myself, all I'm saying is this." She gestured to her breasts. "It's all downhill from here."

I shook my head. "Subtle."

Her comment settled upon us. As it did, I felt in the air that things were changing. Spring was evolving into summer. The evening breeze felt warmer. The sky was marked by an extra brushstroke of light.

Andrew and I had moved into the neighborhood on a night just like it, my stomach as round as a planet, his arms heavy from the crate of literary magazines he'd insisted on schlepping with us, one final reminder of the life we were leaving behind.

We'd looked at only two houses before settling on ours. Andrew had picked it because of the yard. I had picked it because it reminded me of a child's drawing: a perfect square accented by four rectangle windows and a triangular roof. Although we had basically been children when we met, Andrew and I had become adults together—adults who would live in a child's vision of a grown-up home. Somehow, I found logic in that. For reasons I couldn't articulate, it felt poetic.

Neither of us had wanted to leave the city. Our apartment had felt claustrophobic, yes, but also intimate: there physically wasn't room for secrets or personal space. During college, and in the years that followed, our entire relationship had blossomed within the confines of cramped spaces—crowded subway cars, miniature studios, bustling walkways— like a flower you find growing from a sidewalk crack. But then we found out about Tommy, and our crowded life, which we'd once romanticized, began to feel like a potential safety hazard. And so, we left.

We made so many promises to each other back then, promises we knew we'd break but that, at the time, had felt as necessary to us as breath. We'd made promises about following our dreams (*of course we'll keep writing!*) and our interests (*of course we'll still venture into the city!*) and our commitment to our personal identities (*of course we won't shop at big-box stores!*). We made promises to never become so consumed by our new life that we'd forget our old one. But like all our promises, we broke that last one, too.

We made concessions. Once Tommy was grown, there would be time for writing. Once we got through the week, the month, the school year, the holidays, the nonsense, the stress, we'd find time to do the things we longed to do. But then we never did. Life, it turned out, could wait.

"Wait a minute," I said. Up and down our block, the streetlights flickered to life. "You didn't tell anyone it's my birthday, right?" I paused to read Suzanne's expression. A lump formed in my throat. "Oh God. Am I about to walk into a surprise party situation?"

Suzanne deflected by glancing at my platter. "Fresh basil, huh?" She smirked. "That means it's homemade, right?"

I sighed. "I didn't have time to dice the tomatoes. Don't tell the others." A fat drop of oil dripped from the platter and onto my shoe. I tried to shake it off, but it was no use. "They already think I'm a degenerate for forgetting to send Tommy in with cookies for the bake sale." I dropped my voice. "Promise you'll keep my secret safe."

Suzanne smiled in a way that revealed nothing. Knowing some unsolicited birthday celebration was moments away, I followed her inside.

FOUR

Liv!" a chorus of female voices sang out when I entered the kitchen. "Happy birthday!"

I snapped my head in Suzanne's direction; her face was not coincidentally buried inside her refrigerator. "Thanks." I reached for a glass of wine, hoping that was the end of it.

"You're late," Vikki said in a failed attempt at a jovial tone. She laughed awkwardly. "We were preparing to send out the search teams." Another fail.

I set my platter on the island, which was already arranged with an assortment of beautifully assembled, definitely homemade appetizers: dough-wrapped brie, pomegranate-flecked endive boats, that sort of thing.

"We were just sharing everyone's summer plans." Vikki smoothed her white jeans with a tanned hand. The season had hardly started, and already everyone's skin was kissed with a brownish glow, as though they'd all bathed in almond milk. I, on the other hand, was still plain milky, like some Victorian. "Long story short," Vikki continued, "Peter will be at a tap dancing camp upstate." She clutched her wineglass like it was a form of life support. "We had *hoped* he'd be interested in lacrosse camp, but we keep reminding ourselves of the *athleticism* involved in competitive tap dancing."

"Mmm," the group hummed, like we'd choreographed the moment. It was our own collective version of support. We waited then to see if she was ready to say more. Vikki looked away, her invitation for someone else to go on.

"So, what's on the agenda for the big birthday weekend?" Allison Hanley asked, shifting the conversation. Allison lived in a pale-yellow home at the end of our block. She had a reputation for styling her children's meals into elaborate smiley faces (explain to me why a slab of meatloaf requires olive eyes and a ketchup smile) and for wearing yoga pants anytime she stepped outside (note: Allison Hanley has never once taken a yoga class). Everyone turned their attention away from Vikki and toward me. "Suze said tomorrow is the big three-nine!"

"Well, tomorrow I'll be at work." I stabbed a chip into a bowl of dip. "But this weekend, we're going to the zoo," I said. A few nights earlier, while the three of us ate bowls of spaghetti on the couch, Andrew had asked how I wanted to celebrate my birthday weekend. Before I could answer, Tommy shouted, "The zoo! We can visit the flamingos and tell them it's your birthday!" What can I say? I love the flamingo exhibit, and Tommy knows it.

"The zoo?" Courtney Whitehead looked at me as though I'd recently had a lobotomy. Courtney had an opinion about everything: what toilet paper you ought to buy, what recipe you must try. "Oh no, no. You can't celebrate the last birthday of your thirties at the zoo!" She wagged her finger in the air. "You must do something *special*."

What *special* thing were we supposed to do? Go to some okay restaurant where they write *Happy Birthday* in chocolate sauce on the rim of your dessert plate? I felt everyone staring at me. My palms started to sweat. "It's just another year. I don't know why everyone is making such a big deal about it."

"Ignore her, Liv." Suzanne glided around the kitchen and topped off all our wineglasses. "You're the youngest about-to-be-thirty-nine-year-old

I know. You don't even have any fine lines on your face." She set down the bottle and squinted. "Well, not really."

When I was a teenager, I read a magazine article printed in a publication called *Pretty!* (did such publications ever actually exist?) that proclaimed twenty-seven as the best age of a girl's ("young *woman's*!") life. You could tell from all the quirky fonts and makeup advertisements that *Pretty!* was rooted in serious journalism. According to the article, written by a young-at-the-time writer, Jessica Frances, twenty-seven was the age her readers should aspire toward: by then, we'd have checked off all the boxes of adulthood (babies, dreamy husbands, the whole nine) but would still have our teenage metabolism. A win!

It was hard to determine Ms. Frances's point with all the beauty product references getting in her way. However, I had interpreted her takeaway as this: by twenty-seven, all our dreams would be dropped like gumdrops into our well-moisturized hands. At the end of the article was a brief quiz titled Will You Find Your Soulmate by Twenty-Seven? Very highbrow stuff.

For the rest of high school, and then in my early twenties, I recalled this article and told myself twenty-seven would be the year my life snapped into place with all the satisfaction of pressing the final puzzle piece into position. I could take risks and make bad decisions and put my dreams on hold so long as, by twenty-seven, I had everything figured out. The night of my actual twenty-seventh birthday, I blew out a candle on a bodega muffin Andrew had purchased after his bartending shift. We weren't married. We weren't even engaged. My dream job was still off in my future (or my past, I still wasn't sure), while my actual job—a magazine internship—paid me only in free beauty samples and snacks. And so, I edited my plan, reminding myself that I'd always been a late bloomer. Twenty-nine would be my breakout year. When that didn't work out, either, I put all my hopes into my early thirties. And then. And then . . .

"I hate to admit it, but Courtney's right." Vikki scooped up a dollop of hummus. "I mean, once you hit forty, it's all a bit of a mess."

"That's not true." I twisted my simple gold wedding band, an old nervous habit.

"But it is," she continued. "I know people who have *died* in their forties."

I raised my brow. "Name one."

"My cousin's friend's sister." Vikki nibbled a carrot stick. "For months, she had what looked like a smear of mascara under her eye." No one blinked. I shook my head. "It turned out it was melanoma." She paused for the sake of drama. "It spread to her brain." Everyone gasped.

"I know someone, too," Allison added. All the women leaned in. It was beginning to feel like a high school slumber party. "My sister-in-law's college roommate. Or college friend." Allison paused. "Maybe it was her high school friend. Anyway, one day, she woke up fine. The next, she ordered a shrimp cocktail, her throat closed up, and—*BAM*—dead at forty-one." The crowd visibly shuddered.

"That's not a story about getting old," I piped up. "That's a story about an allergy."

"But that's the thing," Allison continued. "She didn't *have* an allergy before that night." She waved to Suzanne to pass her the wine bottle. "The doctor said it was because her hormones were out of whack from early menopause. Basically, aging did her in."

"That's not a real story," I retorted. "I saw that on one of my social media feeds."

"Whatever helps you sleep at night," Allison said.

"Well, this has all been very uplifting." I forced an insincere laugh. "So has anyone purchased their coffins yet?" I asked, a cheap joke, really.

"Go ahead. Laugh." Allison spooned some dip onto her plate. "All I'm saying is that if anyone has unresolved items on her bucket list, she'd better get a move on them, just in case."

"A bucket list?" Courtney laughed. "Sure. I remember when I thought I'd become a ballerina." Everyone echoed her laughter. She touched her forehead. "So embarrassing."

"That doesn't count." Allison sipped her wine. "That's on *every* little girl's bucket list." Courtney's laughter fizzled out. Allison set down her glass. "You *were* a little girl, right?"

Courtney swallowed hard. "Actually, I was in my early twenties," she explained. "I danced in an off-Broadway show before we moved to town." She fiddled with her diamond wedding band. "I helped to choreograph parts of it, too." She looked up, a hint of pride in her expression. "Have I never mentioned that?" No one spoke. Instead, I noticed everyone studying the granite countertop, as though lost in private memories—private bucket lists—of their own. "But that was so long ago." Courtney forced herself to laugh. "Now, I choreograph the kids' sports schedules." Everyone laughed again, too. Everyone, that is, except for Suzanne, who looked away and bit her cheek.

"You know." Suzanne summoned a wide smile. "While we're on the topic of aging . . ."

We understood her subtext. Suzanne herded us around her dining room table, which was arranged with dozens of sleek cosmetic bottles. "So, as you all know, skin care has long been a passion of mine." This, I should point out, was a lie. "Recently, I stumbled upon a line of anti-aging ointments made from a rare Brazilian nut that works wonders for crow's-feet and age spots and all the other problems our friend Liv here gets to look forward to dealing with soon."

My neighbors inspected the products. I contemplated a jar, then peered in a mirror Suzanne had set up with her display. I studied my reflection. The simple sweep of face powder. The collection of faint lines that hugged my lips like unwanted friends. I squinted at my golden-brown eyes. They looked tired, like someone had forgotten to flip the switch and turn them on.

The lights dimmed. I turned and saw Suzanne. She held a single plate in her hand, on top of which sat a single pink cupcake illuminated by a slender candle. "I knew you'd hate it if I got you a cake. But a cupcake . . ." Suzanne handed me the dish. "To the last year of your youth, Olivia Strauss." She smiled and offered me a jovial wink. "Now make a wish."

FIVE

After leaving Suzanne's house, I walked home and reflected on the evening's conversation. Usually the women's talk about aging didn't bother me, but that night it didn't sit right. I stepped onto the porch, ready to go inside and call it a night. Instead, I sat on our stone steps and pulled my palm-size black notebook from my old cross-body canvas bag. I'd carried some version of that notebook with me since college. It was where I jotted down my daily observations in the deluded hope that they'd help respark my creative side. I uncapped my pen and scribbled some thoughts before I quickly huffed my annoyance with myself and crossed them all out. I pressed my phone against my ear. Rectangles of light glowed yellow up and down our block, illuminating sleepy vignettes of my neighbors' lives.

"Are we dying?" I asked as soon as the line clicked to life.

"I mean, technically," Marian shouted. In the backdrop, I heard the buzz of a very different weekday evening, a cocktail of loud music and ambient city noise. "But I just met a *very* handsome, *very* young bartender, so hopefully not tonight."

Sometimes, it felt less like Marian lived in a different zip code and more like she lived in a different universe, one where attractive twenty-somethings simply tumbled onto her doorstep with the same regularity that boxes of toothpaste and cleaning products tumbled onto mine.

"Where are you?" I reached behind our bush and pulled my weather-worn cigar box onto my lap, the one I'd bought at a garage sale shortly after we moved onto our street. I flipped it open and pulled out the pack of cigarettes I stored inside it. "It sounds like you're at a rave."

She raised her voice. "This new place opened on my block." She was still shouting. "It's a renovated gas station with this wild tiki bar, which I'm aware doesn't fit the aesthetic. But here we are." She stopped herself, laughed. "Or here *I* am."

I fumbled to light a brittle cigarette. "Are you drunk?"

"I plead the Fifth."

I could easily imagine Marian at such a place—her dyed blonde hair pulled up in some artfully messy bun, her lips stained red, dressed in a pair of perfect-for-her jeans and one of her signature vintage blouses that she always buttoned in a sexy, but not too sexy, sort of way.

"Anyway, it's my birthday party," she explained. "*Our* birthday party, technically." I forgot to tell you that Marian and I share a birthday, a fact we learned during the modernism seminar we took together our freshman year at NYU. It's June sixteenth, better known as Bloomsday to the literary set, the day when James Joyce's tome *Ulysses* takes place. "In truth," Marian continued, "I'm supposed to be researching the cocktails here for a new article. I figured why not kill two birds, you know?"

"Yeah. Me too," I said. "I'm writing an article about suburban women's love of midrange chardonnay."

"Wait. What? Did you pick up a freelance gig?"

"I'm kidding, Marian."

"Oh. Right." She giggled. "Chardonnay. Good one. They really do love that shit, don't they? Anyway, did you ever email that editor I told you about? Michael. The one from *Hearth*. I've been working with him on some freelance projects. They're looking for essays. They pay pretty well."

"One problem," I pointed out. "I don't write essays."

"From what I understand, these days, you just don't write. End of statement."

"You're a riot," I said.

"And you're a poet," she retorted. "Remember?"

It was a long story.

Shortly after college, Marian, like me, had landed a magazine internship. It was at a publication called *Beurre*—the French word for "butter." It was all the rage back then. Like any intern, she started out shuffling papers. But then, she did the impossible: she parlayed her shuffling into actual bylines. Food, it turned out, was her niche. When the magazine folded, she went freelance. For days, she'd amble around her apartment—the same apartment she'd lived in since our twenties—until she received an email from some editor and then found herself at an under-the-radar bakery or bar that would change your life.

Unlike Marian, it took me a long time to graduate from my interning days. I think it had to do with residual trauma over the fact that I was an intern at all. Anyway, I was eventually hired by *Home Made*, a women's magazine about—you guessed it—modern homemaking. For the next few years, I fell into a sort of alliteration hell and wrote endless roundup pieces about cozy autumn decor ("Five Fun, Festive Fall Finds!").

The job hadn't been my first choice. It hadn't been my last choice, either. I was supposed to be a poet. At least, that had been the plan. Please, spare me your laughter. It was an idealistic dream one can entertain only in one's youth, before things like health insurance factor into the equation. Still, there was a moment when I thought it might work. But then it didn't. It was probably for the best. I mean, who wants to spend her career thinking about *feelings* and being forced into a life of black turtlenecks, berets, and a rotation of strong coffee and croissants?

"I haven't contacted him," I said. "But maybe I will if I come up with a decent idea."

"Well, have you at least read *my* new article? The one I emailed you last week?"

Marian constantly sent me her bylines. "Yes," I lied. "I loved it."

She paused. I heard her suck her teeth. "What was it about?"

I moved the phone from one ear to the other. "Um . . . food?"

"Liv!"

"I'm sorry!" I inhaled a stale drag, which immediately sent me into a coughing fit. "I'm just busy!"

"That's always your excuse."

"But this time, I mean it," I explained. "It's the end of the school year at Blakely. My to-do list honestly looks like a study in insanity."

"You and your damn lists," she muttered. "Maybe you should turn *them* into poems."

"Give me a break," I said in between gasps. I coughed again. "I'm just swamped."

"Wait." The noise around Marian died down. I heard a door close behind her. "Are you smoking a porch cigarette?"

I forced another dry drag. It tasted terrible. "It's been a long night," I explained before hacking into my fist.

Marian cleared her throat. "Speaking of which, let's get back to the beginning. Why the sudden concern with death?"

I stubbed the cigarette out and placed the butt in the box along with the dozens of others that had come before it. "I don't know," I said. "I was at a party with the neighborhood women, and they kept talking about how I'm about to enter the last year of my youth."

"At least they didn't force you to buy any more of that crap lip gloss," she noted.

"True," I said. "Though I did get suckered into buying a bottle of antiaging cream."

"Antiaging. Woof. Feels a bit on the nose, no?"

"Exactly."

I looked out at my tree-lined street and tried to envision Marian's current surroundings, a hodgepodge of strangers and noise. For years, our lives had been so different, Marian's just a more mature version of our twenties, and mine a portrait of suburbia.

"Why do you hang out with those women?" Marian asked. "You don't even like them. Didn't you tell me that more than one has a stick figure family stuck on the back of her car?"

"It's complicated," I said. "We live on the same block."

"Three drug dealers live on my block," Marian offered. "Should I start inviting them over for potlucks?"

I sighed. "It's different. I don't have to like them, but it seems the unspoken code is that I *do*, in fact, have to hang out with them."

I don't know. I wasn't sure *how* I felt about the neighborhood women. I think the issue was that I viewed myself as different from most of them. I still had dreams, though I rarely talked publicly about them. It made me sad the way they spoke about their former ambitions like they were punch lines or relics they'd never dig back up. Prior to that night with Suzanne on the swings, I'd never heard one of them address their passions as things that could still be made real.

Marian huffed. "Have it your way. But do me one favor. Don't listen to them, Liv. Those women are a bunch of old hags. The last time I visited you, one of them told me she admired my confidence for 'dressing so much like myself.' What does that even mean?"

Our foyer light clicked on. "Maybe they're right. Maybe I'm one of those pathetic women who's in age denial or something." I turned and saw Andrew through the screen, his reading glasses pushed onto his head. Like every night, he'd likely passed out on the couch with an old paperback on his chest.

"What are you doing?" His voice was raspy with sleep. "You're not smoking, are you?"

I balanced the phone against my shoulder and held up my hands. "Not guilty."

"I see the cigar box behind you," he said. *Shit.* "You should come to bed, babe. You have a few big days coming up." Andrew leaned against the doorframe, wearing his old Sherpa slippers and half zip. He was all dad. "Speaking of which, has Marian told you yet?"

"Told me what?" I asked, confused.

"You're all mine on Saturday," Marian shouted through the line. "We're celebrating our birthday together this weekend. Consider it a date."

"Wait," I said, already working out a thousand excuses.

"Forget about your to-do list for a day," Andrew said, like he could see inside my brain. "It's your birthday weekend. You should go out and enjoy it." He smiled. "Plus, I already told Tommy the flamingos can wait an extra day."

"I mean, I probably *could* benefit from a change in scenery," I admitted. I hadn't visited the city or seen Marian in months. "I'm not sure if you've heard the news, but based on the neighbors' conversation tonight, I'm officially old."

Andrew smirked. Lines as thin as pencil sketches formed around his mouth. "Those women are a bunch of stiffs. They've been old since their early twenties. What do they know?" Andrew leaned toward the phone. "So, where are you taking her, Mar? Hopefully nowhere too ridiculous." Marian had a history of taking me on bizarre adventures. There was the restaurant where patrons ate in total darkness. The bar that specialized in insect-based snacks. Although we'd known Marian for the same number of years, unlike me, I don't think Andrew had ever grown completely accustomed to her eccentricities. Andrew was the voice of reason in our trio. He didn't buy into things like horoscopes or superstitions, like Marian often did, or fall for trendy gimmicks, like those she often forced upon me. He was our source of logic.

"I promise you, Andy," Marian explained, "there will be no tattoos or trapeze stunts."

"We're thirty-nine now," I said. "Apparently, we're at the height of maturity."

Andrew kissed the top of my head. He smelled like soap and old book pages and sleep. "We'll see," he said and then stepped inside.

When he was gone, I turned my attention back to Marian. "So, what's the plan?" I stopped. "The *actual* plan? This isn't going to be like when—"

"Oh, stop," she said, interrupting me before the memory had a chance to spring back to life. "That was a million years ago. I swear, you get so hung up in the past sometimes." I heard a crowd of people emerge in her backdrop. "Anyway, I'm still weighing out some options," she said. "Though I think this conversation may have given me a good idea."

Before I could question her further, my phone buzzed against my ear. The words Happy Birthday Mama flashed across the screen.

"What is it?" Marian asked.

"Tommy must have set an alarm on my phone to wish me a happy birthday," I told her. "It's midnight, apparently."

"Well then." Marian inhaled a smooth breath. "Happy birthday, Liv. We're officially thirty-nine." She exhaled loudly for drama's sake. "I still feel pretty young. How about you?"

"It's hard to say." I slid my cigar box back behind the bush. "I'm not sure 'young' is the right word." Behind me, our hall light clicked off. Already, a dull ache pulsed in my head from the wine, just another perk of aging. "For the moment, I mostly feel like I need to go to bed."

SIX

I pulled onto Blakely's campus the next morning. Not exactly where I'd hoped to spend my birthday. My bag was stuffed with crumpled essays I'd neglected all week. It didn't matter. The kids didn't care anymore. Neither did I. I could have written anything across those papers. *Timothy—your sentences rely on word clutter. Also, your clothes smell like soup. Therefore, you've earned an F. Sarah—review your pronoun agreement. Likewise, did you really lose your virginity to Timothy? Seriously? The soup kid?*

I walked toward the ivy-covered mansion that housed the English Department. I dropped my bag at my desk. It was a mosaic of end-of-year to-do lists. I picked up a pen but quickly set it back down. I just stared out the window, wondering how I'd ended up there in the first place.

"Our meeting was moved to the library."

Christopher's voice interrupted me. I swiveled my chair. He was dressed in his normal attire—bow tie, gingham shirt, thick-framed eyeglasses. Christopher was twenty-six and an aspiring poet who liked to remind everyone that he'd already earned *two* master's degrees.

"Sebastian told everyone earlier." He sipped from a mug stamped with the words I'M SILENTLY CORRECTING YOUR GRAMMAR. "I said I'd inform you since you were probably running late."

"Oh, thanks." I turned back to my lists so we'd stop talking. Christopher was perfectly nice—pretentious, yes, but nice enough. Still, he irritated me. "I, um, appreciate that. I guess."

I left the office to go teach my morning class. It was no use. The kids kept leaning toward the windows to flirt with the early-summer light, like plants twisting toward the sun. It was hard to blame them. To be honest, I was distracted, too. I kept thinking about what Marian had in store for us the next day.

We were freshmen the first time she took me on one of her little excursions. We'd known each other for only a few months, but already it had felt like years. College is unique in that way. Time is compressed. Friendships are fast-tracked. One minute, you're strangers; the next, you eat greasy takeout together every night and shower in the same hallway.

"Let's go somewhere," Marian had said. I was hunched over my desk with a thousand textbooks one afternoon. "You look like you need a break." I grabbed my bag. I didn't need much convincing.

We strolled downtown. "So, why'd you come to the city, anyway?" she asked. "No offense, but you seem like you might have liked one of those quiet schools upstate."

I slapped her arm. "What's that mean?"

"You hardly take advantage of being here." She shrugged. "You're always studying."

"I'm *here* because I want to be a writer," I told her, plain and simple, even though she already knew that. It was the reason we were both there. "I just want to do well so I can—"

"You don't need to *study* to be a writer." Marian spread out her arms and twirled, right there in the middle of the crowded sidewalk. "What you need to do is to get out and live."

I'd had a passion for writing poetry for as long as I'd been able to breathe. It felt like more than just what I liked to do; it felt like who I was, in many ways. An only child, I grew up in a quiet town with parents who were okay living quiet lives. If they'd had their own passions or interests, I didn't know about them. But me? I didn't want a life like that. I wanted noise. I had ideas and observations I wanted people to hear. I just didn't know how to put myself out there.

"What do you like to write about?" Marian had asked me as we moved up the block. "You haven't let me read any of your work yet. What's your specialty?"

"I'm not sure." I was just getting started and already felt behind. "I'm still trying to find my voice."

A sliver of a smile appeared on her face. It was a smile I'd eventually know well, one that meant she was up to something. "You want to come somewhere with me?" We stopped on the corner. A thousand cars zipped past. "There's this exhibit I've been dying to see."

I didn't have time to decide. Already, she was dragging me forward.

A few minutes later, we stepped out of the sunlight and entered the exhibition space. It was dark, except for a single light. I blinked away the shadows and then realized the entire room was lined with mirrors—the floor, the ceiling, everything. There were a dozen mirrored walls in the center of the exhibit, too.

"It's a maze," Marian explained. "According to the artist, it's a comment on identity. You're supposed to follow the thousands of reflections of your face to find your way out."

"Um." I turned for the exit. "This place is making me kind of nauseous."

"It'll be fun." She tugged my hand. "Plus, maybe it'll give you the inspiration you need."

By the time we'd finally navigated our way through the exhibit, I was simultaneously queasy and thrilled. My mind raced. "I want to go write," I told her, lines of verse already unfolding in my head. "I think something about that place just gave me an idea."

We stepped back onto the street. "Don't forget that you're here for the experience, Liv." We both shielded our eyes from the sun. "You're not going to find your voice inside a textbook."

That night, I wrote what felt like the first real poem of my life.

~

When I was done teaching my morning class, I walked to the faculty lounge, poured myself some burnt coffee, and then headed toward the library. It was my favorite room in the mansion: bay windows, infinite bookshelves, a fireplace, and a robin's-egg-blue ceiling.

"So, we agree?" Sebastian, our longtime chairperson, said as I took a seat. Sebastian had a thick graying beard and a penchant for elbow patches. He reminded me of Hemingway. "No notable curriculum changes for next year."

There were never notable curriculum changes. I'd taught the same books so many times that I had entire pages memorized. It was like *Groundhog Day*. I just kept sputtering off the same allegedly meaningful anecdotes and bad jokes year after year. It was depressing.

"Then it's settled." Sebastian slapped his hands together. "Everything remains intact."

Meetings that could have been emails. They were our departmental specialty. "Olivia." Sebastian stopped me at the door. "How do *you* feel about these changes?"

"Um." I didn't know why he was asking me. "I thought we weren't *making* changes."

Sebastian nodded, like I'd said something profound. "Exactly."

"Right." I adjusted my bag strap. "I mean, whatever works. It's not really up to me."

He touched his beard. "I'd like to talk to you about something." He glanced at an antique clock on the fireplace mantel. "We're short on time for now," he said. "How about next week?"

I nodded my agreement, but I was only half listening. As he spoke, I caught my reflection in the large brass mirror above the mantel. I looked at it for what felt like a long time. "Sure," I said and tried to disregard the fact that, thanks to the light or the angle or some other trick of the eye, it hardly looked like me at all.

SEVEN

The next morning, my train lurched into Penn Station. I glanced at my watch—an old flea market thing I'd bought in college. For once, I was on time. I navigated the labyrinth of underground corridors and emerged at street level, the whole world awake with neon and noise.

I took a cab to the address Marian had sent and found myself standing outside a hipster brunch spot that looked like it'd fallen straight out of some influencer's social media feed. You know the sort of place: subway tiles, cascading plants, trendy neon, sliding garage doors, mason jars for everything. I found Marian, who was seated in the back. She looked so cool and beautiful, so "like herself." Almost instantly, I felt better. She waved. No matter how much time had passed between our visits, she never appeared to age a single day.

I squeezed through the maze of other guests. "Brunch. How tame."

"Consider yourself lucky." Marian smirked. "You were in such a panic when you called me the other night, I almost suggested we meet at our bench."

Our bench. I laughed. During college, whenever one of us was in meltdown mode—an upcoming exam, some boy drama—we'd call or leave a sticky note on each other's desks. *Meet me at our bench.* The bench in question was situated inside the MoMA, right in front of Monet's *Water Lilies.* I don't remember why we picked that painting, other than that on our first trip to the MoMA together we both *swore* we'd always been *so* inspired by it. (I'm sure the fact that it was *huge* or that it had been reproduced on every poster and coffee mug in the museum's gift shop had nothing to do with it.) Either way, when we were in crisis, that bench became our shared place of solace, both of us believing that if we sat together and stared at that painting long enough, we could solve all the world's problems. No matter how many years passed, as far as Marian and I were concerned, that bench would always belong exclusively to us.

Marian stood and wrapped her arms around me, her flowy blouse caressing my skin. I breathed her in. Her hair was laced with jasmine, as though she'd just blown in from someplace exotic. "I miss you," I whispered and then pulled back to take her in. I averted my gaze to the table and noticed two shot glasses. "Am I right to question if it's legal to serve booze this early?"

"Ehhh." Marian shrugged. Her earrings—some funky metal things I'd never have the confidence to wear—brushed against her shoulder. "It's a minor technicality." There was something relaxed about the way she spoke, her whole demeanor as cool and effortless as good denim. She bit her cherry-stained lip. "But the guys here owe me." She smiled. "I wrote a pretty well-received article about the chef a few months back." She lifted a brow. "Speaking of which, are you still too busy, or have you finally read that new article I sent to you?"

I sighed. "Which one?"

"Liv—" She whacked my arm. "Why don't you ever read my stuff anymore? We always *used* to read each other's work. Remember?"

I didn't respond. Marian was a natural storyteller. She could write a hundred pages about a bowl of rice and make the reader want to keep turning the page. Still, I just didn't connect with that world. I mean, craft cocktails and artisanal Popsicles? The topics she wrote about were indulgences that just didn't fit into the rhythm of my life. But it was different for Marian. Ever since that first internship almost two decades earlier, she'd learned to sustain herself through food—physically, financially, creatively. Me? Most days, I ate a package of Tommy's animal crackers and called it lunch. When it came to food, I was basically starving.

"Anyway," she continued, "I had the pleasure of interviewing some suburban types about a new cooking club they founded. You should read it." She smirked. "They reminded me of your neighbors. But not in a good way."

I settled myself at our table, adjusted my glasses. A chambray-clad waiter, some beautiful twentysomething, his skin flawless, his black hair as thick as rope, appeared beside us.

"So, what gives?" Marian put her hand to her chin. Some gorgeous, vintage-looking costume ring shimmered on her finger. "You usually laugh at your neighbors' ridiculous antics."

Our waiter poured our coffees. "I don't know," I sighed. I both hated and loved how well Marian knew me. "Maybe they're right. Maybe my youth really is behind me."

"Your youth?" Marian shook her head. "I met a woman recently who just had her first child at forty-nine. Naturally."

My emotions on the subject felt so jumbled. It wasn't my age that bothered me. It was that I knew I wasn't living up to my full potential. "You don't feel any sort of big emotions about this birthday?" I asked her. "Thirty-nine doesn't feel a bit strange to you?"

"I slept with a twenty-two-year-old this week." She smiled. "I'm good."

I swirled the contents of my mug. "I don't know." I chipped away some of my weeks-old nail polish. "Maybe I've spent too long putting off certain things."

"Like what?" Marian touched my hand, the gesture soft yet strong enough to carry the weight of my words. "Not to play devil's advocate here, but you have a pretty decent life. I mean, your job sucks, but you *do* have one. And obviously Andrew and Tommy are the best."

"I know. I'm aware of how good I have it." A pang of guilt bloomed inside me. "I just feel sort of stuck. Like I missed out on something or like some piece of my life is still—"

"So, let me guess. This is about your career? Again."

"Maybe?" I kneaded the pad of my thumb. "I'm not sure. I just thought certain parts of my life would be different by this age. That's all."

Marian rested her elbows on the table. "That, my darling, is because you have spent years writing out silly lists that detail what you think your life *ought* to look like." The light from the window illuminated her face. "You know, it's okay to be happy and to still have things about your life that you want to change." She spread a napkin across her lap. "You still have time to travel the world and leave your job and dye your hair pink if you really want."

"Well, the joke's on you." I felt like I wanted to cry. I was so damn grateful for her. "Because I don't want to dye my hair pink." It was a last-ditch effort at sarcasm. "I'd look like a bad pop star or an anime character."

Marian squeezed my fingers. "Ignore those women, Liv. Really. They're just sad because they don't have anything driving them anymore."

"That's not true," I countered. "They have their kids and—"

"I'm not talking about their kids. I'm talking about them. Their dreams." Marian tapped her spoon against the rim of her mug. "I know you know what I mean."

I did. You see, there's a great secret to motherhood: no matter who you are or who you used to be or who you'd once dreamed you'd become, you were supposed to pretend that your children were enough, that you weren't multifaceted, and that your dreams weren't three-dimensional. You weren't supposed to admit that you had any dreams reserved exclusively for yourself at all.

Marian squinted at me. "What? I can tell you want to say something."

I bit my cheek. "Remember when we were in college, back when everything felt so fun? When the whole world felt possible?" I sighed. "When did life stop feeling like that?"

Marian grinned. "I remember when *you* were a bit more fun."

"Hey!" I swatted her hand.

"Do you want the truth or something else?" Neither of us spoke for a beat. "But let's forget about the past for now." She slid my shot glass closer to me. "You still have your whole life ahead of you." Marian smiled. "We both do." She lifted her glass and clinked it against mine. "Here's to us, Liv."

We both downed the shots. Instantly, I felt the liquor go straight to my head. "Here's to us, Mar," I said, already feeling a touch buzzed. It was the youngest I'd felt in years.

~

"I want to take you somewhere," Marian said a short while later. We were paused outside a secondhand bookshop—the same one we used to frequent in college. "But I'm not telling you where," she informed me, an old paperback copy of *Through the Looking-Glass* in her hand.

After brunch, we'd spent time getting lost in the city. Marian and I had always liked doing that together. For a long time (minutes? hours?), we just wandered with no real sense of direction. The conversation was the only thing guiding us. We talked about our past—about highs and lows and old drinking holes and former fashions and friends who came and went so quickly we no longer remembered their names. Don't get me wrong. Ours was not one of those sad friendships where the only thing that kept it burning was a shared set of dusty memories. It was just that sometimes it felt important to remember the person you used to be and the person you'd once told yourself you'd eventually become.

"Well, can I ask why you won't tell me?" I knew it was because she knew I'd say no.

"Because you'll say no," she said.

I picked up a yellowed copy of a familiar book titled *Poems for Every Season*. I flipped through it and realized it was the same anthology Marian and I had been assigned to read for our old modernism seminar. "Hey, do you remember this?"

Marian squinted. "Vaguely." She bit her lip. "Professor Buck Something or Tuck or—"

"Luckman," I clarified and then allowed the memories to pour over me like rain. Maybe thirty-nine would be the year I felt inspired by poetry—inspired to actually *write* poetry—again. I reached for my wallet. "So, any hints about our outing?"

"Let me think about it." Marian flicked my hand and paid for both our books. "No."

She guided us up the block. Ever since Andrew and I had left the city, anytime I returned, it was a nostalgic, albeit bittersweet, experience. It felt like time travel. So much of the setting looked the same as when we'd left—the same brick buildings, the same people, it seemed, out walking on an endless loop. At first glance, it felt like that time in my life was still preserved there, all my dreams petrified in a slab of golden amber just around the next block. But then I'd stop. Upon closer investigation, the signage above that old store I'd once admired would be different. That cozy restaurant or bar I'd once frequented would be gone, replaced by some newer establishment I didn't recognize. I'd pause and look at my reflection in a window and realize I wasn't the same, either. The city had moved on without me. Sometimes it felt like *I'd* moved on without me, too, if that makes any sense.

We stopped at the corner. "I guess I can't convince you to close your eyes, huh?" Marian asked. I shook my head. She grabbed my hand and hurriedly led us both across the street.

"Wait," I interjected as she guided us toward the subway. "Where are we actually going? I still have a million things to do today. I need to get back."

"I'm not telling," she shouted as we dashed down the stairs and disappeared underground. We arrived on the empty platform, both of us breathless. Marian let go of my hand. I blinked hard, my eyes adjusting to the dark. "But I promise it will be life changing," she said, and I believed her. A speeding train came to a halt before us. "My lady," she said as she gestured to the door, our hair blowing across our faces. "Your chariot awaits."

"Okay." I stepped inside. The air smelled like garbage and perfume and opportunity. For reasons I could not define, the whole experience felt like chaos. Like poetry.

"You ready to have some fun?" she asked as the doors shut.

"No," I admitted.

"Perfect." She smiled. "Then it looks like this adventure arrived right on time."

The train moved forward. And then, like magic, we were gone.

EIGHT

"Where are we?" I asked when we emerged aboveground. I adjusted my eyeglasses. A faint image of Manhattan's skyline was visible in the distance. I looked around for other notable landmarks. There were none. "What neighborhood is this?"

Marian walked ahead of me. Her head swiveled like a periscope in search of something. "Does it matter?" she asked as she guided us up the block. "Just enjoy the adventure for once."

Up ahead, a trio of ageless women sat at an outdoor café and contentedly sipped some nuclear-colored beverage. Their beauty was alien-esque—strikingly long necks, impossibly slender arms, saucer-shaped eyes just like cartoon princesses. They seemed like the sort of people for whom things such as sipping vinegars and juice detoxes had been invented.

"Wherever we are, it looks like the wellness crowd has already discovered it," I said as I eyed them. They looked like members of some fabulously stylish cult. "I'm assuming that means it's trendy."

Marian ignored my comments. Instead, she peered at something in the distance. "There it is," she said and hurried us up the block. We were both panting by the time we stopped. "Ta-da!" Marian said as she gestured toward some nondescript building, its whole facade painted a sleek white.

I just stood there, waiting for something to happen. A gentle breeze blew, rustling some leaves overhead.

She tried again. "Ta-da!"

"Are you moonlighting as a part-time magician?" I wasn't clear what point I'd missed. "What's with all the 'ta-das'?"

"Very funny." Marian stood in awe. "This is it. This is where we're going."

I better positioned myself beside her on the sidewalk to take in the building from her precise angle. Upon first glance, it easily could have been any other structure in the neighborhood. And yet, as I stood there directly beside her, I couldn't deny that there was something about it—some energy, perhaps—that pulled you in.

"I don't understand," I admitted. "What is this place? A spa?"

"Not exactly." Marian stepped forward. I followed her lead. As I did, I noticed perhaps the only distinguishing detail about the place: a small white neon sign placed at the bottom corner of one of the windows. NETTLE CENTER, the sign announced.

From the corner of my eye, I saw the women from the café, all dressed in flowy, watercolor kaftans, gliding toward us. I glanced down at my basic crewneck, rubbed my thumb across the cotton fabric. "To be clear, this place isn't fancy, right?"

Marian cocked her head. "Um . . ."

"Shit." I quickly smoothed my hair and tucked in the front of my T-shirt.

"Come on." Marian took hold of my hand. "I'll explain more inside."

I inhaled a long breath to prepare myself, as though I already knew in some deep, mystical part of my being that something significant was about to unfold.

Marian smiled. "Here we go."

"Here we go, I guess," I said.

And then, like always, I followed her.

NINE

The first thing I noticed was the light. Somehow, the sunlight seemed brighter inside than it had out on the street. I rubbed my face and let my eyes adjust. The vast ceiling was lined with oversize skylights, which invited beams of honey-colored light into the space. The entire back wall was made of glass and offered an unobstructed view of a lush green courtyard. Still, it wasn't just the natural light. For reasons I couldn't identify, the whole place seemed to glow.

"Quick question." Without the need for signs or formal announcements, it was clear it was the sort of space that demanded a whisper. "What universe are we in?"

"Be careful." We moved across the gleaming white floors and past a collection of potted palms. "You can get kicked out of places like this for having bad energy."

We paused in front of a modern circular desk, behind which sat a woman who, based strictly on appearances, I had to assume owned a personal collection of healing crystals. "You're our twelve o'clocks," the woman said, her voice as airy as the space itself. "We've been waiting for you." She handed us each a slender, metallic packet. Her hands were smooth with youth, her nails cleanly polished. I pulled my own chipped fingernails away from the counter. "You can enjoy these at the wellness bar while you wait," she informed us.

"Wellness bar?" I jabbed Marian's side when the woman looked down. "What in the hell did you sign us up for?"

"Here you go." The woman handed us some papers. "I just need you both to sign these."

I looked at Marian, raised a brow.

"I told you you're not allowed to ask questions." She scribbled her signature, then handed me her pen. "Just sign it."

I scrawled my name and handed back my sheet.

"Thank you," the woman said. "The doctor will be out to see you soon."

Marian guided us toward a stylish counter accented with bowls of exotic fruits—the wellness bar, I had to assume.

"Doctor?" I grabbed her wrist, questioning the sleek designs with new suspicion. "Is this a plastic surgeon's office?" I situated myself in front of a bowl of papayas. "I've never even had a facial. I'm not sure a face-lift is the best introduction to the world of antiaging treatments."

A man approached us from the opposite side of the bar. He had a serene energy about him, like the human equivalent of warm chai. "May I have your packets?"

"What's in these packets, anyway?" I looked up at him. "Vitamins?"

"It's your alkaline drink. It helps to maintain the body's preferred pH levels."

"Did you say pH levels?" I asked. "Like in soil?"

He looked at me with a new expression of pity. "It's good that you're here."

Marian plucked away my packet and handed it over. The man nodded and then briefly disappeared. Once he was gone, she cleared her throat. "So, this is the Nettle Center."

"Yeah. I'm going to need more explanation than that."

"Well, based on the pamphlet, it's a 'holistic, integrative, whole-body clinic,'" Marian explained, like that was normal. She tilted her head to gauge my reaction. I just stared at her.

"That woman back there said something about a doctor." As I spoke, the man quietly reappeared, set down two dirt-colored drinks, then disappeared again. "Any thoughts on that?"

"Fine," Marian admitted. "It's kind of a doctor's office, too."

"False," I announced. "A doctor's office is a boring white room with outdated lamps, elevator music, and a dusty archive of *Good Housekeeping*."

Marian sipped her dirt drink. "I suspect my timing is less than ideal here, but have I mentioned that you and Andrew ought to find a new doctor?"

"Marian, why in the hell are we celebrating our birthdays at a doctor's office?" I looked questioningly at our beverages. "And why are we being encouraged to drink dirt?"

"Try it." She took another sip and tried not to wince. "It's good."

"You're a terrible liar."

"Fine." She looked at the floor. "But you kind of *have* to drink it before our appointment." I drummed my fingers across the counter. "Listen." Marian set down her glass. "I was here on assignment not too long ago. Apparently, they make a matcha smoothie that changed Gwyneth Paltrow's life."

"So, we're here to drink matcha?"

"Not exactly." Marian paused and leaned closer. "They have this . . . test."

"A test?" I felt like someone had slapped me. "A test for what?"

"Well, it's kind of, um, well, it's a genetic test."

I squeezed the bridge of my nose. "Marian, what the fu—"

"Just hear me out. It's *just* a blood test. It's not like they're going to saw you in half."

"A blood test for what?"

"It's a little complicated." Marian bit her ruby lip. "I'll let the doctor explain it." She picked at her cuticles. "I think the results could give you some mental relief." A strand of blonde hair fell in front of her face. She tugged on it. "I don't know." I could see her starting to doubt herself. "I thought it'd be fun to find a way to prove that we're still as young as we feel."

I felt a little bad when I saw Marian's disappointment. Initially, I had assumed our visit was just meant as some quirky, don't-take-this-too-seriously, we're-only-here-for-the-story sort of outing, like getting matching navel piercings. For better or worse, I'd become well accustomed to those sorts of silly jaunts—as well as others—with her over the years. But the more Marian spoke, the more I sensed that our current visit meant something more to her.

"Wait a minute." I squinted and inspected her expression. "This isn't just about me, is it? You lied. You're feeling uncomfortable by this birthday business, too, aren't you?"

"That's ridiculous." She waved her hand through the air. "I'm like a good wine, babe. I just keep getting better with time."

I pursed my lips. Slowly, I felt myself beginning to cave. Marian had always had that effect on me, and she knew it. "I assume you already know how absurd this is?"

Marian pushed my dirt drink closer to me. "I do."

I sighed, then took a microscopic sip. "Ugh." I smacked my lips and set down my glass. "What's in this stuff?"

"Herbs?" Marian absently touched her drink. "Actually, it might be dirt."

"That would make sense, based on the pH concerns," I said. Marian tapped the bottom of my glass. I forced myself to take another sip.

Nearby, a door slid open. A slender woman in a fitted medical coat appeared. "The doctor is ready for you." She gazed at the counter. "You can bring your alkaline tinctures with you."

"Tinctures?" I looked to Marian and shook my head. "I hate this place," I whispered.

"False." Marian winked. "You're going to love this." She paused beside me and raised her glass. "You think two thirty-nine-year-olds can still chug together like they did in college?"

I raised my glass to meet hers, already regretting my decision. Before I could stop myself, I welcomed the mystery concoction. I swear my whole body shook from the taste. "In case I've never formally told you, I'd like to officially let you know that you're the worst," I said. "My tongue tastes like lawn clippings."

Marian dramatically shook her head. "Yeah, that wasn't great."

We handed over our empty glasses, and I followed Marian through the doorway.

~

"Marian and Olivia?" The door slid open. A woman, about our age, entered the room. She wore fashionable jeans, a tailored lab coat, trendy eyeglasses, and a bold red lip. She spoke with a subtle, indeterminable accent, which made all her words sound like they ended in curlicues. "I'm Dahlia."

Dahlia? I mouthed to Marian. She pursed her lips. "I'm sorry. That woman out there said something about a doctor."

"I *am* your doctor," Dahlia stated, already unimpressed with me. "Make yourselves comfortable," she said in a way that made me think she didn't actually mean it. She pointed toward a pair of stylish rattan chairs. "So how much do you both know about our testing services?" She paused, seemingly for effect. "It's important that you're familiar with our—" Dahlia stopped abruptly. A significant clatter rang out from the hallway. She tilted her head, assessing the noise, then inhaled slowly. "As I was saying, our test is—"

Before she could complete her thought, another woman—a younger, more frazzled version of Dahlia—literally stumbled into the room. "I'm so sorry," the girl said, breathless. She clutched a stack of files against her chest, which did not entirely cover the beige coffee stain on her lab coat. "I was just . . . I couldn't find—" She produced two glass vials. "I finally found the right ones," she said. Dahlia's lips tightened. The girl's shoulders slumped. "Right?"

"This is Poppy," Dahlia said, sounding exasperated.

"They're really pushing the floral theme," I whispered to Marian. She kicked my leg.

"She'll be helping me during your visit." Dahlia retrieved the vials, looked them over, and then shook her head *no*. "Today is Poppy's first day." I pinched Marian's thigh. "But back to our tests." Dahlia picked up a sleek metallic pen. "How much thought have you both put into your deaths?"

"Um, what?" I sat up straighter, assuming I'd misheard her. "I don't think I—"

"Your death," Dahlia repeated, plain and simple. "Have you thought about it?"

I turned to Marian. She just shrugged. "In terms of what?" I asked.

Dahlia lifted a brow. "In terms of when it will occur."

I sucked in my cheeks and exhaled loudly. "Yeah, I don't follow." I shifted uncomfortably in my seat. "Do you sell life insurance here or something?"

Dahlia tapped the pen against her chin. "Not exactly." She moved across the room, positioned herself beside the window, and stared out at the courtyard. "For most people, death comes as a surprise. We all know it's coming, and yet none of us ever expects it." She turned back toward us. "However, I have a solution."

I darted my head toward Marian. "Is this a prank?" I wondered if I'd been drugged via my dirt tincture. "What in the hell is this about, Mar?"

Before Marian could explain, Dahlia, likely sensing my trepidation, moved closer to me. "Based on my research, most people put off thinking about their deaths in order to ignore the fact that they might die sooner than they anticipate." She leaned down, her face just inches from mine. "Humanity feels so disconnected sometimes, doesn't it? However, every human on this planet, no matter what walk of life they come from, navigates this earth with the same invisible question weighing on their shoulders: 'How much time do I have left?'"

No one spoke. Poppy fumbled with some papers, making a mess of them.

"I don't understand what you're getting at," I finally said. "What's the point of all this?"

"The *point*," Dahlia continued, "is that our test offers our clients an opportunity to gain a better understanding of their deaths so they can make more informed decisions about how to live their lives." She looked me over. "If you decide to move forward, we'll use epigenetic data to methylate your DNA in order to determine your genetic expiration date."

"My what?"

"Your death date," Dahlia said, as casually as one might discuss the weather. "In addition, the test results will offer us a glimpse into your biological age so we can suggest recommendations for you to follow to enhance the quality of your remaining years." She narrowed her eyes into slender crescent moons and pursed her cherry lips. "Don't we all want to believe that we have multiple decades left on our horizon? Don't we all want to believe that we'll die well into old age?"

It was official: I was hallucinating. "Yeah, I—"

"Don't you understand?" Dahlia lowered her voice. "I can help to eliminate the biggest stressor from your life." She straightened her posture. "You see, inside each of our body's genes are the answers to some very vital questions." She looked me right in the eye. "I'll put it simply." Dahlia spoke slowly. "If you decide to move forward with my test," she explained, "I can tell you how much time you have left to live."

"And, I'm out of here." I picked up my tattered cross-body bag and looked at Marian. "Despite the fact that I asked that we *not* do something like this, I'll admit that you've devised a very creative—very bizarre—outing for us here. One of your best, in fact. However, I'm not in the right mood." I stood. "I'll meet you—"

"How valid is something like this?" Marian asked, ignoring me.

"You can't be serious," I said as I set down my bag with a thud.

"I mean, can't some doctors already do this?" she continued. "Think of oncologists. They tell people every day how many years their patients have left to live."

"I see." Dahlia tapped her pen against her mouth. "I think you've misunderstood me. Our test doesn't allow us to tell our patients about a range of years. It enables us to tell our patients a date. *The* date."

"Marian, this is absurd," I interrupted.

But Marian kept talking. "How is that possible? Sure, maybe our genes can offer insight into the world of diseases and someone can surmise a date based on that. But not everyone in the world dies from a disease." As Marian spoke, I kept waiting for her to burst out laughing. But she never did. "What about things like car accidents? Or suicide. Or tumbling down a staircase? How could your genes ever predict those sorts of things?"

"To be clear, the test results do not indicate *how* someone will die. Only *when*." Dahlia bit her ruby lip, thinking. "We're still working on the 'how' part."

"I'm sorry." I glanced around the room in search of the framed medical degrees I was accustomed to seeing in doctors' offices. "Where did you say you went to school?"

But Dahlia ignored me. Instead, she turned to Marian, whose eyebrows were knit. "I understand. You don't believe me."

Marian swallowed hard. She fiddled with one of her rings. "I'm not sure."

Dahlia crouched down. "When it comes down to it," she said in a hushed voice, "don't all medical procedures rely on a little bit of belief?"

Marian took my hand in hers, her clunky jewelry brushing against my skin. She looked up at Dahlia. "Can we have a minute?"

Dahlia nodded. "Of course."

I remained standing while Dahlia and Poppy exited the room. I kept rubbing the underside of my wedding band with my thumb. Once we were alone, I released Marian's hand. "Mar, I understand that it's kind of your *thing* to take us on strange outings like this," I said. "But this pushes the limits, don't you think?" I paused to give her a chance to consider my statement. She just looked at me, played with her nail. "Even for you."

"Listen." She gestured for me to sit. "There is a ninety percent chance this is bullshit."

"That seems generous."

"Just think of it like a new age form of a palm reading," Marian suggested. "Remember when we had our palms read after college, when you were freaking out about whether or not Andrew would ever propose?" She smiled. "Of course you knew that woman was bullshit. But when she told you that you and Andrew were soulmates, you felt better. Not because you believed in her psychic abilities, but because she offered you confirmation of something you already believed."

"Mar, I thought we agreed we weren't going to do ridiculous stuff like this anymore," I pointed out. "I thought you said—"

"This is completely different. This is—"

"Absurd?" I offered. "Ludicrous?" I stopped. "I can keep going."

"Please don't."

"Marian, this woman can't predict the exact date of someone's death," I continued. "If she could, she'd be all over the news. Every person on the damn planet would flock to this place."

"Fine. So, we agree. This test is bullshit. But that's even more of a reason to do it, right?" She squeezed my hand. "But what if . . ." Marian trailed off. I could see her heart beating beneath her silky blouse. "I mean, if you had the chance, wouldn't you want to know?"

"No!" I spat out. "Of course not!" I furrowed my brows. "Wait. Why? Would you?"

Marian remained silent for a beat. "I'm not sure."

The door slid back open. "Have we made a decision?" Dahlia asked.

Marian looked at me with a sense of longing. I glanced at my watch. It was getting late. Birthday or not, I still had a hundred things to do. "I love you, but I need to head home," I decided. "I really don't have time for a gag like this. Not now, anyway."

Behind me, I heard Dahlia step forward. I turned. Her red lips were puckered in thought, making her look both beautiful and villainous. "But isn't that exactly the point?"

I looked at her, scrunched my brows. "What do you mean?"

She crossed her arms across her sleek lab coat. "Time," she said. "Perhaps you're right. Perhaps you *don't* have the time left in your life for something as—oh, I don't know, as *trivial* as this." She locked eyes with me, dipped her hand into her coat pocket, and pulled out the vials Poppy had given her at the start of our visit. She turned them in her palm. "Or maybe you do."

"Come on," Marian pleaded. "Forget that last trip. This will be fun. It'll be just like—"

"One issue." I tried to ignore the look of yearning in her eyes, as well as the voice inside me that whispered to stay. "I'm too old for this kind of fun," I announced and then swung open the door. "Next year, maybe we ought to stick to brunch instead."

TEN

We arrived at the flamingo exhibit early the next morning. Tommy and I, like always, took a seat on our favorite bench while Andrew bought us our obligatory popcorn. For a while, we quietly watched those bold coral creatures strut through their man-made lagoon, the exhibit's artificial palm trees softly swaying in the balmy, pre-summer breeze. I tried to focus on their exotic beauty and lose myself in their fictitious tropical world, like I normally did during our visits. But I couldn't relax. I kept thinking about the strange world I'd just barely left.

"Look, Mama," Tommy said, forcing me out of my own thoughts. A group of children were gathered nearby, their heads accessorized with party hats. A little universe of balloons floated above them. "They're here to celebrate someone's birthday, too." Tommy waved to get the group's attention. "Hey! Heeeeey!" The children turned. "Yesterday was my mama's birthday!" he shouted. Everyone clapped. I smiled and offered a bow. "She's one hundred!"

Andrew reappeared and handed us bags of buttered popcorn. He pulled his favorite black sunglasses from his pocket and slipped them onto his face. He'd worn some version of those glasses since our twenties. They were classics, like a nostalgic album or a good, strong drink. Like him. "How's the flock?"

"Still flamboyant as ever," I said. That's just one thing I love about flamingos: that they're collectively referred to in the zoological community as a "flamboyance." I audibly sighed. "Must be nice, right?"

"What's wrong?" He tossed a handful of popcorn into the air and tried to catch some in his mouth. "You still seem out of sorts."

Since I'd returned home the night before, Andrew had asked me roughly a hundred times about my day with Marian, but I'd yet to give him a single straight detail. "Nothing," I lied. I don't know why I resisted telling him about it. I think the whole experience just felt too strange to even describe. "I'm fine."

Andrew threw more popcorn toward the sky. A flock of pigeons gathered at our feet. "She didn't take you to a pants-less disco, I hope."

I dipped my hand into my popcorn bag. "Worse."

"Oh boy." Andrew shooed the birds with his feet. "Why do you still let her drag you along for stuff like this?"

"I don't know," I told him. Sometimes, friendships were impossible to explain. "For better or worse, over the years, it's just kind of become our thing."

He lowered his sunglasses. "Lately, it feels more like it's *her* thing, no?" Andrew loved Marian; I knew that. He just didn't like seeing me get all twisted up because of her antics. He slid his sunglasses back onto his nose. "Do you want to talk about it?"

"Not really," I said. "It was just a ridiculous, typical Marian afternoon." I smiled at him. "Really." I waved the memory of it away. "It's not even worth getting into."

Andrew tossed another handful of popcorn overhead and then paused, giving the conversation a chance to shift. "I forgot to tell you. The zoo is hosting that Art in the Park thing again. The paper wants me to write a little piece about it."

Before we had left the city, Andrew worked for a literary magazine called *Smith* (as in "wordsmith," a not entirely clever name for a magazine about, well, words). Writing about and curating fiction had been his dream. Until we moved and something strange happened: Andrew *liked* his job as a culture writer at our local small-town newspaper. (By "culture," I mean he wrote mostly about high school theater productions and magic shows at the library.)

Unlike Andrew, I didn't know what to do. Ultimately, we agreed that I'd stay home with Tommy. Don't get me wrong. I loved being home with him; however, I missed pursuing other parts of myself. I know. Mothers aren't supposed to admit that. But it's true. In a moment of weakness, I'd mentioned these feelings to a woman in Tommy's movement class (that happens when you relocate to the suburbs: you tell yourself your infant needs a class to learn to move). Anyway, the woman mentioned an English opening at Blakely. It had taken everything in me not to visibly scoff. Instead, I nodded, which somehow landed me an interview. And that was that.

"By the way." Andrew dropped a small bag onto my lap. "I bought you something."

"What is it?" Tommy nearly slid off the bench. "Is it a flamingo?"

"In so many words," Andrew explained.

From inside the bag, I pulled out a plastic key chain molded to look like three flamingos who inexplicably held a banner printed with the words *Birds of a feather* in their beaks. "Fancy."

Andrew shrugged. "It reminded me of the three of us. Birds of a feather, you know?"

I should probably explain my admiration for these strange, beautiful creatures. It started when Tommy was a baby on one sleep-deprived night. I'd been pacing his darkened nursery for hours, his body cradled in my arms. Finally, I clicked on the lamp and, half-delirious, pulled a book from his bookshelf. We settled into the rocker. I squinted at the cover. I wasn't familiar with the title. But I was too tired to pick again.

The book was called *Franny the Flamingo Finds Her Flock*. In it, the title character, Franny—a sassy and eccentric young flamingo—tires of the day-to-day routine at her local lagoon and decides to set out in search of a more flamboyant life. Franny flies to exotic lands (on a flamingo-inspired airplane, no less) in search of somewhere that will proverbially set her feathers on fire! Eventually, she lands in the animal kingdom's version of New York City, where she finds a diverse group of animals who take her—wait for it—under their wing and who help her discover her true calling. Franny, it turns out, isn't meant to be a boring old lagoon flamingo; rather, she's *meant* to be (get ready for the word-play) a "flamingo" dancer! The final page features a vibrant illustrated dance scene, where animals laugh and lift cartoon champagne coupes (appropriate?) toward a sherbet-colored sky, all of them celebrating the fact that Franny has finally found her way.

The pages were ripe with zoological inaccuracies and forced rhymes. Yet, I must have read the book to Tommy a dozen times that night, my exhaustion melting into joy as he clapped along to the story. I admit that I'm still not clear on the author's point. Regardless, I liked Franny's bravery and her willingness to seek out a bold and memorable life. Don't judge me for this next part, as I'm aware I'm discussing a fictitious cartoon bird. But in some ways, I think I sort of looked up to her.

"Can I ask you something, Andy?" I said and then finished my last buttery bite.

"Uh-oh." He lifted my empty popcorn bag. "Is this about yesterday?"

"No." I sighed. "Yes." I looked down at my old leather flip-flops. "Maybe."

Andrew moved toward the garbage can. "Okay."

I tucked a loose strand of brown hair behind my ear. "Am I still fun?"

He tossed our trash. "I mean, yeah." He cuffed, then uncuffed the shirtsleeves of his favorite worn-in button-down. It was his signature nervous habit. "Sure."

"Very convincing," I mumbled.

"I didn't mean it like that." Andrew sat, wiped his hands off on his khaki shorts. "Why? Where did Marian take you?"

"It doesn't matter," I told him, even though I knew that it did.

Tommy snuggled up beside me. "I think you're fun, Mama," he said and then ate a piece of stray popcorn off my lap. "You let me have ice cream for dinner last week."

I kissed his head. "Thanks, buddy," I told him, even though *fun* hadn't been my motivation. I'd been too burned out to make us anything real to eat.

The three of us remained quiet and watched those graceful creatures move before us, their whole existence like some colorful fairy-tale fantasy.

"What do you think flamingos do for their birthdays?" Tommy asked, snapping us all back into the present. "Do you think they have secret flamingo parties?"

"Probably," Andrew said. "I hear they like shrimp-flavored birthday cake."

"Ewwwwwww!" Tommy screamed. "That's disgusting!"

"Don't say 'disgusting,'" I reminded him. I tossed my key chain into my bag, feeling both mad at and sorry for myself all at once.

"Why? You say 'disgusting' all the time," Tommy said.

"I'm allowed to," I explained as I cuffed my T-shirt sleeves past my shoulders. I felt desperate to get some sun on my skin, to add some color to my life. "I'm older than you."

"Mama's old!" Tommy shouted loud enough for everyone, even the flamingos, to hear.

I gazed at their beautiful pink bodies. "He's lying," I yelled.

"No, I'm not!" Tommy retorted.

"Fine," I said, accepting my fate. "I'm a has-been." For a minute, I swear they swiveled their perfect coral heads and looked at me in, well, disgust.

ELEVEN

Later that night, after the three of us had rounded out my birthday celebrations with dinner at the local diner and an ice cream date, Andrew and I found ourselves alone on the couch, both of us dressed in our favorite old sweats and matching slippers. That happens in middle age; your relationship turns into a slumber party. Anyway, we were watching some mindless cooking show we loved, which was hosted by an eccentric British gentleman who had no time whatsoever for an improperly executed scone.

"So, do you want your gift?" Andrew asked as a contestant ranted about salted butter.

"Didn't I already get it?" I asked.

Andrew shushed me. He stepped into the hallway, opened and shut the closet, and then rejoined me on the couch. "Here." He handed me a small gift-wrapped box.

I could tell from the weight and shape of it that it was a book, but I tried not to give it away. I shook the box next to my ear for the sake of drama. "Is it a car?"

"Yes," Andrew said. "A very small one."

I unwrapped the metallic paper, slid off the lid, and—*surprise!*—discovered a book. I assumed it would be some bestseller or obligatory beach read, but I was wrong.

Andrew looked at the couch and squeezed his neck, his under-stated wedding band—which he never took off—hugging his finger. "I remembered how much you loved it in college."

I ran my fingertips across the familiar cover, an illustration of a Victorian woman staring through a window. "*A Room of One's Own*," I said. It is a classic feminist text in which Virginia Woolf argues that female writers need both literal and figurative spaces to compose their work. When we were undergraduates, I had read the book at the start of every summer. The habit was meant to inspire me to carve out the time and space I felt I needed to immerse myself in the creative process. Apparently, it hadn't done me much good.

"Do you like it?" Andrew tilted his head, his face all youthful charm, despite the signs of age that had begun to etch themselves there.

"I do," I said.

"I know you've been wanting to write again." He stopped, swallowed. "I saw the rejection from that literary journal in the trash." Andrew paused, second-guessing himself. "I just thought with it being the start of summer and all . . ." He trailed off.

I glided my fingers across the cover. "Thank you," I told him, and I allowed my mind to flood with memories. "I love it."

It felt like yesterday when I'd ride the subway alone for hours, my old Discman headphones covering my ears. I liked to watch the world unfold around me. Everything felt so inspired and meaningful back then. Maybe that's just true of youth. Anyway, later, in my cramped apartment, I'd turn my observations into lines of verse. I loved the feeling of my fingers flying across my keyboard to craft something from nothing, like a pianist of words. I don't know. Maybe it was about control. I liked having the ability to shape the world in ways I saw fit.

Andrew moved into the kitchen. Our life together had become so routine I could determine his exact actions just by a series of otherwise insignificant noises: the soft plop as he uncorked a bottle of wine, the gentle rush of sloshing liquid. Andrew handed me a glass. "Cheers." He smiled. God, I loved that smile. When Andrew smiled at me like that, I felt like a lovestruck kid. "Hopefully this will hold you over until we go out on a proper birthday date."

"You don't have to take me on a birthday date, Andy," I said. "We're a little past that."

Andrew clinked my glass. "I don't think that's true." He rejoined me on the couch. "So, are you finally going to tell me about yesterday?"

He must have sensed my mixed emotions. Ever since Marian and I had left that place, an uneasy feeling had settled upon me, like a residue I couldn't wash away. "If you had a chance to find out when you'll die, would you want to know?"

"Yikes." Andrew gulped a heavy sip. "So, it *was* the gypsy palm reader again?"

I sighed. "Not exactly."

Tommy stirred upstairs. Andrew set his glass on the coffee table. "I'll check on him."

Once alone, I stared blankly at the television. I knew the Nettle Center was a sham, just another in a long string of unconventional excursions Marian had connived me into over the years. Still, I couldn't deny that something about it kept pulling me in, like a rip current I couldn't outswim. Marian had always had that impact on me, too.

I picked up my phone and sent her a message. I'm sorry I left, I wrote. Maybe you're right. Maybe it would be fun to hear more about that test.

See! she replied instantaneously. I knew you were still young and cool.

To be clear, I typed, I'm not getting it. But if you really think it will be fun, I'll go back to have a laugh while you get it. Deal?

Whatever you say, she wrote. We both knew I was bluffing.

Andrew rejoined me on the couch in time to hear the British gentleman go nuts over a burnt pastry crust. "Who's that?" He nodded at my phone.

"Marian," I said. "I'm meeting her in the city again tomorrow."

"Tomorrow?" he asked. "For what?"

I didn't know what to tell him. "She bought me this old poetry collection I loved in college. I left it in her bag," I lied, instantly weighed down by guilt. I should have just told him right then and there. I don't know what kept stopping me.

"What about work?" Andrew asked.

I pretended to cough. "I'm sick."

Andrew's eyes narrowed into slits. "What's going on?"

I looked up. "I think it's easier if I use a Get Out of Jail Free card on this one."

Andrew sighed. "Fine. You get one pass." It was getting late. He clicked off the television. "You know, one of these days, you're going to need to tell her you don't want to take part in stuff like this anymore."

"I know." I sipped my wine. "One day."

I kissed Andrew good night and made my way upstairs. I paused in Tommy's doorway. His room was a little cocoon of calm. I moved toward him, adjusted his blanket, kissed his face, and turned back toward the hallway.

"Mama?" Tommy whispered, so softly I thought I'd imagined it.

I moved back into his room and sat on the edge of his bed. "You still up, buddy?"

"I can't sleep." He turned toward me. "I had a bad dream."

I ran my fingers through his hair, expecting him to tell me about a flame-throwing dragon or a monster under his bed. "About what?"

He squeezed his favorite stuffed dinosaur against his chest. "About you."

"Me?" I said, taken aback.

"You were lost," he explained. "I kept looking, but I couldn't find you."

I rested my head upon his child-size pillow. "It was just a dream," I reassured him and then pulled the blanket over us. "There's no need to worry. I'm right here."

He curled against me. "Do you promise you'll never disappear, Mama?"

Already, I felt both our bodies becoming heavy with slumber. I wrapped my arm around his small frame and pressed my face to his so we were nose to nose. "I swear."

TWELVE

The next morning, I sat on the train with my new book from Andrew in my lap. I wasn't in the mood to read it, since it wasn't technically summer yet. Instead, I stared out the window and watched all the towns pass me by. I thought about the people who lived in those towns. Who were they? What made them happy? I pulled out my poetry notebook and made a note. *Little towns and little people as symbols for little lives?* It's strange to think about people you've never met, let alone people you couldn't even see. But suddenly, I wanted to step inside all their brains and find out if, like me, they had unresolved lists of hopes and dreams.

My train pulled into Penn Station with a grating, mechanical screech. My shoulders lurched forward. The commuters—all dressed in black professional garb—hurried off, as though they were rushing to the same corporate funeral. I slid off the train. The escalator carried me to the station's main concourse, where flocks of people zipped past in a thousand different directions. I wondered where they were all going, what sad or extraordinary lives and careers waited for them.

"Here." I turned and discovered Marian beside me. Even at that hour, she looked so effortless, her golden hair expertly piled into a stylish bun, a denim jacket casually draped over her shoulders in that way only select women know how to do. She handed me a to-go cup. "I brought coffee."

"Thank you." I sipped it, grateful for the overly sweetened brew. "Now let's go, before I change my mind."

Minutes later, we found ourselves crammed into a subway car. It was a study in irony—dozens of people crowded together, all consciously pretending no one else existed. The train raced through a dark, unfathomable tunnel. I held tight to a metal pole, like a clumsy stripper. Coffee splashed across my shirt, a casual striped number I hoped might make me look slightly put together. I glanced down at the brown splatters. I was a caffeinated homage to Jackson Pollock. It didn't matter. No one seemed to notice. That was the thing about big cities. You could spend hours on a train or in a café and never be asked your name or your thoughts on the weather; no one cared. In big cities, you could be invisible if you wanted to be. People had the common courtesy to leave you alone.

Marian coolly sipped her coffee. "So, why the sudden change of heart?"

My knees buckled from the train's movements. "To be clear, I still think that test is complete bullshit." I licked my finger and dabbed my shirt. "It's like I said—I just thought it'd be fun to get more information about it." I smoothed my shirt. "It'll make for a good story." I kept my gaze down so she couldn't see my face. "That's all."

The train stopped. Dozens of people scurried onto the platform. "To be clear, you skipped work so you could get more . . . information?" Marian playfully nudged me as the doors closed. "Interesting." We were the last two people left in our car. "You know, it's cute when you pretend you don't like doing stuff like this together anymore."

"Don't harass me." I wiped spilled coffee drips from my chin. "I'm old and fragile."

Marian easily lifted her coffee to her lips. "And apparently young enough that you're still learning to drink from a cup," she said with a smile.

The train stopped again. Marian signaled toward the door. I followed her onto the empty platform and up the steps. We arrived at street level. I blinked hard, my vision reacclimating to the natural light. Beside me, Marian dropped her coffee into a trash bin. She reached for my cup.

"Wait. Can I just—"

Marian tossed it. "Sorry. It's in your best interest." She stepped forward. "I'm pretty sure they view things like caffeine as punishable forms of contraband."

"I forgot how much I hate this place," I sighed and then followed her up the street.

We paused outside our destination. From the exterior, the Nettle Center looked just as we'd left it: smooth white walls, wide panes of spotless glass, that unassuming neon sign, its announcement so quiet it seemed like a secret. I cupped my hand to the window and saw a dozen barefoot women, all dressed in midriff-revealing yoga apparel, situated among the sweeps of exotic plants. "Maybe this was a bad idea."

"Maybe." Marian nudged me forward. "But it was *your* idea."

"You've been waiting all morning to say that, haven't you?"

"I really have," she said.

Together, we reentered the light-filled lobby. Bold triangles of sunlight danced across the space, where pods of women sipped dirt drinks. It all looked peaceful on the surface, like an advertisement for a wellness sanctuary. But something was off.

Marian and I walked toward the circular check-in desk, where the same woman still sat. Her hair was an endless ripple that stretched down her spine. Some crystal amulet dangled at her neck. She looked up, her expression smeared with confusion. I opened my mouth to speak, but my phone rang inside my bag. The sharp electronic ping sliced through the silence like a spray of gunshots. Dozens of eyes pierced me like knives. I quickly glanced at my phone, already knowing it was Andrew calling to check on me. I smiled at his predictability and then silenced the device. The whole room exhaled a sigh of relief.

"Hi." I leaned across the quartz counter. "We're looking for information about one of your tests." The girl's eyes morphed into saucers. She didn't utter a word, just shook her head *no*, like I'd broken some cardinal rule. I looked around. The whole room offered me a collective death stare. I turned to Marian. "What's happening here?"

A door slid open. Dahlia stepped into the lobby, still dressed in her stark, tailored lab coat. Her shoes clicked against the floor. Every woman twisted in her direction, as though they were all meager planets and she was their brilliant, golden sun. "I feel like we're missing something," Marian whispered.

"Tsk!" Dahlia snapped, her tone as sharp as a dog trainer's command. The sound cut through the lobby like shards of broken glass. Marian and I stood at attention. Dahlia's crimson lips settled into a satisfied line. She stepped toward us. She smelled like a mix of medical soap and expensive perfume. For an uncomfortable minute, she studied us like we were aliens who'd arrived from another planet. Finally, she nodded at the receptionist and then silently waved a hand, signaling for us to follow her.

Inside Dahlia's office, she sat at her large, marble desk. A wall of water cascaded behind her, making the space look like a spa or a five-star resort. "We like to begin every new week in silence," she abruptly stated once the door was closed and then gestured for us to sit. "It's valuable to start each week fresh, to remind the body that we are surrounded by calm." She adjusted her fashionable eyeglasses, ready to make an important point. "Our cells are always listening. If there's too much noise in our lives, it upsets them." I bit my lip, anticipating laughter. "Our cells have feelings, too," she continued, as serious as a heart attack. "People sometimes forget that."

I felt my eyes shrink into slivers behind my tortoiseshell glasses. "Right."

Behind us, the door slid open. Poppy rushed in, clumsily balancing a tray of tinctures. She hurried toward Dahlia's desk, set the tray down in an ungraceful fashion.

"So, what can I help you with today?" Dahlia signaled for us to take our drinks.

"We were here the other day." I took a tiny sip. "We were scheduled for a test."

Dahlia picked up a Lucite clipboard and flipped through a stack of papers clipped to it. "I'm sorry. You'll need to be more specific." She peered at us over her eyeglasses. "The Psychiatric Gut Microbe test? The Chakra Analysis test?" She looked up, tilted her head. "You're not the pair who was here for the Alternate Lifetimes test, right? Because, honestly, I blame those results on faulty energy levels and *not* on our—"

"It was the Genetic Death test," Marian interrupted.

"Aha." Dahlia flipped to a different page. "Though we prefer the term 'expiration.'"

Nearby, Poppy wiped some tincture puddles from the floor. From somewhere in the building, a gong rang out a melodious echo. Poppy's shoulders dropped. Her face melted into an expression of relief. "Oh, thank God," she spewed.

"Tsk!"

Poppy looked up at Dahlia like she'd been zapped by a Taser. "But, the gong!"

"We've gone over this, Poppy," Dahlia explained, all her words brushed with some undefined accent. "The *first* gong alerts our cells that the silent period *will* end. Not that it *has* ended." Dahlia inhaled deeply, looked back at Marian and me. "Now I remember." She scanned her finger across a page. "To be clear, you never *had* the test?" Marian and I nodded. "But then you . . . came back?" We nodded again. "To have the test, I assume?" Marian looked at me. I shrugged. "I'm sorry," Dahlia stated. "I'm confused."

I scooted forward, prepared to recite the script I'd rehearsed in my head. "We'd like more information." My foot tapped the floor. "About whether . . . I don't know . . . if that test is . . . *real.*"

"If it's . . . real?" Dahlia's eyes narrowed. "I don't know. Is the Chakra Analysis test *real?*" She lifted her half-empty glass. "Are our tinctures *real?*" She swooped her hand across her desk. "Is any of this *real?*"

"I, um . . ." I sat on my hands like a nervous toddler. "I don't know. I think that's why we're here."

"Reality is a construct. We all believe what we want." Dahlia glided toward a wall of glass that overlooked a verdant courtyard. "Is my test real?" She tapped the window, like we were trapped inside a fishbowl. "That's for you to decide." She turned back to us. "What I *can* tell you is that we have limited availability today. We're running a plant-therapy workshop this afternoon."

"Plant therapy?" I questioned.

"It has surprisingly quantifiable benefits," Dahlia explained. "It'll be a full house." She moved to her desk, picked up her clipboard. "The only time I could even *consider* squeezing you both in—*if* you're interested in more than *information* . . ." She paused. "Is, well, right now."

"I think you've misunderstood," I explained. "*I* don't want to take the test. I just want my friend here to—"

"Do you question everything in your life as much as you've questioned my services?"

I turned to Marian. She raised a brow and smirked. I wanted to kill her, not because I knew the test was preposterous but because she already knew that, regardless of that fact, I'd give in to it. "One of these days," I told her, "you really need to stop with this sort of thing."

"I know," she said, perking up. "Just not today."

I swiveled back toward Dahlia. "Before I agree to anything," I said, "I want to know how you'll test us. Because if it involves heavy medical machinery, I'm out."

"The genetic evaluation," Dahlia explained, "is a very simple test. We take a few samples—blood, hair, saliva. It's fairly harmless."

"Fairly?"

Dahlia stared off for a moment. "Yes," she decided. "Fairly."

I tapped my fingers across my thigh. "Is this legal?"

Dahlia neatly folded her hands. "Do you ask all your doctors that?"

I felt myself deflate. "Right."

Poppy rushed out, came back in, and handed Dahlia a half dozen vials. Dahlia inspected them, shook her head, handed half back, then slipped the rest into her pocket. "Of course, this all comes at a certain price. But when you consider—"

"We paid in advance," Marian interjected.

"What are you talking about?" I swiveled my head. "I haven't—"

"I did," she explained. "When I booked our initial appointments." She smiled her megawatt smile. "You're welcome."

I should have darted out of there again. I already knew I had innumerable years stretched out before me, that I'd die a wrinkled-up old lady, my final meal fed to me through a tube. But still, wouldn't it be nice to have confirmation—even bogus confirmation—of that?

"Should we move forward, then?" Dahlia asked.

Marian looked to me for approval. I hesitated but ultimately nodded. She released a yelp of excitement. "Andrew is going to kill you," I told her.

Marian blew me a kiss. "I think that's a yes."

A Cheshire cat smile spread across Dahlia's face. "I'm so pleased you're both taking this step." She turned to Poppy, who gathered papers from a cabinet. "Poppy, please get them started on their paperwork. And please make sure they finish their tinctures." Poppy nodded and knocked several sheets from her stack. Loose papers floated toward the white floor like leaves. Another gong echoed. The girl optimistically looked up. Dahlia shook her head. "Not yet." Dahlia inhaled a cleansing breath, smoothed her lab coat, and stepped toward Marian and me. "There's just one more thing I'll need before we begin."

I raised my brows. "Please tell me it's not another tincture."

Dahlia shook her head. She reached into her lab coat pocket and handed us each a vial. "What I need from you now," she explained, "is your spit."

THIRTEEN

I have your results." Poppy cautiously stepped into the room alone, two manila folders clutched against her chest. She tugged the sleeves of her lab coat, which was a touch too big for her frame. She reminded me of Tommy when he dressed up in costume—an astronaut one day, a firefighter the next. "I think." She licked her pale lips. "Sorry. Those are the first real words I've spoken all day." Her eyes darted around the room. "You *did* hear the silence gong a few minutes ago, right? That wasn't just me?"

Marian craned her neck toward the door. Her blouse—some cool, secondhand thing—slid across her skin and revealed a sliver of her collarbone. I touched the neckline of my own shirt—the one I'd so carefully chosen—and wondered about the last time I'd worn something that highlighted more than my self-consciousness. "Is Dahlia coming, too?"

Poppy forced a smile, exposing a smear of lipstick on her teeth. "Not at the moment." She cleared her throat. "Another patient had, well, a little *reaction* to the alkaline drink."

I slid forward in my woven chair. "What *kind* of reaction?"

Poppy scrunched her face. "Let's just say his skin looks a bit tie-dyed at the moment."

I kicked Marian's foot. "I could kill you for making me do this," I mumbled to her.

"Make?" She looked at me, amused. "The first trip was all me. But this trip . . ."

In the distance, another gong rang out. "Oh no." Poppy briefly tensed up. "Wait." She settled herself. "We're okay. It's just time for a communal cleansing breath." Marian and I exchanged an uncomfortable glance. Poppy inhaled deeply, then opened the files. "So, the good news is that both your biological ages came back favorable." She flipped through the pages in a way that made it clear she was lost. "Biologically speaking, you're both still—wait, no—yes, you're both still, no—uh—thirty-two." She froze. I wondered if she'd had a stroke.

"What did I tell you?" Marian squeezed my knee. She smiled, pleased with herself.

"Thirty-two," I repeated. "Sure. That's great." I crossed, then uncrossed, my legs. I couldn't admit to Marian how jittery I felt waiting to hear the full results. "But can we hear more about, well, you know, the *date*?"

"One problem." Poppy glanced at the files. "Dahlia said I have to read the results in a specific order. The date part comes at the end." She dropped her voice. "It's supposed to be more dramatic that way."

My foot tapped the glossy floor. "Because if there's one thing death has always lacked, it's a flair for the dramatic."

Poppy looked at me doe eyed.

"She's kidding." Marian swatted my leg, her clunky rings jabbing my thigh.

Poppy scanned a sheet, then locked eyes with me. "It looks like you're up first." I couldn't help it—I straightened my posture, suddenly at full attention for whatever made-up prophecy she was about to feed to me. "Based on your genetic results, Dahlia recommends that you cut down your exposure to air pollution. Things like smoke, smog . . ."

Porch cigarettes, Marian mouthed to me. I slapped her thigh.

"Also, you should eat more cruciferous vegetables to lower your inflammation levels."

"Veggies. Got it." I scooted forward. "Now can we cut to the chase?"

Poppy shuffled through the papers. "One problem."

"Technically, aren't we up to *two* problems?" I said.

Poppy looked at me in a way that suggested she was about to either cry or throw something at me. It was anybody's guess. "Some of the pages are out of order," she noted and then shuffled them into place with all the finesse of the world's worst card dealer. "I had a little blunder in the hallway." She held up her hands like a mime. "Butterfingers."

Marian rested her head on my shoulder. "You know, for someone who thinks this test is bullshit, you're awfully antsy about hearing the results."

"Shut it," I told her. "I'm only here for the tinctures." I smiled sarcastically.

"Wait." Poppy squinted at a sheet. "I forgot to have you both sign our privacy statement." She dropped the file, the papers billowing everywhere, and rummaged through a desk drawer. "Shit," she mumbled as she looked up at us through a wisp of hair. "I always forget that part."

"Always?" Marian sat up. "I thought you just started last week."

Poppy offered a timid smile. "I did." She sorted through the desk. "Maybe one of you should step into the hallway." She shifted uneasily. "For privacy's sake." Poppy moved toward the door, ready to slide it back open. As though on cue, something very heavy fell very hard in the hallway, followed by a shuffle of footsteps and the sound of something large being dragged. "On second thought, you two seem like good friends."

"Let's just get on with it," I suggested. "Frankly, I'm on borrowed time. Plus, I don't expect that my genes will reveal anything scandalous."

"Okay." Poppy nodded. "If you insist, I guess." She continued to thumb through the papers in my file and then stopped abruptly. Her cheeks flushed. "Oh shit," she mumbled and then squeezed her eyes shut, like a frightened child. The girl didn't move. Several long, uncomfortable beats passed.

"Um, hi," I said, waving. "Hello. Remember us?"

"I'm sorry." She peeled open her eyes, one by one. "I don't think I can do this. I'm not really qualified to explain this part." She quickly reorganized the items in my folder and set it on the corner of the desk. "Here." She met my gaze, then tapped my file for emphasis. "Let's just leave this here for now. I think it's best if we save this last part for Dahlia, okay?" I could see that her hands were shaking. "I'm still learning the system for reading files, and this final bit . . ." She puffed out her lips, then laughed nervously. "I don't think I'm reading it right. It's all so confusing and—"

"I'm sorry," I interrupted and looked around the room, as though an explanation for Poppy's bizarre behavior might suddenly fall from the ceiling. "What's happening here?"

"New plan." Marian inched forward in her seat. "How about you read off some of *my* recommendations," she suggested, and she stretched her neck toward the door. "You know, to kill time until Dahlia can tell us the dates?"

Poppy exhaled a dramatic sigh. "Great idea," she said before turning her attention to the other file on the desk. She sorted through it, then looked at Marian. "Well, the test results indicate that you should wean yourself off the Xanax." She stopped, seemingly for effect. "While it might help your anxiety, it's not helping your liver."

"Xanax?" I interjected and then turned to Marian. "Since when did you start taking Xanax?"

"Oh shit," Poppy said again, as though it was her tagline. She dropped the file, rummaged through a drawer, and held a sheet of paper in the air. "Change of plans: you two should *definitely* sign our privacy statements."

"Why in the hell are you taking Xanax, Marian?" I asked, ignoring Poppy.

"Oh please." Marian fiddled with her metal bracelet. "It's practically a rite of passage at our age. Frankly, I'm surprised you're *not* on it."

"I don't understand," I said. "Why didn't you tell me?"

"It's just work," Marian explained. "My schedule is jammed." She pursed her lips to help prove her point. "You're not the only one over-whelmed by the day-to-day minutiae, you know."

"Shit. I knew I should have made you both sign those statements." Across the room, Poppy kept flipping through the files. "Please don't tell Dahlia about this." She looked at us like a lost toddler. "And please don't tell her I said 'shit.' She thinks obscenities invite bad energy into a space."

"Marian—"

"It's *nothing*, Liv," Marian said to make me stop. "This whole test is nothing. Just drop it. Okay?"

"I'm sorry about the wait." Dahlia breezily reentered the space but quickly shifted her attention to Poppy. "What's going on? Something is happening here." A look of confusion spread like a storm across Dahlia's face. "The energy is definitely off."

"I'm not sure if I'm ready for all this," Poppy said. "I don't think I can read off the results. I don't think I should be the one to—"

"Poppy, can I speak to you in the hallway?" Dahlia interjected before Poppy could proceed. "Now." Poppy lowered her head and shuf-fled toward the door. "We'll only be a moment," Dahlia said and then slid the door shut.

They were barely out of the room before I confronted Marian. "So, should we try this conversation again?"

"Are we still on this?" Marian asked, smoothing her brows with her fingers.

I wondered if I was overreacting. I knew women who regularly took the same stuff. But they weren't Marian. Marian and I didn't keep secrets from each other. The first time I'd slept with Andrew back in college, I'd told Marian hours after the fact. When I first found out about Tommy, I called her from my bathroom floor, the positive test still damp with urine droplets. The idea of her taking a medication—and an antianxiety one, at that—and not telling me felt like a breach of our unspoken friendship code of conduct.

"I told you," she continued. "I'm just pressed for deadlines."

I exhaled my annoyance, knowing I wouldn't get much else out of her. Not in that moment. I stood, stretched my legs, and, not knowing what else to do with myself, moved toward Dahlia's desk.

"So, are you going to take a peek?" Marian asked with a nod toward my folder.

"I don't know. This whole thing is so ridiculous." I halfheartedly flipped open my file. "Honestly, I don't think I want to wait for Dahlia to come back. I'm kind of over this whole thing. I think I just want to leave."

Marian sidled up next to me, so close I could hear her breath. "If that's the case, you might as well just take a look before we go," she said as she gestured toward the papers. "I mean, since we're here." She nudged my arm. "And since I *did* pay for it and all."

"Seriously? You're going to play that card?"

"If needed." She smiled, already knowing that she'd won.

I began to sift through the folder's contents. It took only seconds for me to feel overwhelmed. The pages were full of numerals and medical jargon that read like hieroglyphics. Finally, I looked up. "There's nothing here. Or at least nothing that makes any sense to me." I set the file back on the desk. When I did, a small envelope fell from it and onto the floor. "Wait." I reached down for the envelope and found the words "Expiration date" printed across it. "Maybe I spoke too soon." I glanced at the room's dramatic window and the courtyard just beyond it, a mirage right in the middle of the city. "Do you think I'm allowed to open it?" I didn't believe in the authenticity of Dahlia's test. Her whole presentation had felt too theatrical—too rehearsed—to be real. But still, right then, with the envelope balanced on my fingertips, I felt myself being swallowed by my own anticipation. "I think maybe I should put it back."

"It's *yours*, Liv," Marian said, encouraging me to continue. "It was in *your* file."

"Good point." I unfolded the flap, swallowed hard. I was intelligent enough to know Dahlia's statements about that test were riddled with untruths; still, I couldn't silence the tidal wave of suspense that had begun to churn inside me. I inhaled deeply, preparing myself for whatever I thought I'd find inside that envelope, even though it would only confirm what I already knew about myself: that my whole life was sprawled ahead of me and that I'd live long enough to drive some poor nursing home employees nuts. I shook my head, reminded myself that Dahlia was just a glorified fortune teller. Finally, once I'd quelled my nerves, I peeked inside. That's when I pulled out what looked like a small business card.

"Well?" Marian moved toward me. I could tell by her expression that she was even more anxious than me. "What does it say?"

"Nothing." I flipped the card over a few times, as though words might magically appear on it. "It's blank."

"Blank?" Marian paused. She reached for the card to see my results for herself. She stared at the vast nothing on it. "That can't be right," she said as she ran her thumb across the smooth cardstock.

"Is this part of their gimmick or something?" I took the card back from Marian so I could reexamine it, as though my results might be written in invisible ink.

"Maybe you were right," Marian said. "Maybe we should just put it back."

Before I had a chance, the door slid back open. Dahlia entered the room alone. "I'm sorry about that." She waved, brushing the whole thing off. "Poppy is still . . . *acclimating* to the unique nature of our services."

"Where are my results?" I asked, and I held out the card. "This is blank."

Dahlia paused, taken aback. "Why do you have that?"

My muscles tightened. "It was in my file," I said defensively. "It's mine."

Dahlia's nostrils flared; she sucked her teeth. "May I have that, please?" Before I could stop her, she plucked the card from my fingers, walked toward her desk, and tucked it into my folder, which she then shoved into a drawer.

Marian took a step closer to me. "What's happening here?"

"Why would you want a blank card?" I asked. "There's nothing on it. Where are my results? The results we *paid* to receive."

Dahlia crossed her arms, as though deciding on something. "Of course." She offered me a tight smile. "Unfortunately, there was an issue with your test," she said. "I see Poppy didn't fully explain the—"

"An issue?" I questioned, my breath suddenly syncopated.

"Yes." Dahlia pivoted toward us. "An issue." She smiled a phony smile, some lie hiding just beneath her vibrant lips. "It seems something occurred in our lab, and so we can't provide you with your complete results at this time." Trios of fine lines formed around her eyes as she assessed me. "Our receptionist will mail you a refund."

"Well, what about her test?" I pointed at Marian. She looked at me in surprise, as though I'd said something inappropriate. "We only heard a sliver of her results," I continued. "I want to hear the rest." I widened my eyes at Marian, waiting for her to say something. "We both do," I answered for her.

"Let's just go, Liv," Marian finally chimed in. "We really don't need to do this." She picked up her belongings. I couldn't help but notice the way her eyes and lips had begun to sag, like a pair of arrows that pointed straight to her disappointment. "I don't care about my results all that much. This whole thing was just meant to be . . . fun." She glanced around the room. "Though it's not really panning out that way. We can just leave."

I looked to Dahlia, waiting for her to interject and to offer Marian her folder or a verbal rundown of her complete results or, well, something. She didn't.

"No way," I said. "*You* paid for this, so we're not leaving without *both* of our results."

Dahlia exhaled loudly, like she could blow me right out of the room. "Unfortunately, as I've already explained, we won't be able to provide you with all of that information today."

Marian began to inch toward the exit. "Really, Liv. Let's just get out of here, okay? This isn't worth all the back-and-forth."

"This is bullshit," I interjected, surprised by my own annoyance, before Dahlia could respond. "I guess I expected bullshit results. However, to give paying customers *no* results . . ." I trailed off and swiveled toward Marian. "I told you this whole thing was a scam."

"I'm sure there's a reasonable explanation for everything," Marian said and then looked at Dahlia. "Right?"

Dahlia's lips leveled into a straight line. "I assure you, nothing about this is *bullshit*," she announced, disregarding Marian's question. Marian and I stood there, waiting for Dahlia to offer some additional explanation that never arrived.

I adjusted my bag strap. "I never should have suggested we come back here for some made-up medical test." I slid my eyeglasses up, rubbed my hands across my eyes.

"Believe what you like," Dahlia said, surprising me. I'd assumed we wouldn't get much else out of her. She pressed her hands against her desk and leaned forward, as though to further extend her point. "But I assure you our test is not made up." She spoke slowly, cautiously, as though to defuse a hostage situation. "As I mentioned, belief is a powerful thing." Her stylish shoes clicked against the floor as she moved toward me. "Think of the placebo effect." I couldn't determine if she was trying to threaten me or teach me. "Medicine isn't always rooted exclusively in science. Sometimes it is rooted in what we *believe* about that science." She placed her slender fingers upon my hand, the gesture startling me. "When it comes to medicine, you should be careful of what you convince yourself is fact versus fiction." Her eyes narrowed. "Based on my experiences, misbelief can be a more dangerous ailment than disease."

I wanted to look away but felt like I'd been put under a spell.

"Come on." Marian grabbed my hand, breaking my trance. "Let's go." She tugged me forward. "I think it's safe to say that I owe you a proper, nondirt drink." Before I could object, Marian led me into the hallway. We walked past several lithe women who tenderly set trailing, apparently therapeutic, plants down on white yoga mats. We kept walking. A disquieted feeling followed me like an unwelcome shadow. "So, about that drink," Marian said over her shoulder. She smiled, though it felt forced. "What are we in the mood for?"

But I never answered; before I had the chance, we heard footsteps behind us.

"I'm sorry." Dahlia appeared, her gaze cast on my face. "About your test." Beyond her, a series of crystals dangled from the high ceilings and cast geometric rainbows across the floor, making everything feel a touch unreal. "These things happen," Dahlia said. "Unfortunately, when they do, they're out of my control."

An uneasy sensation settled over me, like a fog that made everything hard to see. I shook the feeling away. "You should be ashamed of yourself," I said as we moved toward the exit.

"Ashamed?" Dahlia asked, as though both the word and the concept were foreign to her.

"Yes," I confirmed. "Ashamed." Dahlia looked at me through slitted eyes, still processing my comment. "For trying to convince people that something as ludicrous as this is actually real," I said.

Marian tugged my arm, and we stepped through the door.

FOURTEEN

Out on the street, the air felt cooler. Above us, the sky was a wash of crisp blues, like a Grecian sea. Marian and I walked toward the subway. The whole neighborhood felt so strange. Pods of people, all of whom looked like they belonged in advertisements for expensive yoga studios, breezed past us, their faces marked by soft smiles. I wondered how many dirt tinctures one had to consume to reach that level of serenity. Too many for my tastes, I had to assume.

Marian walked beside me. "I'm guessing you don't want to see my last birthday pit stop?"

"You're kidding, right?"

"I am." Marian smiled. "I feel like that little fiasco would be hard to top, even for me."

I pulled my hair away from my face. "You could have stayed to get your results." My phone vibrated inside my bag. Andrew, I knew without the need to look. But I ignored it. He'd have a hundred questions about where we'd been, and frankly, I was too frazzled to formulate a normal-sounding response. "You didn't need to rush out of that fun house just because of me."

"It's fine," she said, and I knew from her tone that she was lying. Her body was cast in silhouette, the sun a bold orb behind her head. "I can go back and get them some other time."

"Wait!" a familiar voice shouted out behind us. We turned. Poppy rushed toward us, her lab coat rolled in a ball and tucked beneath her arm.

"This really is the gift that keeps on giving, huh?" I mumbled to Marian and then looked in Poppy's direction. "Just tell her you couldn't find us!" I yelled.

"Dahlia didn't send me." Poppy ran until she reached us. Finally, she stopped, rested her hands on her knees as she caught her breath. "I need to talk to you about that card."

"Here we go," I said as I pivoted away from her.

"Hang on." Poppy reached out and touched my arm. "Just give me a chance."

I swiveled my head. "What could you possibly need to tell me about some blank card?"

She became quiet then. *Too* quiet. "Maybe we should sit," she suggested.

"Honestly, I think I'm sort of over this whole experience," I told her.

"I swear. I'll only take a few minutes of your time."

"This is the worst birthday present you've ever given me," I informed Marian.

"I know it is," she sighed. "I promise I'll make it up to you next year."

I glanced at my watch. "You have ten minutes."

We moved toward the café and settled at a table. Poppy waved over a waiter. "Three waters, please." She looked up at us. "I'm assuming you're over the whole alkaline thing?"

"What is this all about, Poppy?" I asked.

"Here's the thing." She fumbled with some bohemian charm necklace. "Dahlia is incredibly smart." Poppy paused. "Too smart, maybe." Our waiter set down three glasses and a basket of seeded crackers that might as well have been birdseed. "Her genetic test—"

"Is a load of garbage?" I suggested.

"Not entirely." Poppy twisted a lock of her hair. "Actually, the data suggests otherwise." She locked eyes with me. "There wasn't an issue with the lab." She looked away and touched her glass. "It was your results." The ice cubes jangled from her trembling hand. "Your *actual* results."

Marian and I exchanged a glance. "What sort of problem?" I asked.

"Yeah," Marian echoed. "What *exactly* do you mean?"

"How do I best explain this?" Poppy huffed. "Sorry. I'm so nervous." She lifted her glass. "The thing about Dahlia's test is that, typically, the results bring her patients comfort. They confirm something her patients already believe: that they'll die in old age, that they have their whole lives stretched before them." She set the glass back down without taking a sip. "But, sometimes, when the results won't bring her patients, well, comfort . . ." She looked at us as though we should fill in the blanks. "Do you understand?"

"I don't follow," Marian said. Our waiter reappeared and set down three menus. She shooed him away. "What's your point?"

"How do I simplify this?" Poppy's fingers drummed her place mat. "What I'm saying is that it all comes down to our genes." She looked right at me. "*Your* genes, specifically." She willed herself into semipermanent composure. "Based on Dahlia's research, our genes are preprogrammed to expire on a certain day. People can smoke like chimneys or run marathons or become vegans or alcoholics or throw themselves out of airplanes. None of it matters. We're all just ticking time bombs. Our end dates have already been set for us. The test just—"

"And, we're done here." I forcefully pushed out my chair. I felt so foolish for having ever cared about that absurd, make-believe test, even for a split second. "Thanks for all the information, Poppy, but unfortunately, you're out of time. I need to—"

"That's the thing." Poppy stood. "I'm not the one who's out of time, it turns out. Not according to the test, at least." She reached into her pocket and pulled out a small envelope, similar to the one I'd discovered in my file. "Here. Maybe this will help." She handed it to me. "I believe this is yours." I took the envelope from Poppy. "I'm sorry. I never should have left those files unattended." She gathered her things. "I should go." She tucked her lab coat back beneath her arm. "Please don't tell Dahlia I gave you that envelope." Poppy turned to walk away. "In fact, maybe just try to forget about it entirely."

Marian and I watched her glide toward the end of the block and turn the corner. Marian scooted closer to me. "So?" A pre-summer breeze blew and billowed her blouse. "Aren't you going to open it?"

I shrugged nonchalantly. "I guess. Not that it matters." I lifted my brows. "You do know by now that this whole thing is nonsense, right?"

"I do. But so are palm readers, which I guess I don't need to remind you—yet again—that you once—"

"I was in my twenties," I reminded her. "I believed a lot of silly stuff in my twenties." I unsealed the flap cautiously, as though something might jump out at me. Slowly, I pulled out the card and read the neat text printed across it. "Wait." I blinked to ensure that I could see clearly and then read the print again. And again. "This doesn't make any sense." I rubbed the heels of my palms across my face. "Why is the date of my *next* birthday printed on this?" I looked up at her. "This is a joke, right?"

"That can't be right. Let me see that." Marian took the card. For a moment so brief I nearly thought I'd imagined it, her face turned pale. Briefly, she closed her eyes, as though to decide on something. She opened them and handed back the card. "Happy now?"

I eyed her skeptically. "Why would I be happy?"

"Isn't it obvious?" Marian laughed. "She made it up. She probably gives everyone the same damn card or something." She laughed again. "It's like you said: she's obviously just some bullshit fortune teller."

"Minor issue." My gaze kept shifting back to that card and the date printed on it—the date that was less than one year away. "Fortune tellers don't typically take blood samples."

"Liv, come on. The Nettle Center's whole gimmick is obviously a parody." She rested her hand on her hip. "Right?"

"Says the woman who dragged me here in the first place." I looked around. "Wherever *here* actually is."

"You know, *you're* the one who insisted we go back. You. Not me."

I felt my face twisting up in question. "I don't understand why you didn't demand she give you your results. Why didn't you ask her yourself?"

Marian sighed out what sounded like a lifetime's worth of annoyance. "Because I don't get wrapped up in stuff like you, Liv. This was just some fun, silly thing for us to do. The tension in that room was already thick enough. I'll just go back and get them in a few days or something."

I couldn't shake my aggravation. "It must be nice to be so relaxed about all this."

"Come on, Liv." She threw up her hands, a look of concern spreading across her face like a disease. "Do you really think Poppy got all that information right?"

But I didn't want to hear it. I shook my head, more frustrated with myself than with Marian for falling victim to yet another of her ridiculous schemes. "Grow up, Marian," I yelled. "We're thirty-nine years old. Enough with these outings. I told you the last time that I don't want to do this stuff anymore, that I don't have time for this sort of thing. Close the damn yearbook!"

"What does that mean?" Marian scrunched up her face. "Why are you so mad? I thought we agreed that Dahlia's test isn't even real."

"This isn't about the test. It's about you, still dragging me along for this sort of nonsense." I kicked the concrete. "Stop living in the past, Mar. You're still visiting the same shops we visited as undergraduates." I rolled my eyes so far into my head the gesture instantly gave me a headache. "You still rent the same apartment you did when we were twenty-two." I tried to sigh, but my breath had become so jagged that it sounded more like I had choked. "Maybe I'm not the one who should be freaking out about this birthday," I finally said.

"Liv, I—"

But I didn't give Marian a chance to respond. Without another word, I rushed up the block, down a set of stairs, and onto the subway platform. An empty train sped into the station and stopped before me. I jumped inside. The doors closed. As they did, I saw a forlorn Marian appear alone on the platform. We just looked at each other through the glass.

"Liv!" I heard her shout through the door. "Just wait. We can—"

But she was too late. I fell into a seat. Before I could help myself, my eyes began to flutter closed, one and then the other, like a doll's eyes.

Happy birthday, I thought to myself, right before I fell into a deep sleep.

The train began to speed through blackness.

And then, just like that, I was gone.

LIFE

FIFTEEN

Babe?"

I blinked my eyes open. Triangles of sunlight filtered into our bedroom. Andrew stood above me. He was dressed for work—a button-down, jeans, a canvas messenger bag. I swatted my hand toward the nightstand and stumbled upon my glasses. I slid them onto my face. "Shit." I pulled myself up. "What time is it?"

"Late." Andrew moved toward the dresser. "But there's coffee."

I turned and saw my favorite coffee mug—an old blue speckled camp mug stamped with the logo of the writers' retreat we'd attended together after college—placed on my nightstand. I inhaled deeply. My lungs filled with the scent of artificial hazelnut creamer. Probably not a good thing for my body, but an absolute necessity for my morning mental state.

"What happened yesterday?" Andrew sat on the edge of the bed and tied his shoes. "I thought you'd be home for dinner." He adjusted his pant leg and stood. "Was your phone dead?"

I didn't know how to explain it. I sipped my coffee and glanced around the room. Last week's work clothes were still draped over our old rocker. Old photos of Tommy hung from the wall. It all looked so predictable—so *normal*. It was hard to imagine that, just yesterday, I'd been God knows where drinking dirt smoothies with some hipster fortune teller. "It's a long story."

"Well, you'll have plenty of time to tell us an *extra*-long story later this week." He shut the drawer with his rear end. "Tommy is mad that you were late." He straightened his bag strap. "As retribution, he's insisting that you make homemade rainbow pizzas this weekend to mark the end of the school year. No boxed stuff. Apparently, it will be our summer kickoff meal."

"We're already planning for the weekend?" I pushed aside the blanket. Life. It never just happened in the moment; it was always three steps ahead. "Also, what in the hell is a rainbow pizza?"

"Beats me." Andrew picked his keys up off the dresser. "While you research that, I'll drop Tommy off at school."

"Oh God." I never missed Tommy's drop-off. "Is it really *that* late?"

"It is."

I picked up my watch from my nightstand and glanced at its scratched face. "Shit."

"Tommy's dressed downstairs." Andrew grabbed his old NYU baseball cap and kissed my forehead. "It's not, by chance, Wacky Wardrobe Day at the ole elementary school, is it?"

"No." I slid my feet to the floor. "Do I want to know why you just asked me that?"

"No reason." Andrew moved toward the hallway. "Good luck with the pizza." He stepped through the door, then swiveled his head. "One last thing. At what age do you think Marian will stop forcing you to participate in all her ridiculous shenanigans?"

"There were no shenanigans." I pointed to the secondhand poetry anthology on my nightstand. "I was just getting my book." Andrew lifted his brows, a challenge. "What?" I forced a smile. "You don't believe me?"

"No, I do," Andrew said. A clatter rang out from downstairs, followed by the sound of Tommy skidding across the hardwood floors. "There's just one problem." He tilted his head. "Don't take this the wrong way, babe." One corner of his mouth lifted. "But you look like shit."

SIXTEEN

I arrived at Blakely several minutes behind schedule. I rushed across the central quad. The bells chimed. I hustled into the building with a straggling group of students and then flopped down in my desk chair. I stared out my window. Grading papers was completely off the table. I couldn't get past my frustration with Marian. I knew the test—as well as Poppy's absurd warning—was fake. I mean, death in a year? *Pfffft.* I'd have to get struck by a train or tumble overboard on a cruise ship or . . . something. Still, that place had seemed extreme, even for Marian. I didn't understand why she still insisted on wasting my time—*our* time—with that sort of thing.

"Sebastian wants to see you."

I swiveled my chair and discovered Christopher behind me. He adjusted his bow tie, which was embroidered with tiny crustaceans—his nod to the new season—a coffee mug in his free hand.

"He waltzed in earlier and requested your honor," he continued. "I let him know that you usually don't arrive until *after* the morning bell rings."

"Thanks. Really appreciate that."

"One more thing. As the great Bard wrote, 'Could beauty, my lord, have better commerce than honesty?'" I looked at him blankly. He slurped his coffee. "A translation: you have Cheerios in your hair."

I swung open our office door. "Great."

I walked down the hall and into Sebastian's private office. I took a seat across from him while he finished reading what I surmised to be the world's longest page.

"You'll have to forgive me." He finally set down his paperback. "Do you enjoy Joyce, Olivia?"

"I feel like I have to." I glanced at the wall clock. I had a class in ten minutes and no lesson plan prepared. "I was born on Bloomsday."

"Bloomsday!" Sebastian threw up his arms and, in the process, knocked over a mug of tea. He retrieved a handkerchief from his pocket (an *actual* handkerchief!). "How fortuitous." Sebastian tended to the spill. I glanced around his office. Hundreds of books occupied the bookcases. A half dozen cardigans were draped over an old wingback chair. There were empty mugs everywhere. "However, that's not why I wanted to talk this morning."

"Is this about the curriculum?" I considered my end-of-year to-do list, which was shoved in a desk drawer. "Did I forget to submit something?" For a second, I thought maybe he'd fire me. I pulsed with jubilation. It would be so much easier to get canned than to quit.

Ever since the day I'd started at Blakely, I'd told myself the job was temporary, just something to keep me afloat until Tommy was grown or until I could finally get my poetry career off the ground. I knew it was a good gig—a great one, even. I wasn't naive. Still, I'd known from the start that it wasn't for me, wasn't what I wanted to do. I didn't want my whole identity to get wrapped up in that place. That happened with careers if you weren't careful. As time passed, they became more than just what you *did*. They became who you were. You got stuck.

Sebastian cleared his throat. He produced a thin folder from a bookshelf, gestured for me to open it. Inside was a pamphlet that featured an image of a river nestled among mountains. "That's the Rhine, of course," he said. "Have you and Andrew been?"

"We went to France once in our twenties," I told him, unclear of his point.

Sebastian looked toward the ceiling. "I've wanted to travel by river my whole life, Olivia. Think of the sights. Swiss villages. The Black Forest. Germany at Christmastime and those charming wooden ornaments." He pretended to pull the string of one.

"I don't understand." I handed him the folder. "Are we going to teach European literature? I thought we agreed on no changes." .

"That's up to you," Sebastian said. "My wife and I depart in the fall."

"I'm sorry?"

A smile emerged from beneath Sebastian's beard. "I'm retiring, Olivia."

"Oh." I began to sweat beneath my creased button-down. "That's . . . nice."

Sebastian crossed his legs. "I've already told the administration that you're my pick."

Sebastian had sometimes joked about me becoming chair. When he did, I usually just smiled politely and reminded myself that he was likely in the early stages of dementia. "But I've only been here a few years."

"You know the subject better than anyone here. And you're the only one who has ever published," he noted in reference to my onetime claim to temporary poetry fame.

"Thank you." I felt my face turn red. "But that was a long time ago."

I frequently thought of that afternoon at the end of college. Marian and I had skipped classes and spent the day at an outdoor table of a local bar. After a long, frozen winter, it was finally spring. The sidewalks bustled. The sun beat on our exposed shoulders, like it belonged exclusively to us. "So, what are you going to do now that this is all almost over?" Marian had asked me.

I swigged my draft. "I know what I *want* to do. But I also know I *need* to get paid."

Marian signaled to the bartender. "It's not impossible to get paid to write poetry."

"We'll see." I looked out at the city and its many untapped opportunities. "I just know I don't ever want to settle. I want my life to always feel as full of possibility as it feels right now."

Marian handed me a pint glass. "Then what are you waiting for?"

That night, Marian helped me draft a dozen query letters. By dawn, we'd sent my poem—a quiet villanelle about life and chasing dreams—out to a dozen poetry contests. A few weeks later, I received a call. "Holy shit." I dropped my phone on my apartment floor. "I fucking won." That first year out of college, it felt like my whole life happened. There were readings and cocktail parties and poetry panels. There was an agreement with a literary agent and the promise that the life I'd wanted could actually be made real.

Those first few months, I took a million odd jobs—bartender, waitress, anything with an apron—so I could spend every free minute writing a book-length poetry collection. I had only a short time to complete it. We had to strike while the iron was hot, my agent had explained. If we waited too long, everyone might forget about me and that villanelle. Dreams, it seemed, had a limited window. If you wanted to go after them, you couldn't afford to wait.

I practically chained myself to my desk, the whole world bustling just beyond my window. But the inspiration wasn't there. Marian tried a thousand times to convince me to step away and to go grab tacos or drinks or to go out dancing. But I was too consumed. I didn't want to end up a fraud, just a hyped-up writer with only one real work inside her, the literary equivalent of a child star who peaks before puberty. Most nights, Andrew read on the couch next to me while I worked, the city buzzing several stories below us. I rarely made it to bed.

Several weeks after I'd completed my collection, the three of us were at our favorite dumpling spot for a quick meal when my agent finally called. The manuscript wasn't working. The themes, she'd explained, fell flat. The writing felt forced. In short, it was a miss. I cracked open my fortune cookie, unscrolled the tiny paper inside it. "I'll start again," I told her. "I'll start tonight. I have some new ideas. I just need a little time." But it was too late. She had other clients. Other projects that required her attention. That villanelle—the one that had been so celebrated—was already a thing of the past. Before we ended our call, I glanced at my paper fortune. *Your days will be filled with sunshine,* it read.

That night, I made a list. It was a step-by-step plan for how to try again. It seemed so simple. I just had to take it one bullet point at a time, and I could reclaim that version of myself—the one I had thought was about to bloom. But life was never that easy. The list was as far as I got.

Sebastian kept talking. My phone vibrated inside my pants. "Excuse me," I mumbled, grateful for the distraction. I slid out the device and discovered another voice mail from Dr. White's office.

"The position starts in September," Sebastian continued. I tried to tuck the phone away, but it vibrated again in my hand. *Marian.* I quickly skimmed her message. Just checking in to make sure Poppy didn't confuse your big date. You're still alive, right? It was her attempt at a joke, an olive branch. If you're dead, don't text back, okay? Sarcasm had always been our love language. But right then, I wasn't in the mood. I tucked the device away.

As Sebastian carried on, stress crept through me and spread itself around like ink. My hand drifted toward my shoulder. I squeezed my muscles, which were as tight as new leather. That's when it happened. My body went stiff. I pressed my fingers into my skin to be sure I hadn't imagined it. *Oh shit.* I'd found a small, marble-shaped lump at the base of my neck.

The discovery arrived swiftly, unexpectedly, like a heart attack or a bullet to the back of the head. I frantically pressed at it, as though I could diagnose it. My mind flashed to that test, though I quickly disregarded it. It was a coincidence. That was it. While Sebastian rambled about the future I had never asked for, I told myself there was a rational, completely benign explanation—one that had zero correlation to Dahlia or Poppy.

"Olivia?" Sebastian scratched his beard. "Are you okay? You look a bit . . . pale."

"I, um . . ." I probably looked like I was trying to strangle myself. "I have a class."

"Of course." Sebastian resettled himself at his desk. "Well, I hope you'll celebrate your new position with a glass of something sparkling tonight." He picked up his book, signaling the end of our meeting. "You've earned it." The school bell chimed. "But for now," he said, "you'd better get going." The hallways buzzed with voices. "You're running late."

SEVENTEEN

Early Saturday morning, I found myself paralyzed beside a table arranged with an abundance of bunched greens. I'd been standing there, awkwardly fixated on them, for far too long to seem like a functioning human.

"Need help finding something?" An older woman—maybe twenty years my senior (i.e., ancient!)—approached me from the opposite side of the table. She wore a dirt-covered tank top, graying hair swept back. "Those are dandelion greens." She picked up a bunch. "To tell you the truth," she said and dropped her voice, "they're not very good."

"Oh." My fingers palpated my neck, just like they had all week. "Dandelion greens." I thought of the overgrown weeds in our yard that Tommy used to make wishes. "Right." My phone rang, saving me from the conversation and my self-imposed medical exam. "Excuse me," I said and then shuffled across the pavement.

"You never called me back," Marian said the moment I answered. "I messaged you days ago. I was starting to wonder if Poppy's little prediction had been right."

I balanced my phone against my shoulder, my free hand clutching my neck. "Not funny."

"It wasn't meant to be funny." Through the line, I heard a symphony of traffic.

"So, what did yours actually say?" I asked her.

"What are you talking about?" Marian asked. "My what?"

"Your results," I said, like it was the most obvious thing on the planet. It was, wasn't it? "You said you'd go back to get them." I wanted to compare our full results in order to prove that the whole thing was completely inauthentic and absurd.

"Yeah, I meant eventually, when I'm back in that neighborhood or something. I didn't mean right away," she clarified. For a beat, we just listened to the background noise of each other's lives. "Liv, you're not seriously pissed that I brought you there, are you?" I allowed my silence to fill in the blanks. "You've got to be kidding me." Cars beeped in her backdrop. "You know, you *used* to have a sense of humor. Need I bring up the psychic we visited sophomore year? The one who told *me* that I'd meet my end thanks to a faulty manhole cover. Because you found *that* prediction—as well as my yearlong fear of sewers—pretty hysterical back then."

"That was completely different," I reminded her.

"You know what?" I heard her suck her teeth. "You're right."

My shoulders tensed; the bump pressed my finger. "What's that supposed to mean?"

"Nothing." In the background, the whole city swirled past her. "I just forget sometimes that you were a different person back then."

Lately, Marian liked to remind me of all the ways I'd changed, as though growing up and into adulthood had been some kind of unforgivable sin. "I have to go," I finally announced. "I need to get home to Tommy. School is finally over. It's finally summer break, and there's this recipe . . ." I trailed off. "It's a whole thing."

"Hey, Liv," Marian said. "Do yourself a favor." The line fritzed out, and I knew she was stepping underground. "Try not to take that test—or life, for that matter—quite so seriously."

We hung up. I moved back toward the table. The woman was still there, sorting through a crate of produce. I cleared my throat. "Do you know how to make a rainbow pizza?"

She dropped a bunch of greens, like I'd deeply offended her. "Another one, huh?" I lifted a brow, confused. "Wait. Weren't you here last week?"

I'd visited the farmers' market on occasion with Andrew and Tommy, but only to visit the baker's table and load up on hunks of crumb cake. "Sorry," I said. "Not me."

She inspected my face. "All the moms in this town are starting to look the same to me."

Her words pierced me like a million tiny pins. I fumbled with some kale, looked at her through a drape of my hair. "So, then you know what it is?" I tried, my fingers still at my neck.

She reached into her pocket, tapped her phone to life. "Apparently, it's all the rage." She showed me an image of a perfectly styled pizza topped with colorful, cubed vegetables arranged in a precisely symmetrical rainbow pattern.

"Shit." I adjusted my tote. "My kid doesn't even like half that stuff. He refuses to eat bell peppers because he thinks they're made of actual bells."

"If it means anything, my daughter only ate vegetables if I gave them ridiculous names. We ate a lot of 'superhero salads' and 'magical celery wands' during those years." She smiled. "She's probably about your age now." She shook her head at the memory, extended her hand. "I'm Sunshine."

I'd had my fill of women with absurd bohemian names. I turned, ready to walk away.

"So, how'd you get stuck with rainbow pizza?" Sunshine asked, oblivious to my attempt to dismiss her. I looked back. "Rumor is it's a form of parental punishment."

I figured it'd be alarming to tell her my best friend took me to a pretend medical center to have the equivalent of our genetic tarot cards read. "I got home past curfew last week." I left out the part in which a twentysomething predicted the date of my death. "My son is still pissed."

"Well, good for you." Without asking, she lifted my bag from my arm and filled it with produce I didn't have a clue how to cook. "People forget sometimes that mothers deserve that time for themselves, too." Her ridiculous name aside, after that remark, I fell in love with her.

Nearby, I heard familiar voices. I noticed Allison and Courtney at another stand. "Crap," I blurted out. Sunshine squinted. "Sorry. I just don't want to say hello to those women."

Sunshine swiveled her head. "Who? The yoga pants crew?"

"They don't even do yoga," I huffed. "It's like they're always in costume."

"Liv!" From across the market, Allison and Courtney shouted my name in tandem.

"Are they that terrible?" Sunshine asked through gritted teeth.

"They're the human version of rainbow pizza," I whispered. "Decidedly sunny, but in a suspicious sort of way." I adjusted my bag. "They want me to host one of their absurd makeup parties," I admitted, unsure if Sunshine would even know what that meant. "Apparently, part of being middle-aged is selling tubes of lipstick in your living room."

"Some things never change, then." Creases formed around Sunshine's eyes. "In my day, the women in this town were obsessed with selling Tupperware." She shrugged. "That was before we knew about BPA." She laughed. "I gave in to their peer pressure once. I mean, it was better than having to host one of those *awful* Mary Kay parties."

For the first time in a long time, I felt seen. "I'm Olivia," I said, and I offered my hand.

Sunshine shook it, then reached beneath the table. "Here." She produced a glossy postcard. "This is the yoga studio where I teach." She handed me the card. "You can pretend you're reading it to avoid them." I raised a brow. "Let's just say I get it." My neighbors beelined toward us, their arms flapping above them like they were birds about to take flight. Sunshine smiled at me. "For what it's worth, I spent years trying to avoid the women in this town, too."

EIGHTEEN

I spent the rest of the afternoon tangled up in research, like a grown-up version of Nancy Drew. I felt compelled to prove that the test was fake so I could completely write it off as nothing more than Marian's offbeat brand of fun. For hours, I sat hunched over my computer at our kitchen island, my bag of untouched vegetables beside me, and typed in every imaginable combination of search terms. *Nettle Center + Death Date. Dahlia + Nettle Center + Real. Nettle Center + Expiration Date + Scam.* The only thing my search turned up was a link to the Nettle Center's website, which featured a single image of the building's exterior and a complete absence of pertinent details, such as a phone number or an address. *Zing!* If that test had even a shred of authenticity, there'd be virtual heaps of reviews and write-ups—sermons written by other patients either praising or belittling it—all over the internet.

By the time Andrew and Tommy arrived home from an afternoon playdate, the kitchen was a haze of smoke. The three of us stood around the island in mourning. Tommy poked a charred piece of bell pepper, its blistered skin crumbling beneath his light touch. Andrew kept tilting his head from left to right, as though to view my creation from a less disastrous angle. "It looks . . . great," he finally decided without offering to try a bite.

Tommy dropped his chin into his hand. "Can we just have regular pizza?"

I forced myself to smile. "Sure, buddy." I couldn't admit that I'd burned it because I'd been too caught up in my research. "I think there's ice cream in the freezer, too."

Tommy, pleased by the prospect of sugar, skidded into the living room, the rainbow pizza already erased from his mind. I pressed my fingers to my neck. I kept hearing my neighbors' voices and their comments about aging every time I touched it.

"Tears over a pizza?" Andrew appeared behind me, placed his arms around my waist.

"No tears." I distracted myself with a dish towel. "I had a rogue lash in my eye."

"I've known you for twenty years, Liv." Andrew turned me around so we were eye to eye. "Why are you acting weird?"

I considered telling him everything in one stream-of-consciousness burst. *That obviously benign bump. The Nettle Center. That ridiculous test.* "I'm fine," I said instead. I didn't want to sound unhinged.

In the other room, a pile of Tommy's plastic blocks crashed across the floor. I turned from Andrew, grabbed some pizza slices from the freezer, and slid them into the microwave. We were both quiet while the machine hummed. After an eternity, it finally beeped. I slid the steaming slices onto plates. Andrew stopped me. "Really, though," he said, "are you all right? You haven't been yourself in a few days."

I shoved a piece of cheese into my mouth to avoid the need to speak. I nodded and moved into the other room. Andrew followed me, clicked on the television. The opening credits for one of Tommy's favorite cartoons blared through the house. On the screen, a superhero space cowboy jabbed his fist toward the sky.

Tommy snuggled against me with his plastic dinosaur plate. "Mama, I have a question."

I assumed he would ask a typical Tommy question. *Do frogs have families? What do you think the moon tastes like?* "Chew your food," I reminded him.

He made a gulping sound. "Why are you mad at Aunt Marian?" he asked, surprising me.

I shifted uncomfortably. "Who said I'm mad at Aunt Marian?"

"Daddy," Tommy said between bites. "I heard them on the phone."

I set my plate on the coffee table and turned to Andrew. "Spill it," I demanded.

Andrew took a bite. "She called earlier and said you're annoyed about something that happened on your birthday outing." Tommy jumped off the couch and bolted toward his toy baskets. Andrew picked up the remote. "So, what happened?" He surfed the channels and stopped on our favorite cooking show. On-screen, the same handsome British gentleman catapulted a pan of baked goods at a contestant. Puff pastry smashed against a wall in a brilliant, buttery burst.

"It was the eggs," I said. "At our age, brunch can get pretty feisty."

"Liv."

"What?"

Andrew turned down the volume and met my gaze. "Come on."

Obviously, Andrew knew I was lying. That happened when you were with one person for so long. You lost the ability to pretend. Andrew saw right through my bullshit. I was like a human Tootsie Pop; he always knew when I was hiding something else in my core.

"You know, this happened the last time she took you out," Andrew said, like I needed the reminder. "You came home and were lost in your head for days."

He was right. But I didn't want to think about it. "Can we talk about this later?" I asked. "I just want to take a shower. It's been a long week."

Andrew nodded. "Sure," he sighed. "By the way, Suzanne dropped something off for you earlier. It's in an over-the-hill gift bag, so I'm sure it's tasteful." He flipped back to one of Tommy's hallucinogenic cartoons. "I left it on your nightstand." His voice dropped. "Something else came for you in the mail today," he said, his expression apologetic. "That's up there, too."

I knew what he meant without the need for him to expand. "Okay." I kissed him and Tommy. "There's one more thing I've been meaning to tell you," I said. "I think I got promoted this week."

"Oh yeah?" Andrew turned to me. "Congrats?" His eyes narrowed. "I think."

Upstairs, I sat on our unmade bed. A thin envelope lay on our nightstand. I read the return address—*Rhyme and Reason Literary Journal*—then sliced it open. *Dear Mrs. Strauss, Thank you for the opportunity to read your poetry; unfortunately . . .*

I didn't talk about it much, though I still often thought of that first time I saw my name in print. After I'd won that contest, I bought a half dozen copies of the journal my poem had appeared in anytime I spotted it on display in a bookstore around the city. If it was a youthful dream to think I could turn that single accolade into a fully fleshed-out career, it didn't feel that way at the time. Seeing my name printed on the same table of contents page as so many writers whom I admired felt not only like confirmation that my talent was real but that I was real, too. Finally, I'd found my voice. I wish I'd known at the time that it was possible for me to lose it again.

I sighed out my frustration and turned my attention to Suzanne's gift bag. Inside was a small card. *Hope you had a great birthday! And I hope you don't need these . . . yet.* I lifted sheets of tissue and discovered something called over-the-hill breast suspenders. The packaging featured an illustration of an old woman whose nipples dragged across the floor. I shoved the gift back into the bag, too mortified to even look at it. Suzanne. She really was the queen of subtlety.

I carried the bag into the bathroom and set it on the counter, beside the antiaging cream I'd bought at Suzanne's party. I turned on the shower. From downstairs, I heard the echo of Tommy's laughter. I glanced up at the mirror. My reflection had already disappeared behind a veil of vapor. I wiped away a streak and looked myself in the eye. "They're wrong," I said out loud as I gripped the edge of the sink. "Suzanne. The neighbors. Poppy. They're all wrong." I tossed the gift bag and cream into the trash. "You still have time, Olivia Strauss," I told myself. "You still have all the time in the world to be who you want to be." And then, without another thought, I stepped into the shower and lost myself in the steam.

NINETEEN

I'd canceled and rescheduled my appointment with Dr. White three times. The first time, I'd told myself that my cancellation was valid ("It's the last week of the school year—I'm swamped!"). I easily validated my second cancellation, too ("It's the first nice summer day!"). By my third cancellation, I knew I was stalling ("If I don't clean the house today, I never will!"). Finally, one month later, I caved.

"I have good news." Dr. White sat behind his mahogany desk and plucked pistachios from a bowl. A detailed illustration of a vagina hung behind him. "You're not dying."

I blinked hard, recalling his nurse's many voice mails. "Did you suspect that I might be?"

"It's just a joke I make sometimes," he explained before popping more nuts into his mouth.

"Right." I shifted uncomfortably and thought of Marian. She'd been right: I really did need a new doctor. Fast.

"Overall, your labs look good." His hand floated back to the bowl. It was strange that he casually consumed allergenic snacks, considering where his hands ended up during every exam. "However, there is one thing." He lifted a sheet of paper. "Your thyroid levels are . . . off."

My heart beat like a toddler banging his first drum set. "What do you mean by 'off'?"

Dr. White clapped his palms, sending a cloud of nut dust across his desk. "It's medical speak for 'not right.'" He really was a budding comedian. "Why don't we have you throw on a gown, and we'll take a look under the hood?" He smiled. "I'll know more then."

A few minutes later, I found myself dressed in a flimsy paper gown, my body spread across a cold examination table. Tissue paper crinkled beneath me. Dr. White positioned himself near my feet. "How old is your son now, Olivia?" he asked, shifting topics.

"He's five." I tried to avoid eye contact. There ought to be strict rules among physicians about when—and when *not*—to talk to patients (see: when your hand is probing their insides).

"Five!" Dr. White smiled from between my legs and inserted a metal instrument into my body. "We'd better start talking about kiddo number two." He removed the device, which made me wince. "I hate to be the bearer of bad news, but you're no spring chicken."

"Is that one of your jokes, too?"

He peeled off his gloves. "It's not, unfortunately." Dr. White pressed his fingers into my breasts, like I was made of Play-Doh. "Is a second child something you want, Olivia?"

Here's a fact about motherhood: people aren't satisfied with one child. The minute you pop out one kid, the entire universe feels entitled to inquire about the state of your uterus all over again. It's infuriating. "I'm not sure."

Anytime Andrew and I had talked about a second child, I tried to seem on board, like it was something I'd *love* to consider, only at a later date, like scheduling lunch with an old friend you had zero intention of seeing. Honestly, Andrew seemed more invested than me. Who could blame him? He'd only need to have some fun, then wait for an infant to be placed in his arms like a trophy. Meanwhile, I'd have to watch my body morph into some unrecognizable form.

Dr. White helped me sit up. "Well, if it's something you'd like to consider, you ought to get a jump start on it." He made a note on my chart. "Unfortunately, your window is closing."

"I'm assuming that's not a joke, either."

He set my chart on a counter, right beside a plastic mold of a uterus. "It's not, sadly."

I pulled my gown tighter around my body. Dr. White sidled up behind me and pressed his fingers into the base of my neck. "What are you doing?" For weeks, I'd both obsessed over my bump and tried to ignore it.

"Ah, what's this?" Dr. White's fingers pressed against it. *Busted.*

"Yeah. Um, that's new." I cleared my throat. "Any idea what it is?"

He stepped forward. I felt the heat of him against my back. He made a series of noncommittal sounds—*um-hmm, mmm*—as he palpated my body.

"What is it?"

He looked at me with a somber expression. *Oh shit.* For a moment, I forgot how to breathe. "Cyst," Dr. White finally announced, plain and simple.

"Seriously?" I said, and I literally gasped.

"Seriously," he confirmed. "I did feel something else, however." Dr. White made some notes on my chart. "You have a small nodule on your thyroid." He squirted a pump of hand sanitizer into his palm. "It's likely benign, but you should still see an endocrinologist." He scribbled something on a notepad. "Here's the name of a friend of mine." He handed me a sheet. "Try to get an appointment soon. I imagine he'll want to biopsy it, so you shouldn't wait."

It was official: I'd never breathe normally again. "Why would I need a biopsy if you think it's benign?"

"Protocol," he said, matter-of-factly. Dr. White moved toward the door, glanced at my chart, and then turned back toward me. "One last thing. My nurse called you several times but couldn't reach you. Is your contact information the same?"

I was too focused on that word—"biopsy"—to speak. "Why did you n-need to reach me?" I finally stuttered.

"You're due for your first mammogram, Olivia."

"A mammogram?" I felt like I was suffocating.

"Yes," Dr. White said. "It's an ultrasound performed on your breasts to test for—"

"I *know* what a mammogram is," I clarified. *Christ.* I couldn't find a new doctor fast enough. "I thought women went for mammograms in their forties." I forced a smile, as though trying to sell him something. "I'm still technically in my thirties."

"Not for long." He paused, perhaps waiting for a laugh track. "Plus, this one is just a baseline." He nodded. "Think of it like the mammogram *before* the mammogram." He smiled, entertained by his own comment. "But you do need to go soon. You're already late for this one."

I sat up straighter. "How can I be late for something I don't need to do for another year?"

Dr. White opened the exam room door. "Technically, I wrote you a script to go for this one when you were thirty-five."

TWENTY

The next week, Tommy and I were playing in the yard with Zippy, one of his many imaginary friends—a sassy cartoonish T. rex—when I took a break to finally brainstorm ideas for *Hearth*, even though I felt intimidated by the task. It made sense for Marian to write essays. Her perspective—her whole existence—was marked by excitement. *Of course* people wanted to read what she had to say, wanted to pay money to immerse themselves in her stories, her world. But mine? I gave up before I even started. I set down my notebook and pen.

In the yard, Tommy threw a handful of grass and laughed at some invisible hilarity. "Mama, me and Zippy want a snack!" he shouted and pretended to whisper to someone beside him. "Zippy wants to know if we can have chips."

I looked toward him. (Or was it "them"? I wasn't clear on the correct pronoun usage for imaginary friends.) "Tell Zippy he can have fruit," I shouted and moved into the house, Tommy trailing behind me. In the kitchen, I dropped a handful of berries onto a plastic plate. Tommy tossed some in the air for Zippy. They dropped to the floor. Tommy scooped them up and swallowed them.

That's when we heard a knock. Tommy and I looked up. Without a word, we moved toward our home's entryway. I swung open the door, expecting to find Suzanne or one of Tommy's neighborhood friends.

Instead, I saw an inconspicuous white van backing out of our driveway and pulling away from our street.

"A delivery!" Tommy proclaimed while pointing to an equally inconspicuous white box on our porch. "Can I open it?" he asked, already reaching for it.

I knelt down and examined the package, which was free of any sort of marking. Except for one: a small, practically translucent sticker, stamped with two words. NETTLE CENTER. "Shit," I muttered under my breath.

"Time to feed the curse jar," Tommy proclaimed and knelt beside me.

I picked up the box, looked around. Everything on our street seemed typically pedestrian. "Come on, kiddo." I guided Tommy toward the door and peeked over my shoulder to make sure no one had seen us. "Let's take this inside."

I dropped the box onto our broken table. The damaged wood creaked from its weight. Tommy and I just stared at it, like it had arrived from another dimension. "I know what we need," Tommy said and fled from me. When he returned, he handed over his favorite primary-colored safety scissors, my three-and-a-half-foot partner in crime.

I sliced through the packing tape and found another smaller white box inside the original package. Cautiously, I opened that box, too. Arranged inside it were dozens of metallic packets of tincture powders, as well as a white postcard marked with several lines of black type.

> To Our Valued Patient:
> Congratulations on your upcoming death! According to our records, your genetic expiration date is less than one year away. As such, we've included several of our favorite detoxifying supplements to help you to feel good during your final months. On behalf of everyone at the Nettle Center, we wish you the best on your end-of-life journey.
> In peace and serenity—Dahlia

The world started to spin. I blinked hard.

"What does it say, Mama?" Tommy asked.

I shook my head. "Nothing," I declared and then tossed the postcard back into the box. "It's all nothing." I pulled Tommy's petite body against mine and tried to disregard my frustration with Marian, at least for the moment. In all the years she'd dragged me along on her unusual tours, never once had those experiences been made concrete by turning up on my doorstep. It felt too close for comfort, like a bit too much effort for a place that specialized in services rooted in pretend. "Do me a favor, buddy." I uncurled my arms and concealed the box behind a wholesale-size package of cookies I still hadn't put away. "Let's not mention this to Dad, okay?"

Tommy nodded and then raced through the kitchen. He paused beside the counter and pulled down a stack of paperwork I'd neglected for weeks. "Mama, can me and Zippy use these papers for our art?" he asked, his concern with the box—unlike mine—already dwindling.

"Hang on." I squinted. "Let me see that, buddy." Tommy waved my mammogram script through the air, like a reminder from the universe. "Why don't you and Zippy get some construction paper." I grabbed my phone and made a writing note in my head. *A poem about . . . breasts. Reason for babies wanting to devour you, then men, then . . . cancer? (In the end, I guess your cells want to devour your breasts, too.)* "Mama has some calls to make."

Back on the deck, I learned that mammograms were VIP tickets. Forget days—I couldn't get an appointment for months. Plural. "You've got to be kidding me?" I grumbled after I called the breast center back just to be sure I hadn't spoken to someone incompetent the first time around.

"I'm not kidding, ma'am," the receptionist said. Through the line, I heard her fingers click her keyboard. "Breast health is no joke. That's why, nowadays, most women come in for their baselines at thirty-five." And then she hung up.

Nearby, Tommy (and Zippy) sat at our plastic kiddie table and engaged in a fierce art contest. Poor Zippy and his lack of opposable thumbs. He didn't stand a chance. The glass door slid open. Andrew stepped onto the deck. He kissed us, then slid half his rear end onto the kiddie table's plastic bench. He inspected Tommy's artwork. "Dinosaur on a giant golf ball?"

"Close," Tommy said and then scribbled all over a new sheet. "It's the moon."

"That explains the stars." Andrew nodded toward my notebook. "Speaking of creative endeavors, it looks like Mama did some writing today," he said, already reaching for it.

"That's a matter of opinion," I said.

Andrew loved to read my writing. In college, we'd lay on an old futon for hours while he listened to me read drafts of my poetry, like I was the damn poet laureate.

"You forgot to say hi to Zippy," Tommy said, his gaze cast on his drawing.

Andrew side-glanced me. I just shrugged. "Sorry, Zippy." He kissed the air.

Tommy added some finishing touches to his art. "Mama got a package today!" he shouted, then immediately looked to me. "Oh, wait. I wasn't supposed to say that."

A slow exhalation exited my body. "It's fine, buddy," I said with a smile.

Tommy, satisfied by my response, darted up, grabbed Zippy's pretend hand, and ran inside the house.

"Order something special?" Andrew asked as he unfastened his cuff buttons.

"Not exactly."

It was completely ridiculous that I still hadn't told Andrew about the test. I'd had plenty of opportunities, but I'd talked myself out of the conversation every time, reassuring myself that the whole thing was so fake it wasn't even worth my breath. But right then, with a piece of the Nettle Center hidden inside our home, my reasoning felt different, like I was hiding something versus just dismissing it. For the first time, I began to wonder if there was some small chance that the test actually *had* been real.

Andrew sat in an adult chair. "So, in other news, Zippy came over today, huh?" Ages ago, Andrew's newspaper had printed some silly article about how only children have more imaginary friends because they're lonely. I guess the author hadn't considered the role of imagination.

"What?" I still hadn't mentioned Dr. White's stance on my biological clock. "You're not a fan of Zippy?" I asked. "As far as imaginary cartoon dinosaurs go, he seems like a good kid."

Andrew sighed. "Marian called me earlier. She said you're still annoyed with her, that you two haven't talked as much as you normally do."

He was right—and so was she—but I didn't want to admit it. Since our birthday, Marian and I had still spoken most days, sure. But the energy felt different. It was like I was holding all our conversations hostage, only giving her a few short words per call when, typically, our back-and-forth banter amounted to hours of dialogue each day. I was still waiting for her to do her part, to go back to the Nettle Center and get her full results so she could share them with me. But anytime I brought up the idea, she blew me off.

"I've been busy." What else was there to say? I mean, how do you tell your husband that you're frustrated with your best friend because she brought you to a place where a stranger stabbed a needle into your arm, shook up your blood like a Magic 8 Ball, and then predicted the date of your death? Answer: you don't.

"Are you ever going to tell me what happened?" Andrew ran his hands through his hair, which had become brindled with gray. "I'm worried about you."

I looked toward the house, knowing that box was inside. "I promise, when I'm ready to talk about it, you'll be the first to know."

Tommy ran out of the house and onto the lawn. Within seconds, he began to flail his arms at the air. "Mama, Zippy is trying to hit me!"

"He can't hit you, Tommy!" I shouted, grateful for the diversion. "T. rexes have tiny arms!" I explained, momentarily forgetting that Zippy wasn't real.

I moved toward the stairs and then looked back at Andrew. His face was etched with concern. "You promise?" he asked. "That you're okay?"

"I swear." I stepped into the grass and reminded myself that none of it was real.

TWENTY-ONE

"Personally, I found it . . . moving." Sebastian stared off at the ceiling. A worn handkerchief peered from the pocket of his brown cardigan. "Thought provoking, to say the least."

I was seated at a Harkness table in one of the English classrooms. It had been Sebastian's parting wish: before I assumed his role, our department would come together for a summer book club. In homage to me, I suppose, he'd chosen *Ulysses*. I sipped my coffee and tugged my sweater sleeves. That building was forever drafty, as though arctic temperatures were a necessary component of literary analysis. Maybe that's why English teachers always wear blazers and cardigans. It has little to do with aesthetics. They are perpetually freezing.

While everyone spoke about the text, I glanced out at the hallway and noticed a bulletin board, its surface still stabbed with pushpins and xeroxed papers from the spring that announced assorted cries for help—*I need a tutor; I need a teaching assistant; I need help in the writing lab.* Although I hadn't pinned my name up there, I knew I needed help, too. Based on the layers of flyers, I got the sense that everyone on campus did.

"Olivia, what were your thoughts on the passage?" Sebastian had a tendency in our meetings to call on people at random, like we were his students.

In truth, I'd only skimmed it. I'd been too busy contemplating that white box to think about symbolism or any of that stuff. "It was . . . interesting," I said noncommittally. My eyeglasses slipped down my nose. I took more time than necessary to adjust them.

"Why don't you expand upon that?" Sebastian suggested.

"Right." I flipped to the page. It was a passage I vaguely remembered from college, one Marian and I had studied though never fully understood. I skimmed the lines. In them, the main character, Leopold Bloom, reflects on his young daughter, Milly, and her youthful enthusiasm for life. "Well, I think Joyce is suggesting the irony of our relationship with death," I said flatly.

"Good, Olivia," Sebastian said, like I was a child in need of praise. "Tell us more."

I glanced at the passage. Unlike in college, the whole thing came into focus like a developing photograph. "Well, when we're young, we live more authentically. But as we get older and become closer to our deaths, our perception changes. We live in a more fearful state." I felt everyone staring at me. "It's ironic because it's when we're older— when we're approaching death and running out of time to live—that we should embrace life. However, most of us do the opposite." I set my book on the table. I didn't want to speak anymore.

"Beautifully said." Sebastian tapped his page and smiled. "You'll do great things for this department, Olivia."

Around the room, everyone nodded like bobblehead figurines. As they did, my mind drifted back to that box. Ever since it'd arrived, I couldn't stop thinking about it. It didn't make sense. Why would the Nettle Center invest time and money into sending me something long after I'd left their facility if the whole thing had been one elaborate prank?

"I'd like to offer an opposing view." Across the table, Christopher chimed in, interrupting my thoughts. "Personally, as *I've* grown older, and discovered *my* poetic voice, I've found—"

"Ha!" I couldn't help it. I laughed out loud. Every head swiveled in my direction. I bit my lip, embarrassed. I blinked, but all I saw in my head was that note. *Congratulations on your upcoming death!* "Sorry." I forced myself to cough and reminded myself that the box was nothing more than a creative marketing scheme. "I had a little tickle." I turned to Christopher. "Please," I said. "Go on."

"As I was saying, personally, as *I've* aged and more fully come to understand who I am as a person *and* a writer, I've—"

"Aged?" *Shit.* The word spilled from my mouth like a prisoner bequeathed with an unlocked gate. "Come on." I couldn't stop myself. "You're what? Twenty-two?"

Christopher pulled back his shoulders. "I'm twenty-six, thank you." He adjusted his glasses. "And might I remind you that I've already earned two—"

"This seems like a good place to end," Sebastian interjected. Around the room, everyone exchanged awkward glances. "We'll discuss the next hundred pages next week."

Ever since we'd met, Christopher had gotten under my skin like an uncurable disease. It wasn't just his age. It was his ambition: it reminded me of my own failures, I think.

In college, it had taken me forever to let Marian read my writing. She asked me constantly, but I was an endless well of excuses. I knew how talented she was at her own craft, how naturally it came to her. I was jealous. A part of me feared she'd read my work and tell me it wasn't any good.

She had finally caught me in the act our junior year. "What are you doing?" she asked when she threw open the door of our shared apartment. I stood in front of our living room mirror, a hairbrush in one hand, a notebook in the other, talking to my reflection.

"Nothing!" I threw the brush like a discarded weapon. My face was on fire.

Marian moved toward me like a sly detective. "It's kind of awkward at this point if you don't finally let me read them." Without a word, she pulled the notebook from my hand, flipped through it. "Considering I just walked in on you reciting verses to yourself."

I felt like I was going to be sick. "Not true. I can easily keep putting this off for months. Years, in fact."

Marian had laughed as her eyes began to skim my scribbled handwriting. She stopped. Her expression morphed into something more serious. She might as well have punched me in the gut. "Liv," she said, her tone tender.

I was instantly mortified. "Don't even say it."

"They're beautiful," she said then, surprising me. "They're really, really good."

"Oh." I plopped onto the sofa. I hadn't expected that.

"You need to get these out into the world," she said and then threw the notebook back to me.

"Well, how do I do that?"

"I don't know," Marian had admitted. "But I'm going to help you find out."

The classroom cleared. My colleagues gathered their things, pulling me out of my memory. "Is everything okay, Olivia?" Sebastian asked, his brows knit. "Your comments to Christopher were a bit unlike you."

"I'm fine." My face felt flushed. "I just got my words jumbled."

"Good. Because as department chair, you'll need to listen to *all* your faculty members' ideas." He winked. "Even the bad ones."

Sebastian departed, leaving me alone in that freezing room. I picked up my book, flipped back to the folded page. Joyce's words soaked through me like an elixir. I thought of Tommy. Before I could stop myself, I reached into my bag for my phone. I'm going back there, I wrote. And I want you to come with me.

Marian replied almost immediately. Liv, you're not seriously still thinking about that test, are you?

A little bit, I admitted. I didn't mention the box. So, when are you free?

I don't know. I'm kind of over that place, she typed. I'm swamped with deadlines. I don't think I want to go there again.

What? No way. I'm not going alone, I insisted. Plus, it'll give us a chance to finally get your full test results, too. I still want to read through them, don't you? She didn't respond. Anyway, you owe it to me.

Owe it to you? she finally typed. For what?

I gathered my things and then looked around that empty classroom. For too many years, I'd stood at the front of it and carried on about the beauty and importance of other people's voices. *Joyce. Eliot.* All of them.

For years of dragging me along for shit like this, I wrote.

I stepped into the hallway and wondered if I still had the time left to find my own.

TWENTY-TWO

A few days later, Marian and I found ourselves back in that neighborhood. We stood side by side, both of us silent, and once again stared at the building's seductive alabaster exterior. At the corner of the window, the center's compact neon sign glowed with artificial life.

"I think I'm going to go grab a coffee while you go in," Marian said, like it was nothing.

"What?" I turned to her. "Are you kidding?"

"I don't know." She looked at the sky. "I've just sort of moved on from this."

"But what about your results? Aren't you the least bit interested in finally getting them, considering that we came all the way out here?"

She sighed, as though in contemplation. "No." She paused. A warm breeze billowed a canopy of green leaves overhead. "That was weeks ago." It took a minute for her red mouth to lift into a U shape. "Unlike you, I try not to get so hung up on the past."

She turned to walk away. Before she could, I grabbed her arm. "Mar, come on," I pleaded. "Don't make me go in there solo." She parted her lips to offer her retort. "Please," I said before she could.

Marian huffed. "Fine," she said, and then we moved inside.

We entered the lobby. "Oh Christ," I spewed. A dozen women, all dressed in colorful robes, lay motionless across the gleaming floors.

"I instantly regret this." I stepped over a pair of women like they were props and headed toward the desk, where the same crystal-loving receptionist sat. I cleared my throat to get her attention. "Before I go any further, can you give me a head nod if you're allowed to speak?" She absently stared at me, her mouth hanging in a wide, empty O. "So, I'm guessing that's a . . . no?"

Finally, after an unnaturally long pause, she shook her head. "Sorry," she said and then blinked hard. "I was finishing my daily face yoga routine." She stretched her jaw like a fish on a hook. "We only practice silence on Mondays. And Fridays." She paused. "And weekends, too."

Marian gestured toward the ground. Some beautiful gemstone shimmered on her finger, like a tempting piece of hard candy. "Then what is all this?"

The woman tilted her head. "That?" Apparently, having bodies spread across your entryway was just business as usual. "That's our midweek movement retreat."

Marian kicked her foot to free her leather sandal, which had become twisted in the garments of one of the motionless women. "But no one is . . . moving."

A spiral of incense smoke curled around the receptionist's face. "According to Dahlia, when our *exterior* bodies halt movement, our *interior* bodies begin to take shape."

"Right." I leaned across the quartz counter. "So, here's the thing. We were here last month." She looked at me blankly, as though waiting for some distinguishing feature to appear across my face. "Anyway, I'd like to speak with someone about my test results," I explained. "I think there was an error." I looked at Marian, who was preoccupied with staring at the ceiling. "Plus, we never had a chance to see my friend's results on our last visit." Marian lowered her chin and locked eyes with me. I smiled. "We want to see those, too."

"Test results?" she repeated, like I was speaking in tongues. "Oh, I can't help with that."

Footsteps sounded. Marian and I turned and discovered Dahlia moving toward us. "I think what she means is that we don't keep patient files in the building," Dahlia explained. "At all." She pulled a silver bell from her lab coat pocket, shook it. All around us, bodies lifted in strokes of motion, like fashionable zombies. "Holding on to past test results invites complicated energy into the space."

"I don't understand," I admitted. "Where is my file if it's not here?"

Dahlia pointed to the lush courtyard beyond the windows. "We give old files and past test results a second life out there."

I squinted in search of a filing cabinet hidden among the vegetation. "I don't get it."

"It's simple, really." Dahlia's crimson lips arched in pride. "We compost them."

"Oh boy," Marian mumbled, already turning for the door.

Dahlia pressed her hands into prayer and bowed at her other clients. "Come," she told Marian and me. "Let's enjoy a tincture in my office. We can talk more there."

Moments later, Marian and I found ourselves seated across from Dahlia in her office. I kept my gaze cast upon the windows and the many tropical plants my test results had helped fertilize. Nearby, some young, gazelle-like employee set down a tray of electric-green beverages.

"Please, take one," Dahlia suggested. "They're our new chlorophyll elixirs." She sipped hers through a glass straw. "Excellent for cell regeneration."

"How is any of this even legal?" I asked, dismissing her comment.

"The elixirs? Oh, you just need to pitch them in such a way that no one—"

"What?" I immediately pushed away my glass. "No. The files." My face was practically burning. "How can you just destroy them without patients' permission?"

Marian leaned toward me. "I really think we should just—"

"You signed off on it," Dahlia interjected before enjoying another algae-hued sip.

"I didn't sign—" I stopped myself, recalling the paperwork I'd hastily signed on our first visit. I pushed up my eyeglasses. "Look, I received some mail from you that was pretty . . . concerning."

"What?" Marian swiveled her head. "You didn't tell me that." She looked back and forth between Dahlia and me. "What did you—"

"To be clear," Dahlia interrupted, "*I* didn't mail you anything. The mail is so, well, chaotic." She flipped up her hands, as though to block herself from the energy that stemmed from my statement. "Anything you received was sent by one of my assistants. They sort through our files before we dispose of them and send out our complimentary items . . . accordingly."

"Accordingly?" I pressed the heels of my palms against my eyes. "Why did you mail me a damn death box?" I asked. "How am I supposed to interpret something like that?"

"To be honest, I think they're somewhat self-explanatory," Dahlia explained.

Marian tugged my T-shirt sleeve. "Liv, I *really* think we should just—"

"Why are you turning patient files into dirt?" I motioned toward the window and knocked over my elixir, sending puddles of green liquid across the floor, like a reptilian crime scene.

Dahlia brushed her finger across a set of desk chimes. Seconds later, a team of employees, all dressed in white scrubs, tended to my mess. "Don't you see?" Dahlia pulled a sage bundle from her desk. "Just like our files, we all ultimately turn back into dirt, too." She lit the tip and then waved the fragrant, burning stack around her head, presumably to smoke cleanse the space. "It's quite the symbol, really."

"Where's Poppy?" I demanded. "*She's* the one who read me those results, not you. Maybe *she'll* remember some of the details and—"

Dahlia rang the chimes again. "Unfortunately, Poppy was not a good . . . fit."

"So what?" I asked, my voice growing louder. "Did you compost her, too?"

"Of course not," Dahlia said as two muscular, barefoot employees entered the room. She briefly stared into space. "To be honest, I hadn't thought of that."

Dahlia's employees sidled up behind us. "It's time to go," one of them whispered.

"Wait!" I exclaimed. "Are you kicking us out?"

"It's your energy," Dahlia explained as she twirled the burning sage around her body. "It's throwing the whole room off."

~

Back outside, Marian and I walked toward the train. "Well, that was entertaining," she said, brushing away a strand of hair. She looked up at me, offered a half smile. "To be honest, it reminded me of that night you got us kicked out of ABC Bar."

ABC Bar was a certified dive located in a pocket of the city that had attracted artists and writers for the better part of a century. I guess the name was an homage to that. Anyway, Marian, Andrew, and I loved that place, from the cheap beers to the crooked pictures of famous writers on the walls. Instead of bowls of peanuts, they set bowls full of pens on the tables to encourage drunken patrons to spew their creativity across the hot-pink walls.

Marian smiled. "That was a fun night. *You* were fun that night."

"I have absolutely no memory of that."

"Not surprising, considering the amount you drank."

"I guess that's why I was so fun," I said glumly.

"Not true," she corrected me. "It was because you were too busy enjoying the moment to worry about your hundred and one to-do lists."

"If I don't remember it, it didn't happen."

"Don't worry." Marian playfully bumped hips with me. "Lucky for you, I've made a point to hold on to those sorts of memories for us both."

We kept walking. "You were right," I admitted as we crossed the street. "Coming back here was a mistake. We already wrote this place off. I should have just left it at that and—" I cut myself off. "Wait. That's her." I hustled up the block. Marian followed closely behind me. "Poppy! Hang on!"

Poppy stared at us like a startled deer. Since our last run-in, she'd traded her stained lab coat for a pair of torn jeans. "Do I know you?"

Marian and I stopped, breathless. "Don't act like you don't remember us," I said. "We need your help."

Moments later, the three of us found ourselves back at the same café table where we'd originally sat. No one spoke. We all kept peering over our menus, waiting for someone else to start. "I know you know who we are," I finally said. "Am I wrong?"

Poppy set down her menu, looked directly at me.

I adjusted my glasses. "I need you to tell me everything you recall about that test."

"I don't know anything more than what I told you." She gulped her water. "I swear."

"Nothing?" I asked. "Not a single extraneous detail?"

"Liv, come on." Marian reached for her purse. "Let's go. She said she doesn't—"

"Well, there was *one* thing," Poppy said, her statement in the shape of a question mark.

Marian and I both scooted forward. "So," I pressed her. "What is it?"

Poppy hesitated. "I remember overhearing Dahlia in the hallway that day." She breathed deeply, as though to summon her thought. "She was confused by something about—"

"My date?" I interrupted and then smacked Marian's arm. "See? I *knew* those results were—"

"Not the date," Poppy clarified. "It was something else." She scanned the sky, in search of the memory. "It was something about your labs. I don't remember exactly. I only remember that I heard her say that something wasn't quite right. That something didn't match up." Poppy looked like she might cry. "I knew what she meant, but I didn't—" She stopped herself, cupped her face in her palms. "I should have just told her," she said into her hands.

"Told her what?" I questioned.

Poppy swiveled her head between Marian and me. "I shouldn't be talking to you about this," she said. "I'm only twenty-two. I don't even know if any of this is right, honestly."

"I don't understand." I felt like a punctured balloon, my hope quickly deflating.

Poppy pushed out her chair. "I'm not sure I do, either." She pulled a ball of fabric from her bag. "I'm sorry I can't help, but I have to go." She shook it out, revealing a food-splattered apron. "I took a gig at the tea shop up the street. My shift starts soon."

She was gone by the time I tried to stop her. Soon after, Marian and I left the café, too. "I guess that's that," I sighed. "I'll never know anything about those test results for sure."

We moved toward the subway in silence. There was an uncomfortable energy between us, like we were both holding on to things we didn't want to say. "Can I ask you a serious question?" Marian asked. She stopped on the corner and turned to face me. "Would you actually do anything differently? Hypothetically, I mean. If those test results *were* real?"

"Yes," I said. "No," I said, more truthfully. "Why? What would you do?"

"It's hard to say." Marian broke her gaze. "To be honest, I'd probably just ignore them and go on living my life."

"Well, that's good, I guess. You know, since you'll never actually see them."

She ran her fingers through her hair. "But that's me, Liv." She looked at some point beyond us. "We're different people."

I dug my hands into my pockets. "What are you getting at?"

"Just because you have a good life doesn't mean you can't still long to change some parts of it." She squeezed my hand. "You can still want some things you never got for yourself."

I sighed a jagged, heavy breath. "What does that have to do with the test?"

"Nothing," Marian said. "It has to do with you."

I looked at her, my eyes two thin lines. "I don't follow your point."

The sun shone, the sky a wash of gold behind her head. "What are you still waiting for, Liv?"

"I'm not waiting. I'm just—"

"What if?" she jumped in. "What if through some crazy chance it actually *is* true. What then?"

I shook my head at her comment. "So, what is it that you suggest that I do, Mar? I can't go back in the past. I can't—"

"It's not about going back in the past," Marian said. "It's about fixing what you still want to fix right now."

"What does that mean?"

"Test or no test, I think it's time you live like you might be dying." Marian smiled. It was an expression I'd become all too familiar with over the years. "Just in case."

TWENTY-THREE

I didn't know how to start. In my defense, how do you just wake up one morning and make sweeping changes to your life? Survey says: you don't. I mean, sure, maybe *some* people do. You hear about those individuals who just pick up and move across the world simply because they want to hike more or learn to make pasta or something. Personally, I've never met any of them.

For the next week, I went out of my way to find small ways to change. I played infinite board games with Tommy. I cleaned out all our overstuffed drawers. I spent an entire afternoon scrubbing the bottoms of our filthy garbage cans. Eventually, I ran out of ideas.

"I'm going for a run," I announced, like those words were a normal part of my vernacular. I stepped into the yard wearing the closest thing to exercise gear that I owned—an old NYU T-shirt and a pair of moth-eaten yoga pants—hoping to look casual. *Natural.*

"Oh." Andrew tossed a match into our grill. The air filled with charcoal smell. "Um . . . why?"

I figured it would be alarming to tell him about my deep, desperate urge to cross at least *one* item off my birthday list and make a change. "I don't know." Nearby, Tommy rolled through the grass. "I'm always saying I *should* exercise more." I positioned my legs at an unnatural angle

and stretched, even though I had no clue how. "Why not start?" I kissed
Tommy and tried to disregard Andrew's look of suspicion. "Right?"

"This doesn't have something to do with Marian, does it?" he asked.
"Or whatever you two have been keeping from me for a month?"

I tightened the laces on my ancient sneakers. "I have no clue what
you mean."

I walked to the end of our block, already breathless. I guess I had
all those porch cigarettes to blame. "Okay, let's get this over with," I
said aloud to myself, and I imagined crossing off my first bullet point.
"Your new life starts now, Olivia Strauss." Slowly, I picked up my pace.
Every joint in my body ached.

I ran for what felt like a mile, then stopped—panting—and looked
back. In the not-so-far-off distance, Tommy and Andrew were still
perched at the end of our driveway watching me. *Shit.* I'd barely made
it to the end of our street, and already I was covered in sweat.

I jogged a few more blocks and reminded myself of all the people
in our town who regularly ran 5Ks. I picked up my pace and weaved
in and out of different neighborhoods, up and over winding stretches
of unfamiliar streets. *Take that, Dahlia,* I thought as my legs carried
me forward, like I was a celebrated Olympian and not a middle-aged
woman out on her first-ever real jog. *Test or no test, I'm not going anywhere. Not yet!* I moved faster. *I still have plenty of time left to change and
to live and to—*

The front of my foot caught the sidewalk. I flew through the air
with all the grace of a wingless bird. A second later, my body slammed
against the pavement. I just lay there, my face in somebody's lawn.
I tried to move, but every part of me hurt. Maybe, just like my test
results, I'd lie there until I turned into fertilizer, too. *Fuck you, Dahlia,*
I thought. I'd probably never know if her test was real. All I knew was
that, for better or worse, it was the catalyst for why I was spread across
the concrete. I pulled myself up, picked some grass from my hair, and

wiped droplets of blood from my cut lip, looking like I'd had a bad fight with myself. In some ways, I guess I had.

The sun had started to set. I dragged myself to the curb and pulled off one of my shoes, its rubber sole split open so that it smiled at me like some maniacal mouth. "Fuck!" I shouted, loud enough for that whole unfamiliar neighborhood to hear. Without thinking, I chucked my busted sneaker up the street and then watched helplessly as it tumbled into a sewer grate.

"Are you okay, ma'am?" A car stopped in front of me. Inside, a typical suburban dad—neat button-down, fresh haircut, the hum of talk radio—sat in the driver's seat.

I wiped more blood from my lip. "Are any of us?" I asked. I guess that wasn't the response he'd expected. He buzzed up his window and disappeared down the street.

I dropped my head between my knees. Change always looks so easy in movies. Women can just pull out their ponytails or whip off their eyeglasses and step into whole new lives. I have to guess it isn't that simple in real life.

I heard the low rumble of an engine. I looked up. A police cruiser had appeared before me. The officer stepped out of his car. "I can't help but notice that you're missing a shoe."

"Yeah." I pointed to the sewer at the end of the block. "It's down there."

"I know." The officer nodded, like that was a typical place to dispose of unwanted footwear. "One of the neighbors called about that."

I puffed out my cheeks, exhaled a tired breath. "Can I talk my way out of a ticket if I tell you that this whole mess is because I'm trying to change into a better version of myself?"

He nodded. "Aren't we all, ma'am?" He unlatched his radio from his belt, said something into it. "You look like you've had a tough day." He squatted to my level. "Do you need a lift?"

A few minutes later, the cruiser pulled into our driveway. Andrew and Tommy appeared on our porch. Tommy darted toward the car, peeked inside. Up and down our street, neighbors stepped onto their lawns. "I'm fine," I shouted to dispel the gossip mill. "I just took a little spill." I hobbled up our driveway as my new officer friend waved goodbye.

Andrew leaned against the porch post. "So, how was the run?"

"It was good," I said, my voice full of faux cheer. My socked foot dragged across the pavement. "Considering it was my first, I feel satisfied with my time."

Andrew sighed and tucked his hands into the pockets of his shorts. Despite my obvious stubbornness, he helped me up the steps. "In that case, go clean yourself up." He looked at me and shook his head. "Dinner was ready an hour ago." *God.* He had the patience of a saint. One day, I really hoped they canonized him. "Come on." He placed his hand on my aching back. "I'll make you a plate."

TWENTY-FOUR

Twizzler?" Tommy sat crisscross applesauce (his school didn't let kids call it the other thing) beside Andrew and me on our summer blanket and bit his candy with a snap. "It tastes like strawberries," he said in between chewy bites. "That means they're fruit, right?"

My hands were coated in sunblock from slathering his arms. We all stank of coconut and chemicals, like a delicious but carcinogenic cocktail. "We can count them as fruit for tonight."

We'd arrived at the town pool a short while earlier. It had been a last-minute decision after my dinner attempt—*learn to cook*, yet another birthday-list bullet point—went up in flames. (I'm not sure how one scorches nachos, and yet . . .)

"Mama, can I be done with sunblock?" Tommy's cheeks were stuffed with licorice, like a diabetic squirrel. "My arms feel all glue-y."

Andrew peeked at me from beneath his sunglasses. "In his defense, it's practically night."

"Fine," I said. Tommy squealed and raced toward the kiddie pool—less a pool and more a playground with a perpetual leak. I sifted through our enormous canvas bag—God only knows why we needed so many things to relax—and pulled out my notebook.

"Writing anything good?" Andrew looked up from his beat-up paperback.

"Depends who you ask," I said as I flipped to my most recent page. "I sent out some very mediocre pitches to some very C-list magazines last week."

"That's good." Andrew smiled. "It's not poetry, but at least it's a way back in, right? And it pays. Always a plus."

"Yeah." I ran my fingers through the blades of grass. "Did I tell you I looked up the last poetry editor who rejected me? He's in his twenties. He's more or less a child."

"I was in my twenties when I worked for *Smith*," he reminded me. I shook my head. "That was . . . different."

Andrew raised a brow. "Was it?" He pulled out a sleeve of crackers. "Casual change of topic. I finally picked up the right tools to fix the kitchen table."

"You plan to fix our table with a sleeve of Ritz?"

"Very funny." Andrew nibbled a cracker. "I bought some wood glue that should do the trick." Crumbs collected on his bathing suit. "I think."

"Perfect. I can finally host that flaming nachos dinner party I've been putting off." I stole a cracker. "Speaking of which . . ." I nodded toward the snack shack, slid my flip-flops back on. "I guess I owe the three of us a proper meal, huh?"

Andrew smiled and returned to his book. "You don't owe us anything, Liv."

I packed away our Ritz appetizers and then found myself in line. I closed my eyes and tried to focus on the moment—the sounds of splashing, the scent of chlorine.

"Liv!"

Oh God. I opened my eyes. Courtney and Allison stood behind me wearing matching cover-ups, like a pair of middle-aged sorority sisters.

"Oh," I mumbled as I inched up in the line. The town pool was an anomaly. One minute, you might find yourself relaxing poolside; the next, you might find yourself accosted by half-naked members of the town PTA. "Hi."

"Where've you been!" they said in unison and then laughed in unison, too. "Jinx!"

"You know," I said. "Around."

"We just got back from the Cape," Courtney offered, even though no one had asked.

Allison smiled. "We were in Maine." She touched my arm. "So, have you heard?"

"About what?" I asked, half reading the snack bar's handwritten menu.

"About Lillian," Allison said. I must have offered a confused expression. "Oh, you know Lillian. Vikki's cousin. You've met her at a million neighborhood parties."

As Allison spoke, something beyond the snack bar caught my eye: a woman my age, a newborn pressed against her chest, a tote bag printed with Monet's *Water Lilies* on her arm.

"Did you hear me?" Allison and Courtney exchanged a look. "Or were you too busy staring at that sweet newborn?" Allison smiled. "Uh-oh. Babies on the brain?"

A breeze blew off the water. I wrapped my arms across my chest and imagined a child there again. The tiny body at rest on my breasts. The pulsing soft spot. "Actually, I was thinking she needs to put a hat on that kid's head."

We rattled off our orders. "Anyway," Allison explained, "Lillian has ovarian cancer!" She shook her head. "Poor Vikki. It's obvious she's still busy trying to process everything with Peter and now this."

I searched my memory for an image of her, this woman I was supposed to remember. Apparently, I'd met her on several occasions, yet I failed to recall anything about her. Up until that moment, when I learned about her diagnosis, had her life—her mere presence—been so unremarkable that I couldn't even recall her face, that her whole life boiled down to a death warning shared in a snack shack line?

"I don't understand. Ovarian cancer? Isn't she our age?"

"Yes! Can you believe it? One minute, she's busy making babies, and the next, she's a damn tumor factory." Allison reached toward the counter. "But that's middle age. We might wake up fine tomorrow, and then the next"—she snapped her fingers—"that's that." She shrugged the story away. "Let *that* be a warning to us all."

I grabbed my tray and carried our dinner—burgers, melting ice cream bars—to our blanket. I handed Tommy and Andrew their paper boats of food. Above us, the sun began to disappear behind the trees. I set down my food without taking a bite. "You know what? I think I'll go for a swim. I don't want to keep waiting. I want to take a dip before it gets too late."

I navigated my way to a row of diving boards. For a while, I sat on the edge of one and thought about Marian's advice. The air was starting to cool, another day turning in on itself. I pulled my cover-up over my head. I didn't give myself a chance to think. I dove forward in an elegant arch. Once under the water, I parted my lips and screamed, my frustrations and my fears turning into a wall of bubbles. I darted back through the surface. My heart pounded.

"You just about ready?"

I turned and saw Andrew kneeling on the concrete.

"Tommy jumped back in the kiddie pool," he said. "The water's getting cold. His lips are turning blue."

I slicked my hair from my face and swam toward the ladder. "Sure." Andrew reached out his hand. Around us, the sunlight was being replaced by shadows. I picked up my dress, squeezed the dampness from my hair, and turned back toward the pool. Already, the wake from my body had ceased. The water had become still. As we walked away, the surface looked as though I'd never even been there at all.

TWENTY-FIVE

"I want to go out on my birthday date," I told Andrew a few days later when he stepped into the kitchen. He smelled like morning, all soap and toothpaste. Meanwhile, I was straight business. I'd been downstairs for hours, already dressed in my T-shirt and jeans, my birthday notebook set on the counter.

"Okay." Andrew filled his travel coffee mug. The television hummed while Tommy watched cartoons in the next room. "When I get to the office, I'll make some calls and try to get us a reservation someplace next week."

"No." I closed my notebook. "I want to go tonight."

"Tonight?" Andrew tilted his head, perhaps trying to determine if I'd had an aneurysm. "It's a Tuesday."

"We're always *saying* we should go out together." I placed my empty mug in the sink. "Why wait?"

Tommy and I spent the rest of the morning hunkered down in my bedroom while I tore through my closet in search of something decent (a.k.a.—*not* a T-shirt) to wear. Tommy laughed every time I tossed a miscellaneous blouse (stained) or dress (too short) or skirt (my God, was I a *Pilgrim* at one point?) across the room.

From beneath my pile, my phone rang. Tommy answered it before I could stop him. "Aunt Marian!" he shouted and then pressed the speaker button. "Mama is having a fashion show!"

"I still owe you a box of doughnuts, kiddo," Marian said.

"Yes!" Tommy exclaimed and then kicked a pile of my belongings off the bed.

"So," Marian said, shifting her tone. "A fashion show?"

"Not exactly," I corrected her. "More like a fashion meltdown. It turns out I was twenty-five the last time I bought something decent for myself."

"You should have told me. I just purged bags of stuff from back then. Remember that shirt you used to borrow? The one with that weird floral print?"

"Why are *you* purging?" I instructed Tommy to untie a scarf from his neck before he strangled himself. "Did you finally find a new apartment or something?"

"Not exactly," Marian said. "I just want to get some things in order. Just in case."

"In case of what?" I asked and was then immediately interrupted. "Kiddo! The scarf!"

"It's nothing," Marian said, squashing the topic. "I've just been stuck inside my own head a bit. That's all."

"Wait." Nearby, Tommy karate-chopped a box. "Kiddo!" I exclaimed and then turned my focus back to Marian. "What do you mean?"

"It's nothing, Liv," she said. "I don't think I really want to talk about it anyway." She cleared her throat. "Plus, you sound busy. And like maybe you're still a touch pissed."

"What?" Beside me, Tommy knocked over a shoebox full of old costume jewelry. "Who said I'm pissed?"

"I know you, Liv. I know you're still mad that I took you there in the first place."

"That's not true," I countered. "I'm just—"

"It's okay. We can talk about it some other time."

I swept up tangles of old necklaces into my hands. "Okay," I said, partially distracted.

Through the line, I heard a door close behind her. A jungle of city sounds erupted. "So, what are your big plans?" Marian asked me. "For life?" A burst of noise blossomed around her. "Or, at the very least, for tonight?"

I leaned against the doorframe, stuffed my foot into some outdated wedge. "Andrew is taking me out to dinner for my birthday."

"Your birthday?" Marian asked. "The one that was two months ago?"

I stepped away from the closet, took the phone from Tommy. "I'm trying, Mar," I said as I tossed the shoe into a garbage bag. "I really am. And right now, that's the best anyone is going to get."

I met Andrew at some local Italian joint at four thirty in the afternoon. It wasn't exactly dinner. Apparently, despite our promise to pay our babysitter, her evening plans trumped ours. We had until seven, she'd told us. Seven thirty, max.

"You look nice," Andrew said. Our hostess walked us through the empty dining room. She pointed to our table, which was draped in a checkered tablecloth. Nearby, two waiters folded a pile of cloth napkins for the evening service.

"Thanks," I told Andrew and then sat. I'd settled on some blouse I'd discovered in my closet that had been in style three seasons earlier but still had the tags attached.

He handed me a slice of buttered bread, signaled to our waiter for wine. "So."

I took a salty bite. "So," I repeated. Usually, we spent our restaurant visits picking up Tommy's crayons and cutting his chicken nuggets. We sat in awkward silence, looking like a line from a bad poem. *Red-checkered tablecloth / cold bread / the middle-aged couple waits for bad table wine that / like their dreams / never arrives.* It was like we'd forgotten what to say.

"So, why all the sudden urgency?" Andrew asked as he scanned his plastic menu. "We never go out during the week." He swallowed. "Or ever, really."

"It's hard to explain." I shrugged. "I just feel like I need to make some life changes." Our waiter reappeared to take our order, even though he hadn't even given us water yet. "I'm done putting things on the back burner. It's time for me to become a whole new Liv."

Andrew ordered, handed over his menu. "What's going on with you?"

"Nothing."

"Nothing?"

"Nothing." Before I could formulate another thought, our entrées appeared. "Jesus. Is there a packed dining room in the back that I missed or something?"

"You're deflecting," Andrew noted as he sliced through a mountain of melted cheese.

I swirled some pasta onto my fork and thought briefly of our first real dinner date. It was right after my poem was published. I was so damn excited you might have thought I'd won a Pulitzer. Anyway, Andrew took me to this under-the-radar Italian place downtown to celebrate. No sign. No fancy name. We both ordered the spaghetti limone and some anchovy appetizer that—I swear to God—practically changed our lives. Or at least it had felt that way at the time.

"How's your food?" I asked.

"Terrible," Andrew said and then helped himself to another cheesy bite.

"Mine too," I admitted, and I set down my fork. I felt like a fool. I don't know what I'd expected to happen—that we'd share an impromptu meal at a glorified pizzeria and suddenly feel like we were twenty-two again. "I'm sorry I forced us to come out."

"Don't be sorry." Andrew sipped his wine, which had finally arrived. "I like being out with you." He reached across the table, sampled my pasta. "Yikes. That really isn't very good."

"Come on. We can get out of here." I reached for my bag. From the corner of my eye, I saw the waitstaff coming toward us with some ridiculous flaming cake slice. "Oh Christ."

"They haven't even taken our food away yet," Andrew said.

"They really have to work on their sense of timing." I swiveled my head in search of an escape route. Before we could make a run for it, we were surrounded. For the longest minute of my life, they serenaded me with some faux-Italian spin-off of the birthday song, complete with an extended chorus that celebrated me by name, which, apparently, they thought was Libby.

"I swear I told them the right name when I called," Andrew said the moment they left our table, both of us mortified by the whole thing.

"At least we finally went out on a date," I pointed out and then forced a smile. "Plus, there's dessert."

Andrew squinted, then shook off my comment. He lifted my fork and sampled a bite. "How do you mess up chocolate cake?"

"Fine. Scratch that last part."

Andrew smirked. "Come on, Libby." He pushed out his chair. "What do you say we ditch the cake and head home to see if anything decent is on TV?"

I dug my fork into the chocolaty slice and instantly spit the unsweetened bite into my cloth napkin. "Okay." I tossed my soiled napkin on the table and looked at Andrew.

That's when I stopped.

It felt like only days earlier that we'd sat across from each other, our mouths full of briny anchovies, in that tucked-away Italian spot downtown. But it wasn't days earlier. It was years. A lot of them. "Wait." Time, I was learning, was a thief. "We're not leaving," I announced. "Not yet."

Andrew side-eyed me, lifted a curious brow. "We're not?"

"No." Nearby, several patrons appeared, marking the start of the evening's dinner service. "It's my birthday," I told him as I lifted my fork. "Well, my belated birthday." Who knew how many more of them I might get? "Either way, I want to stay." I swigged from my water glass, washed away the bitter taste. "I want to finish my cake."

TWENTY-SIX

August has always felt like the beginning of the end for me. There are reminders everywhere that one season is ending while another is about to begin. Precocious leaves that insist on turning to rust early. Sudden whispers of cool air that sneak through windows late at night. By that point in the season, you can't escape the facts: summer is ending, those final weeks of freedom one depressing denouement.

But not that year. Finally, I was starting to make a segue in my life.

"Why is that fruit dressed in paper?" Tommy pointed to a display of pint-size fruit baskets. We'd been meandering around the farmers' market, nibbling on squares of crumb cake.

We stopped beside the wooden table. "I'm going to need a second opinion." Nearby, a group of moms spread yoga mats across the hot pavement. I tapped Andrew. "Tag. You're it."

Andrew wiped his hand across his shorts, leaving behind a streak of white powder. "Those are . . . tomatillos. I think."

"Actually, they're ground-cherries." A woman approached us from the opposite side of the table. *Sunshine.* She placed some of the fruit in Tommy's palm. "Peel off the papery part." She winked. "The sweet stuff is hidden inside."

Across Sunshine's wooden table, piles of late-summer produce were mixed with autumn crops—plump heirloom tomatoes and waxy pink apples—like neat little piles of juxtaposition. "I remember you." Sunshine clipped herbs to her sign. "Rainbow pizza mom, right?"

"You must say that to all the moms in this town," I said.

"Not all." Sunshine slapped some dirt off on her loose jeans. "How'd it turn out?"

"I'd tell you it became part of our compost pile, except we don't have a compost pile."

Sunshine nodded. I couldn't tell if my inability to care for the planet had offended her. She turned to Tommy. "Do you like dinosaurs?" Tommy's face lit up like neon. Sunshine produced a bunch of greens from beneath the table. "This is called 'dinosaur' kale."

"Can we get it?" Tommy nearly choked on the ground-cherries. "Zippy will *love* it!"

Sunshine passed the bunch to him. "Zippy?"

"Don't ask." Andrew tucked the prehistoric kale and paper cherries into our tote. I looked to Sunshine. "You don't by chance know what I'm supposed to *do* with that stuff, do you?"

Sunshine smiled. "Oil. Salt. Pop them in the oven for a few minutes. We used to call them 'dinosaur chips' in our house." She took a basket from another customer. "Unlike rainbow pizzas, they're practically impossible to mess up."

"My kind of recipe." I smiled, grateful for the tip and another way for me to try to change. I nodded toward the neighborhood yogis. "By the way, what's that all about?"

Sunshine balanced her soiled hands on her hips. "They set up here some weekend mornings." She shrugged. "It's good publicity." She added some purple potatoes to a basket. "You should come to a class at the studio. I'm there a few mornings a week."

Her suggestion startled me. "I'll think about it." I pointed to my still-cut lip. "I got into a fight with some concrete during a recent exercise attempt. I might not be the best candidate."

Sunshine smiled. "Well, the offer stands." She helped another customer. As she did, I noticed something on her forearm: a tattoo of a single line connecting two black dots. I stared at it, tried to make out its meaning.

Sunshine scooted back toward me. "For the record," she explained, "it's *not* a very thin barbell." She ran her fingers across it. "I hear that one a lot."

"I'm assuming there's a backstory?"

Sunshine swooped a strand of gray hair from her face. "My daughter and I both have them." She smiled. "It's supposed to represent the two of us—an umbilical cord, this idea that we'll always be connected." She became lost in a thought. "I went through a difficult time a few years ago," she explained and then rang up another customer.

I moved to the end of the table and pretended to investigate some melons. In reality, I looked down at my legs, exposed through my old denim shorts, and the small tattoo on my inner ankle—the one I always forgot was there.

Marian and I had gotten the tattoos in college, after she'd experienced her first—her only—real heartache. They met on one of those drunken city nights when the world felt like a movie. Their separate lives immediately became tangled into one cohesive existence for a stretch of time.

A few months after it started, Marian told me it was over while we were seated on our MoMA bench. She broke down in tears and then swore off love, commitment—all of it.

"We need to do something," I had told her. Before she could stop me, I grabbed her hand. An hour later, we sat in adjacent red vinyl chairs at a tattoo studio downtown. "We both want this," I told a bearded man and then pointed to a coin-size heart in his illustration book.

"Thank you." The needle pricked Marian's flesh. "I needed some spontaneity today." She didn't say anything after that; instead, she just closed her eyes and squeezed my hand.

I pulled my phone from my pocket, ready to send her a message and share the memory.

"Liv!"

A familiar voice jolted me from my thoughts. I pivoted and saw Courtney and Allison rushing toward us, bags of produce at their elbows. I opened my mouth to voice my complaints about their appearance, my typical protocol. Before I could, another smaller voice chimed in.

"Fucking shit."

Andrew and I darted our faces at Tommy, who innocently nibbled ground-cherries. "Tommy!" we shouted.

"What?" He tossed back another palmful of fruit. "That's what *you* always say when you see them." He gazed up at me. "Right?"

"I—" My words froze in my throat. "That's n-not true," I stammered. But, of course, it was.

"Busted," Andrew mumbled and then stifled his laughter.

I crouched down to Tommy's eye level. "Kiddo," I said, "you can't say things like that."

"Why not?" He swallowed his fruit. "You don't even like them."

"Of course I do," I lied. From my periphery, I saw them move closer. I forced myself to smile and wave. "They're my . . . friends," I said, for Tommy's sake.

Courtney and Allison approached us. I stood back up to an adult height. They each offered me obligatory cheek kisses. "Funny seeing you here!" Allison said. It wasn't, really.

Courtney turned a zucchini in her hand. "I'm glad we bumped into you. Did you get my messages about tonight?"

"Messages?"

"I'm having a little get-together." She winked. "It'll be the usual. Wine. Apps." She leaned in. "Some friendly gossip." She smiled. *Here it comes,* I thought. "Plus, I just started to use these amazing essential oils that I'm dying to tell you all about." *Bingo!* "Can you make it?"

I looked down at Tommy, bit my lip. I released a long huff of air. "Sure," I said and then smiled at him. My sweet, overly observant boy. "I can't wait."

TWENTY-SEVEN

That night, I freshened up the blouse I'd worn to dinner with Andrew, then swiped on some rosy lipstick. In the kitchen, I kissed Tommy and Andrew goodbye and then headed outside. It was that blue-gray hour when the sky can't commit to night or day. The streetlamps flickered to life and cast floating islands of light across the pavement.

I reached the end of our block and stood at the foot of Courtney's driveway. The windows of her pale-gray home were all illuminated rectangles of light. Through one of them, I saw the women gathered around a table, wineglasses in hand. I imagined the root of their conversation. Aging. Lillian's diagnosis. I didn't want to think about that stuff. I turned around and continued to move across the sidewalk just as Courtney's sprinklers clicked to life.

"Liv?"

I swiveled my head and found a familiar, shadowy figure behind me. *Suzanne.*

"Aren't you going in?"

I shifted on my feet, then sighed. "Yes," I told her as I stepped forward. "I am."

Courtney's kitchen island was covered with pyramids of essential oil bottles. Around me, women engaged in light chatter. Courtney swung open her stainless steel refrigerator, pulled out a half dozen professional-looking appetizers, and set them across the granite. "I have a confession, ladies," she announced as she sliced herself a hunk of brie. "My contributions tonight are all store bought." She filled two glasses with white wine. "Let's just say time has not been on my side today. Or any day in recent memory." Without asking, she slid the glasses toward Suzanne and me.

I sidled over to Suzanne. "Is she okay?" I whispered. "I've never heard her say something, well, quite so . . . vulnerable."

Suzanne sipped her wine. "Rumor is the show she danced in ages ago is finally heading to Broadway. Apparently, she just found out this week." She leaned closer. "Personally, I think she's on the brink of a breakdown." She indulged in a more significant sip. "I can't blame her. Unfortunately for me, I understand the feeling," she said, though she didn't expand.

I pressed my glass to my lips.

Courtney fussed with a platter and turned to Vikki. "Anyway, what were you saying?"

"Right." Across the island, Vikki scooped up a dollop of vegetable dip. "So, Peter is home from dance camp," she offered.

"Mmm," the group hummed, an impromptu support group.

Vikki visibly inhaled. "I guess what I mean to say"—her hands shook—"and I think this might come as a surprise to everyone . . ." She lowered her voice and leaned in, as though Peter were in the next room. "I think Peter might be *gay*." She straightened her posture once she'd made her announcement, the one we'd all anticipated for months. She stared at the ceiling, exhaled, then looked back at the group and began to speak, slower this time. "My son is gay." An aura of calm settled upon her. "He finally told me himself, but obviously I already knew."

No one said a word. We all just stood there with her, which sometimes is all you can do. Finally, Suzanne reached across the island, touched Vikki's hand. "Peter is going to be okay," she whispered. We all nodded our agreement. "Peter *is* okay. You know that, right?"

Vikki sighed. "Of course. I'm not evil. It's just that . . ." She stopped herself. "When Peter was a baby, I used to keep this notebook." My heart beat faster. "It was meant to be like a vision board, I guess. Late at night, when everyone was finally asleep, I'd glue in pictures from magazines of things I imagined Peter might want to pursue." She closed her eyes. "I think it was my way of visualizing his future." She opened them. "Or maybe I was trying to visualize mine." She studied the tiled floor. "I know I'm not supposed to say any of this aloud. I just don't want him to face any hardships in life." She wiped her cheek. "Plus, it's that, well, with everything going on with my cousin, Lillian, I . . ." She looked up. "I just thought his life—no, *my* life—would look different at this stage, that's all. I'm still just wrapping my head around our new normal, I think."

A sense of quiet settled upon the room. "I used to keep a book like that, too," Courtney admitted. "I was in college." She smiled at the recollection. "I'd tear out magazine pages and tape them inside." She set down her glass. "It's still tucked at the bottom of my underwear drawer. I flip through it from time to time." She smirked. "I've flipped through it a lot recently."

I'd heard the women talk about their former ambitions before, though the conversations typically unraveled in joke form, their once-upon-a-time plans turned into puns. Maybe that's why I'd never divulged much about that part of myself to them. I didn't want my passions turned into a joke. But that night, for the first time, it became clear that their humor was simply a cover for something else. Fear, maybe. Or sadness. Regret. Sentiments I understood.

"Well, this conversation took a turn," Suzanne said as Courtney distributed glass bottles of lavender oil for us all to sample. "Nothing says 'Happy end of summer' like some light chatter about our abandoned aspirations."

For a stretch of time, we all sat in silence, drinking our wine and feigning interest in the fragrances while we quietly wondered what had happened to them: our dreams.

When I arrived home, I sat on our porch. I wasn't ready to go inside. I reached behind the bush, knowing Tommy was already asleep. I hadn't touched my cigar box all summer. I pulled out a brittle cigarette and inhaled a dry cloud. I closed my mouth and held the smoke inside me for longer than was needed. It was hard to explain. I felt desperate to fill myself with something.

I stubbed out my cigarette and reached in my bag for my black notebook. I just wanted to have something worthwhile to write. *Will we just drown in our white wine / all of us / victims of these unremarkable suburban lives?* But it was no use. I tucked my notebook away, then stood. That's when I noticed a familiar white box on our porch. "You've got to be kidding me."

For what felt like a long time, I sat and stared at that package. I didn't even want to touch it, as though its suggestions about my life were contagious. It didn't make sense. Dahlia already had my payment. Her marketing efforts were a waste on me. There was no reason for her to continue to—

I felt something shift inside me then, slow and then fast, like when the sky turns from day to night. Our street hummed with insects, like a white noise machine. The quieter it became, the louder my neighbors' comments began to echo in me. Dahlia's comments, too. My hands began to shake.

Despite my better instincts, I realized maybe she had been telling the truth.

I pulled my notebook back out and turned to a fresh page. Instead of a poem, I made a list of all the ways my life could end in the coming months. A heart attack. A car accident. An insect sting. My thyroid. A slip in the shower. A newly developed allergy. My breasts.

I closed the notebook. I wasn't invincible. The possibilities were infinite.

~

Inside, Andrew was squatting on the kitchen floor beside our table.

"I'm guessing I shouldn't ask," I said.

He slapped a piece of duct tape against the wood. "How was the party?"

I moved to the sink to wash the smoke from my fingers. "I've been home for a while."

Andrew set down the tape and sat at the island. "I know. I smelled the smoke through the door after I put Tommy to bed." He looked down at the countertop in search of answers, then back up at me. "What's going on with you, Liv?"

I dried my hands on a dish towel. "I'm not sure," I admitted. "Midlife crisis, maybe?"

"I don't buy it." Andrew shook his head. "You're more creative than that."

The house was quiet. From the other room, I heard the low, comforting hum of the TV. "Do you remember right after college, when we used to take those long walks around the city together?" I asked. "We'd talk about our future and who we wanted to be when we grew up."

"I do." Andrew smiled at the memory. "We used to stop at that little coffee shop."

I nodded, remembering. "That's right. The one with those huge burlap bags of beans all over the place."

Andrew smirked. "You'd get a caffeine buzz the minute you walked through the door."

"I'd forgotten about that." I stopped. "Anyway, I don't know why, but I was thinking about those walks tonight." I studied the countertop.

"I think maybe I forgot to grow up and become that person." I briefly looked away. "I think maybe a lot of us did."

Andrew sighed. "Liv, you—"

"Don't." I tried to smile, but it came across as a frown. "It's fine," I said unconvincingly.

Andrew looked at me, tilted his head. "Liv," he said again, like a promise. Or like a question. *Liv. Live?*

I set the towel down beside my curse jar, the one that was overflowing with loose change. "I'm going to bed." I moved toward the stairs, touched my hand to the banister.

"She sent you something," Andrew called out. I turned. "Marian." His face softened. "She told me that the last time you two talked, she felt like you were still annoyed with her about something." He smiled. "Anyway, I put it on your nightstand."

Upstairs, I checked on Tommy. It was an instinct from early motherhood that never faded. Every night, before I could rest, I had to pop into his room a hundred times. *Is he breathing? Is he still there?* His dinosaur night-light glowed. I rested my hand on his chest. My palm lifted and fell with each of his soft breaths.

In our bedroom, I clicked on the lamp and sat on the bed. Beside me, my stack of books—Woolf, Joyce, the poetry collection Marian had bought me—sat practically untouched, along with my notebook in which I'd tried—and failed—to write more pitches for *Hearth*. Unlike Marian, my life wasn't some bold-faced exclamation mark. When it came to essay writing, it turned out I just didn't have anything noteworthy to say. I sighed. On top of the stack was a postal mailer marked with my name. I immediately recognized Marian's familiar script. I unsealed the flap and shook out the contents. A bottle of hair dye fell out, along with a note. *No one is ever too old for pink hair,* it read. *Not even you, Olivia Strauss.*

In college, Marian loved to dare me to step out of my comfort zone. Usually, she won. Once, she challenged me to get onstage at an open mic night and read something from my poetry notebook. Onstage, I panicked. I wasn't ready after all. I closed my eyes and recited a poem I'd memorized for a seminar course instead.

Marian's smile was wide with laughter and alcohol when I stepped offstage. "Joyce?"

"Eliot, actually," I said and then self-consciously examined all the confused faces in the room.

She squeezed my arm. "You'll be up there reading your own work soon. I know it."

Back in my bedroom, I set the bottle and the note on my nightstand. Our friendship had felt strained all summer, like some secret existed just behind it. I tried not to think about it. Instead, I changed into sweats, clicked off the lamp, and then closed my eyes.

That night, I dreamed of her. In the dream, we stood together on the edge of a vast cliff. She didn't speak, but she kept motioning toward me. I couldn't tell if she was trying to push me over the edge or to pull me toward her.

It wasn't until I woke in the middle of the night, my chest slicked with sweat, that I realized she'd been trying to do both.

TWENTY-EIGHT

"Olivia, hi!"

I was half concealed behind our bush a few days later, in the hopes of tossing that white box and the lingering what-ifs that had arrived with it. I looked up, surprised to see Annie and her dog, Jack, moving up our driveway.

"Hi, Annie." I kicked the box back beneath our hedges and looked skeptically at Jack, hoping he wouldn't leave any surprises on our lawn. "Is something wrong?"

Annie reached into the straw bag that hung from her elbow, her linen shirt hem waving with the breeze. She handed me a bunch of cobalt hydrangeas. "I just wanted to bring you these."

"Oh." I accepted the flowers. I'd only spoken to Annie a handful of times. Exchanges about the weather and neighborhood potholes. The only intimate detail I knew about her life was that she lived alone and was probably lonely. "Why?"

She set down her bag. "I thought you might like them." She peered over my shoulder at our minimal landscaping. "Plus, I get the sense that you don't have much of a green thumb."

"Thank you," I said. "I'll try not to kill them."

"You won't." A million wrinkles formed across her face. "Enjoy them. They don't last."

Back inside, I dropped the hydrangeas into an old vase Andrew had given me after we'd moved into our first apartment. Every few days, I'd stop at the bodega for flowers, which I arranged in an empty marinara jar. Finally, one night, Andrew had presented me with a shopping bag. "What can I say?" he'd said. "The combined fragrance of sunflowers and tomato sauce hasn't grown on me." For years, no matter how broke we were, I always kept that vase full.

I set the vase on our island now and looked around. Our house was a perpetual disaster. Piles of paperwork. Toys everywhere. I stepped back. Those flowers felt like a quiet burst of beauty among the chaos. *They don't last long.* I didn't want things to feel so chaotic anymore.

I moved through the room and recycled some old mail. I carried the plastic laundry baskets upstairs and put everything in its right place. I sat on the living room floor and organized a million plastic toys. I grabbed an old tote bag from a drawer and then dumped the contents of my curse jar into it, knowing that Tommy deserved better. I did, too. When I was done, I rinsed the jar out, set it on the counter, and dropped the tote bag onto the pantry floor. It was a start.

Outside, I began to jog up the street in the new sneakers I'd picked up a few days earlier. Before I reached the corner, I saw Suzanne, dressed in her walking clothes. She spotted me, wiped her eyes beneath her sunglasses.

"Hey," I said as we drew closer. "Are you okay?"

"It's nothing," she sniffled. "I'm fine. *It's* fine. It's just . . ." She swatted the air. "I finally got through to them this morning." She stopped herself, wiped her eyes again.

I looked at her, questioning. "Who?"

"A rep from my old design company." Nearby, neighborhood kids rode by on bicycles. "I finally decided after that conversation the other night that it was time to stop putting it off." She waved her palm through the air. "It turns out I didn't leave as much of a mark on the design world as I'd once thought."

"I'm sure that's not true," I said. "Maybe if you called your old boss or—"

"I called him, too. But he didn't remember me." I guess that's what happens sometimes. You put off a dream too long, and it stops being a dream. It just becomes a memory. "Anyway, don't tell the other women, okay?"

"Okay," I reassured her and, at the same time, silently reassured myself that it wasn't too late for me.

"Thanks." Suzanne cleared her throat, changing her tone. "Anyway, look at you in all that athletic gear. Old age hasn't caught up with your ass already, has it?"

I looked back over my shoulder, that white box still concealed at the foot of our home. "Not yet."

That afternoon, I ran farther and faster than I'd ever run before. Despite my exhaustion, I refused to let myself fall.

TWENTY-NINE

The next morning, I found myself alone on our sofa before anyone else was awake. Usually, the minute Tommy opened his eyes, he darted into our room and catapulted himself on top of me like a professional wrestler. But not that morning. I just couldn't sleep.

"Hey, buddy." I turned before I even heard footsteps. Mom radar. It's no joke.

Tommy, his eyes still half-closed, stumbled toward me. "Mama, I jumped on your bed a million times." His favorite dinosaur pajamas, which he'd begun to outgrow that summer, revealed a sliver of his belly. "Why are you down here?"

"I was all done dreaming, I guess." I set down my coffee. "Hungry?" I pulled myself off the couch and slid some frozen waffles into the toaster. That's when I heard a knock at the door. Tommy and I exchanged a glance. "Was that the door?" The only people who knocked at strange hours were Girl Scouts and Hare Krishnas. *Tap. Tap.* I slid the waffles onto a plate. "Hang here," I told Tommy and then zipped up my old hoodie. "I'll be right back."

I arrived at the end of our hallway, unsure who—or what—waited for me, and pulled my hair into a sloppy bun. I swung open the door.

"Don't be mad." Marian stood there, a pastry box in her hands. "I brought doughnuts." She lifted her sunglasses onto her head. "You can't be mad at the person who brings you an unsolicited box of doughnuts." She smiled. "It's science. Everybody knows that."

"Who said I'm mad?"

"Liv, I know you better than that." Marian looked tired but beautiful, her skin makeup-free yet glowing. "You've been short with me for weeks. We've barely spoken."

I balled my sweatshirt into my fists. "What are you doing here?"

"I wanted to see you," Marian said. "Things between us haven't felt right ever since I first took you for that test. I know you're mad at me. I know you think I took things too far."

"This isn't a great time," I lied. I was still trying to process my own feelings and newfound fears. I wasn't ready to talk about them yet. "I'm on my way out."

Marian tilted her head, assessing me. "Based on your current wardrobe choices, you're either lying or you're much worse off than Andy has led me to believe."

"I'm busy, Mar," I said.

"Still too busy to read my articles, too, I guess?" She shook her head, fast and hard.

"Mar, give me a break. Do you have any idea what it's like to—"

"Why do you act like you're *so* much busier than everyone else?" Marian asked, calling me out. "We're all busy. It's called life."

"Look, I don't want to do this," I told her. "I think maybe I just need a little time to myself."

"Fine," Marian said, flustered. She blew away a loose strand of hair. "Will you at least give Tommy the doughnuts before I leave?"

I took the box from her hand. "Tommy!" Within seconds, he skidded onto the porch.

"Aunt Marian!" he squealed. "I missed you!" He threw his arms around her.

"Here." I handed him the box. "Will you take these inside for me?"

Once Tommy was gone, I closed the door. Marian leaned against our porch post. She crossed one slender leg over the other, her jeans perfectly torn in all the right places. "Liv, you can't possibly still be pissed about that test."

Across the street, I saw Suzanne, dressed in sneakers and stretchy pants, out on her morning walk. She waved. "You had a stranger draw my blood and tell me I'm going to die in ten months," I reminded Marian.

"Come on," she huffed. "Why are you taking this so seriously?"

I bent down, reached behind our bush, and pulled out the box. "Maybe because I'm still getting these."

"Liv." Her eyes stayed focused on the box. "You know that's just for publicity." She lifted her chin. "Right?"

I pushed it back beneath our shrubs. "I'm not so sure." Overhead, an airplane jetted across the sky like an elegant bird. I closed my eyes, pretended I was a passenger on it. "You swore, Mar," I said, my voice elevating. I opened my eyes. "You promised you were done taking me to these ridiculous places. Every time you do, something happens, and I just end up getting stuck in my own head for weeks." I felt my frustration beginning to percolate inside me. "Am I busier than anyone else? I don't know, Mar. But I *do* know that I don't have the time to get lost in my thoughts for whole chunks of my life, all because of these little trips of yours!"

Several months earlier, while I was browsing the shelves at a local bookstore, I saw it: the journal that had first published my villanelle had curated a retrospective issue of their best work from the last twenty years. I waited until I got home to see if my name appeared inside. There it was, on page sixteen, the voice of my youth once again in print, like someone had brought the dead back to life. A few days after I'd told Marian about it, she'd called to say she'd gotten me a gift, only I had to meet her in the city to get it.

A bell had tinkled when we opened the door of the tucked-away new age shop far downtown. "I thought we could take a peek into our futures," Marian had explained as we stepped through a beaded curtain and sat at a small card table. "You go first." She winked. "I want to hear about how your dream poetry career is finally going to unfold."

A woman in heavy eyeliner sat across from us and set a deck of tarot cards on the table. She whispered a prayer over them, her stack of silver bracelets jangling with every movement. Without a word, she met my eyes and flipped cards onto the table. She stopped on the Five of Swords. "You've been fighting for something, yes?" she asked me. "Wishing, maybe? For something from your past?"

I sneered at Marian. "I'm assuming you told her to say that?" She shook her head *no*.

The woman flipped another card. "The Fool." She traced her finger across an illustration of a man dressed like a court jester. "The Fool marks new beginnings." She pointed to the path he stood on, which ended at the edge of a cliff. "Here he is at the start of a new journey. The bag he carries contains everything he needs. But you'll see he stands on this path alone."

"What does that mean?" I asked.

"This thing from your past," the woman said. "It's already over."

"Oh please." Marian looked alarmed and reached for the deck; the woman was quick to stop her. "That's not right."

I turned to Marian, who was already grabbing my bag strap. "Why did you bring me here?"

Marian lifted my cards, as though she could interpret them. "I thought maybe she'd—"

"What? Tell me that my dreams were still out there waiting for me?"

"Well, yeah," Marian admitted. "That's what they always do at these places." She looked at the woman. "No offense."

"You have to stop with this shit, Mar," I had said. "This isn't like in college, when you'd take me somewhere like this to open my eyes to the world or whatever. My eyes are already open. And, frankly, they're tired." I threw the strap over my shoulder. "I don't have time for this stuff anymore."

When I returned home from that trip, I had felt lost in my head for days. Ultimately, the next week, I threw the retrospective issue of that journal in the trash.

I repositioned myself on our porch, the memory burning in my mind.

"That's *not* what this is about, Liv." The smile Marian usually wore with such conviction had faded, melted into something else. Anger, maybe? "If you're going to be pissed at me, at least be pissed about the right thing."

"Fine! It's not about the fortune teller or that test!" I shouted and then rubbed the heels of my palms across my eyes. "Or it is." I was sweating. "Fuck. I don't know! I'm fucking scared, Marian!" I slapped my chest. "What if something *does* happen to me?" I swooped my arm toward our house. "What would happen to *them*?" I stomped my foot against the ground. "What if I really *do* only have ten months? What the fuck am I doing with my life?" I released a loud sigh that sounded like a punctured balloon. "I've put off so many things in my life, and then I got that box and I started to think more about that fucking test, and now, I don't know, it's just—it's too late!"

"Too late for what?" I turned and saw Andrew behind me. I hadn't heard him step onto the porch. *Shit.* He narrowed his eyes. "What is it too late for, Liv?"

"I don't know." My neck dripped with perspiration. "Ask Marian."

Tommy appeared on the porch, his mouth coated in sugar. "Why is everyone fighting?"

I felt dizzy. "We're not fu—" I looked at Tommy's face and stopped myself. "We're not fighting," I lied, and I tried to calm myself even though it felt impossible for me to suck down a full breath. "We're having a passionate conversation about the doughnuts Aunt Marian brought us this morning—completely unannounced, by the way."

"I like to talk about doughnuts," Tommy added. "The chocolate ones are definitely the best."

Andrew patted Tommy's head. "Why don't you go in the house and eat another one, buddy?" Tommy disappeared inside. Andrew redirected his attention to me. "You were saying?" Marian and I both crossed our arms across our chests, like two disgruntled children. "Someone needs to tell me what in the hell has been going on with you two." Andrew squeezed the bridge of his nose. "And for the record, if someone blames it on the doughnuts, I'm going to lose it."

I felt my neck and face start to flush, as though the emotions of the whole summer—febrile and angry from being bottled up inside me for too long—were finally ready to explode. "Apparently, I might be dying, Andy!" The words burst from me, like water from a geyser. I lifted my arm and pointed straight at Marian. "And it's all her fault!"

"What?" Marian's jaw dropped. "It's not *my* fault you're dying!"

"So, then you admit it's true?" I snapped. "That fucking test was right?"

"I'm sorry." Andrew looked confused. He squeezed his temples. "What?"

"Marian took me for some ridiculous medical test for my birthday—which, let's pause and acknowledge the level of insanity that guided that decision—and the results suggested that I'm going to die, probably in a few months. Only, here's the kicker: no one knows how!"

"Wait." Andrew blinked dramatically. "What are you talking about?" He shook his head and turned to Marian. "I thought you two were done with stunts like this? Is this true?"

"Which part?" Marian stood there with her fists in her pockets. "The part about the test or the dying bit?" She wanted someone to laugh. No one did. "It was a gag," she finally mumbled to the ground. "It was supposed to be something fun to do to mark the—"

"Fun?" I didn't want to hear it. "I want you to go," I told her. "Preferably, now."

Marian absently kicked the grass. "Fine." A tear slid down her cheek. "Andy, can you give me a ride to the train? I think there's another commuter line that leaves for the city soon."

The three of us stood there in silence for a long minute. Finally, Andrew stepped inside for his keys.

"Can I ask you something before I go?" Marian said when we were alone again. "Why do you keep coming to these places with me?"

"Because you—"

"Because I what?" she countered. "Force you? Hold you hostage?" Marian's words just levitated there, like air. "Did you ever think that maybe this isn't actually about me, Liv?" Andrew reappeared on the porch. "Maybe," she continued, "it's about you."

"That doesn't make any sense."

"Look in the mirror, Liv," she said. "Just accept the fact that you're not the same person you once were."

Marian moved toward the car. I watched them pull out of our driveway and disappear down our block. I turned back toward our house. That's when I saw her: Suzanne, positioned behind the oak tree at the edge of our property. Our eyes met. *Damn it.* I didn't have to ask her a thing. I knew from her expression that she'd heard everything. That, for better or worse, she'd heard it all.

THIRTY

Andrew dropped his keys on the counter. "Go upstairs, Tommy." Tommy and I were snuggled on the couch, our bellies full of doughnuts. "What about my cartoons?" Tommy asked, his lips rimmed in chocolate, and pointed to the TV.

"I need to talk to Mama," Andrew said. "Alone." He tossed Tommy his phone. "If you go upstairs, you can play any game you want." Tommy was no fool. He grabbed the device and darted. Andrew moved closer to me. "Where should we start?"

I took a bite of frosting, my gaze still cast on Tommy's show. "Well, that's no way to speak to a potentially dying woman."

"You're not doing this." Andrew clicked off the television. "You're not making jokes to avoid having to actually talk." He squeezed the bridge of his nose again. "Liv, what the fu—"

"I know," I interrupted. My eyes started to sting. *Damn it.* I looked at the ceiling, hoping to prevent tears from spilling down my cheeks. "This whole thing—"

"Just stop." Andrew put up his hand. "Marian filled in a lot of the gaps in the car." He shook his head at some thought occupying his mind. "You don't actually believe that—"

"No." I looked at the carpet. "Of course not." I wiped the tears from my lashes. "Fine," I admitted. "Maybe I'm starting to believe the test results just a little."

Andrew rubbed his temples. "Why didn't you tell me?"

It was the question I knew he'd ultimately ask, the one I'd tried to avoid for too long. "I don't entirely know," I finally said. "Initially, I didn't want to admit that I'd willingly gone along with Marian's plan. I think I wanted to believe I was past all that."

"That was initially," Andrew said. "What about now?"

I rolled my neck. "The more I thought about that test, the more I started to worry that, perhaps unbeknownst to Marian, it might have been intended for more than just a laugh," I admitted both to Andrew and to myself. "I didn't want you to worry about it, too."

"But that's my job, Liv."

"To worry?" I asked.

"When it comes to you and Tommy, yes."

I sighed. I knew he was right.

"I hate to state the obvious here," Andrew continued, "but have you tried to look the place up? See if any other people had the test?"

"I researched it earlier this summer," I explained. "It wasn't much help."

Andrew exhaled. It sounded like he'd been holding it inside him for a long time. "What is this really about, Liv?" He sat on the edge of the coffee table and rested his hands on his knees. "Is it really about this ridiculous, obviously fictional test?" He shook his head as he searched for meaning. "Your birthday and getting older?" He met my gaze. "Is this about us somehow?"

"What?" My voice cracked. I looked up at him. "No! Why would you say that?"

He leaned toward me, his stance softening. "Then what?"

"I just thought some parts of my life would be different by now," I said, and I hoped he'd understand. "It has nothing to do with you or Tommy. You guys are my whole world." My lip trembled. "I don't know.

There are just so many things I wanted to accomplish and change about myself by now." I rubbed my hands across my face and discovered a bit of frosting in my eyebrow. *God.* I really was a mess. "Sometimes, it just feels like it's too late."

From upstairs, I heard Tommy skid across the hallway, followed by the sound of toys smashing against the ground. "I'm okay!" he shouted.

Andrew studied my face. "What kinds of things?"

"I don't know." I played with my fingernail. "I'm a thirty-nine-year-old mother who doesn't know how to cook a meatloaf!"

Andrew smirked. "So, this whole summer has been about meatloaf?"

"Yes!" I exclaimed and then changed course. "I mean, no." I shook my head, frustrated with myself. "It's just, well, do you remember when we lived in the city and we used to shop at that artisanal cheese shop downtown?"

Andrew nodded. "So, this is about cheese?"

"No." I wiped my cheek with my sleeve. "I just mean, well, when did I start buying our food in a damn warehouse?" I gestured toward our kitchen and the enormous boxes of bulk, prepackaged snacks stacked on the floor. "When did everything start to change?"

Andrew smiled. I could tell he didn't know what to say. "Keep going," he said.

"I think when Marian took me to that place, and that woman told me my time might be running out, I initially wrote it off. But then the more I thought about it, the more I began to realize it actually could. That I don't have forever to put all the pieces into place." The words poured out of me now. "What if it *is* true? What would happen to you and Tommy? Would you guys be okay without me?" I stopped myself. "Wait. Don't answer that." My breath caught in my throat when I thought of Andrew as a sad widower or, worse, finding someone to replace me. "I'm old, Andy. You are, too. We're not kids anymore."

Andrew moved onto the couch and pulled me against him. "There are no timelines in life, Liv. You don't have to become this perfect person by a certain age. People change. They evolve." He squeezed my shoulder. "You still have a whole second act ahead of you."

I rested my tear-streaked face against Andrew's chest. My breath started to even out. "I'm not sure what I believe about that test," I admitted. "The only thing I know for sure is that I want to know that I still have time to do all the things I want to do."

"Like what?"

I pulled myself upright. "I really need to quit smoking."

He nodded. "I agree. The porch cigarettes have got to go."

"And I want to leave my job," I announced.

"Seems like a big jump from the cigarette bit," Andrew joked. "But I see your point."

I rubbed my temples. "I should have really read through my test results. I glanced at them, but I should have reviewed them more seriously so I'd have tangible proof that it was all phony."

Andrew peered at the wall clock. "You know, Marian's train doesn't leave for another half hour. She's probably just sitting on the platform, alone . . . sad . . . missing her best friend."

"No," I said and then nibbled doughnut crumbs. "I'm still pissed about the whole thing."

"I know. You should be." Andrew licked sugar from his fingertip. "But I'd be willing to bet she'd take you back there if it meant you'd speak to her."

"Take me back there?" I asked. "For what?"

"Isn't it obvious?" Andrew's eyes widened. "Just have the test again. This way, you can compare the results."

"Oh." It'd never even occurred to me that it was an option. "Right." I laughed to myself. "I hadn't thought of that." I bit my lip, thinking. "Will you think I'm completely ridiculous if I have it done again?"

Andrew shrugged. "It depends. Will it give you closure?"

I waited a minute before I responded. "I think so."

"I hate to state the obvious here, but even if you prove that the test was fake, it doesn't mean you'll live forever. You could get hit by a bus on your way home."

"Thanks," I told him. "You're like the human version of an inspirational coffee mug."

"It's true. That's the problem with life. We never know when our time is running out."

We were both quiet. Finally, I nodded. "I hadn't really thought about it like that."

Andrew carried the empty doughnut box into the kitchen. "So, are you going to give it a go?"

I followed him and glanced at our wall clock. "You've got Tommy?"

He tossed the box into the trash. "You already know the answer to that."

I cupped my hand around his face and kissed him. "Thank you," I whispered and then pulled away and hustled down the hallway.

"Hey, Liv," Andrew called out before I rounded the corner. I turned back to him. "You know, it just occurred to me that you never told me about Marian's results." His head fell toward his shoulder, his thought curling up into a question. "What did hers say?"

"I, um, I d-don't know," I stammered. "She never got to see them, actually."

Andrew looked at me, some uncertainty framing his expression. "Oh," he finally said. "That's . . . weird. Right?"

I shrugged my uncertainty. "I guess," I said and then dashed up the stairs. I didn't have time to think about his comment at that moment. After all, I didn't want to be late.

THIRTY-ONE

Marian was seated on a bench at the end of the platform. She looked forlorn, not like her normal self, her gaze cast on the tracks. A sense of sadness radiated off her.

"I'm not mad at you," I shouted across the platform. "I'm mad at me." She looked up in question. "For waiting too long," I finally admitted to us both. "For not being able to get out of my own way. For making so many excuses." I felt the tears coming. "I'm sorry for being so short with you these last few months. It's just—"

"Liv, you don't have to—"

"I want you to take me back there," I interrupted. "To the Nettle Center," I clarified. "I want to take that test again. It's the only way I'll ever know about those results for sure."

"Hang on. You want to get the test *again*? When?" I tapped my watch face in response. *"Now?"* she asked, and it was clear that we were both surprised by my urgency.

"I thought we could both have it done again," I said, thinking of Andrew. "We can both finally see our full results."

"Liv, we really need to talk first," she said. "I'm not sure I want to go back to that place. Maybe we need to think this through."

"Aren't you the one who always tells me to be more spontaneous?" I asked. "To stop making lists and just go have fun?" At the far end of the tracks, the train rumbled toward us. "We can talk about it more later."

Marian breathed heavily. I could see she was hesitating, that our roles had reversed. "So, what's the plan once we arrive?"

"Right. A plan." I scrunched my lips in contemplation. "I've never been good with making them. Well, following through with them, anyway."

The train screeched to a halt. "Plans are overrated." Before the train doors opened, Marian produced a plastic pill case from her bag. She placed a small blue pill on her tongue. "Based on my experiences," she continued and swallowed hard, "despite our best efforts, even the best-laid plans rarely work out in the end."

~

Later that morning, we emerged aboveground, just like we had in June. Marian and I moved up the same block. I looked around. Something had changed since our last visit. I wasn't sure if it was a quality to the landscape or if it was me. Either way, something about that unexceptional neighborhood suddenly felt ominous.

We turned the corner. My heart rate increased. Up ahead, I saw that familiar white building, like a mirage. *The Nettle Center.* Together, we hustled toward the entryway.

We stopped.

"Shit," Marian mumbled.

I froze beside her. The front door was boarded up with a piece of plywood. In the window, the neon sign, which had previously beckoned us like a juicy secret, was turned off. I cupped my hand against the glass. The lights inside the building were turned off, too. The once-vibrant potted palms that decorated the airy foyer were all dead.

I banged on the door. "Open up!" I shouted. "I know you're in there," I yelled. I pulled the knob so hard I thought I might shatter the glass. I pivoted toward Marian, my hands still accosting the door. "I'm not going home without more details about those results," I cried out as I continued to jostle the handle. A few minutes passed. Finally, I released my grip. "I can't go home without any new information," I cried. "This wasn't part of the plan."

"Maybe they're just closed," Marian suggested, and she pressed her face against the window. It was clear to me from her sudden tenacity that she was just as disappointed as me. "Or maybe they just open really late." She pulled back. "I've heard new age types require a lot of extra sleep. They're like babies, but with more whining and bigger bank accounts."

She wanted me to laugh, but I didn't have it in me. I sat on the curb and dropped my head between my knees. "I knew this was a bad idea." We sat quietly, perhaps hoping it had all been an oversight, that if we waited, Dahlia would eventually turn the corner. Finally, I lifted my face. "So, what do I do now?"

"You mean about the test?" she asked, and I knew she was just stalling.

I nodded. "Does this mean I'll never know anything for sure? That neither of us will?"

Marian picked up a smooth white stone and turned it in her hand. "I don't know," she admitted, and she tossed it across the street. In silence, we watched it somersault over the pavement. "You already know everything you need to know about it," she said without looking at me. "We both do."

"What do you mean?"

"It was fake, right? We've already established that. What other information do you really need?"

"You were there, Mar," I reminded her. "You saw her draw my blood, too."

Marian blinked, releasing a single tear down her face. "I know."

For a while, we sat there together. "So, what am I supposed to do?" I finally asked. "What are *either* of us supposed to do? Who's to say your results didn't have some error, too?"

Marian glanced at the door, but nothing had changed. Finally, she turned back to me and lifted her sunglasses. "I'm not sure," she said. "But I think it's time that you stop screwing around." She wiped her face with the back of her hand and looked away. Together, we studied the ground. "That maybe we *both* stop screwing around."

And in that moment, I understood that Marian shared my fears about that test. That she'd wondered not only about *my* results—the ones we'd both seen—but about *her* results—the ones we'd never had the chance to view—too. Like me, deep down, in a place she hadn't wanted to admit to, she'd had fears about that test all along.

AFTERLIFE

THIRTY-TWO

Sleep was an impossibility. I might as well have tried to dig a hole through the earth or learn a language on a whim. I spent that whole night focused on the ceiling, like it was a damn movie screen. I kept waiting for some answer about my life to appear there among the shadows. It never did. At some point, I finally accepted the truth. There was no answer. No easy way out. My test results were gone, ground up into dirt. Dahlia and her whole operation were gone, too. There was no magical confirmation of my mortality. I might have days. Or years. It was a crapshoot. Only one thing was certain: in the end, death would find me.

The trouble was that I had no clue when.

I moved into the kitchen, the world still cloaked in black. The coffee machine bubbled. I spent the rest of the night at our island with my poetry notebook and artificial creamer, and I transferred the montage of thoughts in my head down onto the page. I wanted to make sense of them, like a difficult passage I needed to translate. I wanted to understand what they all meant.

"You're up early." Andrew stumbled into the kitchen like a drunk, his eyes still half-closed. He adjusted the drawstring on his favorite pajama pants. "What time is it?"

I looked up. The sun slowly revealed itself in a seductive orange sliver through our window. "When was the last time I did something fun? Something that lit my soul on fire?"

"Oh boy." Andrew shuffled across the room. "I'd better get some coffee." He filled his mug, then settled beside me. "I'm guessing you didn't find out more information about that test."

I took a hazelnut-infused sip. "You were right." I set down my empty mug. "The test never mattered. No one has a damn clue. Not me. Not you. Not some pretend doctor."

Andrew rubbed his hands across his stubble-marked face. "About what?"

"When." I closed my poetry notebook. "Which is why I need to start now. *Really* start. Just in case."

Andrew pressed his palms against his eyes. "I'm going to need more caffeine."

Above us, I heard the light shuffle of Tommy's footsteps. I moved across the room for the carafe and topped off our mugs. "I'm not so sure that test is as silly as I once thought."

"Liv—"

"Just humor me." I sat back down beside him. "Let's say it *is* real. Is this the legacy I want to leave for you or Tommy? Or for me?" I swept my hair from my face. "I need you to not take offense to anything I'm about to say here, because it has nothing to do with you two." I bit my lip, finally accepting some bitter truth. "It has to do with *me*. Just me."

Andrew left his mug on the island. He studied my face. "Okay."

I exhaled audibly. "I don't want to be remembered as some tired, overbooked, boring suburban woman who never took the damn time to become the best version of herself."

Andrew didn't budge. "Is that really how you feel?" He shook his head, some recognition sweeping over him. "About yourself, I mean."

"I think so." It felt like an invisible weight had been lifted off my body.

"Okay." Andrew didn't take his eyes off me. "So, what's the plan?" He squeezed my hand. "What do you want to do, Liv?"

In the other room, the television clicked to life. The familiar sound of Tommy's favorite cartoon filled the space around us. I squeezed Andrew's fingers with all the strength I had. "I want to get out of my own way and finally learn to live my fucking life again."

THIRTY-THREE

September. My whole life, it had always felt like the *real* beginning to the New Year, as though Labor Day and New Year's Day were one and the same. I don't know. I think my feelings were rooted in my childhood, back when a fresh school year felt like an opportunity to create a new identity. New binders. New wardrobes. New *you*. It was the perfect time to begin.

"Mama, what do you want to be when you grow up?"

I glanced in the rearview mirror. Tommy was strapped into his booster seat, his favorite stuffed dinosaur snuggled on his lap. "*When* I grow up?" I lifted my travel mug. "I think I'm already there, buddy." I stopped the car at a red light. "Why do you ask?"

Tommy shrugged. "We talked about it in school yesterday. I told my teacher I want to be a dinosaur hunter." He squeezed his plush toy. "She said there aren't a lot of jobs like that."

"What?" The engine hummed. "Don't listen to your teacher." I forgot to mention that I'm an expert in the field of parenting advice. "You can absolutely be a dinosaur hunter." I wanted to strangle her. "You can be anything you want."

I watched Tommy in the mirror, his little face all scrunched up in thought. "But dinosaurs are huge, Mama. And scary." He glanced up at my reflection. "Maybe she's right. What if I'm no good at hunting them? What will happen then?"

I stretched my arm into the back seat and squeezed his leg. "Then you'll brush yourself off, kiddo, and try again."

For a while, Tommy seemed satisfied by my reply. He peered through the window. "Did you always want to be a teacher, Mama?"

I turned the car into a circular driveway. Dozens of tiny humans, dressed in colorful, mismatched ensembles, poured onto the sidewalk. "No," I admitted.

"Then what *did* you want to be?" Tommy asked.

My mind drifted to a thousand moments from my past. I smiled at Tommy in the rearview. "I wanted to be something else," I told him.

"Well, how come you didn't become that?" he asked, like life was that easy.

I unclicked Tommy's booster seat, smiled, and then kissed him. "Because I wasn't a very good dinosaur hunter, I guess."

~

That night, while Andrew stayed downstairs to read, I lay in our bed alone. A warm breeze blew through the window, like honey on my skin. Tommy's comments continued to fill my mind. I was ready for bed, but instead I leaned toward my nightstand, pulled that second-hand poetry anthology onto my lap, and spent a chunk of time rereading those once-familiar lines of verse. I had forgotten—or maybe I hadn't realized—how many were about the same burdens that had been weighing on me. Love. Death. Time. Maybe I wasn't the only one carrying those fears with me. Maybe doing so was just part of life.

I had finally shared one of my poems publicly our senior year. The three of us had been at ABC Bar, testing the strengths of our livers. While Marian and Andrew staggered back to the bar for more drinks, I sat in my sticky vinyl banquette and studied the setting. The flashing lights. The loud music. Life felt electric in that moment. I felt electric, too. I dipped my hand into the bowl of pens on our table, then twisted toward the bright-pink wall.

My lips had spread into a warm, drunken smile when Marian and Andrew returned with a round of neon shots. I dropped my pen back in the bowl. "What?"

They practically pushed me out of the way to read it. Marian turned to Andrew when she finished. "Now?"

"Now," he agreed.

Without asking my permission, they dragged me out the door. We downed the shots on the street, then raced to the open mic night a few blocks away. We stepped into the crowded room. They directed me to the stage. If I was nervous, I was too drunk to feel it. I closed my eyes and recited my poem the way I'd practiced it in my head. When I was done, I opened my eyes. Everyone in the room was standing.

Back in my bedroom, I set the poetry anthology on my nightstand, Tommy's voice still rippling through me like a gentle wave. I pulled an accordion folder—the one that contained all my old writing—down from the top shelf of my closet. I sat in bed and dug through it. Old journals graffitied with my scribbled half thoughts. Floppy disks I'd never be able to open again. Printouts of completed poems, ones I'd spent months scrutinizing, that had never seen the light of day. Dreams I had allowed to just sit there, collecting dust.

I reached for my laptop, finally ready to do the thing I should have done years earlier. When it illuminated with life, rather than type up my recent observations and attempts at verse, I typed up my old poems instead—the ones I'd abandoned all those years ago. Hours later, I listened as our printer hummed. I folded my screen shut. That was the thing I was learning about death. Once you acknowledged that it was coming, you didn't have time to feel afraid anymore.

THIRTY-FOUR

I arrived at Blakely the next morning and fielded a dozen concerns—*Parents are upset we're teaching a book that includes the word "breasts"; a group of senior girls refuses to read* Moby Dick *because they find the title sexist.* The bell rang. Everyone disappeared. I embraced the silence and pulled my stack of printed-out poems from my bag. I began to neatly fold them up and then slide them into envelopes, which I marked with the names and addresses of literary magazines I hadn't considered in years. Right as I was licking the last envelope closed, the office door swung open.

"Greetings, Olivia."

I looked up and found Christopher in the doorframe. "Hi." I set my pile of envelopes on the side of my desk and willed myself not to give in to my annoyance with him.

"I'd like to speak to you about my book list." He adjusted his cardigan. "*Your* book list, technically." After I was named chair, I'd had to bequeath some courses to select colleagues to accommodate my new role. Christopher was one of my victims. "I'd like to eliminate a text."

I reached for my coffee, already knowing I would need it. "What book?"

Christopher opened his leather knapsack. "This one."

I felt like I'd been slapped. "*A Room of One's Own?*" I'd added it to my course list at the last minute, set on making at least one small change to things. "Why? It's not exactly smut."

Christopher straightened his woven tie. "Personally, I find it offensive."

"Offensive?" I reminded myself not to laugh. "You're kidding?" He failed to respond. "Right?" I inhaled deeply, knowing my quiet morning was officially over. "Okay. Which part?"

Christopher sat across from me and crossed one leg over the other. "The part about *female* writers needing a space to create their art." I caught a glimpse of his socks, which were predictably decorated with a book motif. "What about *male* writers?"

"I think maybe you've missed the point of the text."

Christopher adjusted his eyeglasses, perhaps to prove his intellect. "I believe I'm *more* than educated enough to comprehend Woolf's point. I've already earned *two*—"

"Master's degrees," I interrupted and then squeezed my temples. "You've mentioned that."

"Right." He tapped his loafer.

"Look, I'm sorry the book offends you." I spun around. "But it's your job to teach it." Suddenly, I felt grateful for my age and the sense of authority it granted me. "And it's my job to make sure you do."

"I won't do it," Christopher whined.

"Oh, cut it out," I snapped, feeling like I was arguing with Tommy about some toy. "You're acting like a child," I said, and I instantly regretted it.

Christopher's expression swiftly transformed. "I know you've long had a problem with my youth, Olivia. However, I won't be the subject of ageism."

"Ageism? Stop it. You know that's not what I meant," I said, knowing I'd already crossed some important boundary. "I simply meant that I'm more experienced and—"

"Well, if *that's* not discriminatory . . ." He trailed off and then smiled smugly. "I guess it's *my* fault that I haven't lived enough years to match *your* level of experience."

Apparently, it didn't matter if you were young or old. We all just wanted to rewind or fast-forward to a different era of our lives. I felt tempted to laugh but stopped myself before I could start. Instead, I looked at Christopher, as though for the first time. When I did, I noticed something about him I'd failed to notice before: the fact that he wanted this—the job opportunity that had been so casually handed to me—in the same way I had wanted certain things for myself at his age. "Can I ask you a question, Christopher?" I said, my tone softened. He looked at me with an expression of surprise. "What is it you want out of life?"

He cleared his throat. "I don't know what you mean."

It was the big question no proper adult had ever stopped to seriously ask me at that age. "Your job. Your future." I waved my hand before me. "What do you want from all this?"

He shifted uncomfortably in his desk chair. "Um, I just . . ."

"You can be honest."

He straightened his posture. "I'd like to have your job," he admitted. "Eventually."

Briefly, I believed that I understood him better. "That's what I thought." In the hallway, the bell rang. "In that case, can I give you a tip?" Christopher nodded. "Stop complaining so much," I said. "Take it from me. Otherwise, you're just going to get in your own way."

Christopher stepped into the hall. The office returned to a state of silence. I looked at my envelopes. Another teacher entered the room. "If anyone asks, tell them I'm taking a half day," I said, and I grabbed a booklet of stamps from my desk drawer. "Something came up." I couldn't field any more questions or listen to any more grievances. Finally, I had to take the time to deal with my own.

THIRTY-FIVE

By midfall, I finally secured an endocrinology appointment. I'd never visited a specialist in my life. I figured the point wasn't for the doctor to insist that you're special and give you a gold star. Euphemism at its finest. I thought about that—not the fact that I was special, but the fact that the doctor would tell me all the ways I was broken—while I sat in the waiting room, anxiously ruminating. The word "waiting" is misleading. They ought to call them worrying rooms instead.

"Do you want the good news or the bad news?" Dr. Greene pressed a phallus-shaped device against my throat.

I was in a darkened exam room, my neck coated with sticky goop. "Considering the circumstances, the good news, preferably."

He slid the cold device against my skin and pointed to an ultrasound screen. "It's twins!"

"Wait." My heart dropped like lead. "What do you—"

"Your thyroid nodules." He gestured to a pair of grainy dots. "It's a little joke I make when there are two of them." He wiped my skin with a rough paper towel. "I suppose I don't need to tell you that if they were fetuses, I wouldn't be able to view them in your neck."

It seemed Dr. White wasn't the only physician in our town moonlighting as a stand-up comedian. "So, what's the bad news?" I asked, disregarding his humor.

Dr. Greene lifted a long, thin needle from a metal tray. "That I'm going to need you to remain *very* still." He placed a hand on my forehead to steady me and then pierced my skin. "All kidding aside, I need to biopsy them."

My gaze shifted to that glowing ultrasound screen. It wasn't the first time that twins had taken up residency in my body. It happened right after Andrew and I were engaged. We'd nearly passed out when we learned the news. We weren't ready for one child, let alone two. Slowly, we came around to the idea, but by the time we returned to that darkened examination room, the two little balls of life inside me were slumped like deflated balloons at the bottom of the ultrasound screen.

Dr. Greene set down his medical tools, clicked on the lights. "I'll call you in a few weeks with the results. Assuming things are benign, we'll periodically keep an eye on them," he explained, like they were rambunctious children in need of monitoring. "Figure we'll check in again right around . . ." He glanced at my chart. "Aha! How about the week of your fortieth birthday?"

"Thanks for the reminder." I blinked, my eyes adjusting to the artificial light. "So, what did I do to earn these?"

"The nodules?" He flicked his wrist, like they were nothing, even though they came with the threat of disease. "They're just a fun perk of aging." He squirted a pump of hand sanitizer into his palm. "Think of them like barnacles. Eventually they just develop over time."

I tilted my head, gauging him. "Did you just compare my thyroid to a clam?"

"Or a very old sea rock." He smirked, amused by himself. "Your pick."

I pulled my gown tighter around my body, feeling too exposed. "But I'm not that old," I protested. "Not old enough to have the human equivalent of barnacles growing inside me."

"You're not that young, either," Dr. Greene pointed out.

∽

When I returned home, Tommy and Andrew were on the couch, plates balanced on their laps. "I'm the human version of a middle-aged clam," I said as I tossed down my bag.

"Mama's a clam!" Tommy shouted and then choked down a mouthful of food.

Andrew looked up at me and licked a bite from his fork. "Do I want to know?"

I peeked at the island and the half-eaten casserole set upon it, which was so brilliantly assembled it looked like it ought to appear in the pages of a magazine. "Who made that?"

"Suzanne." Andrew set his empty plate on the coffee table. "It was on the porch when we got home." He gestured toward the counter. "There was a card, too."

Other than a quick wave, I hadn't seen Suzanne in weeks—not since she'd overheard my encounter with Marian. I reached for the card and unsealed the flap. *Dear Liv—here's a little something to help lighten your load. Thinking of you. XO—Suze.* It was vague enough that she could pretend she hadn't been eavesdropping, but specific enough that—if she'd overheard correctly and I *was* actually dying—I'd be touched.

Andrew entered the kitchen. "You want to eat?" He helped himself to another serving. "It's really good."

I stole Andrew's fork and dug it into the casserole. "Maybe later." I indulged in a perfect creamy bite. "I'm going to shower first." I offered a sarcastic smile. "I need to wash all the salt water and seaweed off of me."

Upstairs, I sat on our bed, picked up my phone, and sent a message to Marian. Do you think there are senior communities built inside anemones? I figured we'd laugh about my barnacles before she settled my nerves about the biopsy. That was how our friendship worked: I navigated some existential crisis, and Marian talked me down off the ledge. While I waited for her response, I moved to my dresser and slid off my jewelry. I glanced at the items in an old trinket dish I kept there. Andrew had helped Tommy paint the dish flamingo pink as a gift for my first Mother's Day. I smiled at Tommy's erratic brushstrokes, then picked up the item that had caught my eye—a spiral seashell I'd brought home from our family's only real vacation. I ran my fingers over its surface, remembering the clear water lapping my ankles while Tommy was strapped to my chest. I'd felt so young on that trip, the whole world still spread before me like the horizon. Why hadn't we taken the time to go back? I turned the shell in my hand and noticed several calcified barnacles adhered to its pearlescent underside. I placed it back in the dish.

I glanced at my phone. Marian still hadn't replied. I tossed the device on the bed and moved into the bathroom, ready to wash the day away. Before I disrobed, my heart nearly stopped. I leaned closer to the mirror and squinted at three silver hairs—each of them as gray as those damn barnacles—that had sprouted along my part. "You've got to be kidding me," I said to my reflection. I tugged open a drawer in search of scissors so I could snip the rogue hairs away. And that's when I saw it: the bottle of pink hair dye, mixed in with all my other rarely used beauty supplies.

I thought about that bottle the rest of the night. I thought of it when I returned downstairs and indulged in a generous dish of Suzanne's casserole. I thought of it as I tucked Tommy into his bed. I thought of it later in my own bed as I stared at the ceiling while Andrew snored next to me. I thought of it when I threw back the covers in the middle of the night, headed into our bathroom, and locked the door.

I knew it was a bad idea. Still, I couldn't stop myself. I twisted open the bottle, squeezed a thick line of magenta gel across my center part, and gathered my hair in a heaping fluorescent pile. The dye burning my scalp, I thought of all my old birthday lists.

Year twenty-three: Do something dramatic with my hair!

My lips parted into a smile. Finally, after years of missed chances, I could definitively cross something out.

THIRTY-SIX

Mama turned into a cartoon!" Tommy literally tumbled over himself when he arrived in the living room the next morning and saw the loose strands of cotton candy hair framing my face. He pounced on me and tugged on it. "Is it *real?*" His eyes were two wide disks, as though his sugary cereal had come with a hit of hallucinogens. "Can I do that to my hair, too?"

"Do what?" Andrew shuffled in from the kitchen, his sleepy, Saturday-morning gaze set on his steaming coffee. When he looked up, he physically spat a spray of it through the air like a character in a bad comedy film. "Holy sh—"

"It's only semipermanent," I said. "I think." I bit my lip. "I actually never read the bottle." Andrew just stared at me, wide eyed. "You can tell me I'm a fool."

"I—I, uh, I d-don't understand," he stuttered. "When did you—"

"You've always been a heavy sleeper," I said, finishing his question. I looked down at my hands, feeling self-conscious. "So, um, what do you think?" I peered up at him, suddenly a shy schoolgirl.

"Actually—" Andrew's lips lifted into a half smile. "It's kind of sexy."

"Sexy?" I repeated, as though the word—as well as the concept—were new to me.

Tommy relinquished my hair and reached for the cereal box. "What's 'sexy' mean?"

"I didn't say 'sexy.'" Andrew's cheeks flushed, like a teenager's. "I, um, I said 'pretty.'"

"No, you didn't." Tommy shoved a fistful of marshmallows into his mouth.

I pulled the box from Tommy's grip and then moved toward Andrew. I touched my hand to his jaw, closing his mouth for him. *Birthday list—0. Liv—1.* My lips lifted into a wide smile.

Later that morning, my head still stinking of chemicals, I threw on my running shoes. Our neighbors stared while I sprinted (stumbled?) past. I ignored them. I just kept running, like a happy, but woefully ungraceful, gazelle. Strands of peppermint-pink hair flapped across my face. Nothing about the scene looked different. Nothing about the scene *was* different. Except for me. Voilà! A new Liv! A new life! Finally, I'd taken the leap.

I circled back to our block and spotted Suzanne walking up our driveway. "Hey." I pressed my hands to my knees while I caught my breath. Suzanne turned. Her body stiffened when she saw me, like she'd been shocked by something, her eyes as round as her china dinner plates. I touched my sweating, candy-hued head. "It was a bit of an impulse decision."

"Oh, uh." She kept swallowing, like she'd forgotten how words worked.

"So, what's up?"

Suzanne coughed for no reason. "Um, I'm scheduled to host the next ladies' get-together in a few weeks." She shook her head. "Uh, we're having work done. In our kitchen, I mean." She kept tilting her head in confusion. "Any chance you can host it for me? I know you hate—"

"Sure," I said. I think my answer surprised us both. "I'll do it. I'm in."

"I'm sorry." Suzanne's face wrinkled, like she'd eaten something sour. We still hadn't talked about the lawn incident. Regardless, it wasn't the right time. "What's happening here?"

Before I could answer, Andrew stepped onto the porch. He had a million bags strapped to him, like he was a donkey. "Tommy wants to go to the playground," he said as he pulled a strap away from his neck.

Tommy appeared behind him wearing a pair of neon sunglasses. "I packed supplies," he said, pointing to his dad's many nylon nooses.

"Apparently, we're knee deep in investigative journalism," Andrew explained. "Tommy wants to research some things he can be when he grows up." He adjusted his shoulder; a bag plunged off his body. "It seems his teacher said being a dinosaur hunter won't work out." Andrew flung open the car door. "I'm assuming you know something about this?"

"Tommy's teacher is a fu—" I stopped, revised myself. "She stinks," I said and then locked eyes with my son. "By the way, don't tell her I said that."

Suzanne just stood there, her eyes still cast on my bright-pink head. "I'll, uh, I'll send you the details for the get-together," she said and then deliriously stumbled back to her yard.

I watched her walk away. "I think I shocked her," I told Andrew.

Andrew clicked Tommy into his booster seat. "I think you may have shocked more than her." He gestured to several neighbors, hoses and stacks of mail in their hands, their heads all swiveled toward our lawn. "You're the talk of the town." Andrew closed the door. "You make a midlife crisis look good, Olivia Strauss."

"I thought you said I was too creative for a midlife crisis."

"You're right." Andrew slid into the car. "Maybe this is just thirty-nine-year-old Liv." He buzzed down his window. "By the way, Marian called while you were on your run."

"Okay." I made a mental note to contact her later that morning.

Andrew backed the car out of our driveway. I stepped inside, wandered around the living room, and cleaned up Tommy's explosion of toys. A ball of fury burned inside me as I thought about someone telling him that his dreams were already an impossibility. That's when I picked up his favorite stuffed dinosaur, ready to drop it into a basket with all his other plush friends. I stopped myself and investigated its stitched face, wondering what great and extraordinary things Tommy saw when he looked at it. I wanted to know what fantastical dreams swirled around in his sweet little head.

For the remainder of the morning, I gathered every plastic dinosaur toy Tommy owned and hid them around our front yard. Dozens of tiny T. rex arms popped out of our bushes. Brachiosaurus heads peered through trees, like plastic prehistoric periscopes. Herds of triceratops tromped across our lawn. When Andrew pulled the car back into our driveway, our property looked like a bizarre plastic zoo. I was seated on the porch with a pair of toy binoculars strung around my neck. Tommy ran up to me, his face all excitement. I handed him a second pair of toy binoculars. "Don't listen to your teacher, Tommy," I told him, and I pressed my binoculars against my face. "Don't listen to anyone, actually."

"Not even you, Mama?" Tommy said as he slid his binocular strap over his head.

"Well, maybe me." I stepped off the porch. "But we don't need to worry about that right now." I grabbed his sweet, small hand. "For now, we only have one thing to do." He looked up at me, his eyes full of wonder. "It's time for us to go hunt some dinosaurs, kid."

THIRTY-SEVEN

Everyone at Blakely probably thought I was dying. I must have called out sick a dozen times that fall. It's hard to explain. I knew I *needed* to work. It's not like Andrew and I had duffel bags stuffed with money hidden around the house like mobsters. Still, the more I thought about my life and my lists, the more I realized I needed to be selfish with my time.

October. Another weekday spent with a made-up stomach flu. Tommy and Andrew were off at school and work. I spent the morning reading poetry in bed. For hours, I studied those old lines of verse like a bread-crumb trail that could lead me back to my former path in life. In a way, they did. Each stanza felt like a flashback, like those words could help me to piece myself back together and make me feel whole again.

I picked up my phone and called Marian. We hadn't spoken in days. I wanted to read her some of our old favorite stanzas, to reminisce. Finally, after a million rings, she picked up. "Do you remember that poem we loved in college?" I said as soon as the line came to life. "The one with those final lines about the mermaids that we felt like never really made much sense?"

Marian laughed before she spoke. "The one where everyone was drowning?"

"Exactly." I wanted to keep talking about the poem, but instead I set the book aside. "Where have you been? I've been trying to get in touch with you."

"Sorry." From somewhere behind Marian, I heard a group of women politely giggle at something I'd never see. "I've just been busy," she explained.

"Where are you?" I asked, and I tried to listen to the distant laughter for further clues.

"You wouldn't believe me even if I told you."

"Try me," I said, intrigued, assuming she was on assignment at some new bakery or bar.

"I'm in one of those baby boutiques near my apartment," she said, surprising me.

"A baby boutique?" I couldn't help it. I laughed at the thought of Marian browsing displays of tiny pastel rompers and layette sets. "Why? Are you lost?"

"I don't know," she said. "I was just thinking, I guess."

"About babies?" I puffed out my lips, tried to make sense of her comment.

"Partially," she explained as the laughter behind her died down. "I guess I was more just thinking about life. My life, specifically."

I glanced at my wrist and my old, scratched-up watch, knowing I needed to leave soon. "But why babies?" I pressed the phone against my shoulder while I searched for my shoes.

"It's silly." Above her, the shop bell chimed as she exited the store. "I was just reading this thing the other day."

"About what?" I asked as I dog-eared a page.

She paused. "About the idea of legacy."

After we hung up, I ventured outside and up our block, to a porch I'd never set foot on before. I knocked on the door.

"Olivia?" Annie stood in the doorframe, holding Jack back with her knee. "Hi." She cocked her head, taking in my hair. "That's quite a . . . statement."

"I know this is a bit late, but I brought you something," I said, disregarding her comment, and pulled a folded piece of paper from my pocket. "You were right. I don't know much about plants," I admitted. "But I do know a lot about this." I handed her the creased sheet, on which I'd written the lines from a poem I'd rediscovered that morning in my old anthology. "It's about flowers," I explained. "But it's really about life." I tucked my hands into my pockets. "I can tell you more about it sometime, if you'd like."

Annie accepted the paper, let her eyes skim the lines. She looked up. "Thank you, Olivia. It's been a long time since I've read something like this."

"Good." I took a step back, ready to turn and go. "I'm happy you like it." I moved down her walkway. "Thanks again for the flowers."

Annie pet Jack's head. "You're welcome to cut more for yourself anytime." She reached for the wall beside her, clipped a leash to Jack's collar. "You know, I was wrong about you, Olivia." I pivoted back toward her. "When you and your husband first moved here," she explained. "I'm not sure I got the best read on you back then." She stopped herself, perhaps to gauge if she should continue. "You seemed a bit unsure of yourself. Like maybe you weren't certain if you wanted to be here."

I paused on her walkway, vibrant bushes of flowers blooming all around me. "And now?"

Annie closed the door as Jack dashed ahead of her. "You seem more at home."

Back inside, I dug in my purse for some loose bills. I sat at the island, a feeling of satisfaction pulsing through me, and reached for my old curse jar. I dropped one bill inside it for every small step toward change that I'd taken in recent weeks, and then headed back out the door.

Later that morning, I finally found myself standing outside the local yoga studio, which Sunshine had invited me to visit weeks earlier. For the first time ever, I stepped inside. I'm not sure what I'd expected. When I entered, I was greeted by a dozen women's rear ends jutting high in the air, like acute triangles made of flesh. I tiptoed across the wood floor and found a vacant spot behind a woman I vaguely recognized from around town, her huge, glorious derriere just inches from my face. I didn't know what to do. Do you start a conversation with someone when they're in a position like that? I unrolled my rented mat, slid into a cross-legged position, and closed my eyes, hoping I looked like I belonged there.

"Hello, yogis." I opened my eyes and saw Sunshine at the front of the room. She nodded her recognition at me and motioned to my hot-pink head. She smiled. "Let's begin."

I could barely see what I was doing. The lights were dimmed so low that I began to wonder if there'd been a power outage. I just kept moving my body up and down and folding it like origami in the hopes that something significant might happen.

At the end of class, once we were done twisting ourselves like pretzels, Sunshine instructed everyone to lie on their backs and close their eyes. Quiet music played in the background. The room filled with the scent of lavender. It was the modern woman's version of nap time. The music clicked off. I had no clue how much time had passed. I just lay there, my eyes closed, and listened to the sound of muted movements around the room.

"You're not like the other moms in this town, huh?"

I opened my eyes and saw Sunshine standing above me. Before I spoke, I paused long enough to notice the calm, even feeling of my breath. "Hi," I said, feeling delirious.

"I like the new do." Waves of Sunshine's hair fell toward me like the tendrils on a jellyfish. "It's different."

"Thanks." I sat up and rubbed my eyes. I hadn't realized until that moment that I'd been crying. I blinked and looked at my wet fingers, confused. "It's just something I'm trying out."

Sunshine offered me a rag to wipe down my mat. "So, what made you finally come?"

"Um." I wiped the rest of the wetness from my eyes, hoping it just looked like sweat, and tried to determine the source of all those tears, if they had welled up from a happy or a sad place. Either way, I felt a sense of release as I dabbed them away. Whatever their root, it felt like they'd been trapped inside me for a long time. "I've been trying to cross items off my life to-do list, I guess."

Sunshine nodded, then moved across the room and stubbed out a stick of incense. "I can relate to that."

"Plus, the little nap-time bit at the end was a big sell," I said, hoping my joke would distract from my obvious emotions.

"Ahh, the Savasana." She winked playfully. "That's our little yogic secret."

I dropped my used rag into a basket. "Well, thanks," I said. "I'm glad I came."

"Me too." Sunshine rolled up some mats. "You should come again."

"Okay." I placed my mat into a plastic crate and moved toward the door. "So, any other big, juicy yogic secrets?"

Sunshine's face filled with warmth, like a sunrise. "You're not the first person to cry on one of those mats." Her bare feet made a faint squeaking sound as she moved across the wood floors. "And, based on my experiences, I suspect you won't be the last."

THIRTY-EIGHT

"We're going out."

I'd been seated at our island, a stack of torn-open mail in front of me, when Andrew walked into the kitchen earlier than normal, surprising me. I pushed one of the envelopes to the side and raised my brows in inquisitive curves, like someone had sketched mirror images of the Arc de Triomphe across my forehead. "Oh yeah?"

He dropped his messenger bag on the floor, unfastened the top buttons on his shirt. "Go get dressed," he instructed me, his voice laced with an urgency I hadn't heard in ages. "The babysitter will be here in an hour." He reached into the fridge and pulled out a can of beer, like a clichéd sitcom dad. "I promised to pay her extra if she'd stay past sunset."

A little while later, we found ourselves on the local commuter train. It was the first time in years that we'd traveled that path together. I noticed we both kept drumming our fingers across our thighs. "Did something happen at work today?" I clutched my bag against my hip, the one that contained the envelope I'd waited all day to share with him. "You seem . . . tense."

Andrew turned toward the window. I followed his gaze and observed our reflection—Andrew in his grown-up button-down, me with my candy-colored head and new black blouse. "It was nothing," he explained as he continued to stare through the window. The train lights flickered. In seconds, we disappeared into a tunnel and raced beneath the river. When the train emerged, a forest of silver skyscrapers surrounded us. Andrew turned to me. "You look great, by the way."

We arrived at street level. I held up my arm to hail a cab. Andrew pulled it down and took my hand. "Let's walk instead," he suggested.

Together, we navigated all those once-familiar city blocks. There was that old café we loved to frequent on Sunday mornings. There was that tucked-away park, where we'd set up a blanket and blow off classes. There was that liquor store. Our favorite record shop. It was all still there: our past life.

We stopped. Andrew smiled at the nondescript brick building before us. The memory arrived to me slow, and then fast. "I figured after that last dining disaster," Andrew said as he pulled open the wooden door, "this was the least I could do." Together, we stood in the door-way, expecting one thing but discovering something else. We tilted our heads. "Shit," he finally said.

Instead of a cramped dining room, we found bare concrete. A man appeared from the narrow back hallway, a measuring tape in his hands. "You two need something?"

"Wait." Andrew kept blinking. "Didn't this used to be—"

"That old Italian place?" the man interrupted. "Yeah, what a gem." He pressed his measuring tape against a wall. "Closed up a few months ago. It's a shame. They're putting one of those quick-service salad joints in here next spring."

Andrew and I moved back up the block in silence. "I'm sorry," he finally said. "I should have called." He shook his head at himself. "I was trying to be spontaneous."

We kept walking, the autumn air crisp against our skin. "You miss this part of our lives, too, don't you?" I asked.

Andrew shrugged. "It's hard to explain." He shook his head, as though he was trying to release some memory from his thoughts. "Come on. There's that old burger place up the—"

"Wait." I pressed my bag against my hip, turned in the opposite direction. "I have an idea." Andrew spun around, too. I grabbed his hand. "Come on."

From the outside, it looked exactly the same: black brick exterior walls painted with a white alphabet pattern, an oversize black flag printed with the letters ABC mounted above the doorway, like a confused preschool. "So?" I turned to Andrew. "Want to go in?"

Nothing had changed. Hot-pink walls graffitied with drunken scribbles. A long, black bar. A giant disco ball at the center of the ceiling. The only thing that had changed was us.

"Christ." Andrew paused in the entryway and rubbed his temples. It looked like he'd seen a ghost. A few twentysomethings sat at the bar, sipping cocktails. Outside, it was still daylight. "I guess we should get a drink, huh?"

"Yeah," I agreed and then glanced around at all those bowls full of pens that still lined the tables. "Or, like, three."

We slipped into the same sticky vinyl banquette where we once always sat. Our server, an attractive blonde who couldn't have been a day past twenty-three, approached us. "Two beers," Andrew said. The girl looked at him blankly, waiting for more direction. Andrew pressed his hands to his forehead. "Literally anything," he offered as clarification. "And two shots," he added. "Of something—anything—strong."

An hour later, we were drunk, the tabletop littered with empty bottles and shot glasses. "I do miss it," Andrew finally said while he doodled some silly sketch—three stick figures and a happy dinosaur, like the kind he always drew for Tommy—on the tabletop. He put down his pen and looked up at me. All around us, the music had become louder. There wasn't an empty seat left in the place. Andrew swigged his beer. "The feeling of it, at least."

"I get it," I said and then reached for my bag. From inside it, I pulled out the sliced-open envelope I'd carried around for hours. "I've sort of been thinking that same thing all day." I slid the envelope across the table and watched as Andrew pulled out the letter I'd first read hours earlier. "It's an old poem," I clarified. "One I wrote in my early twenties. I actually think I wrote the opening lines when we were seated in this exact spot." I shrugged. "Either way, they're publishing it this spring."

Andrew set down the letter, looked up at me. "This is huge, Liv." He squeezed my hand. "This is a good literary magazine."

I bit my lip. I'd waited so long to receive an acceptance letter again, to feel like I was back on that path. "Is it weird that I'm publishing something I wrote so long ago?" Across the bar, more patrons filtered in. "I feel like I'm cheating, holding on to my past voice."

"What's wrong?" Andrew narrowed his eyes. "Aren't you excited?"

"I am," I said, though my tone wasn't convincing. "I don't know." I bit my fingernail. "I just thought I'd feel . . . different or something."

Andrew stood and took my hand. "Don't overthink it." He guided us away from our banquette. "For now, let's just celebrate."

And so that's what we did. For the rest of the night, I let my thoughts temporarily melt away and allowed myself to feel as carefree as I had been the last time I'd twirled across that same sticky bar floor. We danced and laughed and drank like we were twenty-five again. Lights flashed around us. That old disco ball glittered above our sweating heads. I closed my eyes and listened to the sounds of my former life. I threw my arms above my head and let the music guide me, my body pulsing with a sense of freedom I hadn't felt in decades.

"Do you know that girl?" Andrew shouted through the music. I opened my eyes. Everything was a touch blurry, like the whole world had been smudged with an eraser. Andrew lifted his arm and pointed to some twentysomething at the bar. "She keeps looking at you."

I squinted, trying to make her out. The lights kept flashing, making it impossible to see her clearly. Finally, my vision adjusted. Everything started to slow down. Her face, which had previously been a blur, began to take shape, like one of those Magic Eye pictures I loved as a kid. *Poppy.* Our eyes met. Instantly, I shoved through the crowd, my celebratory mood extinguished. Andrew trailed behind me. I tried to keep focused on her, but I could barely see straight. By the time I reached the bar, I was sweating. "Where did she go?" I pushed past strangers, but she was nowhere. I wondered if I'd imagined her. "She was just here."

"Who was that?" Andrew asked as he wiped his forehead.

I stopped and looked out at the dance floor. Suddenly, the same scene that had felt fun and exciting moments earlier looked sad. I set my bottle on the bar, feeling out of place. "No one."

Outside, the autumn air had become frigid. Andrew and I stumbled through our old neighborhood, eating pizza on greasy paper plates. We stopped on a street corner. "What do you miss the most?" Andrew tossed his plate in a sticker-marked garbage can. "About being here. About this whole part of our lives."

I looked around us. The glittering yet grimy buildings. The pockets of privacy and the perpetual noise. The whole city was just an experiment in contrast. Young and old. Rich and poor. Dreams and failures. Life and death. "The energy." I tossed my paper plate; my previous, celebratory mood had deflated the moment I saw Poppy across the bar, all my earlier elation transformed into a pattern of question marks in my head. "The feeling that everything in my life was just getting started, that anything was possible."

Once, when I was a teenager, I wandered downstairs late one night after I couldn't sleep. I had assumed my parents were in bed, that I'd be greeted by a dark, quiet kitchen. When I reached the bottom of the stairs, I heard music. All the lights were turned on. In the kitchen, my parents were dancing. "What are you guys doing?" I said, partially disgusted by their display of affection, and poured myself juice. "Why are you still awake?"

They stopped, both of them laughing. "You know we have a whole life we keep just for ourselves after you go to sleep," my mother said and then gestured for me to sit at the table. She pulled some crackers down from the cabinet.

"I used to take your mother out dancing every Saturday night," my father chimed in. He turned down the music. He looked at my mother, some secret unfolding between them. "Remember when we thought we'd open that little music lounge?" He turned back to me. "We went to look at the space and everything."

"So, what happened?" I asked while nibbling my cracker.

My parents glanced at each other. "We had you," my mother said through a quiet smile. "Life changed."

Andrew wrapped his arm around my waist. We walked a few more blocks before it occurred to either of us what street we were on. "Wait." Andrew pointed to a building beside us. "Isn't that Marian's apartment?"

We looked up at her darkened windows. Marian and I had only talked in brief, intermittent spurts in recent weeks. Lately, no matter when I reached out, it seemed she was too busy for my calls. I picked some rocks up off the street and pelted them at the glass, expecting her to magically appear there like when we were young. "Where in the hell has she been?" I mumbled and then launched another stone. It slipped from my fingers too fast and ricocheted off a terra-cotta planter on her fire escape, sending it on a free fall before it exploded against the concrete. "Don't tell her I did that."

Andrew slipped his fingers through mine. Together, we made our way toward the train. We didn't talk about that night again. Instead, like so many moments that had come before it, we just let it slip away into our collective past.

THIRTY-NINE

A few days later, we waited in line for baked goods at the farmers' market, the air marked by a prewinter chill. I wandered a few feet behind Andrew and Tommy. Ever since I'd received that letter, I'd been in a daze. Something deep inside me that I'd hoped would feel fulfilled upon receipt of it still felt empty for reasons I didn't understand. Andrew and Tommy stopped. We each grabbed our cellophane-wrapped baked goods and then browsed the stands and took in the late-autumnal produce— dirt-covered beets and purple globes of cabbage, earthy pints of mushrooms and bins of slightly bruised pears. That's when I spotted Sunshine. She looked up at me from her pumpkin display and waved.

"Do you still have paper fruit?" Tommy asked right away, his mouth coated in sugar.

"Sorry." Sunshine reached under the table, set a box before him. "But I do have these."

Tommy dipped his hand into the box and pulled out several seed packets. Before I could object, I heard a familiar voice call out my name.

"Liv!"

I swiveled my head just in time to see Courtney and Allison rushing toward me, their arms flocked with woven bags of leafy greens. I swallowed the urge to mumble something inappropriate under my breath. Instead, I lifted my arm and waved.

"Seems right on time." Sunshine smirked and tended to some squash. "You sure they don't have a tracking device on you?"

"I haven't entirely ruled out that possibility," I said, and I smiled as they moved closer.

"Ahhh-mazing!" Courtney applauded as she approached me. "Suze gave us the scoop!"

Allison swooped in and kissed my cheek, her tote bag smacking my side. "I mean, way to embrace the *cause*, Liv!" She gestured to my rose-colored head.

"The *cause*?" I asked.

Courtney and Allison exchanged a glance. "Breast cancer awareness!" they announced and then laughed. "Jinx!"

"Oh boy." Andrew grabbed Tommy's hand. "Let's go take a lap, kiddo."

"You *did* get my messages about the fundraiser I'm organizing." Courtney tilted her face. "Right?" She gestured to my head. "I mean, you—"

"The fundraiser," I repeated, and I made a mental note to start taking my inbox more seriously. "Yes!" I punched my fist into the air. "Exactly."

"Well, I'm happy we're all so enthusiastic about this." Courtney leaned in closer. "You know, thanks to old Father Time, we're all at an increased risk." She kissed my cheek. "We're still on for your little soiree?" I nodded. "Good. I'll see you soon."

Courtney and Allison walked away. Sunshine approached me, her demeanor quieter than it had been moments earlier. Without a word, she pulled up the sleeve of her flannel and showed me the small pink ribbon tattooed on her wrist. "I don't know if that's why you did it, but if it is, it's worth mentioning that I've been in remission for three years."

Her words practically stabbed me. "Oh God," I said, like a fool. "I'm so—"

"It's fine." She rolled up her other shirtsleeve. "I kind of threw that on you." There, on the opposite arm, I saw her umbilical cord tattoo once again. "It's why my daughter and I got these a few years back," she said as she pointed at it. "Things were touch and go for a bit."

I felt like someone had knocked the air out of me. "Are you . . . okay now?"

Sunshine smiled, several age spots lifting toward her eyes. "That's what they tell me." She dug her hands into a basket of greens. "I have a follow-up appointment in a few months. In the meantime, I run a weekly support group for other women at the studio." She smiled. "It's not much, but it helps."

I didn't talk the whole ride home. I just kept thinking about Sunshine.

Andrew pulled the car into our driveway. We gathered our bags.

"What's that?" Tommy pointed to a large envelope on our porch. Andrew and I shrugged. "Maybe it's for me!" Tommy raced toward the house, skidding past several dinosaur toys that still peered through our bushes from weeks ago. He shook the envelope beside his ear. "It sounds like paper!"

Andrew squinted, then turned back to me. "Are you expecting anything?"

I shook my head. "Not that I can—"

"What's 'nettle' mean?" Tommy shouted.

My heart dropped like a cinder block. My tote fell from my grip. I raced toward Tommy and took the envelope from him. "That's for me." I shot into the house and ran upstairs to our bedroom like a fiery adolescent. Once alone, I ripped open the envelope and pulled out a stack of papers, the Nettle Center's clean, modern logo printed just inches from my name.

"What are you doing?" Andrew appeared in our bedroom doorway.

I stopped and looked up at him. "I'm not sure," I admitted. I didn't know what I'd find within those pages. An autopsy report for my future death? A minute-by-minute playbook of how my life might end? "Here." I handed the papers to Andrew. "I changed my mind. I don't think I want to go through these."

Andrew stepped back, assessing me. "But isn't this what you wanted? To have confirmation about that test?"

I felt my heart rate settle. "I did." I closed my eyes, invited a long, deep breath inside me. I opened them, glanced at my nightstand and the other envelope I'd recently received. "But I don't think that's what I want anymore."

Ever since my most recent trip to the Nettle Center, something had started to change in me. It was a quiet shift, more a whisper than a shout. But I heard it. In the days that led up to that visit, I had started to think about death. My death, specifically. What it might mean if it really was only a few months away. That's when something strange had started to happen. Some of the fear had started to dissipate. In its place, I was slowly beginning to find my life.

Andrew sat beside me. He tucked a strand of pink hair behind my ear. "Are you sure?" I nodded. He flipped the stack of papers over in his hand. "So, what should I do with all this?"

A clatter rang out. "I need help cleaning up my LEGOs!" Tommy shouted.

"Get rid of them," I instructed Andrew. I stood and moved toward the doorway to go help Tommy. For once, I was too busy trying to live.

FORTY

Liv!"

I'd been crouched beside our porch, tucking more of Tommy's dinosaurs into our shrubs, when I heard a pair of familiar voices. I pulled myself from the branches, a plastic Branchiosaurus tangled in my hair. Courtney and Allison glided up our driveway, platters balanced in their hands.

"Are we early?" Allison looked at me from beneath her wide sunglasses. The hem of her quilted autumn coat caught the breeze. "Suze said we should come around—"

"Oh." I adjusted a palm-size velociraptor, glanced at my watch. "I didn't realize the time."

Courtney tilted her head. "Are you sure this is okay?" She looked me over, perhaps expecting me to cancel on the spot, to offer some excuse. "I know you've never hosted."

For a minute, we all just looked at each other. Finally, I stood to meet them, smoothed the front of the new blouse that I'd picked up for the evening, and tucked strands of my pink hair behind my ears. "It's fine," I assured them. "I just had to finish something for Tommy." Up the block, a half dozen other neighborhood women, all holding their own platters, marched toward our house, like members of some unannounced parade. "You can go ahead inside." In the distance, I saw Annie and Jack out for their afternoon walk. I waved them down, knowing there was one more thing I wanted to do. "I'll be right in."

A few minutes later, I stepped into my kitchen. Half the neighborhood sat around my island, which had become a mosaic of platters. I dropped a large bunch of Annie's freshly clipped flowers in my vase and set it in the center. Everyone looked up at me, suddenly unsure what to do, like we'd all stepped into the twilight zone or something. That's when I realized they were waiting for direction from me.

"Maybe we should eat?" Suzanne suggested and then pulled back a sheet of cellophane.

"Yes," I agreed as I followed her lead. From across the island, I smiled my appreciation at her before I unwrapped several platters. *Thank you,* I mouthed. She smiled, too, and offered me a friendly wink as, all around us, everyone fell into a pattern of familiarity.

Once the group felt comfortable, I disappeared upstairs and sat on the edge of my bed. Below me, the floorboards hummed with noise. It was the first time in all the years Andrew and I had lived there that our house was full with people other than our small family. For a while, I just sat and listened to it: the sounds of life echoing through our rafters. I grabbed my phone and texted Marian. In case you were wondering, the whole neighborhood is currently in my kitchen. How's that for living? I waited for her response, but it never arrived. From downstairs, I heard an eruption of laughter. I tossed the phone on the bed. I couldn't wait forever. There was another burst of excitement. I lifted a box from the floor, the one I'd assembled that morning, and headed for the stairs. I didn't want to miss whatever was happening.

Back in the kitchen, I set down the box and took a seat. The room buzzed with chatter. "So, what'd I miss?" I asked. For the first time ever, I leaned in.

A little while later, once the conversation had died down, Courtney scooted to the edge of her seat and glanced at the box I'd carried down earlier. She rested her chin in her hand. "So, do we get to see what you're selling?"

"Oh, right." I'd been so caught up in conversation that I'd nearly forgotten. I pulled the box onto my lap, then dropped an armful of metallic tincture packets across the island. "Have at them, ladies," I said.

"Are they antiaging supplements?" Allison asked, already intrigued.

"In a way," I said as I began to pour water into all my wineglasses. I ripped open a packet and dumped it into Allison's drink, then watched her take a miniscule sip.

"It's . . . interesting." She visibly winced, nibbled a cracker. "But if it will help to diminish my new set of unwelcome smile lines, well, I guess I'm in."

I sat back as the whole neighborhood sipped those tinctures, like I'd offered them the powdered version of the fountain of youth. Who knew? Maybe I had.

Courtney polished off her glass. "I know about this company," she said, always the expert.

I lifted my brows. "You do?"

Courtney smiled. "They're one of those charitable businesses. For every packet they sell, they send a pair of shoes to some third world country. Isn't that right, Liv?"

I mean, what was I supposed to say? "Yes," I said, even though it wasn't true. "That's definitely them."

Courtney reached for her wallet. "Perfect." She dropped some wrinkled bills inside my old curse jar, the one I'd recently begun to refill with all the small ways I'd tried to move forward in my life. "I'll take a dozen." I looked at her and wondered if she'd recently suffered a head injury. "I mean, if it's for charity," she said as she glanced around the island.

"Oh, um, you don't have to pay me for them," I said, and I pulled Courtney's money from the jar. "They were, well . . ." How to explain it? "They were given to me. They were free."

Courtney shooed me away and stuffed the bills back inside the glass. "Don't be silly, Liv," she told me and then snapped her wallet shut.

I looked up. "What do you mean?"

"No matter how one tries to sell it, there's always some fine print somewhere. I'm sure you paid *something* for them."

"Maybe," I said. "To a certain degree."

"That's what I thought." She took the last sip of her tincture, set down her empty glass. "After all, *nothing* in life is free."

FORTY-ONE

A few days later, I woke to the sound of something smashing against our bedroom window. I pulled down the blanket, shuffled across our room, and wiped the condensation from the glass. Our neighborhood looked like a doily, the whole world coated in a thin quilt of white.

"Did it snow?" I shouted once I'd forced the window open. I couldn't help it. People, by nature, love to ask the most painfully obvious things.

Tommy and Andrew, dressed only in their pajamas, ran across our driveway, smacking each other in the backs with snowballs. "Nope!" Andrew yelled and then pelted our window again, a little snowstorm exploding just inches from my face. "This is all just an elaborate movie set."

"But how?" I yelled, like a fool. "Isn't it too early for that?"

"It's magic, Mama!" Tommy shouted, his hair dusted with snowflakes. "Come play!"

It was the end of the term at Blakely, and my desk was a mess of papers. "I should get dressed." Behind me, my phone buzzed. I pressed it against my ear. It was a voice mail from Dr. Greene's office, letting me know my thyroid results were benign. I didn't overthink it. I grabbed an old NYU hoodie and glanced at my watch. I knew I'd be late for some meeting or a colleague's list of questions. But I also knew I couldn't wait. "I'll be right there!"

My phone buzzed again. It was a message from Marian. Sorry I've been out of touch. I've had a lot going on. I need to talk to you. Can you call me? I paused, about to dial her back. However, knowing Marian, I assumed she just needed to talk to me about some amazing new recipe. *Later,* I thought. Through the window, Andrew and Tommy called out for me. I threw my phone on the bed.

FORTY-TWO

By the time I arrived at Blakely later that morning, classes were already in session. I sneaked through a side door like a sleuth and made my way toward the English Department office.

"Good morning, Olivia." *Busted.* Christopher was seated at his desk, a smug expression settling on his face. "Trouble navigating the snowy roads?"

I settled myself at my desk. "Yes," I lied. "They're pretty slick." I shook my head and reminded myself that I had nothing to hide. "Plus, I don't have anything important scheduled until later this morning, so I decided to play in the snow with my son."

Christopher eyed me over the top of his computer screen. "I see we're still enjoying our interlude with blush locks." He loved to do that—use "we" when he actually meant "you."

"It's for breast cancer awareness," I said, as though to confirm the fact that my midlife crisis was actually a charitable deed. I grabbed my red felt-tipped pen, ready to work. I couldn't get settled. The energy wasn't right. I rummaged through my belongings, wondering if I'd misplaced something.

"Looking for something?" Christopher clacked away on his keyboard, like he was sending out a message in Morse code. "Your calendar, perhaps?"

That's when I remembered. "We were supposed to meet a while back to talk about your book list again, weren't we?"

Christopher looked up. "Oh, that?" *Clack. Clack.* "It's nothing." He smacked his laptop shut and gathered his things. "Good luck to you, Olivia."

"Good luck?" I scrunched up my face. "What do you mean?"

"Did I say good luck?" Christopher laughed. "I'm sorry." He adjusted his bow tie. "What I'd meant to say was goodbye," he said and then left the room.

Once Christopher was gone, I peered through my office window. The whole campus was dusted with white, like a decadent pastry. A group of students ran across the green, their faces wide with laughter.

"Do you have a minute?"

I swiveled my desk chair and saw Geoffrey, Blakely's longtime headmaster, in the doorframe. Geoffrey was the sort of man who made a navy-blue blazer seem casual. "Of course." I turned back toward my desk and glanced at my teaching schedule. "I'm free during—"

"I was thinking now," Geoffrey said.

"Now?"

"Right now," he confirmed.

I glanced over at Christopher's empty desk chair. *Good luck to you, Olivia.* "Sure." I closed the window and followed him into the hall.

Geoffrey sat in a leather wingback chair in his vast office. "Your hair is pink." He leaned back and crossed one khaki-clad leg over the other. "I suppose you know that it falls out of line with the dress code outlined in the faculty handbook."

My palms were slick with sweat. "It's for Breast Cancer Awareness Month," I said.

Geoffrey nodded. "Wasn't that last month?"

I readjusted myself in the buttery leather chair. Nearby, an ornate gold clock ticked on an expensive-looking bookcase. "I'm not sure, actually."

"So, we have a minor issue." Geoffrey reached toward his desk and handed me a familiar paperback. *A Room of One's Own.* "We've received some . . . complaints."

I took the book and examined it, as though it were a hologram. "Is this a joke?"

Geoffrey took the book back from me. "It's not, unfortunately."

"Look, if Christopher is *that* set on not teaching it—"

"There's more." Geoffrey produced a manila folder, just like the one that had instigated so much trouble at the Nettle Center. He tapped it. "Quite a bit more, in fact."

For the next half hour, I listened as Geoffrey read off dozens of complaints Christopher had filed against me. *Perpetual lateness. Excessive absences. Obscene language. Breach of dress code. Questionable taste in literature. Ageism.* He set down the folder. "I can overlook most of this. However, in today's climate, I can't brush something potentially discriminatory like ageism under the rug."

"That's absurd. I wasn't being an ageist." Nearby, the clock continued to tick. *Click. Click.* "I was trying to help him, to offer him advice and guide him on his path."

"Unfortunately, Christopher didn't see things that way." Geoffrey sighed. "The administration would like to use this as an opportunity to reflect on ageism as a community. We'd like you to craft a statement and present it at our next school-wide meeting."

"What? I'm not going to pretend I acted discriminatorily. Christopher just wants to have an opinion and be the smartest person in the room, even though he's a kid."

Geoffrey bit his lip. "Comments like that aren't really supporting your case."

I don't know why I stayed at Blakely so long. For ages, I thought it was because it gave me the chance to consider good writing every day, to keep myself at least somewhat submerged in that world, to find inspiration for my own work. But I'd held on to my passion too tightly, desperate not to let it float away. What I'd done was suffocate it instead.

"I don't want to do this," I said.

I'd always told myself I'd leave one day. It was always one day, meaning some other day, meaning not the current day or the one after that. But here's the sneaky thing about life: all those one days compile pretty fast. I looked around. My gaze stopped on that ticking clock. *Click. Click.*

Geoffrey audibly sighed. "If you're that opposed to making a public statement—"

"I don't mean the statement. I mean *this*." I gestured at his office. "Let Christopher be the chair. Honestly, I think at this point in his life, he's a lot more passionate about it than me."

Overhead, the bell rang. "Olivia, what are you saying?"

"I think I quit," I announced. "I just don't think my heart is in this anymore."

Geoffrey was taken aback. "Surely you don't mean that."

I peered through the window and thought of the students I'd seen earlier. I wanted to be on the other side of that window, too. I glanced at that manila folder. "I do," I said.

The night of the last poetry party I'd ever attended in college, we had ended up back at Marian's apartment, drunk on champagne and our youth. Andrew had passed out on Marian's couch. Marian and I, left to our own devices, crawled onto her fire escape. We drank cheap wine from paper cups and looked out at the city—*our* city, as it'd become over the years. A million windows glowed, like constellations, and lit up the night. The mix of traffic and voices filled the air like a song. It felt like the whole big, beautiful world existed right there below us.

I had taken my last sip of wine, a big drunken smile spreading across my face.

"What is it?" Marian had asked before pouring herself more to drink.

"Nothing," I said and then shook my head. "It's silly."

Without asking, Marian refilled my cup with the burgundy liquid. "Tell me."

I bit my bottom lip. "I just never knew that I could be this happy. That life could actually feel like this." I peeked through the window at Andrew, asleep with his shoes still on. "Just promise me that if I ever get old and boring—that if I ever get off track from this path—you'll help me find my way back." I looked out at the nightscape around me. "No matter the cost."

Marian balanced her cup between her knees. A few splashes splattered the metal grating. She held up her pinkie and locked it with mine. "You have my word."

I blinked the memory away, finally realizing something about that night: it wasn't the poetry or the publication or the publicity that had made me feel so illuminated. It was the inescapable feeling that I was present, that I was living, that I was *alive*.

Only a few months after that night on Marian's fire escape, my agent and I parted ways, my dream over before it'd even had a real chance to begin. That's when my reliance on my lists had started—my quest for what I believed would be my perfect life. But they hadn't ever provided that for me. Instead, they'd made me feel perpetually tired and rushed—not because I was busier than anyone else, but because I was constantly seeking out a better, more elevated version of myself, like I could run and catch up with my past identity, even though it was already behind me.

"So, you're going to just *go*? And do *what*?" Geoffrey fussed with his leather watch strap. "I thought poetry was your passion, Olivia. I thought you lived and breathed literature."

"I did," I explained to Geoffrey and then exhaled years' worth of pent-up tension and grief. "A long time ago." A weight lifted from my body. "But I'm not that person anymore. I don't want to teach other people's voices. I want to try to find my own." Outside, the snow was coming down harder. I moved toward the doorway, then turned back. "When you see Christopher, tell him I said good luck."

I stood at the door and listened to that crowded hallway. I second-guessed myself for only a minute. *It's now or never, Liv,* I said over and over to myself, just like when I tried to write poetry in my head. Only, what I was writing at that moment wasn't poetry. It was something else. Something better, maybe. Something I couldn't yet define.

I opened the door. "Goodbye, Geoffrey." I stepped forward. It felt like the whole world waited for me on the other side.

FORTY-THREE

When I got inside my car, I let out the world's loudest, most glorious scream. I felt reborn, reinvigorated, revitalized. I buzzed down the car windows and turned the radio up. For the first time in as long as I could remember, I felt alive.

On the drive home, I stopped and picked up supplies. I wanted the whole world to feel like a celebration. I tied balloons to the porch. I taped streamers across the living room. I hung a construction paper garland from the kitchen wall. HAPPY MONDAY FUN-DAY, it read. What can I say? I quit my job and instantly became a comedian.

"Balloons!" Tommy squealed when he stepped off the bus. He ran to meet me on the porch, his giant book bag slapping his back. "Is it someone's birthday, Mama?"

I kissed his head, which was covered in a knitted winter hat. "In a way." I pulled him in for a squeeze. "Let's have fun together today, okay, kiddo?" I rested my hands on his shoulders. "Tell me something extra special you want to do. No rules. Just me and you."

Tommy squinted, assessing me. "Anything?"

"Anything." I nodded. "It's your pick."

"Okay," he said, thinking. "I want ice cream for my snack," he said, a clear test.

I didn't say a word. I just guided him into the kitchen, swung open the freezer, and pulled out a pint. "Deal." I handed him a spoon. "What else?"

Tommy dug his utensil into the container. "I want to play in the snow in my underpants!"

"Really?" What can I say? The kid knew how to live. "Okay. But only for a few minutes. And only in the backyard. I don't want the neighbors to call the authorities." I licked his spoon. "What's next?"

Tommy quickly looked around for inspiration. "And I want to plant those!" He pointed to the seed packets we'd received weeks earlier from Sunshine, which were still on the counter.

I pulled some used cans from the trash. "Voilà! Your own personal planters." I handed them over but quickly pulled back. "On second thought, maybe let's give them a quick wash." It's one thing to ask a woman to celebrate life. It's another to ask her to embrace botulism.

By the time Andrew walked into the kitchen hours later, every bowl we owned was covered with pancake batter and spread haphazardly across every surface in sight.

"Happy FUN-Day!" Tommy splattered batter across the floor. "Mama made a sign!"

Andrew set down his bag with a thump. "I don't get it." He sounded uncharacteristically drained. "Are we having a party?" He looked around the kitchen. "And pancakes?"

"Yes!" Tommy exclaimed. "With rainbow sprinkles!"

I looked at Andrew, his face an expression of exhaustion. "What's wrong?" I wiped my hands across my apron, like a TV housewife. "Not in the mood for a party?"

Andrew accepted a plate from Tommy. "I'm confused."

"Come on." I set my apron on the counter and guided everyone into the living room. "I'll explain more while we eat." We settled onto the couches. In the backdrop, Tommy's favorite cartoon blared from the television. "So, I have an announcement."

"Okay." Andrew narrowed his eyes. "Go on."

"I think I had an epiphany today."

"An epipha-who?" Tommy asked.

"A light bulb," I explained and then turned to Andrew. "For a long time, I thought I knew what I wanted out of life. I kept trying to force it."

"Okay," Andrew skeptically noted.

"I guess what I mean is that I don't have a clue what I want to do. I just know that I want to take some time to figure it out, to find my passion—my *voice*—again."

"Liv, I'm unclear what you're getting at here."

I swooped some sprinkles from my plate. "I made a big decision today."

Andrew picked up the remote and turned down the volume. "In terms of what?"

I inhaled and let the words fall freely from my lips. "I quit my job."

Andrew indulged in a fluffy bite. "Very funny."

Tommy reached over and stole some sprinkles from my plate. "What does 'quit' mean?"

I stroked Tommy's batter-coated hair. "It means Mama will have more time for fun."

Andrew nearly choked on a piece of pancake. "Liv, you're kidding." He forced down some water. "Right?"

"Um . . ." I set down my plate. "Yes?"

"Was that a 'yes' with a period or a 'yes' with a question mark?"

"Which one do you want it to be?"

"Liv—" Andrew's voice cracked. "Don't you think—" He tugged at his shirt collar like it was a noose. "Were you planning on telling me that was part of your plan?"

"Shhhhh." Tommy turned up the television. "I can't hear my show."

"Christ." Andrew kept pulling at his button-down. "Is it hot in here?"

"Andy," I said, growing defensive, "I told you I wanted to finally live my life and—"

"So, take a pottery class or something. You can't just quit your job. Especially without even consulting with me." He squeezed his temples. "Do you have something else lined up?"

"Well, I—" I stumbled over my words, the reality of my choice sinking in.

"We need money, Liv," he interjected.

I felt like a stabbed balloon; all the excitement rushed out of me. "I mean, maybe I—"

"Did it not occur to you that this was an incredibly selfish move?"

Tommy kept clicking up the television volume.

"How is trying to carve out time to find my passion selfish, Andy?" I begged.

"How?" Andrew stood abruptly and nearly knocked his plate off the coffee table. "Because it didn't even occur to you that your big heroic choice would have an undeniably negative impact on Tommy and me." Tommy, bored by our antics, grabbed some toys and moved into the next room. "You know, Liv, I don't even know what this is about anymore. For months, you've been having some kind of breakdown because you've suddenly become gobbled up by this realization that, eventually, this will all be over." He shook his head. "Well, welcome to the club. Because, guess what? That's a reality for every single person on this planet. Eventually, we're all going to drop like flies. Maybe today. Or next week. Or in a hundred years. No one knows, Liv! But in the meantime, people don't just quit their jobs and screw over their families because this universal truth finally just occurred to them."

My lip quivered. I didn't know what to say.

"I think I need a minute." Andrew took a step and half stumbled. "I'm going to go rinse off," he announced and then left the room.

It turned out a minute meant hours. After I put Tommy to bed, I cleaned up the batter and stepped onto the porch. I sat on the stone steps, beside Tommy's plastic dinosaurs, and slid out my old cigar box. I inhaled a cold, stale drag.

"I'm sorry about my reaction earlier." Andrew stepped onto the porch and sat beside me. Without asking, he reached into my cigar box and pressed a cigarette to his mouth.

"I haven't seen you smoke since we were in college," I said and then flicked a lighter.

He coughed so hard I thought he'd get sick. "Seems like a good day to start."

Along our street, the houses were a mosaic of darkened windows. "For the record, I didn't wake up this morning with this as my plan." I rested my head on my knees. "It wasn't premeditated. That's usually helpful information in the case of murder."

Through the darkness, I saw Andrew's shoulders slump. "They're cutting my column."

I sat up. "What are you talking about?"

"It's some funding issue." He let out a sad, quiet laugh. "I'm done in the spring."

"But you love that job," I said, feeling a sort of grief for him.

In the distance, a set of car tires crunched across ice. "I do?"

"What do you mean?" I turned to him. "Of course you do."

"I wrote about gingerbread festivals. Not exactly gonzo journalism."

"So, what does that mean?" I asked.

Andrew shrugged. "I don't know." He turned from me, stood up, and then stepped inside.

I picked up his cigarette butt and tucked it into my cigar box. Across the street, a lamppost flickered and died. I took it as a sign. I slid my cigar box back under a snowy bush and watched a plastic T. rex fall from the branches. I untied the rest of the balloons. "Some party," I mumbled to myself.

FORTY-FOUR

It's just not sustainable," Andrew told me a few weeks later, before he left for work. A detailed spreadsheet glowed on his computer screen. "Not for the long term, at least."

"So, what do I do? What do *we* do?"

Andrew rubbed his eyes with the heels of his palms. "Can you call Geoffrey?"

"Come on, Andy."

He sighed heavily. "Then you need to find something new." He gestured at our house. "Otherwise, *we* might need to find someplace new." He tossed up his hands. "But maybe that's what you want. It's no secret you've never loved it here."

"That's not—"

"It's true, Liv." He closed his computer as Tommy literally somer-saulted into the room.

I dropped my face into my hands. I felt like a fool. "What are we going to do, Andy?"

"I'm not sure." He slipped his arms through his jacket sleeves. "But we need to figure it out." He slid on his old baseball cap. "Because pretty soon, I'll be on the job hunt, too."

After Andrew and Tommy left for work and school, I headed back to the yoga studio. I don't know why. Following my conversation with

Andrew, I felt like I couldn't breathe. I opened the studio door and was confronted by a wave of heat. I stepped into the balmy room, expecting to find women's asses, all in salute. Instead, I discovered a circle of frail-looking women, their eyes all closed, their sallow cheeks marked by streaks of tears. I stepped back.

"Olivia?" Sunshine spotted me before I could leave. "What are you doing here?" She looked at me as though she was trying to gauge something. "The next yoga flow class doesn't start for another hour. This is our weekly support group."

I froze while a dozen different forms of death looked back at me. "I should g-go," I stammered. "I'm not supposed to be here."

"Now wait a minute." She paused, reconsidering. "That's not true." Sunshine motioned for me to join them. "We all need support for something, right?"

Against my better judgment, I joined them. Sunshine instructed the whole group—myself included—to lie on our backs and then told us how to breathe. *Inhale for the count of four. Hold. Exhale for the count of four. Hold.* Despite Sunshine's best efforts, my breath felt like broken glass. *Now visualize something you still want to do. Something that, despite your unique circumstances, you still have* time *to do.* I wanted to run, but my body felt too heavy for me to move. Sunshine tapped a gong. The echo of it drifted into my head and turned my thoughts into a sea of soft black waves. A boat appeared, and in it, a set of infant twins. I was suspended above them until suddenly I saw myself seated inside the boat, too. The twins were gone. I glanced into the dark water and discovered something else. A child. Tommy, I assumed, and I cradled him in my arms. But then I looked closer and realized it wasn't Tommy. The child was me.

Everyone opened their eyes and sat back up. I couldn't shake the image. It was the first time I realized the effect that loss could have on me. That the twins, just like so many of my other dreams, had died inside me.

"Why doesn't everyone take a moment to share their thoughts?" Sunshine suggested.

One by one, all those voices around me—the ones that definitively knew they would be gone from this earth in weeks or months—described the things they wanted most from their final days. Their answers were different and yet the same. They wanted time. To make good on old grudges. To relive their favorite days. To laugh. To love. Not one of them spoke about uprooting her whole life, of starting over or tearing down walls or chasing old professional ambitions or turning everything in her world on its head. Rather, every woman's dying wish was to simply spend her final days—however many of them she had left—being able to exist in the simple quietness of her life. To have more time to enjoy and appreciate the beauty in that. Andrew's words ebbed and flowed through me. He was right. I was acting selfishly. When it came to death, it seemed I was going about it all wrong.

"I want to see the ocean," one woman, who looked to be about my age, said when it was her turn. "I want to dip my toes in the waves once more with my husband and son." She stopped herself, focused on some private memory. "We kept saying we would take a trip." She looked at the floor. "But life happened, and we kept putting it off." She lifted her chin. "Then I got sick." She breathed heavily. "It was too late."

When the woman was done speaking, everyone parted ways. Quietly, the group gathered their belongings and began to exit the studio. Before I left, I approached Sunshine. "I'm sorry," I told her. She looked at me in confusion. "That you were sick. I wanted to say that when you told me everything that day at the market, but I didn't know how."

Sunshine's lips parted into a kind smile. "Thank you." She rolled up a mat.

"Can I ask you something?" Sunshine looked up at me. "Back when you were first diagnosed, did you sense that something might be . . . off?" Sunshine tilted her face. "I'm sorry," I muttered. "That was insensitive. I actually can't believe I just asked that question."

"Go ahead." Sunshine tucked the mat beneath her arm. "It's okay."

I inhaled a deep, yogic breath before I spoke again. "Did you have any sense of intuition that you might be sick?" I looked at the floor, embarrassed by my question. "I know it sounds strange, but I've always wondered if people have some kind of sixth sense about stuff like that. If they know something is about to go wrong."

Sunshine sighed. "It was like a freight train derailing," she said, her voice soft. "I didn't have a clue." I lifted my chin. "One day, I felt something, which I assumed was a nothing. A few weeks later, I learned that I was wrong." A look of concern spread over her face. "Is everything okay, Olivia?"

"I'm fine." I could tell she didn't believe me. "Really." Quietly, we drifted toward the studio's glass door. "So, any big takeaways, now that you've come out of things on the other side?"

Sunshine paused beside me. She dropped the mat into a woven basket and considered my question. "I'm happier now than I was before my diagnosis." I watched her lose herself in a thought. "I'm more aware of how good I have it." Her expression changed as she conjured some private memory. "I don't take normalcy for granted anymore," she explained. "As clichéd as it sounds, I take greater value in the simplicity of my daily routine."

I stood there for a beat too long, just considering her words.

"You're sure you're all right?" Sunshine asked.

I nodded. "I'm just working through some stuff."

She looked as if she wanted to question me about something. "Well, in that case, whatever it is you're working through, I hope it all turns out okay."

"Thanks," I said and then reached for the door. "Me too."

FORTY-FIVE

The next day, I ran for miles. My lungs felt frozen every time I inhaled an icy breath. I needed time alone to think. I knew Andrew was right. I had to find another job, not only for the money but for myself. I needed to understand who I was in that moment, not who I was according to some past list.

"Looking for a ride?"

I turned and discovered a familiar car had slowed down beside me. Andrew smiled, his hands casually draped over the steering wheel. I paused and looked around. I didn't even know what neighborhood I was in. "How did you find me?"

Andrew unclicked the door locks. "Lucky guess."

I slid inside and pressed my hands against the heating vents. My whole body felt frozen. "Wait." My fingers started to defrost. "Why are you here?" I felt my spine straighten. "Where is Tommy? Is everything okay?"

Andrew reached across the center console, squeezed my thigh. "Tommy's fine. He's with a friend," he informed me. "I just felt like I owed you a proper date." He smiled. "ABC Bar was fun. Or at least it was at a certain time." He shifted the car back into drive. "But I thought we might both be in need of something slightly more our current speed."

A minute later, Andrew turned the car down an unfamiliar dirt road at the end of an otherwise manicured neighborhood block. He kept navigating us farther until finally we drove past a small, unassuming sign that read SCENIC OVERLOOK. He pulled into an unkempt gravel lot. There wasn't another human in sight.

"Why are we stopped?" I asked. "You're not going to murder me here, right?"

"I don't think so." Andrew reached for something in the back seat. "At least that's not my plan." He produced a canvas tote bag, turned toward his door.

"Wait," I said. "Where are you going? What are we doing? It's freezing out."

Andrew side-eyed me. "Weren't you just running outside?"

"That's different. It doesn't count."

He grabbed a blanket from the floor behind his seat. "We're middle-aged parents who need to pick their kid up in an hour. We don't get to be picky when it comes to dates." He smiled. "Plus, I feel confident that, regardless of the temperature, you'll like this place." He winked, then opened his door. "Now come on."

Andrew slipped out and wiped a thin sheet of ice from the car's hood. He smoothed the heavy flannel blanket across it and took a seat, then gestured for me to do the same. It wasn't until I'd joined him that I saw his point. Spread before us, just past the brush at the edge of the lot, that unassuming road at the edge of our sleepy town gave way to an entirely unexpected cliff. The trees stretched out to the horizon. It felt like we'd traveled a million miles from our real lives, as if, for the moment, we existed in some alternate space—not quite the past or present, but something in between.

"Where are we?" I blinked, like I was dreaming.

Andrew offered me a wax paper–wrapped sandwich from his bag. "I read about it in the paper archives," he said as he unwrapped his own sandwich. "The town was supposed to build a highway overpass here years ago, but the residents protested it. They claimed it was a 'place of beauty.'" He took a sip from a glass bottle of iced tea; his hands shivered from the cold. "But I guess they all forgot about it. They all got too busy to ever come and actually appreciate it."

A chilly breeze blew. I tucked my knees against my chest, allowed myself to indulge in a long, silent pause. "I'm sorry I've been such a mess these last few months, Andy," I finally said, my gaze cast out on the icy tapestry of trees. "You were right. I've done a lot of selfish things, and they were all for naught. I quit my job without even talking to you. I left my students and my colleagues high and dry." Tears clung to my lashes. "I've even been terrible to Marian."

"Well, I think she kind of asked for that when—"

"Even before that test," I clarified. "For ages, she's sent me her articles to read, but I fed her a thousand reasons why I was always too busy to even glance at them." I turned to him. "I was too jealous. It's always hurt too much for me to read them." I wiped the tears from my face. "I want to make this all up to you, Andy. I'll fix this—everything that I've broken. I swear."

"You don't have to make anything up to me, Liv." Andrew reached out and squeezed my frigid hand. "Plus, I'm sorry, too," he said, surprising me.

I turned to him, scrunched up my face. "What are *you* sorry about?" I pulled my coat tighter around my body.

"I shouldn't have given you a hard time about quitting your job."

I laughed. "You're wrong. You *definitely* should have given me a hard time about that," I countered. "It was a totally rash decision based on the fact that I was scared, even though it now seems my fears were completely unwarranted."

"Still." Andrew paused, lost in a thought. "I shouldn't have given you shit about wanting to pursue your dream." He shook his head at some thought that occupied it. "I don't know. I think maybe I was mad that I wasn't pursuing mine." Andrew turned to me, a look of grief on his face. "I caught wind months ago that they might cut my column. It wasn't a completely out-of-the-blue thing."

"What?" I sat up a little straighter. "When? Why didn't you tell me?"

"I'm not sure." He shrugged. "I guess I didn't want you to worry about me."

A feeling of familiarity washed over me. "Been there."

He broke our gaze and stared out at the mosaic of wildness before him. "I want you to keep trying," Andrew said. "I don't care about that bullshit test, Liv. I care about you. Whatever it is you're hoping to do for yourself, I want you to finally go do it."

I looked down at my lap and shook my head. "Andy, that's sweet, but—"

"We'll figure it out," he insisted. "Money. Jobs. Whatever it is, we'll figure it out."

I locked eyes with him. Andrew. The same boy I fell in love with all those years ago, now a man. "How?"

Together, our bodies freezing, we gazed out at the trees, temporarily lost in their infiniteness. I wanted to reach out my hands and touch their branches, see how far into the future they stretched.

"I don't know," Andrew admitted. "I just know that we will."

FORTY-SIX

I wanted to take the time to read all of them.

The next day, I spent the morning scrolling through months of Marian's emails—all the ones I'd always been too busy—too envious— to read. One by one, I clicked open each of her article links. For the next few hours, I sat and finally listened to all the stories—all the other parts of herself—that Marian had wanted to share with me. By way of her writing, I sat across from her as she told me about a briny bowl of littleneck clams she'd once sampled on the Maine coast. I followed her through Chinatown as we dashed to her favorite dim sum restaurant, the one that we'd never visited together in real life. I hustled behind her as she guided me through Barcelona's largest food market, both of us laughing as we ducked when the local purveyors tossed entire fishes over our heads. Together, we sat side by side on a Floridian beach, where we sipped tropical cocktails and ate conch fritters while the sun slowly set.

It'd been years since I'd engaged with Marian's writing. For so long, I'd brushed it off, certain that her subject matter was an extravagance that simply didn't have a place in my world. But that morning, as her voice carried me from page to page, I realized I'd missed the point. Food was only a part of her stories. What those articles were really about was how, through her relationship with food, Marian had developed a unique understanding of what it means to truly sustain oneself, to nourish those you love, and to embrace life. I glanced up at the bowl of Tommy's cheddar-flavored, dinosaur-shaped snack mix I'd been absently nibbling while I read. I pushed the bowl away from me. Perhaps when it came to food, and my life, I still had a thing or two to learn.

Finally, I clicked open the last article, which Marian had sent to me a few months earlier. It was about a group of middle-aged women who founded a weekly cookbook club as a way to rediscover themselves in their second acts of life. Please swear you'll never become the sort of sad, suburban woman who finds her purpose in life by way of a tuna casserole, Marian had written to me in her email.

I finished reading the article, along with the recipe for a roasted-vegetable lasagna that accompanied it. "You wouldn't have sent it if you didn't want me to at least try it," I said out loud, as though she could hear me. Then, before I could overthink it, I pulled out the tote bag from our pantry—the one that contained the contents from my original curse jar—and headed for the door.

By the time Tommy and Andrew returned home, the kitchen was thick with the scent of roasted tomatoes and bubbling cheese. I slid on my oven mitts, opened the door, and peeled back a corner of the foil wrapping.

"I don't know if it's any good," I said as I carried the casserole dish to the island. "But, hopefully, it's a start."

Andrew kissed me and then moved toward the sink. "This looks fancy." He squirted some lemony soap into his hands, glanced down at his T-shirt and jeans. "I feel like I'm underdressed."

I pulled away the foil. The kitchen bloomed with a comforting, savory scent. I cut through the crisp noodles with a serving spoon and portioned out pieces for Tommy and Andrew.

Andrew lifted his fork to his mouth. "It's good." He set down his utensil. "What's the special occasion?"

"No occasion." I indulged a taste. "Just life."

FORTY-SEVEN

Marian finally called a few days before Thanksgiving. I was in the kitchen testing out a cranberry sauce recipe when the phone rang.

"I saw her," Marian said when I picked up.

I set down my wooden spoon. My body, which only seconds earlier had been at ease, grew tense. "What do you mean?" I asked. "Saw who?"

I heard Marian's quickened breath, like static through the line. "Poppy," she confirmed. "It turns out she's a barista in my neighborhood."

My throat tightened. "Whatever it is," I told her, "I don't think I want to know." I looked around at my house, my life. "Listen, I get it. You took me to that place so that I'd finally open my eyes, make some changes. And I have, okay? We don't have to keep doing this. I don't want to think about that stuff anymore."

Horns blared behind Marian. "I really think I should tell you what she said, Liv."

I didn't speak. Instead, I touched my face and realized it was wet with tears. "Where have you been, Mar?" I asked, hoping to shift the topic. "I've been calling and calling and—"

"I've been busy," she explained. "Believe it or not, I've been trying to make some changes. I've been trying to live my life, too."

"What are you talking about?"

"I'm dating someone," she said, which stopped us both in our tracks. "I don't want to jinx it, but so far, things are good. I'm actually on my way to go meet him now." I could tell from the lift in her tone that she was smiling. "But that's not why I called," Marian reminded me, her tone shifting. "I called to tell you about Poppy." She made a strained noise, like she was choking. "You're fine, Liv," she said. "You've always been fine, okay? You don't have to think about that test anymore." I could tell that she was holding something back. "That's all I wanted to say."

"Wait. What?" I began to untwist the strings of my apron. "What did she say, specifically?"

"She said you're fine, okay? That's it. That's all—" The line grew choppy. "Liv? Liv? Can you hear me?"

"Mar?" Across the room, my recipe reached a rolling boil. "Wait. What did she say about your test?" It was all static. "You never heard about your results."

"Sorry. I'm heading underground." Her phone began to cut out. "I can barely hear—"

The line went dead. I moved to the stove top, but it was too late. The sauce was already burnt, crystallized, and stuck to the pan. I carried the steaming pot outside. Our neighborhood glistened beneath a veneer of ice. I moved down the driveway and opened our plastic trash bin.

"Tossing the evidence?"

I turned. Suzanne stood behind me. She was dressed in her walking clothes—tight leggings, baseball cap, one of those puffy winter coats that makes everyone look like a fashionable marshmallow. "I'm hoping I can toss it before the Thanksgiving police send out a forensics team," I said as I dropped it into the trash.

"I once scorched our turkey so badly that I ran to that twenty-four-hour grocer and bought a dozen rotisserie chickens while everyone was having cocktails in my living room. No one knew the difference once I sliced them up and put them on my bone china platters." We stood in awkward silence. "I've been meaning to say that you did a nice job at the party."

"Oh. Thanks."

"Everyone had a good time," she said. "I'm not so sure about those tinctures, but . . ."

I shifted uncomfortably in my slippers. "I've been meaning to send you a thank-you note for the casserole," I said. "I'm sorry. I've never been great with all that Emily Post stuff."

Suzanne nodded. She fumbled over her words. "So, um . . . how are . . . things?"

A cold breeze rattled icy branches overhead, like a set of wintry wind chimes. "I'm not dying, Suze. I know you overheard me talking that day to my friend." I paused. Suzanne looked at me, awaiting more information. "It's a long story," I explained. "But I'm fine." I hugged my arms tighter around my body. "Unless you count a midlife crisis as a form of death."

"That explains the hair," Suzanne said through a quiet laugh. "But at least you can dye it back. When I hit forty, I had a yearlong meltdown that ended with a tribal tattoo."

I placed the lid on the trash bin. "That's not true. Not even your collection of pastel cardigans could cover up that kind of secret."

"Believe what you want." Suzanne shrugged. "Either way, I'm glad you're okay." She began to walk back in the direction of her house. Before she crossed the street, she turned back. "It gets easier, Liv. Getting older. I know I complain about it a lot. But there are some parts of it that are good." She slapped her gloved hand across her chest. "I swear. Tribal tattoos and all."

"Thanks, Suze." It was getting late. "Good luck with your turkey."

"Turkey. Rotisserie chicken." Suzanne shrugged again. "Promise you'll keep my secret safe?"

I nodded my agreement. "I promise."

FORTY-EIGHT

I finally went for my mammogram right before Christmas. The hospital's breast center had rescheduled my appointment a half dozen times. Apparently, that place was the middle-aged woman's version of a coveted nightclub. The only difference was that flashing your cleavage at the door wouldn't help you snag a spot inside.

Another waiting room. They were all the same. Elevator music. Dusty pamphlets. Daytime talk shows you'd never watch in real life. I sat and filled out paperwork about my breasts' history—until then, I hadn't realized they even *had* their own history. Around the room, other women sat waiting, too. Periodically, I'd catch one peering over her magazine. It was like prison. Everyone wanted to know what you were in for. Something routine? A nothing? Or worse: to become a statistic, a story shared among friends as a warning.

"Liv?"

Allison sat on the opposite side of the room, half her face hidden behind a copy of *Good Housekeeping*. She stood and moved closer to me. "What are you doing here?" she whispered. "Aren't you a little young for this?"

I absently flipped through a magazine. "That was my thought, too."

For an interlude, we sat in silence. An awkward energy filled the space between us. "I should have known," Allison finally whispered.

"The pink hair. Blakely." She clicked her tongue, like a detective who'd just cracked an impossible case. "It all makes sense."

"What makes sense?" I continued to skim the glossy pages. "What do you—" I turned the page and stopped. There, nestled between an article about DIY holiday decor and a roundup of festive fashion finds was a picture of Dahlia beneath the words New Year—and New You— Resolutions from the Doctor Who Knows How Long You'll Live. I had no doubt that it was her—the white lab coat, the ruby-red lips. I quickly skimmed the text and discovered another surprise at the bottom of the page. Written by Jessica Frances. "You've got to be kidding me."

"You know," Allison said as she squeezed my hand, "I had a scare last year. It was fine, though. It turned out they just needed some extra scans."

I barely registered Allison's comment. "Do you think it's okay if I tear some pages out of here?" I lifted my face and saw that Allison wore an expression of pity. "I just—"

"Oh, honey." Allison's eyes were glossy. She released my hand. "It'll all be okay."

"Wait." I squinted at her. "What are you—"

"Olivia Strauss?" A nurse appeared in the waiting room. Allison and I swiveled our heads. She smiled the timid smile of a woman who regularly delivered bad news.

Allison patted my arm. "Good luck."

In real time, the procedure was brief. In my mind, it lasted for hours. Days, even. That happens when you're forced to stand in a darkened room with your breasts sandwiched between two hunks of medical-grade plastic. Go figure. I tried to remain calm, but it was impossible. The machine made a menacing whirring noise that made it sound like it might saw my body in half.

"You'd think they'd have figured out a way to make this sound less like a drill was about to pierce your body, huh?" I said to the technician through a nervous laugh. She kept clicking her magical radiology keyboard and staring at electronic cross sections of my breasts. "So, how long have you been doing, um, breast work?"

That one got her attention. "I know you're nervous, but I really need to focus." Her fingers stroked the keyboard. "I need to take some extra scans."

She didn't need to say another word. I kept my mouth shut after that.

A short while later, my breasts freed from their plastic torture chamber, I slipped out of my paper gown, got back into my heavy winter clothes, and moved toward the checkout desk. A nurse looked up at me from beneath two curtains of purple eyeshadow. I knew she was the type who called people by pet names and got away with it. "Doc'll call you in a few days, sugar."

I stood there. "Is that . . . normal?"

She nodded, a pair of hoop earrings slapping her neck. "You're good, sweet pea. If something's wrong, Doc usually talks to you before you leave."

I navigated the hospital's infinite corridors, grateful that the experience was behind me. I didn't want to see another medical facility for months. Years, maybe. Nearby, a woman my age was wheeled past on a stretcher. I looked away. I hated hospitals. The antiseptic smell. The fluorescent lights. The constant reminder that the line between visitor and patient was terrifyingly thin.

"Mrs. Strauss?"

I turned. My nurse friend stood at the end of the hallway. I felt like I might get sick. "I'm sorry, sugar," she said and then batted her purple eyelids. "Turns out Doc wants to speak with you for a minute."

Shit.

A shadow. That's what the doctor called it. As though my own body had gotten in the way of life's natural light and created a darkness inside me. The doctor didn't know what to make of it. He was only human. It could be nothing. Or something. He wasn't sure. I'd need to come back in a few weeks so he could run more tests. "Until then," he told me, "try to relax."

I rushed into the hallway. In my mind, it all flashed before me with the speed of a flip-book. I reached the exit and paused in front of the automatic doors. They opened and closed and opened again. I couldn't move. I just stood there and pulled out my phone.

"I need you to come to the hospital," I announced the second Andrew picked up. "I don't think I can drive."

"I'm already here," he said, his voice faint.

"You're *here*?" I instantly felt a wave of relief knowing he was nearby. "But how—"

"I'm not here for you, babe," he whispered. "I'm here for me." He paused for what felt like a hundred years. "I'm in the ER," he finally said. "I think I'm having a heart attack."

My phone fell from my hand and ricocheted off the shiny linoleum floor. And then, in the flash of a second, my whole world went black.

~

I pulled open the curtain and found Andrew on a hospital cot, a million tubes connected to his body. His salt-and-pepper hair was frazzled, his skin gray. I shut the curtains and rushed to him. "What happened?" I pressed my ear against his chest, as though I could hear his heart and diagnose it. "Where's your doctor?"

"It was a false alarm," Andrew said. He picked up a packet of saltines. "The doctors just confirmed it." He nibbled his sad little cracker. "They think I had a panic attack."

"A panic attack?" I asked, feeling simultaneously relieved and confused. "From what?"

On the other side of the curtain, a drunk person screamed the lyrics to a Christmas carol before a team of nurses silenced him. Andrew sighed. "It's been a long year." He patted the vacant spot beside him. I curled myself against his body. Machines beeped around us.

"Did you ever think we'd end up here?" I whispered into his chest.

"Yes." Andrew ran his fingers through my hair. "But not for a few more decades." We lay there in silence, the only sounds the quiet cadence of medical machines. "What happened at your appointment?" he finally asked.

"They found something. Or nothing." A tear slid down my face. "Let's talk about it later." I wiped my cheek. "I don't want to worry about anything else right now."

Other than Tommy's birth, the only time we'd been in a hospital together was with the twins. I hadn't known before that morning that an invasive surgical procedure was something that could be sprung upon you in early pregnancy, a bundle of infinite grief handed to you instead of an actual baby. I guess that's one thing you learn with age: the fact that our bodies and our hearts are capable of taking on so much. Birth. Death. All the events that unfold in between.

"When did we get so old, Andy?" I asked him.

"I'm not sure," Andrew admitted. Through his shirt, I heard his heartbeat evening out. "But it feels like it happened slowly at first and then painfully fast."

The curtain opened. A nurse stepped into the space. "You're free to go, Mr. Strauss."

I darted up, desperate for more information. "Is he—"

"He's fine, ma'am," she interrupted. "He just needed to take a little time out." She smiled and left some papers on the bed. "Take care, Mr. Strauss." She stepped back through the curtain.

I collected the papers. "Are you ready?" Andrew nodded. I ran my fingers through his hair. "Today has felt impossibly long," I said. But that wasn't really what I meant. What I meant was that some days—like this one—life felt impossibly brief. You blinked and it was over. It was a blip. A drop. Before you'd even had a chance to figure out the purpose of the plot, the closing credits were already on the screen. I squeezed Andrew's hand. "I want to go home."

FORTY-NINE

We spent New Year's Eve at Suzanne's house, along with every other family on our block. Once you hit a certain age, you run out of options for how to mark the ceremonial turning of the calendar page. Every part of that night—from the campy accessories to the lists of sanguine resolutions to the painfully late bedtime—was designed for the young. Still, you couldn't sit home in your sweatpants eating takeout food, even though that's what everyone wanted to do.

Andrew and I were crammed like sardines around Suzanne's recently renovated island. Everyone in our neighborhood regularly saw each other at their worst. Braless trips to the curb. Sweaty mornings spent pulling weeds. Still, we all dressed up for each other. The men wore crisp shirts and blazers, like they were all part of an advertisement for the same store. The women wore black pants and sparkly shirts, like guests at a disco ball funeral. Adulthood is hard to explain. Maybe we all thought we could trick the New Year into believing we were better than we really were.

We all drank champagne and engaged in banal banter—kids' schedules, holiday gripes—while our children launched throw pillows at each other. The whole time, I felt Allison and the other women staring at me. "They've all been talking about me," I whispered to Andrew, my hand linked through his arm. Ever since we'd left the hospital, I'd barely let go of him.

"Who?" Andrew asked through a mouthful of crudités.

"Them," I said with a discreet nod toward our neighbors. "I can feel it."

"No offense, but it looks like they're just eating appetizers." Andrew wiped his mouth with a cocktail napkin. "They're not even speaking."

Across the room, Vikki's son, Peter, broke out into a dance. "You don't know women." I nibbled a cracker and then applauded his performance. Nearby, Vikki and everyone else applauded him, too. "We speak with our eyes."

"Sounds a lot like witchcraft or—"

"Hello to my favorite neighbors!" Suzanne swooped into our conversation. "Don't tell the others I admitted you're my favorites." She was a touch drunk, her tone as light and airy as the bubbles in her champagne flute.

"I think the other women are talking about me," I said and then sipped my drink. "They keep looking over at me like I have something smeared across my face."

"Hi, Suze." Andrew ate some shrimp. "Please tell my wife no one is talking about her."

"No can do." Suzanne set down her glass. "Full disclosure: you've been the focus of everyone's conversation for days."

"I *told* you," I said to Andrew as I refilled my glass. "About what?"

"The breast center," Suzanne explained.

"I *knew* it!" I exclaimed.

"Allison told the whole group that she saw you there," Suzanne continued. "She's working out about a million theories. Boob job. Cancer. The whole nine."

"I don't get it." Andrew crumpled his napkin. "If she saw *you* there, then doesn't that mean that *she* was there, too? Couldn't you be working out these same theories about her?"

"You don't get women," Suzanne said. "It doesn't work like that. Allison jumped to conclusions first, so now her word is gospel." She shrugged. "Plus, she's older. She had a reason to be there." Suzanne leaned in closer. "Off the record, why *were* you there?"

"I don't know." I swigged my champagne. "It's the mammogram *before* the mammogram. Or at least that's what my doctor said."

Suzanne continued to greet her guests. Andrew moved across the room to search for Tommy. That's when I felt someone squeeze my arm.

"Liv." Allison stood beside me, a timid smile sketched across her face. "How are you?"

I swallowed hard, forcing down a cube of cheddar. "What are you telling everyone?"

Allison straightened her posture. Her shirt sparkled when she moved. "About what?"

I rested my hand on my hip like a disgruntled teenager. "Allison, come on."

"Look, I only told them so we could help you." She combed her fingers through her hair. "We already started to organize a meal train."

"I don't need a meal train."

Andrew reappeared beside me. "Tommy is insisting that he's only eating dessert for dinner tonight. Apparently, it's his New Year wish."

"Can you please tell Allison there's nothing wrong with me?" I asked him.

"Oh boy." He tried to walk away, but I grabbed his arm. "She's fine, Allison. Really." He pointed to his temple. "Maybe a few screws loose, but that's about it, I'm afraid."

Courtney meandered toward us, a champagne flute in her hand. "Liv. I'm so sorry. Allison told us." She squeezed my shoulder. "I'm happy to make as many casseroles as your family needs."

Andrew stuffed a canapé into his mouth so he wouldn't have to speak.

"I don't need any meals," I explained and then dabbed a cocktail napkin across my forehead.

Allison and Courtney exchanged a glance. "Liv," they said in unison, making my name sound more like a question than a certitude. *Liv? Live?*

From the corner of my eye, I saw Tommy run toward me. Before I could tell him to slow down, he slammed into me, spilling my champagne down the front of my silly, sparkling shirt.

"Fu—" Andrew and Tommy side-eyed me. I puffed out my lips, like I was having an allergic reaction to my own thoughts. "Fudge," I said, revising myself. "Fucking fudge." I kissed Tommy, handed him a stack of cookies. "I'm sorry. I think I need to get some air."

Outside, I walked back to our porch, the windows of Suzanne's house illuminated with vignettes of the party. It was getting late. Soon, the ball would drop and everyone would explode with acclaim. I reached for my phone and called Marian. It took a few rings before she finally picked up. "Did you really see her?"

The backdrop hummed with indistinct chatter and loud music. "Happy almost New Year to you, too," she said, and I could tell that she was buzzed.

"I'm not kidding, Marian." I tugged my glittering sleeves around my fists. "I want to know."

I heard a door close behind her. "I thought you were done with this."

"I am," I said.

"Then why are we still talking about it?"

"I didn't realize it was off limits to simply ask—"

"I told you not to think about that test anymore," Marian spat, surprising me. "It's for me to worry about, not you."

"You?" I removed the stack of metallic party beads from my neck. "Why would you need to worry about it? Why would either of us. I thought she said—"

"Just stop!" Marian shouted. "You want to embrace life, Liv? Then stop circling back to that test. It's enough already. I can't talk about it anymore." She exhaled audibly. "You know, you keep saying you want to find your voice again, to write for real this time. I sent you the name of an editor months ago for actual paid gigs, and you've done nothing except—"

"I'm not like you, Marian. I don't have any wild stories about my crazy, spontaneous life. I don't have anything important to say. Not the way you do."

She stopped. "You're the only person who seems to think that."

I slid off one of my heels and rubbed my foot. "It doesn't matter."

Marian huffed loudly. "When are you going to see what you have, Liv? A home and friends. Andrew and Tommy." She was slurring. "You did it. *You* won the game of life, not me! When are you going to stop with this shit and finally just enjoy it?"

"Are you drunk?"

"Does it matter?" she barked. "What is it you're actually looking for, Liv? You already have everything. You already have this big, beautiful perfect life!"

"I know that. Except—"

"It was a dream you had in your twenties, Liv!" she said, cutting me off.

"It wasn't just a dream!" I shouted. "It was my whole identity. And I just abandoned it. And now I'm lost. I don't know what it is I'm supposed to do."

"Dreams change, Liv. People change."

I took her comment as an insult. "What does that mean?"

She sighed. "It means you're already living the dream. But you're so stuck in the past that you can't see it."

"Marian," I said, carefully weighing out my words. "Where is this all coming from?"

An eternity passed before Marian spoke again. "Did you ever think that maybe you're not the only one who's been trying to reinvent her life?" Through the line, I heard her heavy breaths. "Maybe I've been busy trying to finally live my life, too."

"Stop it." My cheeks were damp. "You love your life."

Marian laughed quietly, even though I hadn't said anything funny. She paused for what felt like too long of a time. "It's almost midnight," she finally whispered, disregarding my comment. Through Suzanne's windows, our whole neighborhood gathered for the countdown. "I should go find my date. You should go find your family. Tommy will be furious if you miss the ball drop."

"No." I inhaled several deep, shuddery breaths. "I want to stay here with you." Through the line, a crowd of people around Marian began to count down. *Ten! Nine!* "I miss you," I whispered, suddenly wishing she were right there beside me.

"I miss you, too," Marian said.

Across the street, I saw Andrew through a window. Tommy was propped up in his arms, their heads decorated with gold party hats. *Eight! Seven!* "Promise me that what you said about Poppy is true," I said. "Tell me that we can really bury this."

"What does it matter?" As she spoke, her voice took on a somber tone. *Six! Five!* "That test was in the past, Liv. It's not like it was real."

"Tell me anyway." *Four! Three!* "Promise me that what you told me is real."

"Fine." *Two! One!* Across the street, Suzanne's house erupted with noise. "I promise."

"Are you telling me the truth?" Through the window, Andrew squeezed Tommy.

"No," Marian admitted, and suddenly I felt more distant from her than I'd ever felt, too far away for me to ever fully reach. "I'm telling you what you want to hear."

FIFTY

I t looks like we've got ourselves a funny duct." The radiologist smirked, his face illuminated by his ultrasound machine. All morning, he'd pressed medical devices into my chest like I was a cadaver. "Get it? A funny *duct*. A funny *duck*." He smiled, amused by his own joke.

I sat on a cold examination table in a flimsy paper gown and wondered when every physician in our town had become a budding comic. "So, what does that mean?"

He clicked off his machine. "It means you're fine." He turned on the overhead fluorescent lights. "We'll see you for your first official mammogram in about a year."

I drove home from the hospital and thought of her. Prior to our phone call on New Year's Eve, it'd never occurred to me that Marian might be unhappy. From the outside, she had everything she wanted. But it turned out that, hidden in a place no one else could see, she had her own list, too.

"Are we okay?" I asked the moment she picked up her phone. "We've hardly spoken the last few weeks." I clicked on my blinker and took the long way home so we could talk. "Are we good?"

Through the line, it sounded like the whole world breezed past her in an instant. "We're okay, Liv," she said, but her tone was unconvincing.

"I just have some things I'm trying to grapple with. But I swear they don't have anything to do with us. It's me. Just me."

"What things?" I asked.

"I'm fine," she said to try to reassure me, though it didn't help. "I'm just not ready to talk about it yet." What else could either of us say? "Thanks for checking in," Marian said. "I appreciate it, Liv. I really do." We said goodbye and left the conversation like that.

I turned onto our street. Up and down our block, our neighbors tended to various tasks. Buckling children into car seats. Collecting rolled-up newspapers. Despite the perfect facades we'd all created, maybe we all had shadows. Secret longings. Dreams present in our minds, even when we couldn't see them. They revealed themselves only when the light in our lives began to shift and our world began to grow dim.

The house was quiet. I breezed into the kitchen and tucked my keys inside my bag. As I did, my fingers grazed the folded-up magazine article I'd tried to ignore for days. I couldn't disregard it anymore. I poured myself some coffee and ran my hands across the pages to smooth out the creases. Finally, when I knew I couldn't wait any longer, I dove in.

> "The issue with life," says Dr. Dahlia Brooks—or just "Dahlia" to her growing roster of A-list patients—"is that most individuals don't really learn to live until they're essentially out of time. We get so caught up in our daily routines that we forget how quickly those days turn into years. We put things off until tomorrow or next month until eventually they just fall to the wayside. In particular, I frequently see patients put their health off until, frankly, it's too late."

> For years, Dr. Brooks has kept the Nettle Center— her sought-after, highly exclusive, integrative well-ness clinic—shrouded in secrecy. There's minimal

information about the center online, and any interview she's given in the past has typically revolved around her assorted, well-known beverages, such as her coveted matcha smoothies. But for a long time, things stopped there. However, it seems she finally feels ready for her operation—and her intriguing, though questionable, services to go mainstream. "I believe in karma and energy," she explained to me when we first spoke on the phone, and I asked her why she suddenly decided to have information about her clinic published in a national magazine. "For years, I have built up positive karmic energy by helping hundreds of clients discover unexpected ways to both enhance and, in some cases, extend their lives," she explained through her subtle, yet indistinguishable, accent. "I now feel that I can help a larger population of people find wellness and longevity, without any karmic consequence."

In recent months, Dr. Brooks has become the buzz of the holistic health world thanks to the Nettle Center, which opened in Palm Springs after she moved her operation to the West Coast late last summer. In addition, she recently launched a line of plant-based alkaline supplement powders inspired by her popular, in-office tinctures. However, if you ask anyone in the know, the tinctures are only part of the story. Dr. Brooks first developed a following thanks to her patent-pending genetic test, which she claims can provide her patients with an estimated life span. It's a complex test, one that has been no stranger to ethical scrutiny, and it's the reason I recently met with her on a sunny Palm Springs morning.

When I first entered the Nettle Center, I felt more like I was at a spa than a medical facility. The space was airy and full of natural light—nothing like the doctors' offices we all grew up visiting—and accented with the sort of modern bohemian touches you'd expect to find at a place famous for its matcha detox massages and biological age tests. After I enjoyed one of her tinctures, it was time for my genetic life span evaluation. It was simpler than I expected (just a bit of my saliva collected in a vial and a quick, painless finger prick). The difficult part was the wait. Despite the Zen-like atmosphere, I admit that this fiftysomething writer was on edge while awaiting her results. However, it wasn't until afterward that I realized how vital the wait is to the whole process.

"For many of my patients, this test—and the period when they're awaiting their results—is the first time they've ever faced a very uncomfortable reality: we're not here on this planet forever. Eventually, there is an end date."

She was right. During the hour I awaited my results—and then in the days and weeks that followed—I was forced to consider the possibility that my time was running out. For the first time, I really thought about my life. Had I accomplished everything? Had I made peace with all my old grudges? Had I lived my life fully enough that I could die happily?

In the end, I was one of the lucky ones. My test results were desirable; based upon them, I'm not going any place anytime soon. Even so, I've spent a great deal of time since that morning evaluating my life. The unusual, and certainly controversial, test—as well as the waiting period that is inevitably a part of it—forced me to consider the what-ifs. What if I hadn't received desirable results? What would I change? That's when the real beauty of Dr. Brooks's tests finally dawned on me. Why wasn't I committed to changing those things now?

So, is Dr. Brooks's test real? That's been the question ever since she first unveiled it. The answer: I'm not sure. However, in the end, maybe the test results aren't the part that matters. Maybe it's the fact that, regardless of how many tinctures we consume, the test forces us to confront the ephemeral nature of our own existence. After all, one thing remains certain: no matter who you are or what you do or how you live, your time—just like mine—is ultimately running out.

I set down the pages. Through the window, the morning light shone into the room, creating a bold shadow of my body. I closed my eyes and allowed the sun to beat across my face. I needed to feel the light on my skin. When I opened them, I saw that the light had changed. I looked down and folded up the magazine pages, ready to move forward with my day. When I did, I noticed that my shadow was gone.

FIFTY-ONE

*B*elief is a powerful thing.

Dahlia had said that back at the Nettle Center when I'd doubted her test. At the time, I'd found her statement annoying, like an inspirational quote stamped on a bumper sticker. But as I sat in my kitchen on that quiet February morning, the phone pressed against my ear, I couldn't help but think that Dahlia had been right. At least about that one thing.

"I don't understand," I muttered into the phone. I felt like a cartoon character who'd been smacked in the face with a frying pan. "Like, *love* love?"

The vibrancy and life that had been missing from Marian's voice was suddenly restored. "I can't believe it, either. But it's true. I think this is it. I think he's finally the one."

I blinked hard, like she'd just woken me from a long dream. "Who is he?"

"Hot bartender," she interrupted. "It turns out his name is Sam. He's young, I know that. It's hard to explain. It just works."

I poured more hazelnut creamer into my coffee. It was the first time since college that Marian had fallen for someone for more than a weekend. She'd never longed for things like relationships or marriage. She'd never really longed for anything. There was a contentedness about her. Once, in our twenties, I told Marian about my birthday lists and asked if she'd ever kept anything similar. She laughed. "Never," she'd said. At the time, I believed her.

"So, you're happy?"

In Marian's backdrop, I heard the familiar sounds of traffic and passersby. "It's the happiest I've felt in a long time." She paused, lost in a thought. "I know it sounds crazy, but I can really see it." She couldn't hide her excitement. "The long haul. We could be a family, you know? Like you and Andy." Marian had never suggested to me that a family was something she wanted. If anything, she'd always suggested that things like marriage and family were roadblocks to her dreams. "I don't want to be alone, Liv. I'm not a kid anymore, you know? I'm thirty-nine." I wondered if it was the first time she'd truly realized that fact. "I don't have a lot of time left to figure this stuff out."

"So, is this what you've been keeping from me?" I asked.

Even through the line, I sensed Marian's lips forming into a question. "What do you—"

"I could just tell," I said, answering the question I knew Marian was about to ask me. "I know you, Mar. I knew there was something you've been hiding." I paused, let my realization breathe. "So, is this it?"

Marian waited a long time before she answered. "Yes," she finally decided, and I could tell that there was still something she wouldn't say.

Belief is a powerful thing.

But I didn't press her. For the moment, I think we both just wanted to believe in the power of happy endings.

After we hung up, I couldn't get back into the swing of my day. My mind was too busy with emotion. I moved across the kitchen to pour myself more coffee. I set down my mug before I took a sip. Upstairs, I slipped into my yoga pants and sneakers. And then, I was gone.

The class was in session by the time I entered the yoga studio. The whole room smelled like sweat and eucalyptus. I unrolled my mat and began to twist my body up like origami. Sunshine saw me and waved.

At the end of class, like always, Sunshine instructed us to lie on our backs for our little yogic naps. I closed my eyes. Sunshine made a point to remind us all to breathe. I kept thinking of Marian. I knew I should be happy for her, but something inside me felt unsettled. I worried about her motivations, that she was moving too fast. I kept breathing. In the backdrop, quiet music played, lulling me deeper into my Savasana. An image kept appearing in my head. It was of Marian and me, the two of us on the Brooklyn Bridge. Back in college, Marian had always made a big fuss over our shared birthday. Dinner at some cool café downtown. Cupcakes from our favorite bakery. Every year, we shared a sunset walk over that bridge together, complete with cocktails concealed in plastic water bottles. At the time, I'd always thought she'd just liked the idea of a celebration. But as I rested on my yoga mat that morning, I finally realized her real intent: she never wanted to spend those sacred days alone.

"I'm starting to think you might actually like this."

I blinked open my eyes. Sunshine hovered over me. "I don't *not* like it, I guess."

She tossed me a rag to wipe down my mat. "I see you kept your hair pink."

"Right." I touched a sweaty strand of it. "I keep forgetting about it," I explained. "At this point, I think it's just become a part of me."

"I like it." Sunshine softly walked across the wood floors. "It sets you apart."

I gathered my things and stepped outside. I began to walk down the street. I was thinking about Marian, about those birthday outings, when I heard someone shout out my name.

"Liv!"

I turned and saw Allison rushing toward me. She looked the same as always—black yoga pants, baseball cap.

"I'm sure you've figured out by now that I canceled the meal train. I know you think I was being a gossip, but I swear I was only trying to do the right thing."

"You could have just asked me if something was wrong."

"Guilty as charged." Allison puffed out her lips. "I know I talk too much," she admitted. "And that I share too much of other people's information." She brushed her hair away from her face to seem nonchalant. "But I really am trying to change those things about myself." She paused. "It's one of my New Year's resolutions." She glanced at the ground. "One of many, if I'm honest."

We looked at each other, as though understanding one another for the first time. "I understand," I said. "Truth be told, I've got a bunch of resolutions, too."

Allison smiled, perhaps grateful to know she wasn't in it alone. "Speaking of which, I'd better get going. I signed up to take my first yoga class today." She fluttered her eyelashes. "I know. February. I'm a bit behind in the resolution department." She paused. "But I'm trying." She fidgeted with her jacket. "Plus, I figure I already own the pants." Life is so strange. At times, it feels so lonely, like we're isolated with our flaws and fears. "I'd better get moving." Allison tossed up her hands. "Better late than never, right?"

But in the end, you begin to learn that, despite our many differences, we're all the same. "Better late than never," I agreed.

FIFTY-TWO

Y ou heard what happened, didn't you?" Suzanne poured everyone a glass of wine. All the neighborhood women were gathered around her island and dressed in conservative black dresses like a bunch of Puritans. Earlier that day, we'd all attended Annie's funeral.

"Maybe we should change the topic." I picked up a square of cheese and then set it down without even tasting it. "You know, seeing as we just buried the woman." I thought of Annie's small act of kindness and how it had brought me such joy when I most needed it.

Suzanne dismissed my comment and continued on. "She fell down the damn stairs while carrying the laundry basket. The laundry basket!" Suzanne clicked her tongue. "The poor woman spent her final moments switching out a load of bath towels." She sipped her wine. "Let that be a lesson to us all. We're not getting any younger, and the laundry pile isn't getting any smaller." She set down her glass. "And the worst part: You know who found her?" We all shook our heads. "It was that damn dog, Jack." Suzanne rolled her eyes so hard it looked like she'd had a seizure. "All his shitting aside, at least he was good for that."

Later that afternoon, once the trays of lunch meats had been picked through and the wine had all been drunk, I walked back home. It was already late March. Spring had arrived. The air was marked by a buttery warmth. The trees had become speckled with green buds. Everything was blooming sooner than planned.

I stopped in front of Annie's house. Despite our recent exchanges, the truth was that I hadn't known her well. I didn't know if she had hobbies outside of gardening, or if she'd accomplished everything that she'd wanted. I just knew that since we'd moved onto our block, she'd lived alone.

I wiped my face with the sleeve of my black dress and pressed my phone against my cheek. "I'm happy for you," I told Marian when she picked up. "I think I forgot to tell you that."

"Thanks," Marian said. "I'm actually in one of those fancy home-ware stores as we speak." Even through the phone, I sensed her smile. "I offered to cook Sam a special dinner tonight." She laughed. "Apparently, I'm secretly a nineteen fifties housewife."

"Don't feel too badly," I told her. "I did the same thing a few months ago, thanks to your lasagna recipe."

"You finally read it?" She seemed surprised. "You never mentioned that."

"I did read it." I sniffled. "I read all of them, in fact. They were great. But, no surprise there." Across the street, a neighbor walked past and waved.

"I know it kills you to read my articles sometimes," Marian whispered. It was a truth that had been so obvious for so long, yet it was one we never discussed. "I know how much it still hurts you that you never gave your own writing a solid second try."

I moved up Annie's walkway. There was no sign of life from the house, just a sad sense of stillness and silence. I thought of the last time I'd spoken to Annie on her doorstep. I wished I'd had the chance to tell her more about that poem. To tell her that, when you peeled back the layers, it was about taking chances, trying again. But I never did. Life moves too fast. "I don't want to interrupt your shopping," I finally said. Before I moved back down the block, I reached my hand into one of

Annie's lush cobalt bushes, which had just recently bloomed, and tore away a large bunch of the early hydrangea stems so I could enjoy their beauty—and Annie's gesture—one last time. I was about to end the call, but I spoke up once more. "I heard what you said when we spoke a few weeks ago," I added. "About being alone. About wanting a family. About wanting someone to spend your life with."

"I know you did." Marian briefly said something to a sales associate, then turned her attention back to me. "You have a damn good life, Olivia Strauss," she said. "I hope you know that."

I stepped into the familiarity of our home, my flowers cradled in my arm like a baby. "I do."

~

Later that night, while I was getting ready for bed, I glanced in the bathroom mirror. Lines as thin as hairs had formed around my eyes. My pink hair had finally given way to a sprinkling of grays. I pulled back and studied my reflection. It wasn't the same as it was all those years ago, when I saw thousands of versions of it reflected back at me in that exhibition space. I was getting older. I wasn't the same person I was back then. I'd evolved. Some of my former desires had faded. Some new ones had taken their place. But I was still me. I was still Liv.

I pulled open a drawer to put away the toothpaste. That's when I saw that half-used bottle of hair dye. I took it out. As I did, my mind drifted back to that memory from my youth, when I'd walked in on my parents dancing in our kitchen. The music. Their smiles. The familiarity and safety of our home. At the time, I'd thought their lives were so settled, their whole existence just a straight line, like that was a bad thing. At the time, I was too young to know what it looked like to be content, but I was finally starting to understand for myself.

For too many years, I'd taken for granted so many aspects of my life while on a quest to check off the few boxes I'd yet to complete. It was like that scattering of blank squares had left a blankness in me. It wasn't until I began to chase them down that I realized that I could still have a full life, even if they remained empty. That I could be content, yet still have dreams. *You have a damn good life, Olivia Strauss.* That I could simultaneously exist in both those spaces and be happy.

"How was today?" Andrew appeared in the bathroom moments after I stepped out of the shower, fluffy towels still wrapped around my head and body.

"Long." I smoothed lotion into my skin. "Weird." I rubbed my hands together. "But mostly sad." I pulled the towel from my head and allowed my freshly colored hair to fall around my shoulders. "All the neighborhood women went," I told him. "I'm glad we were there."

Andrew leaned against the doorframe. "I didn't realize that funerals gave you such an urge for a fresh hairdo."

"Oh, right." I tousled my wet, pink strands. "I thought I'd give it one more go." I shrugged my bare shoulders. "Figured the neighbors will need something to talk about, right?" I glanced in the mirror. "Plus, to be honest, I think I like it."

"I like it, too." He smirked. "It looks good on you." His voice was laced with flirtation as he took another step into the bathroom. "You know," he said as he wrapped his arms around my body, "Tommy is already asleep. The kitchen is all cleaned up."

I rested my head against his chest. "I feel like you're suggesting something."

Andrew placed his fingers beneath my chin and lifted my face to meet his. "That's because I am."

FIFTY-THREE

Everything changed on a Tuesday. Life. Time. All the little microcosms that exist in between. It was the first week of April. I picked Tommy up from school, just like every weekday since I'd left Blakely. We played I spy on the drive, like normal. We talked about his schoolwork and his friends. That part was normal, too. There were no signs anywhere to indicate that the day might be anything other than ordinary. All afternoon, life had run as though according to a script.

It was my own fault. I should have seen that something bad was coming.

When Tommy and I walked through the door, Andrew was seated at the kitchen table with a heavy-looking box in front of him. I tilted my head. "I finally fixed it," he said, his gaze focused on the dozen or so magazines spread before him. "The table." He lifted his chin, gripped the edge of the wood, and shook it. The old thing didn't budge.

I slid Tommy's book bag off his shoulders. "Did you find a special kind of tape?"

Andrew dog-eared a magazine page. "Not exactly." He smiled. "But I did finally find the number of a special kind of handyman."

Tommy mimicked his father, shook the table, too. He nodded his approval and then ran into the other room and flipped over a basket of toys for no good reason.

I sat beside Andrew and ran my hand across the tabletop, reacquainting myself with the knotted wood. "What's all that?" I asked with a nod toward the box. I picked up one of the magazines. "Wait. Are you looking at old copies of *Smith*?"

Andrew lifted his dog-eared copy and flipped through it. "Guilty," he admitted.

I felt my brows furrow. "What brought that on?"

Andrew wasn't like me. He was straightforward, less emotional, more to the point. If we were pieces of punctuation, I'd be a question mark, always second-guessing my life. Andrew would be a period. Simple. Certain. It wasn't like him to get hung up in the past. Nostalgia was a department I typically managed for us both.

He shrugged. "I've been thinking about my next move, I guess."

I set down the magazine. "Your next move?"

In the other room, a million plastic pieces smashed against the floor. "I know I need to get a new job once they cut my column," he said. "A real job. One with money and benefits and all that adult stuff." He turned to me. "But I want to start my own journal," Andrew said. "You know, start spending time with real fiction again." He twisted his gold wedding band. "Not for a job," he said. "I recognize that I'm a bit past that point." He ran his hands through his hair, as though embarrassed about what he'd say next. "I just want to do it for me."

I felt my posture straighten, like a marionette doll. "Oh. I didn't realize—"

"That I still had dreams, too," he interrupted with a half smile.

I looked down at my fingernails. "Well, yeah."

"I'd been thinking about it for a while," Andrew admitted. "Even before word got out about my column." He laughed then at some private memory. "I know it will sound ridiculous, but right after I heard, I was flipping through the paper before it went to print and came across my weekly horoscope and—"

"I'm sorry," I interrupted. "I just blacked out. Your what?"

"I know. That sounds like something Marian would say, huh?" He shrugged again. "Desperate times, right?" He smiled slowly. "Sometimes they make us believe in crazy things."

I just nodded. "I've heard that."

Andrew slid me the box. I pulled out a magazine and studied the cover—a black-and-white photograph of a man on a bench in Washington Square Park, a pocket watch chain dangling from his fingers. The *Time* issue. "I remember putting that issue together. I was in my twenties—a kid—but I felt so old." Andrew laughed. "Time is funny like that."

Anytime Andrew talked about *Smith* or our past life together, it felt like he was referring to some artifact, like our whole existence prior to the day we moved had been a museum exhibit we liked to reference in passing. But right then, as we sat beside each other at our finally mended table, an actual box of relics positioned between us, I think we both remembered that part of our history in a way we hadn't in a while: as something that had been real.

"I remember when you'd come home from *Smith* late at night," I said. "You'd stay up for hours reviewing proofs." I laughed at the memory. "You never seemed unhappy, though."

Andrew rubbed his thumb across my fingers. "So then, I have your support?"

"In case you forgot, I quit my job on a whim," I reminded him.

Andrew moved into the living room. I pulled out another magazine. Behind me, my phone buzzed inside my bag. I pushed back my chair and reached for it. The screen illuminated with a message from Marian.

I need to talk to you, the message read. It's not good.

I ached for her as I imagined what I believed at the time to be the worst: a broken heart. Give me five minutes, I wrote back. I'll call you when I get upstairs.

I was actually hoping you could meet me, she wrote. At our bench.

That's when I knew it was something more.

I threw a copy of *Smith* in my bag and sprinted into the other room. Andrew was building a block tower. He looked up at me. "It's Marian," I announced, already breathless. "I need to go meet her," I told him. "Now."

Andrew glanced at our wall clock. "The next train leaves in twenty minutes." He patted his pockets and threw me his car keys. "You'd better go now. Otherwise, you'll be late."

I tossed the keys into my bag. "I'll be back as soon as I can," I said. And then, unaware of all the ways my life—my whole world—was about to change, I was out the door.

FIFTY-FOUR

When I walked into the exhibition room, Marian was already seated on our black rectangular bench. Her back was to me. Nearby, several other museumgoers wandered into and out of the space. I lingered in the back, waiting for them to leave. Once they were gone and the room fell completely silent, I approached her.

"I think the last time we called for an emergency meeting here, it was because I thought Andy was going to break up with me," I said as I took a seat beside her. Without the need to look at her or to ask, I took her hand in mine. "I think we were all twenty-two."

We kept our gazes on those series of paintings. I'd forgotten their magnitude, the way you could immerse yourself in that watery scene and briefly forget about the rest of the world. If you stared at the oils on those massive canvases long enough, you began to believe there were no edges, that those brushstrokes of blue-gray water flowed on forever. In retrospect, maybe that's why we chose it as our place of refuge all those years ago—not because of the paintings' popularity, but because we felt like we could disappear into that scene.

"We broke up," Marian said, her eyes lost in that quiet image.

"I figured." I squeezed her hand. "It's obviously his loss for ending it. I'm sorry it didn't work out."

"It wasn't his decision," she clarified and then released my hand. "I was the one who called it off." She rested her palm on her thigh and drew in a long, smooth breath. "I just couldn't do it to him. Make him believe that we had a future together."

I studied her profile, which was illuminated in silhouette. "What do you mean?"

My words hovered there in the narrow space between us. Nearby, a group of tourists wandered into the room. They snapped photographs and then left.

"I'm sick," Marian said. A single tear slid down her face. She turned toward me. "I found out last year."

Neither of us spoke. Instead, we stared at the painting, just like we had one thousand times before that moment. But it wasn't the same. I blinked and finally saw the edges. Just like everything, that painting had an edge—and an ending—too.

"I don't understand." I looked away from the artwork, watched her chest rise and fall.

"I found out a few weeks before our birthday." She looked down at her lap. Even through the heaviness of our conversation, her eclectic metal earrings shimmered like a pair of quiet promises. "I just chose not to believe it. It was easier to ignore it, I think." She looked up and met my eyes. "I went for more scans last week. My doctor called today to tell me that I finally have to start believing it. I can't keep putting it off or ignoring it anymore. I need to start treatments. Soon."

Death is not what you'd expect. It's more quiet, less dramatic, than I imagined. After Marian told me the news, we sat for a long time in silence, her words circulating all around us until they'd transformed from sounds and into the air that we both breathed and eventually just became a part of us, like our cells. When I finally remembered how to speak, I asked her for the facts.

She sighed heavily. "I don't think I have a lot of time left."

Behind us, more visitors entered the space.

"So, what do we do now?" I asked, the shakiness evident in my voice.

The group moved in front of us to snap a photograph, blocking our view of the water and ruining the illusion when we needed it most.

"I don't know." Marian dropped her head onto my shoulder, much like Tommy did when the world felt too big and confusing for him to understand. I tilted my face and allowed my cheek to rest against the softness of her hair. "I guess for now," she whispered, "we just try our best to live."

BIRTH

FIFTY-FIVE

I know what you're thinking. I should have been forthright and told you Marian was sick from the start. But it wasn't that easy. Even now, as I look back on that whole year of constant change in my life, I struggle to believe it. It's hard to explain. Up until the very end of that year, I think I still felt like death didn't apply to me or anyone I loved. Maybe I thought I could opt out of it, like unsubscribing from an obnoxious email thread.

Of course, I was wrong.

Once her treatments started, Marian stopped taking my calls. "I don't want you to get all this stuff in your head," she told me. "You don't do well with negative thoughts floating around up there." What she meant was that I wasn't strong enough to handle what she was about to face. That I wasn't strong enough to help her. She wasn't wrong.

For eight weeks Marian called Andrew every few days with a report. Details about her treatments. Summaries of her doctors' notes. Names of medications I'd never correctly pronounce. Andrew began to talk to me in mantras. *Anything is possible. One day at a time. Everything happens for a reason.* He had a bad poker face. I knew, despite everything he told me—and everything I knew he was not telling me—that her prognosis was not good. That my world was slowly closing in on me. He just wouldn't say the words. *Have faith.*

I didn't know what to do with myself. Every day, I called her over and over and over again, but she wouldn't pick up. I sent her endless messages in which I asked what I could do—what I *should* do—to help her, but she wouldn't respond. I didn't know how I was supposed to just go on living my life. Should I just pretend nothing had changed and keep busying myself with all my menial, day-to-day tasks? Should I just sit with my grief—my overbearing, unwanted friend? I didn't know. She hadn't given me an instruction manual.

Most days, I wandered aimlessly around our house. I wanted to be mad at someone. I needed something to blame. The only option was Dahlia. I'd lie awake in bed and wonder if her test had somehow caused Marian's illness. I'd toss and turn, considering if we'd brought it upon ourselves. I couldn't help but wonder if we'd somehow jinxed our lives by questioning our longevity.

The insomnia lasted for weeks. Eventually, I couldn't lie there anymore. During the darkest hours of the night, I began to wander downstairs and stare absently at some mindless show on the television screen. Most nights, I flipped to that silly cooking show we often watched. I needed to not think. For hours, I'd watch a bunch of Brits shape rounds of seeded soda breads and construct neat, savory tarts. It wasn't until the end of May, when Marian concluded her first round of treatments, that my midnight ritual stopped satisfying me.

I needed to connect with her. To sustain her. To breathe life back into her. To bring the world to her, since her world had so abruptly become closed off. But I didn't know how.

Until I remembered her articles.

Suddenly, the path to caring for Marian became abundantly clear. Food, I knew, was the answer. It was the one way I could bring a sense of piquancy back into her life. Maybe, I thought, it was also a way for me to bring some back into my own life, too.

I started to cook. On a Tuesday night, while the world slept, I funneled my anxiety into my first-ever batch of biscuits, the television quietly humming nearby. On Wednesday night, I baked my first loaf of bread. Ever since Marian had told me about her illness, I had felt perpetually starving and yet too nauseous to take a bite of anything. It's hard to explain what I was doing. Maybe, subconsciously, I felt that by connecting with food—the thing Marian had built her career around—I was more deeply connecting with her. Who knows? Maybe I just needed to stay busy. Maybe that's why the neighborhood women always whipped up impressive meals—to keep their minds off the other calamities in their lives. I don't know. Some nights, it felt like I was preparing for an apocalypse. Maybe I was. Maybe we all were.

"I want to see her," I told Andrew when he stumbled downstairs one morning at dawn. Our kitchen island was covered with flour, my old NYU sweatshirt smeared with butter.

"What do you mean?" Andrew blinked away the sleepiness. "Now?"

"Well, I figured we'd shower first." I shut the refrigerator with my backside. "But yes, in theory, now."

"Liv." Andrew nibbled a crumb. "She doesn't want you to see her when she's sick."

"I know." I wiped down the counter. "But I really need to see her."

Later that afternoon, the three of us piled into the car, my cooler of frozen food strapped into the back seat beside Tommy. It was the first time we'd ever driven into the city as a family. Tommy couldn't stop staring through the window at that jungle of skyscrapers.

Andrew drove. I stretched my arm across the console and held his hand. The whole ride was bittersweet. Each street corner held a memory of my and Andrew's life together. Our whole past slid by us. I had to keep reminding myself why we were there.

The car stopped at a light downtown. I turned my head, and there it was: our first apartment. It was hard to say what had aged more since we'd left—that old building or me. I looked up at the fourth-story window and the adjacent fire escape, still decorated with string lights and potted plants, like we'd never left.

"Feels like a lifetime ago, huh?" Andrew said.

I nodded. "I guess it was, technically." I gestured toward Tommy. "It was his lifetime."

A few minutes later, Andrew pulled alongside the curb outside Marian's apartment. "Give me your phone," I told him. He looked at me like I had six heads. "She won't answer if she knows it's me."

"So, you're going to trick her into talking to you?" he asked. "That's not fair."

"You're right." I took his phone. "None of this is fair."

I wheeled my cooler toward her stoop and then called her from Andrew's phone.

"Hey, Andy." Her voice was raspy. "Thanks for calling. It hasn't been my best day."

"It's me," I said. "I'm outside your apartment."

I watched her appear at her window. She looked thin, her head wrapped in some vintage-looking scarf. Even so, she was still so damn beautiful. I waved. She shook her head and waved back.

"I told you I didn't want you to see me when I was sick. I didn't want you to get all wrapped up in this."

"What did you think I would do, Mar?" I studied her quiet movements. "Just go on living my life? Just disregard the fact that this is all happening?"

She shrugged her frail shoulders, her best effort to seem nonchalant. I watched her take a seat on her window ledge. "What's all that?" She pointed to my cooler.

"I can't sleep," I admitted. "I started stress baking as a form of therapy."

"How's it working out?" she asked.

"Well, my scones are too dry, and my butter—unlike more decent therapists—won't write me a script for anything fun."

"You know," she said, "I still have some of those Xanax. Any interest?"

"Can I come up?" I asked, desperate. "I can put all this in your freezer for when your appetite comes back."

She released a long, heartfelt sigh. "Not today, Liv," she said, and it felt like a bullet hit my chest. "I'm too tired. I think I'm going back to bed."

"I'll tuck you in, then." Marian had never once turned me away. "Tommy says I'm the best at that. Way better than Andy."

"Another time," she said, and I heard the real exhaustion in her voice. "Just not today, okay?"

"Why did you first talk to me at that poetry reading all those years ago?" I reached up and wiped the tears from my face. "You must have known we were different, even before we spoke." I felt my lip tremble, the way Tommy's always does when the world overwhelms him. "If you think I'm so weak, then why are we still friends?"

Marian looked down at me. "Because you're stable."

We both stared at each other, all those stories separating us. Around us, life carried on like normal, the city alive with life. I barely noticed it. All I could concentrate on was her. Her life. The one that I had finally seen for myself was fading, like the last flicker of a candle right before it goes dark.

"You're a great friend, Liv," Marian said. "The very best. *My* very best." She leaned her frail body through the window and blew me an air-kiss. I pretended to catch it, like I always did with Tommy. "We'll talk soon, okay? As soon as I'm feeling more like myself."

My youth and my age simultaneously weighed down on me. "When will that be?"

She tilted her head. "I don't know."

I left my cooler on her steps and climbed back into the car. We slowly pulled away. I watched as Marian's apartment became smaller in the rearview and thought about the irony of it all: the fact that I'd spent so much time concerned that something terrible might happen to me, only for something terrible to happen to her.

"Mama," Tommy said from the back seat, "is Aunt Marian okay?"

I turned and handed him his favorite stuffed dinosaur, which had fallen to the floor. He pressed his face against it like a plush, prehistoric pillow.

"I hope so." The car accelerated up the block. I glanced back at the mirror, hoping to catch one more glimpse of Marian in her window before we were swallowed by the tunnel. I was too late. By the time I looked up, the reflection of her was already gone.

FIFTY-SIX

I guess what I need for you to know is that Marian was dying. Just like that. One day, she was fine, her life a blur of cocktails and friendship and limitless days ahead. But the next day, a doctor examined her with some magical device that saw into her future and saw that there was no future left for her to see.

We finally started to talk about the hard stuff. There wasn't time left for us to pretend. According to Marian's doctors, she had a few weeks—maybe a few months—left.

"I made a list," Marian told me over the phone on the last weekend in May. She was alone in her apartment, despite my and Andrew's constant requests for her to stay with us, when she called. "I wasn't going to tell you, since it goes against everything I stand for," she explained. "But considering the circumstances, I figured I'd better shoot it straight while I still can."

I was at the farmers' market, a savory tart in my hands. I'd baked it during one of my midnight cooking sessions, which Marian had begun to call the "Great Witching Hour Cook-Off," like my grief was just a bad reality show and not plain reality. I'm sure it doesn't surprise you that her sense of humor remained intact, even then. I placed a bunch of swiss chard into my bag. "What kind of list?"

"A bucket list, I guess." Through the line, I heard her fumble with paper. "Only I don't have time to do any of it now." She coughed violently, her new habit. "I probably should have made it a decade ago." She coughed again. "Please don't say 'I told you so.'"

I stopped at Sunshine's table, in search of her. I wanted to give her the tart, show her how far I'd come since the rainbow pizza incident. She was nowhere to be found. "Read it to me."

"Some of it is embarrassing," Marian admitted.

"Prove it."

"Fine," she huffed. "But I'm dying, so you're not allowed to make fun of me."

"I make no promises," I said.

I heard her flip through pages. "Go to Paris," she finally said. "I've traveled to a million different places and yet I've never once seen the Eiffel Tower, which I know I shouldn't care about because everyone says it's trash. But still."

"A little trite," I said. "Keep going."

"Run a marathon."

"Really?" I said, unable to hide my surprise.

"No," Marian said. "Not really. But I felt like I should add that one in there so that if someone finds my journals once I'm dead, they'll think I was a better person than I really am."

"Fair," I told her. "Anything else?"

"Fall in love," she said and then remained quiet, her words just hovering there for us both to face. "Sam was great. But I was thinking about it today, and I don't think I've ever actually been in love—with him or anyone else—for real. Not like you and Andy."

I picked up some radishes, held them to my face, and pretended to smell them—as though that was normal—to hide my emerging tears. "That's not true. You've been in love."

"I figured that one would kill you," she said through a quiet laugh that instantly sent her into another coughing fit. "It's so clichéd and sad."

"It's not that," I lied. "It's just that—"

"I'm running out of time, Liv," she interrupted. "I can feel it in my body. I know that I don't have a lot of days left."

"You're not running out of time," I assured her. "You're still here."

"You're right." Her voice was plagued by weakness. "But there's one problem."

"Is this about the marathon again?" I said, my best attempt at a joke at a time when jokes could no longer save us. "Get it? Running."

"No," Marian said. "The problem is that I won't be here for long."

After we ended our call, I set my tart on the table.

"Can I help you with something?"

I looked up and found a woman, about my age, standing before me. I wiped my face. "I'm looking for Sunshine." I gestured to my tart. "I made her something."

"Thank you," she said, her eyes glassy. "I know she'll appreciate that." Beyond her shoulder, I noticed an assortment of other foil-wrapped baked goods.

"Is she here?" I asked, and I watched her cuff her sleeves before she carried my tart away. That's when I saw it: the thin black line tattooed across her skin. "Unfortunately, Mom isn't doing so great." She returned to the table, arranged some of the springtime produce, and then waved to someone behind me. "Hi, ladies." She pointed to the pile of home-made goods behind her. "Do you mind leaving everything back there?"

From behind me, a pair of women—both about Sunshine's age—marched up to the table, their arms practically overflowing with Tupperware. They kissed Sunshine's daughter on her cheek and then quietly disappeared.

"It's funny." Sunshine's daughter spoke to me while she helped another customer. "My whole damn life, those women drove my mother nuts." She smiled at some memory. "She's nothing like them." She handed the customer her bag. "But it turns out, in the end, they've really come through for her." She shook her head, ready to change the topic, and turned her attention to a crumpled piece of paper on her table. She pulled a pen from her back pocket. "I'd better get back to this," she said. "This place has a to-do list about a mile long this time of year."

I observed the stress stamped across her face. "Do you need help?"

A new group of customers wandered toward us. "What do you mean?"

"I'm good with lists." I gestured to her paper. "They're kind of my thing."

"Oh." She looked confused by my offer. "I, um—"

"I could use the work," I admitted. "As it turns out, I'm sort of in between gigs."

She paused, thinking about it. "Yeah," she finally decided. "Okay." I watched her shoulders settle. "To be honest, I really need the help."

I stepped behind the table and glanced at her paper. "Me too." I looked up at her and extended my hand. "I'm Liv."

"Skye," she said, accepting my gesture. "Welcome aboard."

Later that afternoon, my fingernails caked with dirt, I crossed out the final item. Never in a million years had I ever imagined myself there, and yet in that moment, I felt more like myself than I had in a long time.

"Any chance you'd want to come back next weekend?" Skye reached into her cashbox and handed me a thin stack of bills. "Maybe the one after that, too?" she said with a laugh.

I glanced down at the vibrant piles of produce arranged on her table, suddenly wondering where it'd all end up. How might each customer prepare it? What memories might come from those meals? I thought of Marian. If she were there beside me, I knew she'd offer some story—something about a flavor that would inspire me or a recipe that would change my outlook on a particular cuisine or a new experience that was right there, just waiting for me among that earthy display, if only I'd take a step forward and grab hold of it.

"Actually," I said, looking up at her. I reached toward those piles and rubbed some leaves between my fingers. They emitted an unexpected scent—something bright and fragrant and new. It awoke something in me. I rubbed them again. "I think I would."

I started to walk away.

"Thanks for thinking of her." Skye reached into one of her buckets. "Here." She handed me a generous bunch of tender spring onions. "Take some." She smiled the false smile of a woman in horrible pain. "They're Mom's favorite. She's always said spring is the best time for cooking. For living, really." She exhaled heavily. "The only problem is that all the good stuff is so fleeting. You peek out in the fields one minute and they're bursting with this stuff." She clapped her hands together, sending particles of dirt into the air. "But when you look out again"—she snapped her mud-caked fingers—"just like that, it's all gone." She shrugged. "That's the only problem with spring. It's such a short season."

At home that afternoon, I stood at the sink to wash the spring onions. When I did, I noticed Tommy's rinsed-out can on the counter, and the green tendril that had finally sprouted through the dirt. I touched the delicate sprig of life, aware of both its beauty and its fragility.

Spring.

Based on what Skye had said, Sunshine was right.

It really is the most beautiful, and yet the most fleeting, season.

FIFTY-SEVEN

I'm smoking a porch cigarette for the first time in months, and it's all your fault." It was the middle of the night, my pajamas streaked with butter. I pressed my phone against my ear. "Also, I'm aware that it's incredibly selfish of me to call you at this hour." I inhaled a dry, tasteless drag. "But I only had two choices: call you or throw a five-pound box of butter at my kitchen wall in a fit of rage."

"Another tough night with the scones?" Marian's voice was scratchy with sleep and sickness.

"No matter how much butter I use, I can't get a flaky center." I rubbed my cigarette butt out on our porch. "Also, you're dying."

"Right." Through the line, I heard the muffled movements of her body as she pulled herself upright in her bed. "Well, if my years as a food writer have taught me anything, it's that scones are hard," she said. "And so is death."

I changed the topic. "I need you to be honest with me," I said. "Did you know that something was wrong—that you were sick—that day you first took me to the Nettle Center?"

"I did," she admitted. "Though I didn't know *how* sick." Marian sighed heavily. "I first saw the initial scans not long before that trip. Don't get me wrong. The doctor had told me." She laughed, even though nothing about the situation was funny. "It's hard to explain. I just wasn't ready to believe that any of it was real yet. I just kept telling myself those scans were wrong."

I placed the cigarette pack back in my cigar box and set the old, weatherworn thing beside me. "Why didn't you tell me?"

"I'm not sure." Marian paused. "Sometimes lying is just easier."

Up and down our block, it had begun to softly rain, more a gentle mist than a storm. "Did we cause this?" I asked, like we'd opened some metaphysical door the moment we'd questioned our own vitality.

"I don't think death works like that," Marian said and left it at that, which made me think that maybe she'd wondered about it, too. "This is just life," she added. "This is just how it is sometimes, you know?" It was the most truthful statement either of us had spoken in months. "So, what are you going to do, Liv?" Marian finally asked. "When this is all over."

Across the street, a light clicked on in one of my neighbor's homes. "What do you mean?" I asked, even though I knew exactly what she meant. I was just buying time. She wanted to know what I would do with myself once she was gone. If I'd keep evolving or fall back into my old routine. You see, it was up to me. That was the thing I'd only recently come to understand: that we aren't born with one life, but with two. The life we live before we understand loss, and the one we finally live once we realize that, despite our many efforts, our life will ultimately end. "To be honest, I don't think a scone bakery is anywhere in my immediate future," I said.

"Liv, come on."

The rain stopped, leaving behind a trace of dewy freshness. "I don't know," I told her. "I don't know what I'm supposed to do with myself once you're gone."

"I was wrong, Liv." Across the street, the light clicked off. "We're not as young as we think."

In the distance, a faint web of light emerged in the night sky. *Morning.* I watched it spread slowly, like watercolors across canvas, a new day literally dawning before me. "I know."

FIFTY-EIGHT

Marian reached out to me on the first Saturday in June to invite me to brunch. I literally fell out of bed—clumsy like a bad comedy character—when I read her message. I darted off the mattress, anxious to get dressed and jump on a train. Anxious, really, about everything.

I spent the whole train ride staring out the window and imagining Marian. I hadn't seen her since that day I'd dragged my cooler to her steps. The train sped past splotches of towns. I envisioned what it'd be like when I turned up at her apartment. In my mind, she'd magically be better. She'd wear her favorite jeans, her lips cherry red, her blonde hair miraculously grown back as she stood in her doorway, ready to launch snarky banter at me.

"I'm sorry," she said when I arrived, her newly frail body hidden beneath a terry cloth bathrobe. Defeat was branded all across her face. "I really did try."

We spent the rest of the day in her bed. It felt strange to be back inside Marian's apartment—the same apartment she'd lived in all those years ago. I barely remembered the last time I'd visited her there. That happens as you age. Your friendships become public, all your exchanges taking place in crowded restaurants and coffee shops while a million people walk past. It isn't like when you were young, your relationships built upon drunken sleepovers and getting dressed for weekends while pressed against the same bathroom vanity, a certain pride felt in know-ing which cabinet housed your friend's wineglasses or where to find her spare key.

"So, what happened?" I asked, and I pulled an old but familiar book from a shelf beside her bed. *Poems for Every Season*. The one she'd pretended to barely remember. I still easily recalled the two of us in that modernism seminar when we first learned we shared a birthday. After our professor had clicked through a presentation about Bloomsday, I'd tapped Marian's desk with my pen. "That's my birthday," I'd whispered. Marian paused, taking me in through the darkened lecture hall, and pursed her lips—ruby red, even back then. "Really? Mine too," she said as our professor clicked to the next slide. I wondered how such a cool, beautiful person could possibly be so intimately connected to me.

"I don't know," Marian said, snapping me back into the present. "Brunch sounded easy." She pulled her blanket up to her neck. "I woke up feeling better, but when I moved out of bed to get myself dressed—"

She didn't finish her statement. I flipped open the anthology and landed on a work I vaguely remembered. My eyes skimmed the lines—all marked with Marian's ancient annotations. Outside the windows, an explosion of noise floated upward from the street. "Why didn't you ever move out of here?" I set the book beside me. "That's not a judgment," I clarified. "I love this apartment. I mean, the noise pollution alone definitely helps to make it feel 'classic New York.'" I adjusted my pillow. "It's just, well, you've lived here since we were in our early twenties. Didn't you ever get the urge to upgrade?"

Marian's cheek rested against her pillow. "Because I bought it."

"Very funny."

"I'm serious." She smiled weakly. "A few months ago. My landlord presented me with an opportunity. I figured that, in the midst of every-thing, it could be my one source of stability. I had some money put aside, so I just went for it."

I tousled my hair. "Why didn't you tell me?" Outside the window, the noise died down. "I would have bought you champagne. We would have celebrated."

"I tried," she said. "But you were always too busy." Marian shrugged from beneath her sheets. "Plus, I think I was in denial. I didn't want to admit that I was actually a grown-up."

A wave of nausea washed over me. The room started to spin like one of Tommy's crazy topsy-turvy toys. I placed my hands on the mattress to steady myself.

"What?" Marian tried to scoot herself upright; she made it only partway. "What is it?"

I smacked my tongue and briefly closed my eyes. "I'm sorry," I whispered. "This year." I gestured my hand around her apartment. "All of this." I opened my eyes. "It's just so much."

"I'm sorry, too." Marian touched my hand. "For all of it."

Soon after, we fell into a deep sleep, our bodies and minds exhausted in a thousand ways. I don't know how long we were out, only that when I finally awoke—my chin coated with a slick of drool, a thousand messages from Andrew blinking on my phone—it was night.

"Hey." Marian woke beside me. "How long was I out?"

"Not sure." I pulled my hair, matted from sleep, into a messy bun. "I was out, too."

Marian finally pulled herself upright. "I'm starving," she admitted and immediately noticed my face. "I know," she quickly added. "I haven't said that in ages." She smiled, a sliver of her former self right there in her raised lips.

"Should we order something?" I pushed her heavy comforter away from my legs.

Marian pressed her back against the headboard. "Actually, I have a better idea."

For the next half hour, I raided Marian's freezer and pulled out the many cellophane-wrapped creations I'd brought her weeks earlier. They

were labeled with my own familiar penmanship. *Lemon Drizzle Cake.*
Sticky Buns. Currant Shortbread. I carefully unwrapped them and slid
them into her tiny apartment-size oven, each dessert an expression of
my grief.

"I think the drizzle cake wins," she said after she'd sampled
everything.

I untied her old apron and rejoined her on the bed. Without asking, I tore a piece off her cake. "It's good," I said, my mouth full. "But
I feel like it's missing something."

Marian smiled. "The drizzle," she said.

"Damn it." I dropped my feet to the floor, ready to fetch the pot
of sugary liquid I'd been warming on the stove. Before I stood, Marian
grabbed my arm.

"I'm kidding," she said. "It's fine. It's *more* than fine." The corners
of her eyes creased with emotion. "It's probably one of the nicest things
you've ever done for me."

I resettled myself and indulged in another bite of cake, simultaneously warm and frozen in spots. "What made you pursue food writing all those years ago?" Almost two decades had passed since she'd
published her first food piece. It's terrible, but to be honest, I'd never
thought to ask. That's another thing that happens with age. Your career
just becomes a part of you, as much a piece of your identity as your
name. *This is John, the accountant. This is Cindy, the nurse.* We forget
that we were all other people before those titles.

Marian distracted herself with another mouthful of cake. "It's silly."

I raised my brows, a challenge. "Try me."

She wiped her sticky fingers on her bathrobe. "Well, from the start,
I liked the idea of food writing. There's a sort of secret romance to it,
the notion that people would read my articles and then feel inspired
to gather for some celebratory meal, or to share an intimate drink,
or to prepare a special recipe for someone they love." She closed her
eyes, embarrassed by her own words. "I don't know. From early on, I

conjured this vision that one day, I'd learn something new through my writing and that eventually I'd cook that food for somebody, too. That I'd have a table and a partner who sat at it. That all those stories I was crafting might help me to get there somehow."

She didn't expound more on that, and I didn't ask her to. Instead, for the next few hours, we watched bad reruns of once-good television shows we'd loved in college. Outside her window, the city was vibrant with neon and noise, hints of it drifting into her apartment and creating the illusion that we were still out there and a part of it all.

"I have a confession," Marian announced a little while later, our stomachs full of sugar.

"You didn't like the shortbread. I know. I tried it a few times, but I just couldn't get the texture right."

"It's not about the shortbread," she told me. "It's about the envelopes." I looked at her in question. "The ones with the test results," she explained. "Poppy mixed up the cards. She told me when I saw her working in my neighborhood." Marian spoke slowly. "She hadn't realized her mistake until a few days after we'd had our tests. By the time we saw her weeks later at that café, I think she was too scared to say anything." Marian's eyes were wet with emotion. "She finally confessed when I saw her that day at the coffee shop. I guess enough time had passed that she felt okay admitting her mistake." She swallowed hard, unsure if she wanted to ingest her confession or allow it to slide past her lips. "Though, if I'm being honest, she didn't need to tell me anything, Liv. Deep down, I knew from the beginning which card was mine."

I set my plate of crumbs on her nightstand. "What are you talking about?"

Outside her window, a drunk person screamed something incoherent into the night. "I already knew my results. I first had the test done when I was at the Nettle Center to research the matcha piece a few weeks before we ever went." Marian sighed heavily. "It was a few weeks after my doctor told me about my first scans." She closed her eyes as she spoke, as though too tired or afraid to look at me. "Instead of my results on that first visit, one of Dahlia's assistants gave me back a blank card." I watched her chest barely rise and fall as she inhaled a few shallow breaths. "I was so desperate to find out why that I bribed one of the counter girls with an invitation to a big magazine launch party." She peeled open her eyelids. "It only took a few minutes for her to go in the back and get me my actual results before Dahlia ground them up into dirt."

"I don't understand," I mumbled. "You'd already had the test? You'd already gotten results?" I felt delirious. "Why didn't you tell me?"

"I don't know." Marian looked so weak as she spoke, when she'd always been so strong. "I guess because I kept trying to convince myself that the test was fake, and so there was nothing for me to tell you." She stopped herself. "But the problem was that a part of me continued to question if it was real."

"Wait." I sat up a little straighter. "I'm still unclear. Why did we *both* get blank cards?"

"You didn't," she explained again. "It was never your card, Liv. That blank card—that date—was always mine." She stared at her bed. "I found out they give patients blank cards instead of their real results when things turn up undesirable. I guess death isn't a good look in their industry."

"So, you . . . knew?"

She gripped the edges of the blanket for support. "I initially assumed it was all just some freak error, that there was no way my doctor—or Dahlia, for that matter—was right. There was no way my life was closing in on me." She released the blanket and met my eyes. "When you started to express concerns about aging, I figured it was the perfect excuse to go back so that I could have the test redone and prove that it was pretend." I stared at her while she spoke. She looked down. "I never thought my results would come back blank again. I never thought something might actually be wrong."

My vision was blurred by tears. "I spent months thinking about those results, Mar." My heart began to race, while my breath slowed down. I was both fire and water, simultaneously furious and calm. "Why didn't you—"

"I didn't want you to worry about me," she interjected. "Plus, Poppy's mix-up seemed like a good opportunity."

"An opportunity?" I questioned. "For what?"

She took my hand in hers, her grip as frail as a child's. "You were so upset about your birthday. I guess I thought that if you believed for a short time that something was wrong, that you didn't have forever, that you'd finally see how good your life already is, or that you'd stop making excuses. I never thought this whole charade would carry on for this long. I wanted to tell you a million different times, Liv. I swear. But every time I tried, it just felt like you were in the middle of taking steps to make your life even better. I know it sounds strange, but I didn't want to take that from you." Marian stopped herself. She turned toward the window and that wrought iron fire escape, where we'd spent so many nights of our youth. "Do you remember that night when we sat out there after you won that poetry contest? You were so excited, your whole life still stretched out far beyond you. It was like you had all the hope of the whole city bottled up inside of you." She held my hand. "You're still that person, Liv. The one you were that night." She squeezed my palm. "That hopeful girl is still alive in you."

I blinked, as though waking from a long, confusing dream. In that moment, nothing made sense, and yet, for the first time in forever, everything did. "But, the boxes."

"I have a stack of them in my closet," she said, and she pointed across the room. "I started to get them right after my first visit." She adjusted her blanket. "After our tests, someone must have seen my blank card—the one Poppy mixed up—inside your file and added you to the mailing list," she offered, a final point of explanation for a situation that would never fully be clear.

We didn't speak after that. What else was there left to say? Soon, Marian fell asleep again, her head at rest beside mine like we were children at a slumber party. It was getting late. I knew I should gather my things and head home; after all, I had my own child to put to bed. But I couldn't force myself to leave. Some voice inside me just kept telling me to stay. I sent Andrew a message and told him I'd be home in the morning, that Marian needed me. What I really meant—what Andrew already knew—was how much I still needed her. How much I needed these final moments: us, these muted city noises, the soft sounds of her breath.

I set my phone on the nightstand and clicked off the volume. Through Marian's gauzy curtains, the city continued to hum, on and on like a party guest who won't ever leave. I closed my eyes and listened to the world around me until it had all melded together into one quiet song. I forced myself to stay awake and listen to it for as long as I could.

In the end, it was not nearly long enough.

Nothing ever is.

FIFTY-NINE

You already knew this part was coming: the moment where I tell you that my whole life fractured like glass. You probably just didn't want to believe it. Trust me. I can relate.

It was the next weekend, a Sunday. The end of one week, or the beginning of the next, depending on whom you ask. Marian had called the night before. "I'm at the hospital," she said. "I called an ambulance earlier. I don't want to be here. I should have called you instead."

"What happened?" I asked, groggy with sleep. I pulled my phone from my face and glanced at my calendar. It was already June. Not quite our birthday but close enough for that date to matter. "You're not due for your next round of treatments for a few weeks. I thought your doctors said your last scan looked okay."

"I don't know," Marian said. "I just don't feel right." She explained that the doctors would run tests in the morning, conduct extra scans, and consider beginning her treatments early. "Will you come?" It was the first time she'd asked me to attend any of her medical visits. "I don't want to be alone."

"Of course," I said. "I'll come now."

She told me to wait until the morning. By then, she'd be finished being poked and prodded. "I'll call you once my tests are done," she explained. "You can come then."

I'd been late to everything all my life. Late to my job. Late to appointments. Late to making life choices. But not that morning. I took the early train, the one that departs when the sky is still smudged with black. When I emerged at street level, the city was still quiet. I glanced at my old watch. It was too soon to call her. Too soon, really, for anything.

I walked. With no sense of purpose or direction. I didn't know where I was going. Eventually, I accepted that there was only one place left. The museum had opened only moments before I stepped inside the exhibition room and sat on our bench. I was alone. For a long time, I stared at those massive paintings, hoping to lose myself in that watery scene. But it was no use. My mind was too busy. The illusion was finally gone.

My phone rang, breaking the silence of the exhibition space.

"Hi." I pressed the phone against my ear without even looking at it. "It's me," I said, as though it might be someone else. "I'm a few blocks over. Are you—"

"Good morning." An unfamiliar voice echoed through the line. "I'm looking for an Olivia Strauss."

I pulled the phone away from my face and realized that a random local number, and not Marian's number, had appeared on my screen. "Wait. What?"

"Maybe I have the wrong—"

"This is Olivia," I said and cleared my throat. "Who is this?"

"This is Dr. Hamilton," the voice explained. "Your friend Marian had asked me to call you."

I sat up at the sound of her name. "Are her tests done? I can be there in ten—"

"I'm sorry, Mrs. Strauss," he said, and I knew in that instant that nothing would ever be the same again. "Your friend Marian passed away this morning." His voice cracked at the end of his statement. "She gave me your name and phone number weeks ago. She made it very clear that when the time came, you were the person I should call."

I blinked, but all I saw were brushstrokes of water, like I was drowning. "But that's not fair," I said, like a child. "Her birthday is next week. She still had a week," I informed him, even though he wouldn't have a clue what I meant. "She still had time."

In the backdrop, an ensemble of medical machines beeped. "I know," he said. "She made a point to tell me that last night, too."

SIXTY

Just like that, it was over. Marian's life. The last year and its messes. It was a wrap. The curtain had dropped. The producers had left the set. There was no time left for a happy ending.

A few days later, I found myself alone in our kitchen, surrounded by sympathy cards and fruit baskets and potted plants, as though the cure for grief was a hit of vitamin C and some greenery. I didn't know what to do with my hands. Finally, I ripped apart the plastic on one of the baskets and set the citrus fruit into a bowl because it felt like a normal thing to do. But it wasn't normal. Nothing was anymore. I stopped myself and tossed all the fruit into the trash.

I just stood there beside a bin of discarded grapefruit. The smell and the sight of it was making me feel nauseous. I forced myself to swallow the queasy feeling. I tied up the garbage bag and stepped outside. It was time.

Summer would arrive soon. Our block smelled subtly of flowers, as though the whole world had let out one big yawn and then finally begun to bloom again. I took a step. It all looked the same as it had one year earlier, on the night I'd attended Suzanne's party. But it wasn't the same. In my little world, everything had become so unrecognizably different.

I moved down our driveway and dropped the bag into our plastic garbage bin. Pebbles of gravel pressed against my bare feet. Before I started back inside, I pulled open our mailbox, then sat on our porch and sifted through the stack of paper. Junk mail. A summons for jury duty I knew I'd ignore. Coupons for local big-box stores. An overdue notice from the library. I was about to toss it all. But that's when something at the bottom of the pile caught my eye. The envelope was inconspicuous enough that I nearly threw it away by mistake. There was only one distinguishable detail about it: the address was penned in Marian's familiar script.

I peeled back the envelope flap slowly, my hands shaking. I didn't know what I'd find inside it, like I expected a note in which she informed me that it was all a terrible prank.

> Liv—I meant what I said that day at brunch. Your life
> is still just starting. You still have a whole world's worth
> of opportunities out there. You still have enough time
> to actually go live your dreams.

I ran my thumb across the words and tried to imagine when she had written the note. During her final hours at home? In the hospital, her life closing in on her? When I was done reading, I swooped my finger through the envelope again, the weight of it suggesting that something else was still inside it. I pulled out a smaller, business card–size envelope, similar to the one I'd found tucked inside my manila medical folder all those months ago. My heart beat harder. I cautiously opened it and discovered a petite note card and a silver key.

> I tossed the card—my card from my first test, the one
> that was originally inside this envelope. I figured that,
> after everything, we were both better off without it.

That day that I saw Poppy, I asked her: I wanted to know for sure what she knew about your date. Your actual date. I had planned to tell you what she said that day when I called you. But once we started talking, I realized it wasn't right.

I thought about writing that date here. However, in the end, I think it's better that, in life, we don't know certain things. But I'll tell you this: I meant it when I said that you're fine, Liv. Your whole life is still stretched out before you. You're not going anywhere. Not yet.

This time last year, taking you to that place seemed like the perfect gift to show you that you still had your whole life ahead of you. In the end, I thought of something more appropriate instead.

You always said you wanted a room of one's own, Liv. Now you have one. It's yours. The apartment. The noise. The alone time. The quiet. Do with it whatever you wish. All I ask is that you promise me you'll do something. That you'll embrace this second half of your life. That whatever it is you want, you'll stop making lists about it. That you'll actually go do it instead.

When I looked up, my eyes burning, the neighborhood women were perched at the end of our driveway watching me. Allison stood in the middle of the group, holding a stack of Tupperware so tall it concealed half her face.

"You look busy," Allison shouted and then nodded toward the pile of mail in my lap. "We'll just leave this here for you on the curb," she added as she set the meals on the ground. She waved and then, taking the lead for the group, moved back down our block, leaving me alone with my thoughts. It was the nicest thing she'd ever done for me.

You can probably imagine what I did next. Some habits are just impossible to break. Once my neighbors were out of view, I reached beneath our bush and pulled out my old cigar box. I'd never pulled it out in the light of day. It looked less alluring. More beat up and sad. Inside were years' worth of stumped-out cigarette butts. I flicked my thumb against the lighter and watched it spark, the old thing finally too tired and worn out to produce a flame.

I moved down our driveway, pulled the lid off our trash bin, and flipped the box over. When it was empty, I moved back to the porch just as the sprinklers clicked to life, dampening my feet. It sounds strange, but I liked the feeling of it. It made me remember that I was alive.

I set the letter inside my empty cigar box, her final words to me safely tucked away in the same place where my anxieties had once lived. At that exact moment, Marian's life was over. But not mine. I still had a chance to move forward. To break my old patterns. To revise the trajectory of my life. To start over. To try again.

Time.

Despite what I'd convinced myself of, I hadn't reached the end. Not yet.

SIXTY-ONE

The Friday before my birthday, I found myself back in Dr. Greene's office, a cold probe pressed against my neck. He hovered over me, his favorite phallus-shaped device tight in his grip.

He clicked off the ultrasound machine. "Well, I have some positive news." He stood and walked across the room. "Your thyroid looks fine. We can wait two years for a follow-up."

"That is positive news," I agreed.

He squirted some hand sanitizer into his palms. "That wasn't the *positive* news."

I felt my shoulders slump. "Okay." I sat up and mentally prepared myself for one of his stand-up comedy routines. "What do you mean?"

He picked up a manila folder. "I was looking through your lab report prior to our appointment." The mere sight of that folder sent me into an immediate whirlwind of panic. "Overall, everything looks normal."

"That's good." I couldn't shake the feeling that he was about to drop a bomb on me. "I think."

He stopped flipping. "There was *one* thing."

My heart stopped beating in my chest. "What?" Every cell in my body tightened.

Dr. Greene set down the folder. He sat on a metal stool and crossed his legs. "Are you aware that you're pregnant?"

Instantly, the panic ceased. "Very funny." I scooted myself off the table, the thin tissue crinkling beneath me. "I see where you're going with this. *Positive.* Pregnancy." I pulled my old cross-body bag from a hook and waited for him to laugh. Instead, he smiled. "Wait." My voice grew shaky. "You *are* kidding." Suddenly, I felt like I might be sick. "Right?"

"I'm not." Dr. Greene clicked on the lights. "I wouldn't make a joke about something like that," he added, suddenly the poster child of ethical humor.

"I—" My bag slipped from my grip and fell onto the floor in a heap. "I don't—"

"Congratulations, Olivia."

"Huh?" The whole room spun like a fun house. "What do you—"

"On the baby," he clarified. "Congrats."

I fell back onto the examination table and gripped the edges so I wouldn't pass out. "Shit," I mumbled before I could edit myself.

~

It felt like the ultimate practical joke from Marian. With everything that had been happening around me, I must have been too caught up to notice or worry that I was late. I kept driving, unaware of where I was heading. Before me, a traffic light changed to red. I blew right through it.

Up ahead, I saw a familiar-looking street that I was too delirious to place. Without thinking, I clicked on my blinker. My car rolled over the curb and into a practically empty parking lot. I turned off the ignition and dropped my head against the steering wheel, unsure if I wanted to scream or laugh or cry or do all of the above. I probably looked dead. I shouldn't have been surprised when someone knocked on my window. I lifted my face and blinked hard, finally realizing where I'd parked the car.

I buzzed down the window. Sunshine stared back at me. The sun was a splash of gold behind her. I squinted and saw that her face was indented in new places, her whole figure thinner than it had been at our last meeting. Still, if she were a stranger whom I'd breezed past on the street, I never would have known she was sick. Illness, I've learned, is sneaky that way. Sometimes, it fails to truly reveal itself until the very end.

"You know, I owe you a big thank-you." She leaned closer to the car. "Skye wouldn't have been able to run things these last few weeks without your help."

I blinked again and watched as the yoga studio just beyond her shoulders came into focus. I had no idea how I'd even ended up there, and yet in that instant I knew it was exactly where I'd needed to land. Life was funny like that.

"My friend died." The words spilled from me like water through a sieve. "And I'm pregnant." It was the first time I'd stated either fact out loud, the vast juxtaposition between them suddenly abundantly clear.

"I'm sorry." Sunshine's face became sketched with new lines of concern. "But also . . . congrats?"

My eyes began to burn. I braced myself for the tears that I assumed would soon pour out of me. Much to my surprise, I started to laugh instead. My shoulders shook as though my body was trying to release the many conflicting emotions—grief and joy and every nuanced feeling in between—that had taken up residence inside me. "I'm sorry," I said. "It's been a strange couple of weeks. I don't even know what I feel anymore, if I'm being honest."

Sunshine laughed then, too. "I can certainly relate to that." After another brief burst of laughter, we both paused to catch our breath. "You know, the studio doesn't open for another hour." She glanced behind her, as though in search of something. "There's this new little breakfast spot up the street. I was going to walk over there to pass the time." She pressed her hand against the window frame. "Would you like to join me, Olivia?"

A few minutes later, we found ourselves seated across from each other. Our waiter set down my plate of jewel-colored berries, thick-cut toast, and eggs—a hearty-enough portion to nourish my own body and the life inside it. I took a bite and then another, surprised by my own appetite. It was the first time in ages that I felt like I had a real taste for anything.

"That looks good." Sunshine wrapped her hands around a mug of herbal tea. "Unfortunately, I haven't been able to eat much lately." I set down my fork, suddenly paralyzed by guilt. Sunshine shooed away my gesture. "Don't be silly. That isn't what I meant." She pushed my plate closer to me. "Plus, *you* need to eat." She smiled. "Eggs are good for you when you're expecting." She sipped her tea. "Anyway, I'm sure Skye told you I had to undergo a procedure." She stopped herself and inhaled. "It seems some of the bad stuff decided to come back."

A familiar feeling of dread settled upon me. "She didn't tell me anything specific," I said. "I didn't want to ask her. I was afraid I'd make her more upset. I just kind of assumed . . ."

Sunshine set her mug back on the table. I braced myself for the worst. "Well, the good news is that I'm okay. The doctors found it really early this time. They've assured me more than once that this is not a death sentence. It was just a bump in the road, one that, thanks to a successful surgery, is already in the rearview now."

I felt my shoulders settle. I pressed my napkin against my mouth, unsure what to say.

Sunshine tucked a loose strand of gray hair behind her ear. "Anyway, I'm just waiting for my appetite to finally come back. All that worrying, you know? It messes with your insides." I *did* know. I nodded my understanding. She waved over our waiter. He poured more hot water into her mug. "So, do you want to talk about your friend?" She squeezed a lemon wedge into the water. "It sounds like you've had a lot going on in your own life since I saw you last."

One year earlier, I'd sat at a different table, across from a different woman, talking about the state of my life. How could I possibly describe the events that had unfolded in the last twelve months? "I just miss her," I said, plain and simple. It was the truest thing I knew right then. "It's been hard." Neither of us spoke for a few minutes. Sometimes, you just have to sit quietly with your grief and give it room to breathe. You have to acknowledge that it is a part of you, and that it probably always will be. "She would have celebrated her birthday this weekend," I finally continued as I looked down at my half-empty plate. "It turns out I still will. Sunday, actually." I lifted my chin. "We were born on the same day."

"Well then." Sunshine's eyes glimmered with kindness. "Happy almost birthday to you." She unwrapped a fresh tea bag. "Let me guess. The big twenty-two?"

"Close." I smiled. "More like the big four-oh."

Sunshine shook her head slowly, like a wise old owl who knew some secret I hadn't yet been told. "I remember my fortieth." She turned away from me briefly and looked wistfully at something I couldn't see. "That was about a million years ago." A smile emerged across her aging face. "Or yesterday." She shrugged. "It all starts to blend together at my age."

Inside my bag, my phone alarm buzzed. "I should get going," I said. "My son's school has an early dismissal today. It's the last week of the year before summer break." I took one last bite and then reached into my wallet for some bills. "It was good to see you, Sunshine. I'm really glad I ran into you."

Our waiter set our check on the table. Sunshine reached into her own bag, then handed our payment to him. "You know, I've been coming here every Friday morning," she explained. "It's a nice place to have a quiet cup of tea before I lead the weekly support group. Maybe you'd like to start meeting me here for breakfast," she suggested and then paused, weighing out some thought. "And, whenever you're ready, maybe you'd like to join me next door, too." She met my gaze. "It'd be a good place for you to talk about her."

"Okay." Our waiter set our change on the table. "I think I'd like that."

Sunshine nodded, satisfied. "That's great," she said. "I'd like that, too." She took a final sip of tea. "So, same time next week?"

"Sure." I gathered my things and then slid out of my chair. Nearby, a bell chimed as the café door swung open and a new group of patrons blew in. "I'll see you then."

SIXTY-TWO

We arrived at the flamingo exhibit early Sunday morning. Tommy and I sat on our bench. Andrew appeared with striped bags of popcorn. For a while, the three of us sat and watched those beautiful coral creatures breeze through their man-made lagoon.

"Happy birthday, Liv." Andrew reached his arm over Tommy's body and squeezed my shoulder. "It's been one hell of a year."

The leaves on the exhibit's artificial palm trees billowed. "Thank you." I watched several flamingos flap their majestic neon wings. Tommy jumped off the bench and ran toward the exhibit. I rested my head on Andrew's shoulder and watched him. My Tommy. The baby who was once nothing more than a figment of my imagination made real. "I'm pregnant."

Andrew choked on a piece of popcorn. "I'm sorry?"

"You're not going to have a stroke or something, right?" Nearby, a group of children, presumably on an end-of-the-year field trip, walked past in a single-file line, all holding each other's hands. A little blonde girl in a brilliantly mismatched ensemble waved to us.

Andrew turned to me. "You're serious?"

"Unless the three tests I took last night were wrong."

Andrew glanced back at the flamingos. "Shit."

Slowly, a smile unfolded across his face. I smiled, too, then shrugged. I wish I could perfectly explain to you what I felt in that moment, knowing that, in just a few months, my new circumstances would force me to change once more. That I'd become a different person. For a moment, I closed my eyes and thought about what it would mean to have a newborn in our home again. All the chaos and unpredictability. All the sleeplessness and second-guessing. All the breast pumps and child carriers and endless items that ask you to give up parts of yourself. It wasn't easy. No. It was something else. I looked up at Tommy, my whole heart. It was life.

"Mama, the flamingos want to know if they can have some popcorn," Tommy shouted. I shook my head. He pouted, but only for a moment before he became distracted by some noteworthy rock near his feet.

Andrew nodded toward Tommy. "So, when do we tell the flock?"

I watched Tommy collect assorted treasures from the ground. I thought briefly of the twins. Nothing was ever certain. "Not for a while. I need time to absorb the news myself first."

Andrew playfully tugged a strand of my hair. "If I had told you back in college that you'd have pink hair and be pregnant at forty, would you have believed me?"

"Not in a million years," I said as Tommy slid back into his spot between us. "It turns out life is full of surprises." I smiled. "Even at my age." Simultaneously, Andrew and I draped our arms around Tommy, a feeling of contentment surrounding us like a protective dome.

"Mama, I got you a birthday gift!" Tommy exclaimed. Andrew and I exchanged uncertain glances. Tommy reached into his pocket and pulled out his rock, the one he'd discovered moments earlier. He handed it to me, his face marked with pride. "Happy birthday, Mama."

His gesture was so simple and yet, so genuine. I couldn't help it. My eyes instantly filled with tears at his innocence. It was the best gift I'd ever received. My Tommy. My family. My whole perfectly imperfect and messy life. I accepted the rock and rubbed my fingers across its smooth, warm surface. "I love it," I told him. I loved all of it.

Andrew tossed a fistful of popcorn above him. He threw back his head like a baby bird. "You're going to show me up, kiddo. I haven't even given her my gift yet." With that, Andrew reached into his pocket and pulled out a handful of sparkling confetti. He threw it toward the sky.

I laughed out loud like a child and watched the pieces flutter through the air, the flamingos and the turquoise water just beyond them.

"If you squint," Andrew whispered, "it almost looks like we're on vacation."

We needed that again. I wanted to see the ocean and feel the sun. For me. For my family. For the women in that support group and the moments they would lose. The ones I still had. I thought briefly of the many crumpled bills that remained in my old tote bag, all those symbols of my past self. I knew they weren't enough to get us anywhere. But maybe they were a start.

As the confetti settled on my shoulders, I thought back to the first time I'd read about Franny and my fascination with those exotic creatures had begun. I'd felt so lost back then. I didn't know where I was heading or where I hoped to end up. I was so worried about trying to create a perfect life and a perfect ending. But it was only then, while seated on that bench for my private, impromptu party, that I understood that those things don't exist. There is no such thing as a perfect life. There are only perfect moments.

Andrew picked some confetti off his pant leg and playfully nodded toward my flamboyant friends. "You know, thanks to your hair, you almost look like you could be one of them."

Although it'd taken me a while, like Franny, I'd finally found my way. I just hadn't had to fly around the world to find it. The life I'd wanted had always been there. It was only a matter of me finally learning to open my eyes so I could see it.

"Maybe." I collected a pile of the confetti in my palm. When I felt ready, I blew it away and watched it billow all around me. "But for right now," I told Andrew, "I think I'm okay just being me."

SIXTY-THREE

The next morning, I found myself alone on the train. I didn't know where I was going. I just knew that, after everything, I finally needed time to myself.

The train disappeared into the cavernous mouth of a black tunnel. The lights in my car flickered. When the train emerged into the sunlight, infinite skyscrapers stood statuesque all around the tracks, like monuments dedicated to my past life. I stepped onto the platform and navigated the same corridors and escalators I'd navigated one thousand times before until I eventually emerged at street level.

The memories were everywhere.

I began to walk. I saw her reflection in every shop window I passed. On every street corner, some reminiscence was there waiting for me. I followed the memories like a bread-crumb trail until they eventually led me to her door.

I moved up Marian's steps and opened my bag. I unzipped the lining pocket and reached for the petite envelope she'd sent to me. I unfolded the flap and pulled out her key.

The apartment was exactly as she'd left it. Her bed still unmade. Dishes still set out in the drying rack. Television still turned on. I moved across the space and clicked it off, wondering what she'd been watching in those final hours, yet knowing I never would find out.

I set down my bag. The gauzy curtains billowed from a still-opened window. The whole apartment was marked by bold, dust-filled funnels of sunlight. I paced through the room and ran my fingers over everything, as though a part of her still existed on the surface of her material possessions.

I didn't know what to do. Slowly, I began to put away some of her things, as if she might come back for them. I placed her vintage drinking glasses back in the cupboard. I tucked in her bedsheets, like she'd have the chance to sleep there one last time. Soon, everything was back in its right order. Everything—except for her.

I sat on the edge of her bed. Her old copy of *Through the Looking-Glass*, the one she'd picked up the day it all started, was tossed among her rumpled bedsheets. I ran my fingers across it. Through the window, the city sang to me: the jarring burst of sirens, the incessant hum of traffic, the ambient sound of bodies moving against pavement. I closed my eyes and let the noise fill me. When I opened them, something caught my vision. There, on the opposite side of the room, was an envelope marked with my name. My mouth went dry. I moved toward her desk and reached for it. I took great care to open the flap and then slid out the note card inside it.

The funny thing about writing is that, to some degree, it is always rooted in our pain. Seems like a good time for you to start doing this stuff for real then, no?

I left you the last of the scones in the freezer. Also, Michael's email address is written on a sticky note in the drawer. I know it's not poetry, but it's a start. You have more to say than you realize sometimes, Liv. He's waiting to hear from you.

Xx—Marian

I set down the note card, my hands shaking. A half-drunk glass of water—still stamped with her ruby lip prints—sat on the edge of her desk. I reached for it and gulped down the days-old liquid. I dropped my face into my hands and let more emotion seep out of me. My vision blurring, I wiped some of the pain from my eyes. When I could see more clearly, I felt a slow smile begin to appear across my face as I noticed a framed photograph of the two of us on the adjacent window ledge. It was taken on one of our birthdays, about a million lifetimes ago. In it, Marian and I stood with our cheeks pressed together, the vast ironwork of the Brooklyn Bridge framing our backdrop, our hair whipping across our faces, which were marked only by innocence and the youthful promise of infinite life.

I wiped some dust from the edge of the frame and set it back in its place. And then, all out of excuses, I got to work. I tilted open Marian's laptop. The screen flickered, like it was too depressed to do anything, but then changed course and became illuminated with life. A tab was already open and waiting for me. It was a document Marian had been working on—presumably her last. Unlike her other articles, most of which were rooted in research and travel, this one was a personal essay about the relationship between food and death, all framed around the homemade baked treats I'd brought to her in her final weeks.

I read through it and then stopped at her blinking cursor, wondering what thought she'd hoped to write out next. I stared at the screen. The cursor continued to blink at me, like one of Marian's playful winks. That's when I understood. It was my turn. *Our* turn, to write our story—the one that taught me that I did have something worthwhile to say after all.

I moved across the room and clicked on her tiny, apartment-size oven. I pulled several cellophane-wrapped treats from the freezer and slid them inside. Once they were warmed, I made myself a plate and got situated once again at Marian's desk. I unclasped my old leather watchband, set it down before me, and stretched out my wrists. I spent the rest of the afternoon writing with a sort of fury I hadn't experienced since college. By the time I finally looked up—my plate covered only with morsels—dark shadows had started to fill the apartment. I stared at all my words on the screen. It wasn't the poetry I once thought I'd write. Not even close. It was something better. Something that connected me with Marian, with a new part of myself, with the new life I'd learn to live without her. I slid open Marian's drawer and pulled out the sticky note she'd left for me. Without thinking more about it, I saved the file and sent it to *Hearth*.

I leaned back in Marian's chair and pressed some crumbs into my fingertip. At that moment, I didn't know what would come of my efforts. I didn't know that, the next morning, Michael would write me back to send his sympathies about Marian. That, in the same message, he would tell me how much he liked my piece or that, a few days later, I'd find myself in his office to talk about me taking over other pieces Marian hadn't had the time to complete, and to finally make money— make a career—out of my words. That, eventually, our meeting would open doors that I'd been waiting to open my whole life, and give me a reason to spend several days each week at Marian's desk—where I'd finally found a room of my own, like I'd always wanted.

That was all tomorrow. My future was still a whole day away.

~

I finally left the apartment at dusk and walked back in the direction of the train. All around me, the world buzzed with life. People walked past in pairs, their whole night—their whole lives—just beginning. Entire evenings full of important memories and life-changing mistakes were only blocks away.

I stepped into a coffee shop a few streets away from Marian's apartment. Inside, an orchestra of espresso machines hissed with steam. I approached the counter. When I did, a young woman turned to greet me, a linen apron tied around her waist. A flash of recognition swept across both our faces. *Poppy.*

"Can I take your order?" she asked as she squinted and assessed my face.

I placed my hand on my belly. "A decaf latte, please," I said, unsure of how to proceed.

She turned toward her coffee station and began to prepare my order, periodically glancing back at me over her shoulder. I watched her warm my milk, knowing that it was my last chance to finally find out more about the test that had rolled all the events of the last year into motion.

She handed me my coffee. "Do I know you from somewhere?"

I bit my lip. It would have been so easy for me to ask her. To remind her about that blank card. My lips parted, but I couldn't form the words. "I don't think so," I finally told her. In the end, I decided that I didn't want to know any of it. "I just have a familiar sort of face."

She nodded and then wiped her hands across her apron. "Anything else?"

I lifted my to-go cup. "No, thanks," I said and took a slow, warm sip. "I think I have everything I need."

Back outside, the last fragments of daylight marked the sky. I walked toward the train. As I did, I reflected on the last year and all the moments I'd lived through that had carried me to the present scene. One year earlier, I had been so afraid of everything. Back then, it had felt like my life had been defined by an ending. My own self-imposed timeline. I'd boiled my entire existence down to bullet points, constantly trying to hurry through my goals so I could cross them out and be done with them. What I'd done was hurry through my life instead.

I sipped my coffee and paused on the corner until the light changed. I looked beside me and realized I was standing next to the secondhand bookshop Marian and I had visited months earlier. I noticed my reflection in the window. My faded pink hair. The slight bulge in my belly. I was a different person from the one I had been on that day we'd browsed there together.

While I studied my reflection, I thought about my birthday lists. For the first time I could remember, I'd been too busy living to pause and write one for the next year. It was for the best. In the end, I knew there was only one thing I'd need to write anyway. *Keep Moving Forward.* That was it. No lengthy lists. No bullet points. I didn't need them anymore. I just needed one simple goal for the next 365 days. To keep going.

I crossed the street. A streak of yellow taxis raced past. I tossed my empty cup into a trash can and looked over my shoulder, back in the direction of Marian's apartment and all the steps I'd already traveled. In the distance, the sun began to set behind the buildings, illuminating thousands of symmetrical windowpanes with golden streaks of light. A burst of air shot through the subway gratings. A pre-summer breeze blew across my face. For the first time in forever, I welcomed all of it.

I took another step and disappeared into the train station. All around me, the world pulsed with renewed energy. The sights. The sounds. The *feeling.* I stepped onto my train, took a seat, closed my eyes, and thought about all the ways my life had evolved. It had taken forever. It had taken nothing. Time was an anomaly.

I opened my eyes and saw my reflection staring back at me in the window, the whole city—the whole future—just beyond it. But I didn't need to think about what was out there waiting for me. Not yet.

The train moved forward.

For the moment, all I needed was the present moment.

In the end, I still had time.

ACKNOWLEDGMENTS

I never thought I'd write an acknowledgments page because I never thought I'd find the time to write a book, let alone to publish one. Lucky for me, life is full of surprises. It is with sincere gratitude that I thank the following people.

Thank you to my agent, Eve Attermann, for dedicating tireless hours to both me and my writing, for expressing early enthusiasm for this manuscript, and for being so patient with me as I worked to edit it. This is all your doing. I'm so grateful we get to work together.

I'm incredibly fortunate to have Carmen Johnson as an editor. She is smart and insightful, and just when I thought this manuscript was finally finished, she pointed out just the right moments that still needed a touch of TLC, all of which ultimately made this book so much better. I am very thankful that she shared my vision for this story and that she took a chance on me.

I owe a special thanks to Faith Black Ross. I'm so pleased we had the opportunity to collaborate on this project. Thank you for your expert eye and also for your many kind words.

Thank you to Nicole Weinroth for taking that initial phone call and for believing that this book could possibly be something more than just a book.

Thanks, too, to Caitlin Mahony for bringing this story to new readers around the world.

I'm so appreciative of Rikki Bergman, and everyone at William Morris Endeavor, including all those individuals involved in International Affairs and Business Affairs, for helping to carry this book along on its journey, and for the incredible work you all do. I also owe a heartfelt thanks to Suzanne Gluck, who made sure the original draft for this manuscript found its way into just the right hands.

I'm equally appreciative of everyone at Little A, including the many talented people involved in production, for expertly transforming this story into the beautiful book it is today. Thank you, thank you, thank you for taking me on.

I'm very grateful to Sara McFarlane, who shared with me both her time and her vast knowledge, and who helped me better understand the business side of writing.

I'd also like to acknowledge the excellent faculty who comprise the MFA program at Fairleigh Dickinson University, where I studied in my early twenties, particularly the late Tom Kennedy. Tom was the first real writer I knew who believed in my work. He also gave me some of the best writing advice I've received to date: early on, make a habit of saving all the rejection letters so that, one day, when the time is right, you can read back through them and be reminded of how long and hard you've worked at your craft. I wish Tom could read this book. I think he would have liked it.

I'm lucky to have such excellent friends, particularly my "Ski" group, who have listened to me talk about this project for infinite hours, for which they should all probably be given some kind of award.

To my parents: Thank you for always supporting me and for all the opportunities you've worked so hard to give to me. Thanks, too, for instilling a love of storytelling, fairy tales, happy endings, and pixie dust in me. It has inspired me and my writing more than you know.

To my children: You are the center of everything. It wasn't until the two of you entered my world that I understood who I really am and what really matters to me. In so many ways this book is because of you.

Please never settle for anything in your lives. Dream big. Listen to the voice inside you. And keep moving forward. Always.

To Jay: Honestly, I have no idea how we pulled any of this off. I'm so grateful for this life we've created together, and for all the ways you've supported me while I wrote and edited this book (schlepping our daughter to soccer and birthday parties so I could revise a few more chapters; running all the errands so I could read through a draft a few more times; frequently suggesting that I step away and go out into the sunroom to write, and then quietly placing a plate of eggs and a mug of coffee on my desk without my ever having to ask). I'm so glad to share my life with someone who understands the creative process, as well as the importance of not only having dreams but following them. None of this means anything to me without you. xxx

Lastly: To anyone who has a goal she keeps putting off. Stop waiting. There is no perfect time. No perfect circumstance. The time will pass anyway. Don't put your dream off anymore.

You owe it to yourself to write your own story.

ABOUT THE AUTHOR

Photo © 2023 Sylvie Rosokoff

Angela Brown's writing has appeared in the *New York Times*, *Real Simple*, and other publications. She holds an MFA from Fairleigh Dickinson University. Angela lives in New Jersey with her husband and two young children, where she is currently at work on her second novel.